IN THE ARMS OF
AN INNOCENT ACCOMPLICE...

For a moment neither of them spoke, then Cynthia sighed happily and said, "There's never been a man who can do what you've done for me. I feel so good I'm not even going to be jealous of the other women who must've told you that."

"You're a lot more woman than most," he told her.

"I like to hear you say things like that, Longarm," she said throatily. Then her voice grew serious. "You're not fooling me a bit, of course, and I'm not one to fool myself. You didn't come here tonight just to see me, or even because you knew I'd be only too damned ready to fall into bed with you."

"You better sit down," he said.

"Well?" she asked. "What is this bad news you've got to tell me?"

"Cynthia, don't you know you've been working for the Santa Fe Ring?"

TABOR EVANS

LONGARM

ON THE SANTA FE

A JOVE BOOK

First Jove edition published September 1981

First printing

Printed in the United States of America

Jove books are published by Jove Publications, Inc., 200 Madison Avenue, New York, NY 10016

Chapter 1

When Longarm got to the crest of the low ridge that the long-legged cavalry roan had been mounting for the past half-dozen miles, he reined in and waited for his companion to draw abreast. The sun was an hour past noon and no longer shone into his eyes, as it had when they'd gotten their last glimpse of Hoodoo Jack Simms and Big Ed Slater.

While Longarm waited, he studied the expanse of winter-brown prairie that stretched from the ridge to a thin line of trees that marked a creek's bed, less than a mile away. In the bright early-afternoon sunlight, the terrain was bare and deserted. Not even a wintering bird could be seen in the vast canopy of the pale winter sky.

Second Lieutenant Bedford Wheeler, U.S. Cavalry, drew up at Longarm's side and scowled at the emptiness that he saw. There was disappointment in his youthful face as he slowly shook his head, keeping his eyes turned toward the barren reach of grassland in front of them.

An onlooker studying the two men as they sat in their saddles on the crest would have been hard put to find another pair that offered as great a contrast.

Deputy U.S. Marshal Custis Long, whose friends called him Longarm, had a well-tanned face that told of long periods in the saddle, facing all kinds of weather, and his gunmetal-blue eyes were at the moment as cold as the blue ice at the heart of an Arctic glacier. His well-groomed mustache, brown like the sideburns shaved square at the level of his earlobes, swept above his full lips like the horns of a Texas steer. Even in the restricted movements that were allowed a man on horseback, his big frame showed the muscular grace of a strong, active man.

1

Wheeler, wearing the regulation cavalry field uniform, was perhaps a bit more than half Longarm's age, but beside him, Wheeler looked baby-callow. The lieutenant's face was clean-shaven, his skin the bright pink hue that shows before tanning on the face of a man who has spent little time outdoors. The lines that give a man's face character had not yet had time to form on the lieutenant's countenance. His brown eyes were soft, and his lips protruded in a babylike pout.

"Looks like we've lost them again," he said flatly.

Before answering, Longarm fished a cheroot from his pocket, flicked a horn-hard thumbnail across a matchhead, and touched the flame to the tip of the long, slim cigar. A freshening breeze from the north trailed the blue-gray smoke away from his face as he replied, "Not likely. They'll be holed up some-place along that draw. It's the first cover they've come to since we spotted them."

Lieutenant Wheeler gazed at the ragged line of young, leaf-less cottonwoods the ridge had hidden from them earlier. The trees straggled across the flat plateau in a narrow and often interrupted weaving line that stretched southward in the general direction of the South Platte River, still out of sight below the horizon. Between the cottonwood trunks there were low-lying sandplum bushes, almost as bare of leaves as the trees.

"Why do you think that?" he asked, then added quickly, "Even from here, I can see there's not enough brush to hide them."

"You ain't been out here long enough to know what a little bit of cover like that can hide," Longarm answered. "If I was Hoodoo Jack and his sidekick, I'd cut a shuck for those trees and wait till whoever was after me got in range. And from what your man with that payroll wagon said, Hoodoo Jack Simms is a man that won't stand and face a fight when there's anyplace he can hide and bushwhack you."

While he spoke, Longarm was sliding his Winchester out of its saddle scabbard. Wheeler looked at him, frowning.

"You really think those outlaws are as close as that?" he asked. "They had a good five-mile lead when we saw them just after daybreak, and we haven't gained on them all that much, Marshal Long. If you'll remember, they spurred up when they spotted us following them."

"Sure they did. Until they seen us, they didn't know there was anybody after 'em. When you're trailing a man and he sees you the first time, he just naturally kicks his horse up."

"They must've known somebody would chase them."

"Outlaws have got funny minds, Lieutenant. Most of 'em figure they're going to get away scot-free from whatever job they've pulled. Then, when they see they ain't, they got a way of running as fast as they can for a while. But it don't take long for 'em to shake off that first surprise, and that's when they remember they can't afford to get their horses winded. So they slow down."

Wheeler said thoughtfully, "What surprises me is that they were foolish enough to leave that man in Cheyenne. They should have been smart enough to foresee that somebody like you would find him, and that he'd talk. But regardless of that, if I was a criminal running with accomplices from a crime, I'd have taken that wounded man along, no matter what bad shape he was in."

"That's the army way," Longarm conceded. "Don't abandon your wounded, ain't that what the book says?"

"Of course. A primary rule, Marshal."

"Outlaws don't play by rules, Lieutenant. You better get wise to that sooner than later, or you'll be sorry."

Longarm nudged the roan forward in a slow walk. A bit reluctantly, the army officer followed him. Longarm kept his eyes moving along the line of trees and the clumps of sandplum bushes that became visible between their trunks as he drew closer. The range was still extreme, but he didn't know how nervous the fugitives might be getting after the long morning of pursuit. He did know that bushwhacking was Hoodoo Jack Simms' style, and the cover the creekbed offered gave him an opportunity the fugitive outlaw would welcome.

Longarm and Wheeler had been following the two outlaws since early the preceding day, after Longarm had picked up their trail in Cheyenne. Simms and Slater were the last survivors of an ambush in which they and four like them had trapped an army payroll wagon loaded with gold being sent to pay the soldiers manning the forts in northern Wyoming.

Half of the escorting cavalry detachment had been killed in the first volley fired by Simms and his band, and the rest of the escorting squad, as well as three of the bushwhackers, had died in the sharp, short fight that followed. The payroll clerks in the wagon had done their best, but only one of them had survived his wounds and gotten back to Fort Russell. It was

3

this survivor who'd not only reported the payroll theft and murders, but had described the bushwhackers accurately enough to give Longarm the leads he needed to begin running them down.

And if Billy Vail hadn't known you were waiting for a train to Denver at the depot there in Cheyenne right when he got word from the paymaster at Fort Russell about those bastards getting away with the payroll chest, old son, you wouldn't be out here right now, his thoughts ran on, ignoring the presence of the lieutenant. *Out here with a green shavetail who don't know his ass from a hot rock, and ain't smart enough to understand how much he don't know, fresh as he is from the East.*

However, Vail's telegram assigning him to the case had gotten to Longarm before the train for Denver pulled in, and he'd wasted no time in pulling together the loose ends that faced him. After getting the story of the ambush from the surviving payroll clerk, he'd lost an argument with Colonel Blaisdell, the commanding officer of the provost marshal force at Fort Russell, who'd insisted on having Lieutenant Wheeler go with him.

To save time and get on the gang's trail quickly, Longarm had agreed. He'd requisitioned the long-legged roan from the fort's remount station and, with Wheeler accompanying him, had ridden the three miles from the fort to Cheyenne. There, over Wheeler's protests, Longarm had conducted a quick shakedown of the scabby red-light district south of the tracks, and before daylight he had pulled the wounded survivor of the outlaw gang out of one of the dives.

Very little persuasion had been required to get the captured outlaw to start talking. He'd blabbed the names of Simms and Slater and revealed their getaway plans. Because arguing with a greenhorn second lieutenant was easier than arguing with a chicken colonel, Longarm had been able to convince Wheeler that they'd be wasting valuable time by going back to the fort and mustering a squad to go with them. He and the lieutenant had been able to set out on the trail of Hoodoo Jack Simms and Big Ed Slater less than eight hours after the outlaws had ridden out of Cheyenne.

Now, as they neared the draw, a twitching in the yellowed, sere leaves of the sandplum bushes caught Longarm's eye and he shifted slightly in his saddle. In two places, the brush had started to lean against the chill wind that had come up fast in the few minutes since they'd stopped at the crest of the ridge.

Longarm reacted instantly when he saw the sandplum brush swaying in a manner the wind couldn't account for. "Split up and ride fast!" he called to Wheeler.

Without waiting to see whether the lieutenant obeyed, he kicked the cavalry horse into a forward leap just as a pair of smoke puffs blossomed above the low-hanging bushes and rifle slugs raised spurts of dust from the dry prairie soil a few yards beyond them.

Longarm heard the hoofbeats of Wheeler's horse at the same time the sound of the shots reached his ears, their sharp, cracking reports faint in the fast-rising wind. A split second later he sent an answering bullet from the Winchester into the brush where he'd seen the dry leaves shaking.

At the same time he toed the roan into a zigzag lope at an angle that would extend the distance between him and the hidden sniper. Gunsmoke rose from the brush again, and lead whistled past Longarm's head. Longarm didn't bother to reply, though he heard the flat blast of Wheeler's Springfield carbine behind him.

Experience hadn't yet taught the greenhorn that shooting at an invisible target did nothing but waste lead. Longarm concentrated on getting to the creekbed as fast as possible while opening up the range still more between himself and the outlaws who, his senses had told him, were likely to be hunkered down in the bushes.

Another quick shot zipped between the two men as they got to the edge of the draw leading to the creekbed and slid into the brush. There, in the cover of the sandplum bushes and with the trunks of a half-dozen cottonwoods between him and Hoodoo Jack, Longarm reined in to take stock of the situation. At his side, the young officer was breathing hard, the air whistling out of his expanded nostrils.

"That was a close call," Wheeler commented, trying to keep his voice steady, but not quite succeeding.

"There's likely to be closer ones before we get those two fellows corralled," Longarm replied.

He took out a fresh cheroot, but the wind, whistling down the draw in which the winter-shallow creek lay, blew out the first match he struck before he could raise it to light the cigar. Twisting in the saddle to put his cupped hands to the wind before striking a second match, he saw the ominous gray of snow clouds, a high, threatening bank moving down from the northern mountains that were less than fifty miles distant

"What we better do right now is shake a leg," Longarm went on. "If we lollygag around here and let 'em get too much of a lead on us before that storm hits, we're apt to have some real trouble, a kind we ain't been counting on."

"What storm?" Wheeler asked, frowning. He looked at the sky. The clouds still appeared to be far distant, and ahead of them the sun was shining brightly through the bare limbs of the cottonwoods along the creek bank. The lieutenant jerked his head to indicate the blue sky above them and went on, "It's as clear as a bell, Marshal Long. I don't see anything to worry about."

"Maybe you don't, but I sure as hell do." Longarm pointed to the gray clouds sweeping down from the north. "That's a real weather-maker coming at us, and it's moving faster than we can. If we don't step fast, we might lose those two, because I'd imagine by now they're making tracks."

A trickle of water, barely deep enough to cover the stones in the center of its bed, ran in the creek. Longarm reined the roan into the center of the waterway and toed the horse into a walk. Behind him he heard the hooves of Wheeler's horse scraping over the bed of the little stream. The creek's course was almost straight, its banks bordered on each side by the sparse stands of young cottonwoods, interspersed with thick growths of sandplum.

Above the splashing and the scraping, Wheeler called, "We're wasting time following the creek, Marshall! Those outlaws will have started on across the prairie by now! They'll be so far ahead that we'll never overtake them!"

Longarm didn't waste his breath explaining to the inexperienced young officer that he was trying to avoid a brush-fight. He'd decided quickly to flush the fugitives out of their protecting cover. Had he been alone, or with a companion he knew could be trusted to move silently, keep cool, and shoot fast and straight, Longarm would have made a silent approach to the outlaws and tried to take them by surprise. With a tyro like Wheeler, he knew that surprising Simms and Slater was an impossibility. Instead of answering the lieutenant, he simply nodded and kept moving ahead.

Longarm's instincts, honed to a fine edge in countless confrontations like the one they now faced, told him that the out-

6

laws would do one of two things. Either they'd stand ready to shoot as he and the lieutenant approached along the creekbed, or they'd pull out of the draw, rein in, and wait until he and the lieutenant emerged from the gully. For the few moments while their horses were pushing through the brush, he and Wheeler would be sitting ducks. He was betting strongly that the fugitives would choose to run.

When his judgment told him that they'd ridden far enough in the cover of the creekbed to give the outlaws a chance to get in position, while they were still far short of the spot where Simms and Slater had been when they fired, Longarm led the way up the east bank of the creek and out onto the prairie again. Ahead of them, at extreme rifle range, the two outlaws were galloping as fast as they could spur their horses. With a sweep of his hand, Longarm motioned for Wheeler to follow him and headed for the fugitives on a long slant that would intercept them within the next few miles.

Engrossed in the chase, they had paid no attention to the threat of the oncoming storm. Riding out of the draw, Longarm glanced up long enough to see that the scudding cloudbank coming from the north now covered almost the entire sky. They'd ridden only a short distance when the clouds swallowed the sun, and the sudden sharp bite of the air on his face set Longarm's eyes to searching the sky.

He did not like what he saw. The slit of blue to the south was closing fast, and when he looked to the north again he found his vision cut off by an impenetrable haze. When they'd stopped on the ridge, he'd been able to sweep twenty miles of prairie with his eyes; now visibility to the north was only a mile or so. Longarm knew the prairie weather pattern like a book. He'd seen similar storms blow in on the prairie before, and knew the haze was not mist but heavy snow, blowing toward them at a pace faster than their horses could travel.

Swiveling in the saddle, he called to Wheeler, "That storm you didn't believe in is catching up to us. We're going to be up to our bellybuttons in snow before we got a hope of catching up to those men ahead of us."

"What do you think we should do, then?"

"Hell, there's not but one thing we can do. Keep moving!"

Almost before Longarm had finished speaking, the first snowflakes were swirling around them. The already sharp wind took on a cutting bite. Longarm folded the lapels of his coat

7

together and buttoned them across his chest, then pulled his wide-brimmed hat down on his head more firmly. Wheeler was twisting in his saddle to get his greatcoat, which was in a compact roll strapped behind his saddle. He managed to free the long, heavy coat and get his arms into its sleeves without dismounting, and to don his gloves.

Suddenly the air was gray, the clouds so low they seemed to be pressing on their heads, the wind whipping big snowflakes into their faces, where the wet flakes stung like tiny bullets.

Above the whistle of the wind, Wheeler shouted, "How are we going to keep on a straight course? I can't see ten feet ahead!"

"Don't worry about that. I can keep us heading straight. Just don't get separated from me." Longarm put his head down and kneed the cavalry roan forward a bit faster.

Already, Simms and Slater were dark blobs moving through a thickening haze of whirling snowflakes. Their vaguely defined forms disappeared completely before Longarm and Wheeler had ridden another ten minutes. For all practical purposes, the two of them were alone, riding enclosed in an impenetrable veil that extended from sky to earth and imprisoned men and horses in a circle only a few yards in diameter. Underfoot, the ground was already a soft, featureless white.

"What do we do now?" Wheeler asked Longarm.

"We keep on riding straight ahead. That's all we can do. If we stop out here on this damn bare prairie, we'll freeze."

"How the hell do you know you're going straight?"

"If you don't know, Lieutenant, I do. I've been out in these blizzards before. Don't worry. Simms and Slater are in the same pickle barrel that we are. They got to keep moving, they can't go any faster than we do, or see where they're going any better than we can. We'll see 'em again as soon as the snow lets up."

"How long will that be, Marshal?"

"Maybe ten minutes, maybe ten hours, maybe ten days. The longest time I ever heard of a blizzard lasting in this part of the country was two weeks."

"Two weeks!" Wheeler exclaimed. "Why, if it goes on like this for more than a few hours, the snow'll be ten feet deep!"

Longarm noded. "It's been known to happen." His voice was calm. "And that means we better keep moving as fast as we can, while we can."

"It seems stupid to me to move without knowing where we're going. So far I haven't seen any kind of shelter, if that's what we're looking for."

"Like I already said, Lieutenant, if we don't keep moving, we're likely to freeze. And even if you didn't see anyplace up ahead that we can head for, there is one. I think I can find it, with a lot of luck."

"Well, I suppose you know the territory, Marshal. How far are we from this place you're talking about?"

"Maybe six or eight miles. It's an abandoned army post. I don't guess you ever heard of it. The place used to be called Fort Sedgwick. It was put in to guard a ford on the South Platte, in the days when there was a lot of emigrants moving along the Overland Trail."

Wheeler shook his head. "No. Maybe I've heard the name or seen it on a map, but I don't remember it if I have."

"Well, it never was much of a shucks as a fort, just a little outpost. Tents for the men, and two or three soddies for the headquarters and cookshack and stores. There's parts of the soddies still standing, or was, last time I passed by the place. I'm guessing there's still enough left to shelter in."

"And you think we can make it there?"

"I think we *better* make it." Longarm didn't mention that he was already feeling the symptoms of freezing as the wind struck through his clothing. He went on, "I guess we can get there before it's too late, if our horses hold out."

They'd kept moving slowly during their conversation, which had been carried on in shouts made necessary by the increasingly shrill keening of the biting wind. Now Longarm reined in. He fumbled his bandanna out of his hip pocket, the wind stabbing him like an icicle, piercing his midsection when he opened his coat. With fingers that were already growing stiff, he unfolded the big red handkerchief and spread it on one thigh.

As he worked, he told Wheeler, "You better fix that pretty yellow scarf around your neck like I'm fixing my bandanna, Lieutenant."

Longarm had taken out his pocketknife; now he cut two eye-slits in the bandanna. Taking off his hat, he spread the kerchief over his face, positioning the eye openings carefully. The bandanna met and overlapped at the back of his head, and he pulled his hat over the top edge of the bandanna to hold it in place. Then he tucked the kerchief's bottom edge into the collar of his gray flannel shirt. The improvised facemask reduced his field of vision, but it helped to cut the wind's bite. More importantly, it trapped the warmth of his exhaled breath and protected the skin of his face from freezing.

Wheeler had watched carefully, and now he pulled off his cavalry gauntlets and arranged his yellow cavalry scarf as Longarm had fixed the bandanna. After a few moments he was surprised to find that the effect of his exhalations was to make his face feel warm, even though the thin cloth of the neckerchief provided no real warmth in itself.

"Keep opening and closing your hands on your reins, now," Longarm cautioned as he kneed the cavalry roan into motion again. "Those gauntlets you got on wasn't ever intended to keep a man's hands from freezing up."

Slowly they moved forward through the swirling snow, which was falling more thickly than ever. They'd gone only a short distance when Wheeler's horse began to toss its head and neigh plaintively. The young officer reined in after the animal began rearing, threatening to throw him.

"What's wrong with this damned beast?" he called to Longarm, his voice muffled by the snow-covered neckerchief covering his face. "He acts like he's gotten spooked over something."

"He has." Longarm reined in. "You stay where you are and keep a tight rein. I'll see if I can fix your critter's eyes."

"His eyes?"

"Yep. The snow's froze his lashes together. He's panicky because he can't see where he's going."

As he spoke, Longarm was pushing his way through the blanket of calf-deep snow to the head of Wheeler's mount. He fumbled his pocketknife from his pocket as he moved.

"Hold a tight rein, now," he told the lieutenant. "I got to trim his eyelashes so they won't be long enough to catch the snowflakes anymore."

Wheeler watched through the eye-slits of his neckerchief as Longarm pinched the horse's eyelids together and, with infinite care, trimmed away the animal's thick lashes close to the flesh, using the razor-sharp edge of the knife's small blade.

When the delicate job was completed, the horse grew calm once more. Longarm pushed through the snow to his own mount and led it close to Wheeler. He tossed the reins to the officer.

"Hold mine as steady as you can. Might as well fix him so he won't spook later on."

While Wheeler held the roan's head, Longarm trimmed its lashes. He put his knife back into his pocket and started pushing through the snow to mount the animal. A twinge of worry nipped at the edges of his mind as he moved; standing in snow that was almost knee-deep for the time required to tend the two horses had stiffened his legs, and he could feel a numbness creeping up from his thighs into his body. Longarm knew he must find shelter without delay.

With agonizing slowness he led the way toward the banks of the South Platte. The horses could not move faster than a deliberate walk in the deepening snow, and often it was necessary for the pair to detour around drifts, for by now the swirling wind was piling the snow so that in places it formed ridges as high as a tall man's head.

Even though he'd assured Wheeler that he could find the old army post, Longarm was beginning to doubt his own words as they moved forward ever more slowly and the snow continued to pile up deeper and deeper.

Time lost its meaning as they pushed on blindly through the almost impenetrable veil of thickly falling flakes. The horses moved more and more reluctantly, and Longarm could tell that the extreme cold was sapping their vitality almost as badly as it was his own. Though he tried to follow his own advice to Wheeler, and work his hands on the reins, his fingers responded less and less readily to his efforts to flex them and keep them useful.

Doggedly, Longarm led his companion forward in what he hoped was the right direction. He had no choice but to trust the instincts that had served him so well in the past, a sense of direction that he was trusting to lead them to the river, which they could then follow to the abandoned outpost.

As the horses moved slowly through the snow, floundering now and then in spite of the care with which they lifted and planted their hooves, he glanced at his companion from time to time. Though Wheeler's face was hidden by the yellow cavalry kerchief, now encrusted with ice around the mouth and nostrils, Longarm gave the lieutenant credit for a toughness that the young officer hadn't displayed earlier; in spite of their slow progress, Wheeler did not complain.

Old son, Longarm told himself as he stared through the eye-slits into a world of shifting white against a field of gray, *if you got turned around and ain't heading toward the river, you've took too big a bite to chew or swallow. But there ain't much else you can do except keep going, because if you were wrong, it's too damned late to do anything about it.*

Because there was no alternative, Longarm kept moving ahead. The snowstorm showed no signs of abating. The big flakes kept swirling from the sky as thickly as ever, while the horses picked their way forward at a slower and slower pace. There was no way Longarm could judge how much time they'd been moving; he knew that his time sense was disoriented, with the sun obscured and the invisible sky a uniform gray.

Wheeler's horse stumbled and almost went down. Then, just as it found a footing, Longarm felt the hooves of the long-legged roan beginning to slip. He reined in hard and called to Wheeler, "Pull up! It looks like we've finally made it to the South Platte!"

Chapter 2

Longarm dismounted and plowed carefully through the snow to the place where the horses had begun to slide. His feet, already cold, quickly became too numb to feel the ground, and the blowing snow kept him from seeing more than a yard or so ahead. Suddenly the unseen ground below the level surface of the snow seemed to pull him forward, and he had to lean his torso back sharply to keep his balance. Then he realized that he must be standing at the edge of the river, that he had stepped off the level prairie onto the sharp downslope of its bank. Carefully he worked his way back to where Wheeler waited.

"Just like I figured, it's the South Platte, all right," he told the lieutenant. "The bank's pretty steep along here, but it ought to flatten out when we get close to the ford."

For a moment, Wheeler peered through the kerchief's eye-slits, turning his head from side to side. Then he said, "I can't see any sign of a river."

"Not through this snow, you can't," Longarm replied. "Ten feet's about as far ahead as a man can see, and the bank slopes down a lot further than that before it hits the water. It'd be froze over anyhow, and level-full of snow. But I'll guarantee you I know where we are now."

"Your judgment's been good so far, Marshal," Wheeler said. "Well, what's your idea? Should we try to follow the riverbed to the old fort?"

"I'd say so. But we better lead the horses from here on, so we can keep 'em back from where the bank slopes down."

For a moment Wheeler hesitated, then confessed, "I'm not sure I can walk, Marshal. I haven't any feeling at all in my legs and feet."

Though Longarm didn't admit it, he was in much the same

13

shape. Only his superbly conditioned muscles had kept him going this far. He started toward Wheeler, to help him dismount, but the lieutenant was already swinging out of his saddle. He got a foot on the ground, but when he tried to disengage the other foot from his stirrup, he slipped and fell sprawling.

Longarm hadn't realized the young officer was in such bad shape. He got to Wheeler's side and helped him regain his feet.

"I guess you see now why I figure we got to lead the horses," he told the lieutenant. "If one of us was to slip down that slope, he'd be able to get up, but wouldn't have the chance of one of these snowflakes in hell to get a horse back on his feet. Anyhow, walking's going to keep us warmer than riding, even if we still have to go slower."

"Don't worry, I can walk," Wheeler insisted. Then he asked, "How far are we from old Fort Sedgwick?"

"Damned if I know. If I could see any landmarks, I'd be able to tell you, but the way the weather is, I can't be all that certain. At a guess, I'd say we got less than a mile to go."

Wheeler nodded and said, "Let's start walking, then, before we freeze."

As slow as their progress was, the exertion of pushing their way through the knee-deep snow warmed them somewhat as they led the horses along the flat ground bordering the river. Longarm watched Wheeler, and insisted that they stop and rest whenever he saw that the younger man was beginning to tire. Their halts were brief, for within minutes after they'd stopped moving, the below-zero wind and the deadly chill creeping up their snow-encased legs warned them they were in danger of having their feet freeze if they stood still too long.

After what seemed an interminable time, their progress slowed by a number of rest stops and several detours to avoid high snowdrifts, their advance was halted by the biggest drift they'd yet encountered. The snowy mass towered head-high and extended on each side as far as they could see through the blowing flakes that filled the air.

"That ain't any regular snowdrift," Longarm told Wheeler. "It looks to me like we hit the earthworks that the soldiers piled up all around what used to be Fort Sedgwick."

Wheeler nodded. "That's a reasonable guess, Marshal. There'd have been redoubts around the fort, all right. Let's take a closer look."

Turning, they skirted the foot of the huge snowbank for a dozen yards until they reached its end. Longarm led the way along the edge of the massive drift until they came to a break in it, and they plowed through the gap. Suddenly the air was relatively clear ahead; they had reached an area where updrafts created by the earthen breastworks surrounding the abandoned fort whirled most of the falling snowflakes above their heads. In the cleared space that had so unexpectedly opened up, they saw three huge, widely spaced humps, domed hills of snow, twenty to thirty feet apart.

"I'd say you're a pretty good guide, Marshal," Wheeler said. His voice carried the smile that Longarm could not see. "Unless I miss my guess, there'll be buildings under those snow piles."

"Soddies, or what's left of 'em," Longarm agreed. "Well, no need to waste time. Let's see if we can get in out of this damn storm and warm up a little bit."

Inside the sheltered area, the snow was not as deep and they could move more easily, but the cold was just as intense as it had been on the open prairie outside of the earthworks. They led the horses around the three snow humps, and in the last one they came to, they saw vague signs of an opening on one side of the hump. After a brief period of digging into the snow with their hands, the section of the drift they'd attacked crumbled suddenly, revealing what was unmistakably a doorway.

Wheeler stared at the black, rectangular opening for a moment before heaving a sigh of relief. "Let's get inside," he said. "My hands are about to burn up after digging away that snow."

"Rub 'em good," Longarm advised. "We'll take the horses in with us. Be a mite crowded, but whatever heat they give off is about all we're going to have."

By the short-lived light of the matches that Longarm struck one after another, they got an idea of the interior of the soddy. It was just a shell of a building, with a low roof and a packed-dirt floor, but bare ground had never looked so good.

Two horses and two men more than filled the soddy, but once they'd gotten inside and Longarm had covered the door opening with the tarpaulin that served him as a groundcloth, the wind couldn't get at them anymore, even though the cold was still as numbing as before. Their eyes grew accustomed to the darkness enough to see shapes, and the hard-packed earthen floor was at least warmer than the snow-covered ground outside.

Longarm dug into his saddlebags for his reliable standbys, jerky and parched corn, while Wheeler produced some slabs of army hardtack from his emergency-rations pack. They ate, then washed the dry food down with a mouthful or two of snow scooped from the drift outside the door and melted in their mouths.

"What about the horses?" Wheeler asked. "They're overdue for watering."

Longarm was lighting a cheroot, and waited to reply until its tip was glowing. The red coal, tiny as it was, lighted the soddy's small interior with what, to their dark-adjusted eyes, looked like the flame of a candle.

"They'll have to wait, that's all," he said. "But it ain't like it'd be if the weather was hot. They'll make it all right through the night, and we'll see what things look like outside tomorrow."

"We'd better get some sleep, I guess," Wheeler suggested. "Even if it's still daylight outside, I feel as tired as I would in the middle of the night."

"Best thing we can do," Longarm agreed. "And we'll sleep warmer if we keep all our clothes on, boots and everything, and roll up together in all the blankets we got, unless you got some objection to bunking up close with me, that way."

"Marshal Long, I don't have any objections to doing whatever is going to help us survive. You make up the bed. I'll just be damned glad to lie down in it."

Both men were too tired to be restless. They slept heavily until Longarm was wakened by one of the horses snorting, and once awake, the smell of horse urine and freshly dropped manure suddenly assaulted his nostrils. Instantly he was aware of an urgent need to empty his own bladder. Fighting his way out of the tightly wrapped blankets, he hurried toward the wall by the door, noticing, in spite of his haste, that a faint outline of gray showed around the edges of the tarpaulin he'd used to cover the opening.

Standing beside the doorway while relieving himself, he pulled back an edge of the canvas and looked out on a dazzling glare of sunshine tossed back from the snow-covered ground. He opened the canvas wider, and light flowed like liquid silver into the soddy's interior, bringing with it a rush of cold air. A rustling noise behind him turned Longarm's attention to the soddy's interior.

Turning to look, he saw that his movevents had roused Wheeler. The lieutenant was sitting up, staring around, his eyes still glazed with sleep. His face had lost its baby-pink hue, and shone stark white in the sudden light, colorless except for his lips, which were bluish-purple.

"You all right?" Longarm asked.

"I guess so. Or I will be, when I get waked up."

Wheeler pulled himself erect and struggled to his feet. Longarm took a step toward him, intending to help, but on second thought stopped short. Any effort he made to help might be taken as calling attention to the young officer's shaky condition.

"Storm's passed," Longarm said, indicating the bright light shining through the doorway. "Still cold as billy-be-damned, but at least we can see where we're at and what it's like."

Wheeler was standing shivering in the cold air, and Longarm let the tarpaulin drop. Wheeler moved to the door with careful and somewhat unsteady steps. He stood by the door, urinating, looking outside.

"I thought upstate New York had cold winters," he remarked over his shoulder, "but this beats anything I've ever seen. How long is it going to stay this way?"

"It ain't likely we'll be able to move for a day or two. Give the sunshine a chance to work on the snow, and it'll crust over hard enough to hold us pretty fast. But if it's Simms and Slater you're thinking about, it ain't likely we'll lose 'em. They'd have to stay wherever they stopped, just like us, unless they got bogged down and froze to death."

"I suppose we're lucky, at that," the young officer said with a thoughtful frown. "If we hadn't found this place when we did, we wouldn't have had much chance of surviving through the night in the open, would we?"

"Not a lot, but I imagine we'd have managed somehow. Even if we'd have to kill the horses and gut 'em out and crawl inside 'em for shelter."

"You've had to do that?" Wheeler asked incredulously.

"Not yet. But I've known men that did."

"I guess I've got a lot to learn about the West, haven't I?" the young officer asked, somewhat ruefully.

"It's a country that takes some learning." Longarm moved

17

to the piled-up blankets and retrieved his holster and gunbelt, which he'd used as an uncomfortable pillow. He finished buckling on the belt and said, "I'll just step outside and have a looksee before we start thinking about breakfast."

"Is it all right if I come along?"

"Suit yourself."

Pushing through the snow that had drifted into the doorway before the storm ended, they struggled out of the soddy. The tracks they'd made when entering the area enclosed by the old fort's earthworks had been covered, and the surface had not yet crusted, but lay like new-mown grain wherever they looked. Inside the rough circle of the redoubts, the snow was only boot-top deep, and they did not have to struggle hard as they made their silent, shuffling way to the soddy nearest the one they'd occupied.

"What are we looking for?" Wheeler asked when they'd covered about half the distance.

"Nothing special. I don't reckon we'll find much, at that. This place ain't been used for such a long time, anything the soldiers left has likely been scavenged by the emigrants or the Indians. But we might find a busted pot or a bucket we can melt snow in, if we can find some wood to make a fire with."

Except for the rough circle of the redoubts beyond the humps made by the snow-covered soddies, the sun was shining with painful brilliance on an unbroken expanse of white. The South Platte River, frozen, its surface covered with snow, was visible only as a wide, troughlike depression on the south side of the abandoned post, and as far as they could see, there was not a tree or bush of any kind protruding above the surface.

"We better not stay outside too long," Longarm said. "And be sure to keep your eyes squinched up, or you're liable to get snow-blinded."

They reached the snow-buried soddy and slowly started to work their way around it, looking for the depression in the snow that would mark its doorway. Longarm was a yard or so in front of Wheeler when they rounded the last corner of the high drift. He had not expected to see the burly, blue-chinned man who stood, pistol in hand, in the broken snow that extended from the dark rectangle of the soddy's doorway.

Longarm drew as the other man brought up his revolver. The two shots rang out as one, but by the time the stranger had triggered his weapon, Longarm's slug had torn into his chest. The man was falling backward when he fired, and his slug sailed to nowhere over Longarm's head as he sagged downward and lay quiet, his body sprawled darkly on the white snow.

"God almighty!" Wheeler exclaimed from behind Longarm. "Where the devil did he come from?"

"Out of the soddy," Longarm replied. His eyes were darting from the recumbent form of the dead man to the black opening of the soddy's door. "And his partner's most likely just inside that door, so stand clear."

"You mean—" Wheeler began. An impatient flicker of Longarm's left hand silenced him.

Seconds stretched out as Longarm stood watching the soddy door. He had not changed position since the exchange of shots, and knew that where he was standing, whoever was inside would have to show himself to get a shot at him. The seconds stretched into minutes, and there was no sign of movement from inside the soddy.

Longarm risked looking away from the doorway long enough to flick a glance over his shoulder at Wheeler. The young officer was standing a pace or two behind him, his eyes in a wide stare, fixed on the body of the man Longarm had shot.

Returning his attention to the soddy door, Longarm said in a matter-of-fact tone, "You don't have to worry about him, Lieutenant. He ain't going to bother us anymore."

In a hoarse, troubled whisper, Wheeler asked, "He . . . he's dead, isn't he?"

Longarm kept his voice carefully neutral. "He damn well better be."

"How could you be sure he was one of the men we're after?"

"Stands to reason. He was standing there waiting to bushwhack us. Must've heard us talking while we were coming up."

"Of course. I didn't think about that."

"Better start thinking about his partner, in the soddy."

"Are you sure there's another one inside there?"

Without looking around, Longarm replied, "You seen just what I did while we were trailing 'em from Cheyenne. There were two of them then, right up to the place where we lost 'em in the storm. That leaves one, and there's no tracks leading away."

"How do we go about getting him out?"

"Well, he damned sure can't get away without going past us," Longarm reminded his companion.

Longarm waited for several moments, and when no one showed at the doorway, he called out, "All right, Simms or Slater, whichever one of you is in there, throw out your gun and come out with your hands up! Your partner's dead, so don't look for him to help you!"

There was no reply.

"You heard me," Longarm called again. "There's two of us out here, and you ain't got a chance! Come out before we come in after you!"

Silence was still the only answer he got from the dark doorway of the soddy.

Without looking around, Longarm asked his companion, "You didn't put on your pistol belt, did you?"

"No. But I can go get it fast enough."

"Maybe you better do that. We got to settle this thing one way or another. It's too damned cold to stand out here waiting for that other bastard to come out."

"You mean we'll have to go in after him?"

"It's the only way I know of to handle it. And if I'm going inside that place, I want to do it before my fingers get so cold and stiff I can't shoot."

"All right," Wheeler said soberly. "I'll go get my pistol."

Longarm shifted his Colt .44 to his left hand and shoved his right hand through the lapels of his coat, holding it in his armpit to keep it warm. He kept the Colt trained on the black opening of the soddy door while he waited for the lieutenant to return. By the time Wheeler came back carrying his revolver, he'd worked out what seemed to be a reasonable strategy.

"You know how to use that thing, I reckon?" he asked, indicating the heavy revolver the young officer had in his hand.

"On a target. I've got a couple of marksmanship medals. But I never had to aim it at a man before."

"Just see you aim at the *right* man," Longarm told him with a mirthless grin. "Now, I want you to circle around the back of the soddy and come up on the other side of the door."

"You're going in alone?"

"That door ain't wide enough for us both. Anyhow, this job's more along my line of work than yours."

"Whatever you say, Marshal. What will I look for?"

"There's no way to tell you that. Just stand ready to she if shooting's called for."

While he waited for Wheeler to circle around behind the soddy, Longarm busied himself trampling down the soft snow at the edge of the drift that slanted away from the door. He kept the black opening under constant and careful observation as he stamped down the snow under his boot soles. By the time his job was finished, he had formed a narrow passageway below the level of the drift, but had left a thin wall of snow at the trampled area in front of the door where the dead outlaw's body lay.

When Wheeler finally showed up, Longarm pointed to the position he wanted the lieutenant to take, out of the direct line of fire from the doorway, but close enough in front of it to catch sight of any movement inside. Dropping to the surface of the passageway he'd trampled down, Longarm pushed through the thin wall of snow he'd left and began worming forward on his belly, toward the yawning black opening of the soddy.

As he moved, he fished out several matches from his pocket. When he was close enough to the doorway he flicked them quickly into flame on his thumbnail and flipped the matches, one after another, in tiny, smoking arcs into the soddy. Some of the matches fizzled out in midair, but three or four sailed inside.

Inside the soddy, a horse neighed and snorted, but the shot he'd expected did not answer his approach, nor did a voice come from the blackness beyond the door. Longarm took no chances, though. He continued his crawl until he got to the bare earth past the door. When there was still no reaction to his presence, he edged away from the opening and stood up.

One or two matches remained in his left hand. He flicked his thumbnail over one of them and, in the sudden yellow flare, saw the horses, standing with heads down on one side of the interior. Along the wall that extended from the animals, a dark figure of a man's body lay motionless. Longarm could tell at a glance that he was looking at a corpse. His brow knitted into a frown and he holstered the Colt.

Exhaling the breath he'd been holding, he called over his shoulder, "You can come on inside, Wheeler. The other one's in here, all right, but he's dead too."

"How can that be, Marshal?"

"I'm trying to figure that out right now."

Wheeler's form blotted out the light for a moment as he came through the doorway. Just inside he stopped, letting his eyes adjust to the darkness. Longarm struck a match, and together they moved to the body. The match guttered out, and Longarm struck another one. By its light they looked more closely at the dead man. Longarm held the match closer to the recumbent figure, then tried to shift the corpse with his free hand. The body was stiff as a board.

"I guess that's the answer," he told Wheeler, pointing at the dead man's coat. A dark stain of dried blood spread over the left side, shoulder, and arm of the coat the corpse wore.

"But he never did come outside!" Wheeler objected. "And you only fired once!"

"Just now, sure. But that blood ain't fresh. It's been dry a long time, judging from the way his coat looks. And if you'll remember, both of us took a shot at those two when they tried to cut us down back by the creek where they'd stopped."

"But we were just snapshooting, Marshal, not really aiming!"

"After you've been in a few brushes out here, you'll find out that there's more men killed by bullets that ain't aimed at 'em than by careful shooting."

"Either one of us could have hit him, then, with the shots we fired into the bushes along the creek," Wheeler said, his voice hushed.

"That's about the size of it. They didn't dast stop. Hell, when the storm hit, they couldn't stop any more'n we could."

"And they got here before we did," Wheeler said thoughtfully. "We didn't know they were here, and they didn't know about us until the one you shot outside heard us talking this morning."

"That's the way it looks to me."

"And this one must've died fairly soon after they got here," the lieutenant said, frowning.

"Likely that's the way it was," Longarm agreed. He read the undertone of contrition in Wheeler's voice and went on, "Don't feel bad because it might've been your rifle slug that hit him, back at the creek yesterday. He might've got over the bullet, but he kept bleeding and getting weaker. Chances are it was the cold that finished him."

"I . . . I guess that could've been the case," Wheeler agreed.

"Sure." Longarm ignored the relief the young officer's tone carried. "And I'll make a bet that when we search the saddlebags on those horses, we'll find the rest of that gold these two took off your pay wagon."

Wheeler nodded, then said, "Well, Marshal, I'd say we finished our job. What's next?"

"Not much we can do except wait for the snow to melt down a little bit. Tomorrow or the next day, it'll be crusted good and we won't have too much trouble making it back to Cheyenne." Longarm lighted a cheroot before adding, "And this time there ain't going to be a thing that'll stop me from getting on the first train heading for Denver!"

Chapter 3

Longarm sauntered into the U.S. marshal's office in the Denver Federal Building as the hands of the clock touched nine. This time he had a valid excuse for being late. The blizzard that had hit the southeastern corner of Wyoming hadn't reached as far south as Denver, but for the first twenty miles out of Cheyenne it had stalled rail traffic, and his train had pulled in two hours behind schedule.

This time the pink-cheeked young clerk in the outer office didn't try to get Longarm to wait while he checked to see if Chief Marshal Billy Vail was busy. Instead, he said in a gloating half-whisper, "You'd better get into Mr. Vail's office fast. He's very upset because he hasn't heard from you."

Longarm saw that the door to the chief marshal's office was ajar. He pushed it open a bit wider and said, "You can quit worrying about me, Billy. I'm back and on the job."

The pudgy, bald man looked up from his paper-piled desk and raised his bushy eyebrows questioningly. "Why the hell didn't you answer that wire I sent you three days ago in care of the provost marshal at Fort Russell?"

"Why, hell, Billy, that damn blizzard up there froze all the telegraph wires from Canada clear down here to Denver." Longarm saw too late that Vail was in no mood for jokes, and by the time he'd entered the office and taken out a cheroot, he realized that his chief was in no mood to wait for a reply, either.

He put off lighting the cheroot long enough to explain, "The plumb truth is that I didn't go near the fort after I wound up that payroll-robbery case. You remember, the one you wired me to stay there and handle? After I closed the case, I just stayed on in Cheyenne and waited for a train. I left the officer that was with me to handle the army's end of things, and I guess that didn't run to sending you a wire saying I was on the way back."

"I guess it never crossed your mind that I might like to know when to expect you back," Vail said accusingly.

"Maybe the wires were down. There was that little blizzard that blowed in while I was working on the job. The train I come in on was running about two hours behind time."

"Then you did close out the pay-wagon robbery?"

"What makes you think I'd show up if I hadn't closed my case, Billy? You know that ain't my style."

"I'll have to admit it's not," Vail replied. "You'll turn in a report when you get around to it, I imagine?"

"Sure. Soon as my hands warm up enough so's I can write it out. Billy, that goddamned blizzard I run into while I was working on that case was a real ringtailed one. It got colder'n a dry heifer's hind tit up on that Wyoming prairie. It's going to take me a month to get warm again."

"You'll have a chance to get warmed up where you're going. It's a new case I've been holding until you got back."

"That right?" Longarm finally touched a match to the cheroot he'd been dry-smoking. He looked at his chief through a cloud of blue smoke and asked, "Is it one of them jobs that you'll expect me to close out yesterday?"

"Not exactly." Vail shuffled through the papers stacked on his littered desktop and pulled out a telegram. "The fact of it is, I don't know too much about this one. All I can tell you is that you'll be down in Albuquerque."

"Well, I wouldn't call Albuquerque a summer resort at this time of the year, but at least it'll be a lot warmer than Wyoming. How come you don't know all the ins and outs of what I'm supposed to be doing there?"

"Because this wire says you'll be taking your orders direct from Governor Wallace."

"You mean *General* Wallace? Seems like I recall him being put in charge of New Mexico Territory after the Santa Fe Ring got so bad the smell reached clear back to Washington."

"He was. And he still is in charge. Now, I don't know that this assignment has anything to do with the Ring, but I've got a pretty strong suspicion that it might. The governor's asked the Attorney General in Washington to send him a man from outside New Mexico Territory to protect the government's interests in getting some trouble settled along the tracks the Santa Fe Railroad's laying west out of Albuquerque."

"A railroad trying to get track down fast might be willing to do a lot of bribing if it'd help 'em push ahead faster," Longarm observed, frowning. "And that sounds like the Ring, all right."

Vail nodded. "It did to me, too. That's the only reason I can think of why Wallace would ask for a man from outside his own territory."

"It must be pretty big trouble if the Santa Fe can't handle it with their own police force. What am I getting into, Billy?"

Vail studied the telegram for a few moments. "The way I read this, their construction's being held up by local ranchers who own rangeland along the right of way. You know what that means; we've run into it before."

Longarm nodded. Both men were familiar with the law that gave railroads subsidies in the form of land grants along the new rights-of-way that were streaking across the West. Both had been involved in cases where ranchers, claiming more grazing land than the Homestead Act allowed, had tried to oust settlers attempting to establish themselves on land they'd bought on the railroad's grants.

"I'm not sure that's all it is, though," Vail went on. "It seems the railroad sent in a new batch of surveyors who are taking liberties with the original route, shifting it north or south and cutting up private rangeland."

"Hell, Billy, if that's what it is, they don't need a U.S. marshal down there. All I'd be doing is wet-nursing 'em. Tell the railroad what they want is smarter surveyors."

"You're overlooking something."

"Oh?" Longarm asked innocently. "What's that?"

"I don't talk back to the Attorney General the way you talk back to me."

"It might do him a lot of good if somebody talked back to him, Billy, but it's sort of hard to give a man any backtalk over a telegraph wire. Well, maybe it ain't the Santa Fe Ring after all. Not if it's just some kind of fuss going on between a bunch of local ranchers and the Santa Fe Railroad."

"Not exactly a fuss, from what Governor Wallace says in his wire to Washington. He mentions outright fighting between the Santa Fe's construction crews and the ranchers. And you know how important Washington considers that new rail line."

"This is the first I've heard about Washington being concerned about much of anything except politics, Billy."

"Well, there's politics in this, of course. The Santa Fe's got mainline in three or four states now, and those states have all got congressmen and senators to put pressure on the department. And when any congressman starts to squeeze, our bosses say ouch real fast."

"Ain't Governor Wallace got some soldiers or some militiamen there that he can put to work?"

"He probably has. And he's probably got good reasons for not using them. For all I know, they're busy chasing Apaches or guarding emigrant trails, or down on the Mexican border."

"So what it all boils down to is that I'm elected?"

When Vail made no attempt to answer such an obvious question, Longarm asked, "Am I going to have time to take a bath and have a shave and get my laundry done before I go?"

In spite of his effort to keep a straight face, Billy Vail smiled. He said, "Take the rest of the day off, but pick up your expense money and vouchers before the clerk goes home this evening. I want you on the way to New Mexico on the morning train tomorrow. And if you run into any bad trouble down in New Mexico Territory, for God's sake let me know beforehand if you feel like you've got to clear it up by shooting a congressman or a senator."

"Now, Billy, you know damn well I never have shot a real honest-to-God U.S. congressman." Longarm frowned thoughtfully. "Closest I come to it was that state representative over at Leadville, and you remember how that come about."

"Well, you'll handle the case the way you see fit, regardless of any orders I give you," Vail said. "Now get out of here and get your laundry done. Just be on that train tomorrow."

There had been no vacant seats in the smoking car when Longarm got on the D&RG southbound passenger train at Denver's Union Depot. He'd resigned himself to sitting with his long legs folded in the narrow space between the day coach seats, sure that some of the men in the smoker would get off at the Colorado Springs stop. None had, so Longarm had cut his losses and walked back through the smoker and observation car to the back platform, lighting a cheroot as he strolled.

Watching the narrow-gauge tracks recede as the train rocked on the downgrade to the Rockies' foothills, Longarm felt the coach losing momentum as the engineer pulled back on the throttle and began to apply the brakes. He stepped off the platform to the steps and leaned out to look ahead. A buckboard was standing near a loading pen beside the tracks. A woman was on the seat, and a man wearing the faded duck jeans, checked gingham shirt, and wide-brimmed Stetson that marked him as a ranch hand was standing in the buckboard's bed, flagging the train with a flapping neckerchief.

Flag stops were nothing new to those who, like Longarm, were fairly regular riders on the Denver & Rio Grande line between Denver and Trinidad. There were more ranches than towns in the rolling, grassy foothills south of Colorado Springs, and the railroad was always ready to accommodate its big cattle-shipping ranch customers by making an unscheduled stop to pick up an occasional passenger at a ranch's loading pens.

Couplings clanked as the train came to a halt, the sure hand of the engineer playing throttle and brake bar to let the engine and tender slide past the waiting wagon. The train stopped with the buckboard directly in line with the sliding doors of the baggage coach, just behind the tender.

Longarm watched with no special interest as the coach door slid open and the baggageman's head popped out. He was too far from the head of the train to hear what was said, but saw the baggageman step down into the bed of the wagon to help the driver lift a trunk up into the baggage car. The woman in the buckboard's seat turned to watch them loading the trunk. That was the moment the engineer unwisely chose to bleed the cylinders of excess steam.

With a loud, swooshing hiss that Longarm heard clearly at the back of the train, a white cloud spurted from the cylinder, only a few yards in front of the buckboard. The horse in the wagon's shafts reared and whinnied as the steam enveloped the wagon with a loud hiss.

To the panicked horse, the noise must have sounded like all the snakes in Colorado were after it. The animal's front hooves hit the ground and its hind hooves dug in at the same time. Its first spooked jump pulled the buckboard fifteen feet, sending the woman in the seat flying head over heels out of the seat and into the wagon bed, with a flutter of skirts and a fleeting display of white petticoats. That wild leap pulled the buckboard so far from the door of the baggage coach that the men handling the trunk had no chance to jump down to the wagon bed.

Rocking and swaying, threatening to turn over at any moment, the buckboard careened alongside the train. Heads popped from windows as the clatter of hooves drew the passengers' attention. Longarm had no time to drop the cheroot clamped between his strong front teeth. He poised himself on the step of the smoking car, hoping the buckboard would pass close enough in its madly weaving course.

Gauging the distance he must cover, knowing he'd have no second chance, Longarm leaped during those few critical seconds when the horse approached. His shoulder hit the panicked horse's neck and he grabbed for the reins with strong, sure hands before his feet hit the ground.

Longarm bulldogged the reins, but the horse had gained too much momentum to be stopped at once. With the buckboard threatening to overturn and crash at any moment, the horse dragged Longarm with it in a wide arc that took it bouncing across a stretch of the bumpy pasture and back up the right-of-way embankment, a hundred yards behind the train.

Finally, Longarm's constant, steady pressure on the reins combined with the drag of the buckboard as it mounted the right-of-way hump. With a final shrill burst of angry neighing, it came to a quivering stop with its forefeet inside the rails, its haunches braced against the backward pulling of the wagon. The buckboard stopped, still canted upward, leaning at a precarious angle, still threatening to overturn, on the steep side of the bank along which the rails ran.

"Lady, you better jump out of there quick as you can," Longarm called. He was holding the horse firmly, but the animal's panic had not yet subsided, and it was trying to twist away, threatening to break from his grip. He did not dare risk turning his head to look back at the wagon, and when he heard no movement from behind him he raised his voice again. "Damn it, ma'am, get out of there! This critter might bust loose again, and then you'd stand a chance of getting hurt real bad!"

A feminine voice replied angrily, "My hair's all tangled up back here under the seat! I can't get loose!"

"You better figure out a way to get loose," Longarm called to her. "I can't do anything to help you."

"If you Western men are the gentlmen I've always heard

29

you were, you'd come give me a hand!" she replied tartly.

"I'd be proud to do that, but I can't let go of the horse!" Longarm told her. "If I let go of this nag of yours, we're both going to be in trouble!"

By now, several passengers from the smoker were running down the tracks. The first pair to arrive grabbed the reins to help Longarm hold the horse, which was still pawing the gravel of the right-of-way with its forefeet. Instead of trying to explain to them about the trapped passenger in the buckboard, Longarm let go of the reins and vaulted into the wagon bed.

Landing on his knees, he saw a pair of shapely legs clad in knee-length pantaloons protruding from a tangle of skirts and petticoats. At one side of the wagon bed an embroidered carpetbag lay on its side, its contents spilling out. Longarm had eyes only for the woman to whom the legs belonged; she lay half under the buckboard's seat, her body from the waist up somehow trapped beneath the buckboard's seat, which hid it from view.

Longarm tried to disentangle the petticoats, but the jumbled folds of cloth defeated his groping fingers. He thrust his arms forward, his hands following the contours of the trapped woman's pleasantly rounded hips to a tapering waist, but he could reach no farther than the beginning of a pair of billowing breasts.

Lying down beside the woman, Longarm ran his hands up over the smooth skin of her neck and face until he reached her hair. After a few moments of frustrating fumbling, he managed to free the tangled strands of hair from the iron straps that supported the buckboard's seat.

Extricating himself from the cramped space under the seat, Longarm hunkered back on his heels and pulled the trapped woman free. She pushed his hands away and sat up, her long blond hair falling is wispy tangles around her oval face. She looked down at her exposed legs, and her full lips tightened angrily. Before Longarm could speak, she brought her arm around in a wide arc and landed a resounding slap on his face.

"You . . . you uncouth boor!" she snapped. "That's for feeling of me the way you did while I was lying here helpless!"

Too surprised to reply, Longarm stared at her for a moment, then said, "Now, you didn't have any call to do that, ma'am. You asked me to get you untangled, and I had to sort of feel my way because I couldn't see what I was doing."

30

She finished brushing the wisps of snarled blond hair away from her face, uncovering a pair of dark brown eyes, bright now with anger. She was more girl than woman, Longarm saw; he guessed that her thirtieth birthday still lay several years ahead of her. She was paying no attention to him now, as she busied herself with pulling her skirt and petticoats down over her legs. She looked up at Longarm, and slowly the angry scowl on her face dissolved into a smile. The smile grew larger. She shook her head ruefully.

"I'm sorry," she said. "I shouldn't have done that."

"Well, I don't hold no grudges, ma'am. Especially against a lady that's still all upset after a runaway."

"Yes. It's the first time I've ever been in one. And I was too excited to think very straight, I suppose. But please don't call me 'ma'am.' It's a title I don't really admire. My name is Cristina Albee, and I do thank you for rescuing me."

"My name's Long, Miss Albee," Longarm told her. "Deputy United States marshal, out of the Denver office."

"My goodness! If I'd known that, I don't think I'd have had the nerve to slap you a minute ago!"

"No harm done, Miss Albee. Now let's see about getting out of his buckboard before that fool horse cuts up anymore."

Longarm stood up and helped Cristina to her feet. He was surprised at her diminutive size. Her head came only halfway up his chest, and the rest of her was scaled proportionately. In spite of her size, Longarm saw that she was truly a woman; the small but full breasts and flaring hips that filled out her tan broadcloth travel suit were evidence of that. He handed her up to the buckboard's seat, jumped out of the bed to the ground, and gave her a hand down. For a moment they stood by the wagon, gazing at one another, but before either could speak, the ranch hand who'd been driving the buckboard ran up, panting.

"Are you all right, Miss Teena?" he gasped.

"I'm fine, Tom. Not hurt a bit."

"Well, if I'd thought that horse would bolt the way he did, I sure would've stuck with the wagon," he apologized.

"It wasn't your fault," she began. Before she could go on, a sharp blast of the train's whistle interrupted her. She looked at the train, where the passengers who'd left the cars to look down the tracks were beginning to get back into the cars. "Oh my!" she gasped. "We're holding up the train, Tom, and that's what Uncle Roger said we should be careful to avoid doing."

"We better get back there in a hurry, lady," one of the men from the smoker broke in. "If you're all right, that is."

"I'm quite all right," she told him. "You gentlemen go ahead. Tom will help me get aboard."

"If you don't mind me butting in, Miss Albee, you'd best let me see you to the train, and leave Tom look after the wagon," Longarm suggested. He looked at the ranch hand and asked, "Think you can get that horse to back off the right-of-way, or will you need a hand?"

"Oh, I can handle the buckboard all right. And I'd be real obliged if you'll see Miss Teena safe on the train."

A longer, more strident blast from the locomotive's whistle broke the air. Longarm looked at the train. The blue-coated conductor was standing behind the smoker now, and the last of the passengers who'd alighted was just getting aboard.

"We better get a move on," Longarm told Cristina. "We don't want that fool engineer to go on without us."

"Yes, of course," she said. She started toward Longarm, then stopped and turned back. "My bag! Tom, will you get it for me, please? It's in the wagon."

"Sure." Tom leaned over the buckboard, reached the carpetbag, and handed it to Cristina. He said, "I'd be just as glad if you didn't say anything about the runaway when you write your uncle, Miss Teena. Might cost me a job if you did."

"What runaway?" she asked innocently. "Thank you for taking me to the train, Tom. Tell Uncle Roger I'll write him."

"I'll sure do that," Tom called after her as she and Longarm started walking toward the train.

Cristina turned and nodded to him. Longarm took the carpetbag from her as they picked their way over the shifting gravel between the ties. They reached the observation car, and she looked helplessly at the steps leading to the rear platform. The bottom step was just below the level of her waist.

"Hold tight to your bag," Longarm said. He grasped her tiny waist in his big hands and lifted her straight up to the step, then swung up after her.

With a rattle of couplings and a squeaking of steel on steel, the train moved slowly forward. Longarm took out a cheroot and settled it between his teeth, but did not light it.

Cristina said, "I won't impose on you any longer, Marshal

Long. If you'll give me my bag, I'll go find a seat in one of the coaches ahead."

"You're not bothering me one little bit, Miss Albee. I'll be glad to see you to a seat. Matter of fact, I'm the only one in the seat I been using up ahead in a day coach, and I'd be right pleased if you feel like sharing it with me."

"But you're going to want to smoke your cigar," she replied "You'll be stopping in the smoking car."

Taking the cheroot from his mouth, Longarm tucked it back into his vest pocket "The cigar can wait," he said. "Come right down to it, I keep trying to tell myself I ought to stop smoking the cussed things. Except I don't, for some reason."

Cristina gazed at him speculatively for a moment, then said, "You look like an understanding man, Marshal Long. In fact, you've got the kind of face I—" she stopped short and shook her head. "No," she went on, "That can wait. What I started to say, Marshal, is that I indulge in a cigarette now and then. I know people frown on women using tobacco, but I acquired the taste while I was living in Europe, where folks aren't as straitlaced as they are here. After that experience with the runaway, I'd stop in the smoking car with you, if women were allowed to."

"Well, now," Longarm told her, "we don't have to go to the smoking car, Miss Albee, or even go set down in the coach right now. We can stand right here and you can have your cigarette while I puff on my cigar."

"I'd enjoy that. And if you don't mind, I'm not fond of being called Miss Albee any more than I am of being called 'ma'am.' If we're not on friendly terms after what we went through with the runaway, we never will be. And my friends call me Teena."

"And mine call me Longarm. It's sort of a funny nickname but I answer to it better than I do to my real first name."

"Good. Now, Longarm, if you'll hold my bag open while I dig out my cigarette case, we'll stay right here for a while."

Longarm spread the opening of the carpetbag while Teena rummaged around in it until she dug out a silver cigarette case. She took out one of the slim white cylinders and placed it between her pouting red lips. Longarm returned his cheroot to his mouth and lighted her cigarette before touching the flame of the match to his cigar. They stood in companionable silence

33

for a moment, watching the rails slip by behind the gently rocking train.

Teena broke the silence. "I've never met a United States marshal before, Longarm. I don't really even know what they do. Are you looking for a criminal, or on your way to arrest one, or something like that?"

"Well, I'm going down to New Mexico Territory on a case, but I ain't sure yet that I'll be arresting anybody."

"You mean you're going to investigate a crime, but you still don't know whether you'll catch up with the criminal?"

"Something like that. I'll find out more about it when I get to Santa Fe and have a talk with Governor Wallace."

"What an odd coincidence!" she exclaimed. "Governor Wallace is my great-uncle, and I'm going to visit him in Santa Fe. He's promised to arrange for me to do some paintings in the Indian pueblos around there."

"You mean the artist kind of paintings?"

"I'm afraid so. I've spent the last four years in Europe, mostly in France and Italy, studying and learning, and I think I'm ready to strike out on my own now."

"Looks like we'll be traveling together as far as Santa Fe, then. Only I don't know how long I'll be staying there. This case I'm on is . . . well, I'd guess I'll be moving on to Albuquerque or even past there, as soon as I've talked to the governor."

"Have you ever met my uncle, Longarm?"

"No. I heard a good deal about him, though. His name was in the papers a lot, when he was on that court the army set up to try those people who were framing up to kill President Lincoln."

"Yes. I remember the trials, of course, but I was still too young to understand. After the trials ended, he came back to Indiana to rest, and I got to know him quite well. Uncle Lew was the one who encouraged me to go to Europe to study."

"I take it he's a right smart man," Longarm said.

"Very brilliant. And nice. I owe Uncle Lew a lot." Teena took a final puff from her cigarette and flipped it away. "It's nice to know you're going to Santa Fe, Longarm. It makes it easy for me to ask you to do something I've wanted to do ever since I saw you."

"Oh? What's that?"

"I'd like to do some sketches of you. Not on the train—the

cars bump and sway too much for me to work. But later, maybe, if there's a long wait somewhere between trains, or after we get to Santa Fe. Would you sit for me as a model?"

"Well . . ." Longarm felt a bit embarrassed, but tried not to show it. "I never did do anything like that."

"There's got to be a first time for everything."

"Oh, I don't deny that. Except I don't see why you picked me out to draw pictures of."

"That's easy. You've got a very interesting face. Something in the way your eyes look, and your mustache, and the set of your jaw. I know about faces, Longarm. It's my business to know them."

"I guess I can see where it would be. Well, I don't reckon it'd hurt me any. If you can stand it, I can. You tell me when you want me to, and I'll pose for you."

"Thank you, Longarm. We don't have to be in a hurry, since we're both going to the same place. We have to change trains to get to Santa Fe, don't we?"

"Up ahead, at Trinidad. We'll be there an hour or two, making connections."

"We'll wait, then. Maybe not even in Trinidad. I might want to wait until we get to Santa Fe. Because before I start to sketch you, I think I'd like to get to know you better." Teena looked at him thoughtfully and said, "A lot better, the way I feel about it now."

Chapter 4

"Trinidad!" the conductor called as he walked down the aisle of the coach. He made the name into three words: *Trin-eye-dad!* "Change trains for Santa Fe, Albuquerque, Fort Worth, and all points east and south!"

"How long will we have to wait for the train to Santa Fe?" Teena asked Longarm after the conductor had passed them.

"I ain't quite certain how long we'll have between trains," Longarm replied. "It's been a while since I was down this way, and the railroads keep changing their schedules all the time."

"I hope it'll be long enough for us to get a bite to eat. Those butcher-boy sandwiches we had a while ago certainly didn't have much meat in them!"

"Oh, I guess we'll have a chance to find a restaurant and get a bite to eat before we pull out for Santa Fe," he told her. "My belly thinks my throat's been cut."

They'd been chatting casually, and generally impersonally, while the morning wore into early afternoon, and the narrow-gauge was now snailing through the hills between Pueblo and Trinidad. Cristina—or Teena, as she preferred to be called—was still a puzzle to Longarm. He had not been able to decide whether she was a girl just turning into a woman, or a woman who had not yet lost all her girlish traits.

There were moments when her eyes would hold the sparkling, innocent enthusiasm of youth, and other times when they turned deep and sad, and her oval face would seem to lengthen and her soft, pouting lips compress into a sober line that made it look almost sad, burdened with a wisdom beyond her years. Then, a moment later, her features would soften to girlishness again as their conversation took a different course.

Teena had been full of questions about the West, which she was seeing for the first time, and she'd been especially curious

36

about the Indians she'd come such a distance to paint. Like most tenderfeet, she had made little distinction between the warlike tribes of horsemen who inhabited the plains, and the settled, peaceful tribes who lived in the pueblos of New Mexico Territory. Unconsciously, Longarm had been flattered by the interest with which she hung on his words as he explained the differences among the various tribes.

Even though it had been done in an oblique fashion, Teena had given Longarm a number of quick glimpses into her background, with casual references to people she'd known in Paris, Rome, and Florence, and into the bohemian life she'd experienced in other European cities where she had lived as an art student.

She'd also lost him occasionally when she had mentioned the names of artists. From her way of referring to them, Longarm had assumed the men she named were friends or teachers whom she had known abroad, but had learned belatedly that some of them had been dead anywhere from fifty to three hundred years.

If their long conversation had served no other purpose, it had put them on a basis of mutual understanding that was friendly enough for Longarm to tease Teena mildly at one point by saying, "You sure got a lot of names and places and times stored away in that pretty head of yours, Teena. I don't see how you can remember all of it."

"I don't find it hard at all, Longarm. I'm just like you are in the business you follow. How many names of criminals are you carrying in your head? And how many of the places where you've trailed them have you forgotten?"

"I guess you got a point there," he replied after a moment of thought. "Everybody remembers what helps him get along in his trade, I guess."

Since the Denver & Rio Grande had no dining car on the Denver-to-Trinidad run, they'd had to buy their lunch from the basket of the butcher boy who came through the cars at intervals, hawking candies and cigars and the morning edition of *The Rocky Mountain News*. Then, as noon drew close, the butcher boy changed his wares and began to sell sandwiches and apple turnovers and cookies.

It had been Teena's idea to make a picnic of lunch. They'd eaten on the observation platform, not a bit deterred by the flecks of ash and an occasional small, hot spark from the soft

37

Trinidad-mined coal flying back from the engine's smokestack. Now, though they'd eaten only two hours earlier, their stomachs were reminding them that the thin-cut sandwiches weren't quite the same as a full meal.

"Maybe it's this mountain air that makes me so hungry," Teena said. "Whatever it is, I'm certainly famished."

"I could use a bite myself. We'll fix it up to eat in Trinidad, even if it's just at the depot restaurant the Santa Fe runs there."

"Oh! The depot!" Teena exclaimed. "I don't suppose there's a union station in a little town like that?"

"Not likely. The Santa Fe and the D&RG ain't all that close to holding hands. If one of 'em was for a union depot, the other one would be against it. They been fighting over right-of-way as long as I recall."

"You mean real fights? With fists or guns?"

"Fists and guns both. They had a big blowup at Raton Pass, and I guess at just about all the other passes up the Colorado Gorge. What are you so concerned about the depot for?"

"It just occurred to me that I'll have to arrange for my trunk to be transferred, if this railroad and the Santa Fe don't use the same freight depot," she explained.

"Now don't fret over a little thing like that. I'll see to it for you," Longarm assured her.

Getting off the Denver & Rio Grande train at Trinidad, with the afternoon still early, they found that they had almost four hours to wait for the Santa Fe train that would take them the rest of the way on their trip. Longarm had also found that the feud between the two railroads was still very much alive. When he asked the baggagemaster about transferring Teena's trunk to the Santa Fe, the man had said with a surly shrug, "Guess you'll have to handle that yourself, friend. We don't do no business with that other line."

"Well, then, do you know of a drayman I can hire to carry the lady's trunk across town?" Longarm asked.

With another shrug, the baggagemaster replied, "You might find one if you look hard enough. Or you can rent a rig from the livery stable across the way, and haul it yourself."

Teena said to Longarm, "Getting that trunk moved is my problem, Longarm, and I've got an idea. We have lots of time, and nothing else to do. Suppose I hire a buggy, and after we've had an early dinner and taken the trunk to the other depot, we can ride around and look at the town, or maybe even go out in the country a ways and enjoy the scenery."

"That's about as good a way as any to see things," Longarm agreed. "And we sure ain't got anything else to do."

"I'll get a sketchpad and some charcoal out of my trunk to take along," she went on. "We might see a nice mountain scene I'd want to draw. And this may be the only chance I'll have to take a look at this part of the country."

"If that's what you'd enjoy, then that's what we'll do," Longarm said. "It'd sure beat setting on one of those hard benches in the Santa Fe depot, waiting for the evening train."

"Let's not eat at the restaurant in the depot," Teena suggested after they'd delivered her trunk to the Santa Fe's baggage room. "After two weeks at Uncle Roger's ranch, I think I'd like to have something besides steak and potatoes."

"Well, I'm pretty much of a meat-and-spuds eater," Longarm told her. "But we'll see what we can find."

Trinidad was a small, compact town, the old adobe buildings on its main street just beginning to be replaced by newer and more imposing structures of orange-red brick. The valley in which it huddled was wide and shallow, overshadowed on the west by the Culebra Mountains, a score of miles distant, but looking much closer in the thin, clear air of the mild afternoon.

Longarm wheeled the rented buggy beyond the center of town, to a section where no new buildings had yet been erected. Before the street became a trail leading to the hills, Teena spotted a sign reading "Cafe" on a low adobe building and insisted that they stop. They were served *albóndigas*, meatballs simmered in a mild but still peppery sauce; *chilis rellenos,* long sweet green peppers, deep-fried after being dipped in a thin batter; and *sopapillas,* puffy buns filled with tangy local honey.

"Oh, that was delicious," Teena sighed as they came out of the restaurant and stood for a moment beside the buggy. "Now we still have time for a drive. Let's just keep on going up those little hills until we find a place that's high enough to look out over the town and the valley."

Within minutes, Trinidad lay behind them as the buggy rolled over the narrow, graveled road up the slope to the foothills. The day was warm, more like spring than late autumn, the sun flooding the slopes of the distant Culebra Range with golden brilliance. Longarm lighted an after-dinner cheroot, and after looking around as though to be sure there was no one to see them, Teena took out a cigarette.

"All I miss now is a sip of good Maryland rye," Longarm remarked. "But maybe you're a temperance woman who don't approve of a man taking a drink now and then."

"Nonsense! I spent too much time in Europe to have what seems to be a purely American attitude about drinking. I think Europeans have a different view about a lot of other things too, and I guess some of them rubbed off on me."

"Well, now that I know how you feel, maybe I'll find us a bottle of rye to take on the train this evening."

"If you do, I'll certainly join you in a drink. Maybe more than one, if it's like most train rides at night." Teena smiled. "And that's a promise."

They soon passed through the area where the woodchoppers had been at work, and rode through stands of low, gnarled piñons, broken now and then by small meadows studded with clumps of mountain sage. The road was a winding one, and apparently seldom used, for they met no one and saw no signs of life except for a few birds and an occasional chipmunk or ground squirrel scurrying with twitching tail through the scrubby brush.

"Are there a lot of bears and mountain lions in the woods around here?" she asked, watching a chipmunk dive off a rock by the road as the buggy approached.

"Plenty of both of 'em, but this time of year they're up in the higher country, getting ready for winter. You don't have to worry about any of 'em popping up and chasing us."

"Oh, I wasn't worrying about that. I know you've got a gun, and I suppose you usually hit what you shoot at." She dug into her carpetbag and held up the pad and sticks of charcoal she'd taken from her trunk. "I was hoping we might see some animals I could sketch."

"Well, don't give up hoping," Longarm told her. "We might run across some kind of wild critter—antelope or deer, maybe—that you can draw a picture of."

"If I don't see any animals, maybe we'll find a place where we can stop and I'll do a quick sketch of the scenery, the town down there in the valley, or maybe there'll be a rock outcrop or something with good, bold lines where I can get you to pose."

"You mean right out here in the open air?"

40

"Why not? You're certainly an open-air kind of man, Longarm. Somehow I can't imagine you in an office behind a desk, or selling something across a counter."

"I can't see myself doing any jobs like that, either, Teena. I guess the job I got now suits me better than anything else."

"You're good at your work, too, aren't you?"

"Now you're asking me to brag on myself, and that's something I fight shy of."

"You're more modest than my artist friends, then. When one of them paints a picture they think is very good, they can't talk about it enough."

"Maybe that's because they're afraid nobody else will."

"Perhaps. But if I—" Teena broke off and pointed down into the valley, where Trinidad had suddenly come into view, a miniature, fairy-tale town from that angle and altitude. "Oh, look! I'm just going to have to do a quick sketch of that, Longarm. Can we stop here?"

"Sure." Longarm reined in. "We ain't passed a soul since we left town, and I don't imagine there's ten people a week uses this trail, except when the woodcutters come out, or somebody like us goes for a buggy ride."

He pulled the buggy off the road into a small clearing, and without waiting for him, Teena jumped to the ground. She walked back along the trail to where she'd seen the view of Trinidad, studied it for a moment, frowned, and shook her head.

"No. It's not as nice as thought it'd be, now that I study it. But maybe if I can get a little way along that ledge that leads off the road, I'll find a better angle."

With Longarm following her, Teena started working her way along the ridge. It was a wide shelf, covered with curling grama and long-stemmed needle grasses that grew thick and lush, forming a soft carpet under their feet as they moved along the ledge. Teena stopped twice to study the vista in the valley below them, but each time shook her head, dissatisfied.

"No. It's just not what I'd imagined it would be when I saw it back there." She looked ahead, where the ledge ended in a massive formation of cracked and chipped slabs of stone. "But those rocks would make a good background for a portrait sketch of you, Longarm. Do you mind standing in front of them for a minute while I make sure?"

Longarm walked ahead to the stone slabs and stopped in

front of them. He asked, "Like this?"

"Yes, that's fine." Teena studied for a moment and said, "Turn a little bit more this way, Longarm. I want your body facing me and your head looking out over the valley."

"I'm new at this, remember," Longarm reminded her, trying to take the position she'd asked for. "Is this the way you want me to be standing?"

"Not quite. Here, I'll turn you to the right angle."

Teena went to Longarm and clasped his upper arms to turn his body at an angle. As her hands closed around his biceps, she gasped. "My God," she exclaimed, "I've never felt the kind of muscles you've got in your arms! They must really be something to look at."

"Working keeps me in pretty good shape, I reckon," Longarm told her noncomittally, very much aware of the pressure of her hands and the pleasant but indefinable fragrance of her body.

She nodded absently, studying his face, then cupped his chin in her palm and adjusted his head to a new angle, stepped back and studied him for a moment, then nodded with satisfaction. "Yes. That's much better. Now just stand still while I get you down on paper."

Longarm could see her working out of the corner of his eye; she sketched quickly, with long, sure strokes of her charcoal stick, looking from him to the pad, stopping occasionally to rub the surface with a fingertip. Longarm was surprised at the short time it took Teena to complete the sketch. She looked up from the pad with a smile, and nodded.

"It's finished. You can relax now, and come look at what I've done."

Lighting a cheroot, Longarm walked over to where Teena stood. He looked at the sketch, but didn't quite recognize it as being himself.

"Well?" she asked when he said nothing. "Don't you like it?"

"I like it, but that sure ain't the same face I see in my mirror," he replied.

"Of course not. It's how you look to me. If you want to see how you look in a mirror, you'll have to get a daguerreotype made," Teena told him, smiling.

"They don't look much like me, either." he said.

"I don't know," she said. "Maybe I worked too fast."

Teena picked up her carpetbag and fumbled through it, found her silver case, and took out a cigarette. Longarm flicked a match into flame across his thumbnail and held it for her. Teena stood for a moment, studying the sketch, and then looked up at him.

"If you want to know the truth, Longarm, I may not have done a really good sketch because I was thinking about something else. You know what I'd really like to try?"

"I wouldn't even try to guess."

"I'd like to draw you in the nude."

"You mean bare—" Longarm caught himself in time to change his phrasing. "You mean buck naked? Right here in the open?"

"Certainly. There's not anyone around, or likely to be. And when I felt your arms a minute ago, I got the idea that if the rest of your muscles are like your biceps, a nude sketch would be something quite special."

"It'd be something special to *me*. I never did pose for a picture until right now, let alone one with no clothes on."

"Don't let that bother you," she said. "I've seen a lot of models, men and women both, in the nude. It won't embarrass me a bit to look at you, if that's what you're thinking."

"Well, I was thinking more about how *I'd* feel."

Teena shook her head, smiling. "Now don't try to fool me with false modesty, Longarm. If you're the kind of man I think you are, I certainly wouldn't be the first woman to see you without your clothes on."

"Now, Teena, it ain't quite the same—" Longarm caught himself and stopped before finishing what he'd started to say.

"Quite the same as when you're going to take a woman to bed with you?" she finished for him.

"Something like that."

Teena looked at Longarm intently for a moment, then dropped the butt of her cigarette and ground it out with her foot. She put the pad and charcoal sticks beside her bag and dropped her hat on the ground. Still without speaking, still holding Longarm with her eyes, she shrugged out of her short jacket and let it slip to the ground.

Moving with casual deliberation, she unbottoned the waistband of her skirt and let it slide off. Her fingers twinkled over the buttons of her blouse, and in a moment it too lay with the clothing at her feet. She pulled the straps of her camisole over

43

her white, smooth shoulders, gleaming in the sun's rays, and let the undergarments fall.

Now she stood naked to the waist, her small but fully rounded breasts erect, their rosettes pebbled, their nipples protruding. Without taking her eyes off Longarm, she stepped out of her pumps, hooked her thumbs under the waistband of her pantelettes, and pushed them down to her knees before they fell of their own weight on top of the clothing piled at her feet.

She faced Longarm, naked but for her stockings, her small body perfect in its contours, with upthrust breasts, flared hips, rounded thighs extending down in tapered white columns from the dark delta of her pubic hair.

Although Teena had not seemed to hurry, her undressing had been done in only a few moments. Longarm had been so fascinated by her unexpected move that he still stood as though transfixed, staring at her in unconcealed surprise.

"Well?" she said, extending her arms. Her eyes were bright, and there was a challenge in her voice. "Aren't you going to join me?"

"Godamighty, but you're a beautiful woman, Teena!" Longarm exclaimed.

He stepped forward, took her in his arms, and bent to kiss her. Teena's lips met his avidly. Her tongue darted out to seek Longarm's, and while they clung together in their kiss, her hands busied themselves with the buttons of his shirt. Longarm freed one hand and unbuckled his gunbelt, letting it slip gently to the ground while Teena's fingers moved from his shirt to the buttons of his trousers.

Longarm was not quite sure how, between long, clinging kisses, he managed to lever his feet out of his stovepipe boots, or whether it was he or Teena who opened his balbriggans to free his growing erection.

"I was sure you'd be big down there when I felt how big your arm muscles are," she gasped when they had to break their kiss to breathe. She encircled his shaft with one hand and found that her fingers did not meet when she closed them. "But I didn't expect all this much!"

"You're a real tiny woman," Longarm said. There was worry in his voice. "I wouldn't want to hurt you, Teena."

"I'm the same size as any other woman where it counts. You won't hurt me, but I don't care if you do. I've never had a man as big as you are before, and right now all I can think

44

about is getting that big, lovely muscle of yours inside me! Lift me up, Longarm, and let me take you in! Don't make me wait any longer!"

Longarm lifted her. She spread her thighs and straddled him, worked his tip against her streaming juices for a moment, then guided him into her. She gasped with a sharp inhalation when he began to penetrate her, but looking at her face, Longarm saw that the cry was one of ecstasy, not pain.

Teena locked her fingers around the back of his neck and buried her face between his neck and shoulder. Longarm dropped his big hands to her buttocks. Grasping their round softness, he pulled her to him with a quick, hard jerk, and went into her fully.

He felt her moist lips on his neck, then her teeth began nipping him, her head moving down his neck to his shoulder and back up to his jaw, where she took the lobe of one ear into her mouth and began caressing it with the tip of her tongue. Longarm cradled her buttocks in his hands and began to slide her slowly back and forth on his erection.

Teena's mouth left his ear and sought his lips. He opened them to her darting tongue, still moving her back and forth, and a wordless cry formed in her throat, a low-pitched vibration like the purring of a cat, that set her body quivering.

She sucked his tongue deep into her mouth, her lips working around it as she drew it in, while the vibration that was shaking her small body increased in intensity. Longarm stepped up the tempo of his stroking. Now he began easing her buttocks away from him until he almost came out of her, then pulling her to him in a single fast motion until their hips thumped together.

Teena's breath was whistling through her nostrils, and her breasts, pressing hard against the thick brown curls on Longarm's chest, were heaving frantically. She threw her head back and opened her eyes to look at him.

"I'm getting awfully close," she gasped. "And I'm not going to hold back unless you want me to. We'll have to stop for a minute if you do, and I don't want to stop. You're giving me feelings like I've never had before!"

"You let go when you're ready, Teena. I'm sort of long-winded and it won't bother me one bit."

"Just don't stop when I let go. It does something extra to me when a man can carry me through and keep on going all the time. And I'll be ready again in just a few minutes."

45

"It won't matter a bit how long it is before you're ready for the next time. I'll hold on, all right."

Teena nodded and closed her eyes, squeezing their lids tightly together, concentrating on her own sensations. Longarm maintained his quick-paced stroking, and in a moment or two her legs tightened convulsively around his hips, she threw her head back, and her body started shaking like a windblown aspen leaf until the quivers came one after another and merged into one last, shuddering spasm that brought a loud sigh of satisfaction, and her body went limp in Longarm's hands.

She slumped forward, her arms around his neck, while he slowed the tempo with which he was sliding her back and forth on his rock-hard shaft. After a few minutes, Teena began to breathe more evenly. She stirred and leaned back again, smiled up at Longarm, and leaned forward to rest her head on his shoulder.

Her lips close to his ear, she said softly, "You're an amazing man, Longarm. Most big men can't hold out very long, but you haven't stopped yet. I don't see how you can keep going very much longer."

"I'm good for a while yet," Longarm told her, without breaking the rhythm with which he was moving her.

"Would you like to lie down? The grass looks nice and soft, and I'd enjoy feeling your weight pressing on me."

"If it'd pleasure you more."

Holding Teena impaled, Longarm dropped to his knees and leaned forward, lowering her onto the fragrant, yielding carpet of grass without breaking the connection of flesh that joined them. Teena sighed when she felt his weight on her, and spread her thighs wider. He thrust deeply and she raised her hips to meet his.

"Oh God," she whispered gustily, "I think you're going deeper than you did before, and it feels so wonderful that I'm going to be ready sooner than I usually am. Are you going to come with me this time, Longarm?"

"I'm getting close. Hold on just a little while longer."

"As long as I can. But don't hold back this time."

Longarm did not answer her. He was building up to his own orgasm now. He drove into Teena with long, hard strokes that brought her up to meet him. He held back only long enough to feel the ecstatic rolling of her body under his, and then he'd reached the point where his body took control and he pierced her with a final hard lunge and held himself pressed against her while he shook and drained with a deep, satisfied sigh.

They lay quiet for a while in the warm sunshine, Teena holding Longarm in a soft embarce, her head pressed to his muscular shoulder. Finally she stirred and sighed.

"I'd like to lie here this way forever," she whispered. "But I've lost track of time, and we've got to get back to town in time to catch the train to Santa Fe."

"Too bad about that, but there ain't no way to change it," Longarm said philosophically. He stood up and rummaged in his vest to find a cheroot.

Teena propped herself up on an elbow and watched him as he touched a match to the cigar. She said with a smile, "You see? You're not a bit embarrassed when I look at you nude, now. It's too bad there's not enough time left for me to sketch you."

"I still won't promise, but maybe I won't feel so funny about it later on."

"I don't really care about the sketch, Longarm," Teena told him as she stood up and started to disentangle her clothing. "No sketch I could make would be as wonderful as what you gave me instead."

"Maybe that's something we can do in Santa Fe."

Teena corrected him with a knowing smile. "Yes. But I hope what you're really saying is that the sketch is something *else* we can do in Santa Fe. Because I'm still a long way from having all I want of you, Longarm!"

Chapter 5

In the total darkness of the big square room, the glow of the cheroot that Longarm had just lighted enabled him to orient himself in the strange chamber. He stood up, moving quietly to keep from disturbing Cristina Albee, who was sleeping soundly in the wide, low bed that Longarm had found uncomfortably soft. He padded on bare feet to the window and parted the heavy drape a few inches to look out. The opening revealed the vista he'd expected, an oblique view of the tree-studded plaza that he knew from previous visits was the heart of Santa Fe.

Dawn was bringing a translucent gray light to the square and to the narrow, graveled streets that defined its sides. The room from which Longarm looked was on the hotel's second floor, and the hotel stood at an intersection of two of the streets enclosing the plaza. From his vantage point, Longarm could see most of the square itself and two of the intersecting streets that ran along its sides.

On one street the ancient Palace of the Governors stretched across one entire side of the square. The long, low adobe building was in shadow. Under the protruding ends of the *vigas* that supported the roof, its dozen windows were still dark, and the wide double doors set deep in the building's thick walls were closed. At right angles to the Palace, the business buildings that faced the intersecting street were as dark as the Palace.

Three or four women draped in black *rebozos* were hurrying through the tree-studded square; the bells of San Francisco Cathedral began chiming as Longarm watched, suggesting to him that the women were hurrying to early Mass. An ox-drawn, two-wheeled *carreta* was making its way along one side of the plaza, and on the other side a woodchopper led his tiny burro, its back piled with short lengths of piñon he'd cut in the mountains.

Well, old son, Longarm told himself, looking again at the Palace while he savored the fragrant smoke of his cheroot, *it's going to be real interesting to find out what kind of stew Governor Wallace has been cooking up. Most likely there's a few of those mean bastards from the old Santa Fe Ring still lurking around, which means you better keep looking over your shoulder unless you got a hankering for a bullet in your back. They'll be after your hide sure as shooting, soon as they find out you're back in New Mexico Territory. Yes sir, this might turn out to be a right interesting case.*

He and Teena Albee had reached the territorial capital a little after midnight, following a chilly and jolting fifteen-mile ride in a stage from the Santa Fe station at Lamy. They'd taken separate but adjoining rooms at the old hotel called La Fonda, which stood at the corner of the square beside the decaying remains of the corrals where, in colonial days, merchants from Old Mexico and, a hundred years later, traders and emigrants from the Santa Fe Trail, had penned their stock.

Although the hour was late and the trip had been tiring, they'd wasted no time taking up their lovemaking from the point at which they'd interrupted it in the late afternoon on the mountainside above Trinidad. This time they had no train to catch, and their bouts had been more leisurely and prolonged, with embellishments made possible by the comfort of a bed and the warmth of a fire that gradually faded to a soft glow of dying coals in the little domed fireplace that occupied a corner of Teena's room.

Only dead ashes remained in the fireplace now; the fire had gone out during the exhausted sleep into which both he and Teena had fallen after their last protracted embrace, but the room was still comfortably warm. Longarm had slept well at first, but as the night wore on, hunger and a hankering to clear his gullet with a good swallow or two of Maryland rye had conspired with the too-soft bed to make his naps shorter and his sleep increasingly restless.

Turning away from the window, leaving the heavy draperies open in a gap that allowed the gray predawn light to brighten the room, he looked at Teena. She was lying on her back, and at some time had pulled a sheet halfway up her body. Longarm studied her for a moment, recalling the night with a smile. In sleep, Teena's oval face looked as guileless and innocent as a child's, though the avidity and inventiveness she'd displayed in bed had proved to Longarm that she was very much a woman.

Her full, high breasts with their dark rosettes called to Longarm's hands, and her pouting lips, even fuller now, swollen from their kisses of the night, looked soft and inviting, and tempted his lips. He thought of kissing her, and desire battled with duty in his mind for a moment. Then, as had been the case so often in the past when he'd faced similar temptations, duty won. He decided the time had come when he must leave.

His bare feet noiseless on the carpeted floor, Longarm put on his balbriggans, slid into his gray flannel shirt, and pulled on his brown twill trousers. He lifted his gunbelt from the knob on the headboard of the ornately carved wooden bed, where it had hung since he'd come into Teena's room the night before. His coat, vest, and hat were in his own room next door, as was the bottle of Tom Moore. He'd bought the liquor before leaving Trinidad, but Teena had found the bite of the Maryland rye too sharp for her liking when she'd sampled the liquor on the train.

Fishing the key to his room out of the pocket of his pants, Longarm picked up his stovepipe cavalry boots from the floor beside the bed and started from the room. He'd gotten halfway to the door when Teena's voice stopped him.

"Aren't you even going to kiss me goodbye, Longarm?" she asked.

"You were sleeping so sound, I didn't want to wake you up."

"You didn't. I think instinct did. Don't you know all women have a sixth sense that tells them when a lover's about to leave them? As far as I know, I didn't hear a sound, but all of a sudden I was wide awake."

Longarm went back to the bed and sat down beside Teena. She pulled herself upright, put a pillow at her back, and leaned against the headboard. Longarm looked at her in the dim light, and temptation tweaked him again.

"You want me to stay a while longer?" he asked.

"Of course I do, but I realize you've got to start on your case today. But you won't go off to wherever Uncle Lew sends you without saying goodbye, will you?"

"You know I wouldn't do that, Teena. Soon as I talk to the governor, I'll have a better idea about when I'll have to leave to get to wherever he's sending me. I'll hurry on back then, and we can say goodbye the proper way."

"If you mean what I think you do," she smiled, "I'll just wait right here in bed for you."

Longarm bent to kiss her, and she clung to him for a moment, then he stood up and went into his own room. The first thing that caught his eye, even in the dim gray dawn light, was the face of Tom Moore looking at him from the label of the bottle that stood on the bureau. Dropping his boots beside the chair, Longarm went to the bureau and had his morning eye-opener swallow of the sharp-smooth Maryland rye, then lighted a fresh cheroot.

As the warmth of the liquor spread from his stomach, he grew aware of his bare feet, chilling in the unheated room. He sat down and worked his feet into the boots before chasing his eye-opener with a second small swallow from the bottle. The curtains at his window had not been drawn. Looking out, Longarm saw that the plaza was brighter now, with sunrise near, and that a light glowed in one window of the Palace of the Governors. There was more movement on the square and the portions of the streets that he could see from the window.

No use in lollygagging around, he told himself. *Folks are starting to stir, and if there's any worms around, it's the early birds that'll get 'em.*

Lighting the lamp, Longarm adjusted its wick until it no longer smoked. Sitting down, he slid his Colt out of its holster and pressed the cylinder latch. Dumping the five cartridges from its chambers into his hand, he inspected the nose of each shell for burrs or nicks that might cause the slug to yaw, then looked closely at the base of each shell for traces of oil that could seep into the primer and create a misfire. As each cartridge passed his inspection, he reloaded a chamber.

Holstering the Colt again, he took his vest off the back of the chair in which he sat. From its bottom pocket he took his watch and the stubby little derringer that was clipped to the other end of its gold-washed chain. It was the work of only a few seconds to give the two cartridges in the derringer's barrels the same inspection he'd given the loads of his Colt. Longarm slid his arms into the vest, adjusted the watch in the left-hand pocket, and draped the chain across his chest to the right-hand pocket, where he placed the derringer. Then he donned his coat and walked downstairs.

Except for a clerk, bent over the registration desk asleep, with his head resting on his arms, the tiny lobby was deserted.

Longarm went outside into the sunrise-flushed morning. The air was nippy at that more-than-a-mile-high altitude as he cut diagonally across the plaza to the street lined with business buildings, where lights now showed in several of the structures. The cafe that he remembered from his earlier visits was open, but the barbershop a few doors away from it was still dark.

A half-hour later, when he came out of the restaurant after a steak-and-eggs breakfast, the barber was just unlocking the door of his shop. Longarm followed him in, dozed in the chair while water heated over a charcoal brazier, and emerged freshly shaven, his tanned cheeks tingling with bay rum, his mustache trimmed and waxed, restored to its steerhorn curves. He glanced at the Palace and saw lights glowing in all its windows now. He strolled across the plaza again and went through the open doors of the wide entry.

A soldier in dress blues, his sleeves bearing the stripes of a master sergeant, sat at a desk just inside the entry, shuffling papers from one pile to another. He looked up at Longarm.

"You looking for somebody, mister? Or just looking?"

"I'm looking for Governor Wallace, if he's here at this time of the day."

"You're about two hours too early, friend. The governor don't see nobody until nine, and it's just going on seven."

"I'd imagine if you was to tell him I'm out here, he'd want to talk to me. I'm Deputy U.S. Marshal Long, from Denver."

"Marshal, nobody who don't wear two stars on his shoulders is going past me until nine o'clock. Them's my standing orders." Involuntarily, the sergeant glanced over his shoulder at the closed door behind him. "If I was to interrupt General Wallace while he's working on that book of his, he'd have my stripes!"

"Now, I'd be sorry if that was to happen, Sergeant, but the governor sent for me all the way around through Washington, and I can't start my work for him until I get in to talk to him."

Before the sergeant could move, Longarm stepped around the table and put a hand on the man's shoulder, pinning him into his chair. The sergeant looked up, startled, but could not move in time to stop Longarm from tapping on the door of the governor's office and immediately opening the door. Governor Wallace was sitting in the center of the room between a wide desk and a wider table, both piled high with papers. He looked up with a frown when the door opened.

"Sorry to bust in on you this way, Governor," Longarm said quickly. "I'm Deputy U.S. Marshal Long, out of Denver. My chief told me I was to report to you as soon as I landed here in Santa Fe, so I didn't want to waste any time. Now, if you tell me to come back later on, that's sure what I'll do, seeing as you're my boss as long as I'm in New Mexico Territory."

While Wallace was still staring blankly at Longarm, the sergeant managed to slide out of his chair and scramble to the door. He said, "I told him to come back at nine, General, but he—"

"It's all right, Higgins," Wallace told the sergeant. "The marshal's just carrying out his orders. I don't blame you for letting him outmaneuver you. From what I've heard about him, Marshal Long can move faster than most men."

"You want me to—" Higgins began.

Wallace stopped him with a gesture. "Just go back to your post, Higgins. And don't let anybody else interrupt me while I'm talking with Marshal Long."

Taking the governor's words as an invitation, Longarm stepped into the office. His face a study in puzzled anger, Higgins closed the door.

"You seem to have a way of taking charge, don't you, Marshal?" Wallace asked. He looked at the chairs near the table where he was working, but all of them were piled high with books and papers. He told Longarm, "Just clear a seat for yourself. I can't find anything I'm looking for anyhow, so one chairful more or less doesn't matter."

Longarm looked around the office while he lifted books and stacks of paper from the handiest chair. In spite of its size, the big room seemed small because of the books spilling out of the overfilled shelves that lined three of its four walls, and piled in untidy stacks on the floor. The room contained little furniture in addition to the desk and table in the center, with lampstands at the end of each; a coat-rack stood near the door and there were a half-dozen straight chairs. Like the one Longarm was clearing, each chair held a disorderly melange of thick tomes and piles of paper.

Wallace saw Longarm studying the disarray. He said, "I'm not sure whether you're aware of it, Marshal, but I'm an author by choice, even if I have become a soldier and a politician to serve my country, and a lawyer to earn a living."

"I know about your soldiering, Governor," Longarm replied, pulling up the chair he'd cleared and sitting down. "And I guess anybody that gets to be governor of a territory or a state has got to do some politicking. I hadn't heard about the others, but I ain't much at reading, and the only lawyers I run into are the ones I see when I have to testify in court."

Wallace smiled. "A surprisingly large number of people have managed to avoid buying or reading the only book I've had published so far," he said. "I'm afraid *The Fair God* was something less than a literary sensation. I hope the one I'm trying to find time to finish now will do better. It's about a young Roman chariot racer named Ben Hur, and his conversion from paganism to Christianity, back in the days when Christ first appeared on earth."

"Sounds like it'll be right interesting," Longarm said politely.

"My only problem is trying to work on it in the little time I have away from my duties as governor," Wallace sighed. "But you didn't come here for a literary discussion. We'd better get down to business. I'm very glad the Attorney General responded to my request that you be assigned to the job I have for you."

By exercising a great deal of self-control, Longarm kept his jaw from dropping. *Why in hell didn't Billy Vail tell me the governor asked for me on this damn case?* he wondered. *Guess he might've thought if he told me, I'd get too big for my britches. But how'd a high muckety-muck like Governor Wallace ever come to know my name any more'n I know the name of Adam's off-ox?*

Wallace answered Longarm's unspoken question when he went on, "I heard a great deal about you, Marshal Long, in connection with the job you did in beginning to break up the old Santa Fe Ring when you were assigned to a case here before. I didn't make the connection at first between the man they kept calling Longarm and a certain deputy U.S. marshal named Long, though."

"Well, Longarm's a sort of nickname I picked up, Governor. I guess more folks know me by it than by my born name."

"You won't mind my using it, then, I hope."

"Not a bit, Governor." Longarm took out a cheroot, but did not light it at once. He asked Wallace, "Is the old Ring back at work? I know it wasn't busted up all the way when I left."

"If it wasn't broken up, it was pretty badly bent," Wallace replied. "Oh, I've had a bit of trouble with what's left of the Ring, but certainly nothing like my predecessors did."

"It was the Ring that ran the territory, not the governor, when I come here before," Longarm commented.

"So I've heard. And I'm not certain the Ring's involved in the matter we have in hand now. However, my legal training makes me a bit overly suspicious of men and their motives. The Ring was a very profitable thing for its members once, so I'm inclined to suspect that some of them are involved in these problems the Santa Fe Railroad is having west of Albuquerque."

"Billy Vail—he's my chief in Denver—told me a little bit about what's going on down there," Longarm said. "It sounded at first like it was just the old ruckus that folks stir up when they don't want to see their range cut up by railroad tracks, but if you think the Ring's mixed up in it—"

"I'm not all that sure," the governor broke in. "Any more than I'm sure it wasn't the Ring that kept the railroad out of Santa Fe."

"I wondered why we had to take a stage here from Lamy. But what's that got to do with the Ring?"

"As I said, I'm not sure it was the Ring, but I do know the man responsible was closely connected to the Ring, perhaps one of its top men. Do you recall a Señor Emiliano Montemayor, Longarm, from your troubles with the Ring?"

Longarm thought for a moment before shaking his head. "That name don't stick in my mind. But I never did find out the names of all the men mixed up in that case."

"Montemayor was a member of one of the old Spanish land-grant families. He managed to buy up most of the mountain passes in the Sangre de Cristos when the Santa Fe began surveying for its route south from Raton Pass. He didn't have enough money to buy the amount of land involved, though."

"So the cash came from the Ring?"

"That's my suspicion." Wallace noticed the cheroot in Longarm's hand and motioned for him to go ahead and light it as he went on, "Montemayor must have known which passes the railroad would need so they could lay track into Santa Fe most economically, and he offered them his land at a price just enough below the cost of building on an alternative route. But when it came to the last pass between here and Lamy, the Santa

Fe balked. Obviously they had figured out Montemayor's game by then. So they simply established their terminal at Lamy, and now the Santa Fe doesn't have any tracks into the town it's named for."

"So they jumped on down to Albuquerque," Longarm said. "They had to push on west toward California pretty fast to get their land grants along the right-of-way, I'd guess."

"That was their main concern at the time. It's still their main concern right now. There are other roads building, Longarm, you know that, building both west and east. It's a race, and the Santa Fe is set on winning it. From what I've heard, they have to win it to survive. So now you understand why you're here."

"A lot better'n I did before. So you got an idea that what's left of the old Ring is giving 'em the kind of trouble my chief told me they're having?"

"A suspicion, that's all. I don't look on the railroad's trouble as being a lot of individual incidents. I think it's all part of a planned scheme to blackmail the Santa Fe, just as Montemayor did when he held them up on the mountain passes. And if I'm right, that means some single individual or group is at work in the background."

"Meaning what's left of the old Ring?"

"Exactly. But whether or not I'm right about that, Longarm, I want the trouble stopped, and if the Ring's involved, I want whatever is left of it smashed. You're the best man I could think of to finish the job you started."

"Well, I thank you for the compliment, Governor."

"It's not just an idle compliment. You're familiar with the territory and you've tangled with the Ring before. Besides, since you're coming in from the outside, I can be sure you don't have any strings tied to you by the survivors of the old Ring."

"That's one thing for certain you won't have to worry about They don't like me any better'n I like them. Tell me something, Governor. Can you put names to any of the men on your list of Ring leftovers who you figure are still around?"

"You know I can't, Longarm. The men who made up the old Ring never did let outsiders know who they were, or even that such an organization really existed."

"You're right about that. Everybody knew there was a Ring, but nobody was willing to talk about it."

"I was hoping you'd remember some names," the governor said. "If I just had a starting point, I might be able to get rid of at least a few of the troublemakers."

"Oh, I remember a pretty fair number of names from the times I spent here before."

"That's good! Give them to me, and maybe I can connect them with some of the members who are left."

Longarm shook his head. "I don't think that'd help you much, Governor. The names I remember are all carved on tombstones now. Besides, I never could be too certain about the ones that got off free."

Wallace's voice reflected the disappointment that showed on his face. "You'll be starti.ig from the beginning again, then?"

"Pretty much, I guess. First I got to find out where to start, though."

"You might start with Jim Ferrell. He's the Santa Fe's construction superintendent. You'll find him at the railhead, which is about fifty miles west of Albuquerque."

"I'll see him, sure. But the ones I aim to go after ain't the ones that just do the dirty work. Who I'm lookin for are the ones that are paying to have it done."

"You'll still have to find a place to put your starting wedge, Longarm, and the only way I can see for you to find it is to go out to the Santa Fe railhead and get the whole story firsthand from Ferrell."

"If that's the way of it, I best start moving, then. I don't guess the territory's got any government-issue horses? I'll need one."

"I'd suggest you rent one at a livery stable when you get to Albuquerque," Wallace said. "You could get one here from the remount station at Fort Marcy, but you'd have to ride it or ship it to Albuquerque."

"I'd figure the territory might have some kind of office in Albuquerque, or keep a stable there where I could borrow a horse."

"Don't count on the territory to give or lend you much of anything, Longarm. It's close to bankruptcy now, thanks to all the graft and kickbacks that have been paid by the big land-owners to get their taxes reduced."

"Sounds to me like you got some problems."

"More than I like to think about. I've just told you why I

asked for you to be sent here. I know some of the political appointees that I have to rely on are still loyal to what's left of the old Ring, and there are other pockets of corruption that I haven't been able to clean up. I'm hoping you can help me by finishing the job you started before I was appointed."

"I'll do what I can, Governor." Longarm frowned thoughtfully. "How about my reports, Governor? If you got some of the old gang working for you—"

"Don't worry about that. Don't address any letters or telegrams to me, though. Send them to Sergeant Higgins, Terence Higgins. He'll pass them on."

"Seeing as how he's army, I guess you can trust him," Longarm said.

"As soon as I understood the situation here, I asked General Sheridan to give me a few men like Higgins for my personal staff—men I was sure I could trust. I'll instruct Higgins to be watching for anything you send me."

Longarm stood up. "I'll be going, then. No use in me hanging around here if whoever I need to talk to first is out west of Albuquerque."

"If you need expense money, I do have a small contingency fund that I can draw on."

"I'm all right for now, Governor. If I find I need more'n I got, I'll let you know."

Wallace sighed. "I'm feeling better already, now that I know you're going to be on the job. There've been times"—he shook his head—"times when I've felt I was just like a teamster with a wagon stuck in mud so deep his team couldn't pull it out."

"Considering what you run into when you took on the job, I'd say you've made a lot of headway."

"I'm not so sure sometimes. Right now, the army's having trouble with the Jicarilla Apaches up north and the Chiricahuas in the south. The old Hispanic families keep pulling in one direction, the Anglo settlers pulling in another." Wallace sighed sadly. "When the President asked me to take this appointment, I was glad of the chance. I thought I'd have a lot of time to myself so that I could finish my new novel. I'm not one to give up easily, but I'll admit there are times when I get discouraged."

"I might have some news that'll cheer you up a little bit, then. On the train coming down from Colorado, I got acquainted with your niece, Miss Albee."

"Cristina's here?"

"She's at the hotel right now, and I imagine she'll be visiting you pretty soon."

"I knew she was going to visit me, but I wasn't sure exactly when she'd be here. It's been several years since I've seen her, you know. She's been in Europe, studying art."

"That's what she told me on the train. She said she's come out here to paint pictures, mostly of Indians."

"Well, I'll be glad to see her. It'll be nice to have someone from home. At least I can talk to her without having to weigh every word I say." He extended a hand to Longarm. "Good luck. I'll be waiting for your first reports."

"Don't look for much right fast, Governor. I might stop a few days in Albuquerque and nosey around. I been thinking while we were talking. If I was out to make trouble for the railroad, I'd figure it'd be easier to work down there closer to the railhead than up here in the capital."

"It's your case from this point on, Longarm. And I don't mind saying that I'm glad to see you take at least part of my worries off my hands."

With his mind busy filing the scanty information he'd gotten from Governor Wallace, Longarm walked slowly across the now-bustling plaza to the hotel.

Looks like you really got a job on your hands this time, he thought as he strolled along the sun-dappled flagstone walk. *You're going to be right busy when you get to Albuquerque, and you can't get a train out of here until late this evening. But Teena's waiting for you at the hotel, and there ain't a better way to spend the rest of the day than telling her goodbye.*

Chapter 6

Sitting in the cupola of the caboose, facing forward, the setting sun was in Longarm's eyes. He'd long ago gotten tired of watching the raw new ties and the brown steel rails, still unpolished by use, disappearing under the locomotive of the Santa Fe work train that he'd boarded in Albuquerque. Instead of squinting into the sun's bright orange disc, he kept his eyes on the barren country on either side of the newly laid tracks.

There'd been very little to see since the rails began curving west after passing the little Indian pueblo of Isleta, fifteen miles south of Albuquerque. To the north there'd been only the upslopes of a series of high plateaus, humps with flattened tops that cut off any view in that direction. To the south, the shortgrassed prairie undulated to the horizon, a monotonous vista of brown and ocher.

From time to time he'd seen flocks of sheep grazing placidly on the dying grass. Once, a herd of cattle had run from the train, the steers tossing their polished horns as they bolted. Except for the huddled cluster of terraced adobe buildings he'd glimpsed fleetingly at a distance when the tracks had skirted Laguna Peublo shortly after noon, the only sign of human habitation had been three or four dilapidated adobe hovels, and the occasional ruts of a wagon road.

Ahead, the locomotive tooted a signal. The head brakeman, playing a desultory game of casino with his four-man crew in the central section of the caboose, tossed his cards on the table and said, "All right, boys. Let's get out and earn our pay while this old rattler goes up the hump."

Indifferently, the brakemen dropped their cards and followed the foreman to the front of the caboose, where they picked up their brake-bars before disappearing through the forward door. For the most part, the train crew had ignored Longarm's presence except when he'd asked one of them a direct question, but their attitude had not been unfriendly, merely uninterested in their passenger or his business. They already knew his destination, the railhead, which now could not be too far distant, Longarm thought.

From his vantage point in the cupola, Longarm watched the brakemen as they took their stations along the train. He'd seen the brakemen go through their routine a half-dozen times since the train had pulled out of Albuquerque that morning, the men taking places at intervals on the tops of boxcars, ready to tighten up the brakes if a coupling gave way and part of the long string began to roll back down the incline.

Like most work trains, this one was a mixture of boxcars, flatcars, gondolas, stock cars, and tank cars. It carried rails, ties, tools, water, foodstuffs, horses, and mules—all the materials needed by the track gangs that were pushing the Santa Fe's rails west. He'd found out about the work train's schedule from the livery stable in Albuquerque, where he'd rented the horse that now rode in one of the stock cars ahead.

"Hell, mister, ain't no use in you forking this nag for two days if you're going out to railhead," the liveryman had said after learning Longarm's destination. "It ain't that I don't want the extra two bits a day I'd make renting it, but you'll save yourself a damn long ride if you just load the horse on that Santa Fe work train that goes out there every other day."

A brief discussion with the dispatcher at the temporary freight depot, and an exchange of wired messages with Jim Ferrell, the construction superintendent, had resulted in the horse being loaded into a stock car and Longarm being given a seat in the caboose.

And it sure beats setting two days in a saddle, Longarm thought as he watched the engine entering the curve at the top of the grade, only to have it disappear almost at once behind the wall of the cut in the pass that topped the incline.

For a few moments the raw sides of the cut towered over the caboose as the train pulled over the hump and started downgrade. The brakemen on the two rear cars began twirling the brake wheels, and the string began to slow down.

Ahead, in silhouette against the rim of the disappearing sun, Longarm could see the sprawl of the construction camp. It was a motley assortment of tents and shanties stretching along one side of the tracks. The settlement was separated by a wide strip of rutted gravel road from the half-dozen sidings where boarding-house cars, cabooses, two or three yard dinkies, and a clutter of other rolling stock stood waiting to be unloaded or hauled back to the supply depot.

Well, old son, looks like you got where you're headed, Longarm told himself, clambering down the ladder that led to the floor of the caboose. *Now all you got to do is find this fellow Ferrell and see what-all's been happening here, and you can get on with the case.*

Jim Ferrell turned out to be a stocky, bushy-browed man in his middle thirties, when Longarm ran him down in the converted caboose that the construction superintendent was using as a combination office and living quarters. Ferrell sat in a swivel chair between a square table and a desk in the windowed cupola of the car. The desk was strewn with lists, maps, and charts. An acetylene lantern hanging from the ceiling had already been lighted.

Below the lantern, tilted back in his chair, Ferrell was clutching a thick sheaf of waybills in one hand and a well-chewed cigar in the other, and listening to three overall-clad railroad men who were all talking at the same time. When he'd finally finished answering the questions of the trio, he looked around at Longarm.

"You'll be the U.S. marshal that Elmer Parsons wired me about from Albuquerque," he said.

"That's right, Mr. Ferrell. Long's my name."

"Well, I don't know why the hell you've come out here to the railhead," Ferrell said somewhat irritably. "The source of all our troubles is in Albuquerque or Santa Fe. That's where the main office of the teamster company's located, and where most of the ranchers that've been disputing our new right-of-way have offices. They're the ones I want you to get off my back, not my gangs out here. I can handle them myself."

"Now wait a minute, Mr. Ferrell. Nobody's said a word to me about teamsters. I knew you had some trouble about your right-of-way, and if this is like all of the other railheads I've seen, you'll have a bunch of deadheads, gamblers, and whores and their pimps and sharpers and plug-uglies all grabbing at your crews on paydays, trying to get their money."

"They don't worry me," Ferrell said curtly. "I've got our own Santa Fe police to keep them in line. But you're right, of course, Long. This Hell on Wheels is just the same as all the others, but I've bucked the railhead camp followers on construction jobs before, and I can hold my own in the clinches. What's happening here is something new, though."

"I guess the best thing is for you to start and tell me about it from the beginning," Longarm suggested. "You're the only man I've talked to since I left Denver that knows firsthand what's going on."

"Long, I haven't got time to talk, right this minute. I've got to check these waybills before the work train picks up the empties and starts back to Albuquerque, and there's a crew boss I've got to fire before the day's over. Tell you what. I eat supper here in my office. I'll put your name in the pot at the chowcar, and you come back here in, oh, an hour or so. We can talk while we're eating."

"That'll suit me fine," Longarm agreed. "I got a horse in one of those stock cars on the work train. I'll have to get him and find where I can put him up. And I'll have to have a place to sleep while I'm here."

"Put the horse in our corral, since you're on Santa Fe business," Ferrell said. "And we've got plenty of bunks in the car my foremen sleep in. I don't know whether our grub's any better than you'd find in the joints in Hell on Wheels, but if I can stand it, I guess you can. Later, if you want to eat at the foreman's table in the chow car, you're welcome."

"I call that right hospitable, Mr. Ferrell, I'll see you in about an hour, then."

With his livery horse turned into the corral and his saddle gear safely stowed in the farrier's supply car, Longarm started out to look around the railhead camp. As Ferrell had said, it was like those he'd seen before. Longarm's assignments had taken him to many railheads, where the camp followers lived in the movable settlements the railroaders had named Hell on Wheels.

He'd seen the like of the Santa Fe's Hell on Wheels in Wyoming along the Union Pacific, in Colorado on the Denver & Rio Grande, in Montana on the Northern Pacific, in Arizona along the Southern Pacific, in Texas along the Rock Island, and in other places where his cases had taken him.

Everywhere he looked, what he saw recalled places he'd visited before. Almost all the structures lining the chewed-up dirt road that ran parallel to the rails looked as though they'd been put up yesterday and could be knocked down and moved tomorrow, when the rails had moved far enough ahead to take the construction crews out of easy reach.

There were the same frame-supported tents, half hidden behind high false fronts of hastily painted boards, mixed with a few wooden buildings erected by optimistic merchants who hoped that the railhead settlement would turn into a permanent town. There were the same pictures of foaming steins of beer in front of the saloons; the same red lanterns hanging above the doors of the whorehouses and cribs; the same hand-lettered signs—"CAFE" and "NOTIONS" and "DRY GOODS"; the same barber's pole painted in shaky spirals of red and white.

If the jerry-built shelters were the same, so were the people milling around them. Since most of the construction gangs worked from daylight until dark, the Hell on Wheels establishments had their fullest life from early evening until midnight. The rush was just beginning when Longarm strolled along the road.

Longarm could identify almost all the men he saw by the jobs they did. Tie-setters and tracklayers had the broad shoulders and bulging muscles of men who lifted the heavy ties and rails and swung sledges that pinned the fishplates down. The pick-and-shovel workers had bulging muscles too, but most of them walked with a sidewise swinging of their shoulders developed from their constant turning of their bodies on the job. Members of the surveying parties that kept just ahead of the rails moved with the easy stride of men accustomed to long walks that took them over rough, unbroken ground.

Crew foremen wore vests bulging with papers and pencils, and their clothes were less sweat-stained than those worn by the laborers. The few office workers wore coats in addition to vests, and their hands were white and smooth; their clothing had no sweat stains at all. The muleskinners and bullwhackers, whose teams hauled materials from the construction camp stockpiles to the spot where the actual construction work was going on, always carried their whips; to them the whip was both tool and weapon.

Few of the inhabitants of Hell on Wheels were abroad at the moment. The early evening was the time when they tended to their business. There was a constant flapping of the saloons' batwings, and a steady stream of customers entered and emerged from the cribs and whorehouses. The restaurant tents were crowded, and the yellow panels of lamplight that streamed into the road from the few retail establishments were blotted out at frequent intervals by the forms of patrons entering and leaving.

Puffing his cheroot, Longarm strolled unhurriedly along the full length of the road before his time sense told him that Ferrell would be looking for him to show up. He reached the construction boss's caboose-office just as an aproned flunky from the chow car arrived with two food-laden trays balanced on his arms.

"Looks like your nose led you here just in time," Ferrell said as Longarm followed the flunky into the car.

Waiting until the cook's helper had distributed the plates and bowls of food on the table and left carrying the trays, the construction boss rummaged in his desk and brought out a squat black bottle and two glasses. He poured, and pushed a glass across the desk to Longarm.

"We don't observe Rule G in office cars," he smiled. "So I can offer you a small sip to clear your gullet before we eat. It's Gilbey's best Irish, and you'll find it a pleasant whiskey to taste."

Longarm swallowed half the whiskey and said to Farrell,"I'm a Maryland rye man myself, but I'll have to admit, Irish is my second choice."

"And I'll take Maryland rye when I can't find Irish," Ferrell said. "So we're not too far apart in important things, are we, Marshal Long?"

"I'd say we're pretty close, Mr. Ferrell," Longarm replied.

Ferrell went on, "Now if we're going to eat and drink and do business together, let's don't be so damned formal. I'd rather be called Jim, if it's all the same to you, and I suppose you've got a name that goes in front of Long, so if you'll tell me what it is—"

"Well, I got a front name, but nobody much uses it anymore. My friends have got a nickname they call me. Longarm."

"Sit down, then, Longarm, and let's see what the Santa Fe's belly-robber's got for us this evening."

They ate beef stew with hot biscuits and sipped hot black coffee with apple pie, spending very little time on casual conversation. Their plates pushed away, Longarm drew a pair of cheroots from his breast pocket and offered one to Ferrell. The construction superintendent had already reached behind him into a drawer of his desk and produced a fat brown cigar. He waved the cheroot aside.

"No offense, Longarm, but a man's taste in cigars is keener than his taste in liquor. I'll smoke my own, if it's all the same to you."

Longarm flicked a match across his thumbnail and bent forward to hold it to the tip of Ferrell's cigar. He'd just started to lean forward, pulling away from the high back of his chair, when the glass of the dark, uncurtained window on one side of the cupola broke with a crash, the sharp bark of a revolver sounded from outside, and a chunk of lead scored the wooden back of the chair where his broad shoulders had been resting a fraction of a second earlier.

Longarm's instinct triggered his instantaneous reaction to the shot, taking over at the moment the first tinkle of breaking glass reached his ears. He threw himself forward, pushing the table aside with one hand while, with the other, he grabbed Ferrell by the ankle and pulled him to the floor also.

A second shot followed the first, the two reports sounding almost as one. The second slug hit the edge of the chair back, sending the chair toppling to the floor. By the time it hit, though, Longarm and Ferrell were already on their way to the floor. Their bodies were below the bottom of the windowsill, invisible to the sniper outside.

Leaving the construction boss sprawled and sputtering, Longarm rolled across the floor toward the broken window. He turned his body as he rolled, to carry him to one side of the window opening. As he bounced to his feet, safely out of sight beside the window, he was whipping his Colt from its cross-draw holster high on his left hip.

With the wall shielding his body, standing as close to the window opening as possible, Longarm peered outside. A moment passed before his eyes grew accustomed to the dim outside light, broken only by the glare of the sputtering acetylene lamp hanging on the car's ceiling. He saw nobody outside, but hadn't really expected to.

Ferrell had rolled over and was sitting on the floor, gazing at Longarm. He asked, "You see anybody out there?"

"No. Wasn't likely I would. After he missed twice, he wasn't about to hang around, knowing I'd be ready to shoot back."

"And you're not going out to look for him?"

"Wouldn't be much use. It's dark as pitch out there, and he's made tracks away from here by now."

"Whoever it was, you figure he was shooting at you?"

"More'n likely. He'd have had plenty of chances to potshot you, if that was what he had in mind."

"You have any idea who it was?"

"Not right this minute. I took a walk through Hell on Wheels after I left here earlier. Could've been somebody recognized me from a case I worked someplace else, maybe somebody I sent up for a stretch in the pen. There's plenty of such around. He could've followed me here, taken his chance to get even." A second suspicion was also forming in Longarm's mind, but he saw no reason to mention his thoughts to Ferrell at the moment.

Ferrell stood up, dusting off his clothes. He looked at the gaping window opening and said, "I'll get a man from the carpenter shop to set in a new pane tomorrow. But I think it'd be a smart thing if we covered up both windows right now."

Stepping over to the end of the car, Ferrell opened a narrow door, revealing a pair of bunks on each side of an aisle that led to the caboose door. He ripped blankets off the bunks and tossed one to Longarm, saying, "You fix one window, I'll take care of the other."

A few moments later they had the blankets draped over the window openings. Ferrell reached for the whiskey bottle and poured into the glasses that still stood on the desk.

After he'd taken a short sip, Longarm took a fresh cheroot from his pocket and lighted it. Ferrell watched his hands and said, "You've got more than your share of nerve, Longarm. I'm not sure I could hold a cigar right now, much less light one."

"You'll never know till you try." Longarm took another sip of the edgy Irish whiskey. "But I guess after you been shot at a few times, it don't upset you all that much."

Ferrell took another cigar out of his desk and kept his eyes on his own hands as he touched a match to it. "I just surprised myself," he said smiling through a wreath of blue smoke. "I'm not as shaky as I thought I'd be."

Longarm had stooped over to pick up his chair. He set it on its legs and settled into it. "You don't strike me as a man that spooks easy, Jim. Don't downgrade yourself."

"Oh, I'm not. And I have been shot at a time or two, but

this is the first time anybody's shot at me when I wasn't expecting it and wasn't in a position to shoot back."

"I guess there's a first time for everything." Longarm took an appreciative sip of the whiskey. "Well, we were just getting ready to see what we could figure out about the trouble you been having getting your track laid. You want to start from the beginning and tell me why you said what you did about me looking in the wrong place for whoever's back of it?"

Ferrell sat down, cigar in one hand, drink in the other, and puffed thoughtfully for a moment. "I've put down a lot of railroad track, Longarm," he began. "A lot of track in a lot of places, and I guess I've had my share of right-of-way disputes. Now tell me something. In your line of work, haven't you run into a situation where you feel there's something wrong, even if you can't quite put your finger on it?"

"Sure. You get to where you can smell a thing like that."

"Well, that's how it is with me and the trouble we've been having since we started pushing iron west from Albuquerque." He looked thoughtfully at his glass, swirling the whiskey around in it, and asked, "You know much about railroads, Longarm?"

"Not as much as you do, I reckon. I've rode a lot of 'em, and seen a bunch of tracks being laid."

"You know, a preliminary route survey just pretty much hits the high spots. It's simply to establish that there is a route a road can take."

Longarm nodded. "I can see how that'd be. First you find your general route, then you fine it down to the best one."

"That's one way to put it," Ferrell said. He went on, "In this kind of country, the surveyors look for passes through the mountains first. If they do their job right and have a little luck, they may come up with two or three alternate routes. Then there'll be a final survey run just ahead of the track gangs, and that survey might show that if we build a few miles one way or another off the early one, we'd be better off. You know, easier grades, a better route between two key passes, things like that."

Ferrell paused, and Longarm said, "I'm following you so far, Jim. Go on."

"What I suspect is happening here wasn't too obvious to begin with. We had a wrangle over the first pass we cut. I suppose you saw the cut on the way here today?" Longarm nodded and Ferrell continued, "Then I began getting reports back from our survey parties. There's five more high spots we're going to cut grades through between here and Gallup, and at four of them the final survey's relocated the line. And at every one of those four places, there's a rancher saying we can't relocate."

"All of 'em give the same excuse, I suppose?"

Ferrell nodded. "Exactly the same. They claim we'd cut up their land too badly, interfere with them working their stock, or destroy their rangeland if we relocate the line."

"I can see where you'd get the idea they were in cahoots."

"There's a little more to it," the construction boss went on. "You know, we've got to have water for our engine boilers about every forty miles, which means digging wells and putting up windmills to pump them. Now, we'll have something like a hundred and sixty miles of trackage between Albuquerque and Gallup. Four wells, you see. In this damn dry country, water's not all that easy to locate."

"You don't have to tell me that," Longarm interrupted. "I crossed enough desert land to know what you're getting at. You got ranchers all along the line that are claiming water rights to places where you need wells."

"You hit it right on the button. We've been able to get a temporary injunction for the one well that we've already put down between here and Albuquerque, but there's three of them ahead and I don't know how these local judges are going to rule in the water-rights cases that haven't been decided yet."

"Looks to me like the Santa Fe's sort of caught between a rock and a hard place, Jim."

"Of course we are. And it's the pattern these hard places seem to form that's got me convinced we're not just bucking the individual ranchers. There's somebody encouraging them, maybe even backing them, paying for their lawsuits. That's why I said earlier that you're in the wrong place, out here."

"You're figuring there's a boss of some kind behind all of your troubles? Somebody setting back in Albuquerque or Santa Fe, pulling strings?"

"I'd say there has to be something like that going on. It's not a new thing to the railroad, you know. We've run into organized opposition often enough before to recognize it when we see it. And this certainly looks organized to me."

"You said something earlier about the teamsters giving you

trouble too. I guess you're figuring they're in on the same deal the ranchers are pulling?"

"I'm betting it's all in one big package."

"From what I seen while I was walking around Hell on Wheels before supper, there's a lot of teamsters working on your job. All they'd be doing is putting their own selves out of work if you had to stop building. Why'd they do that?"

"Look ahead, Longarm," Ferrell suggested. "The teamsters have been charging ten to twenty cents a pound for freight hauls to California. Once our mainline's in operation, they're not just out of work, they're out of business for good as far as long hauls are concerned. Of course they'd still have short hauls, from the railroad to towns we won't get to, but that's just a drop in the bucket compared to what they've got now."

"I guess I hadn't looked at it that way, but it makes a lot of sense. I spotted a bunch of muleskinners and bullwhackers while I was walking through Hell on Wheels, too. Didn't know you hired all that many."

"More than you'd imagine. We've got to have teams to haul materials from our construction camp here up to the railhead. As soon as we get more iron down, we'll move this camp on farther west, and keep on leapfrogging until we meet the gangs that are pushing east from the coast."

"How're the teamsters doing you dirt, Jim?"

"In a lot of small ways that all add up to big trouble. We might figure on having twenty teams show up of a morning, and get only a dozen or fifteen. And there's too damn many wagons breaking down, a lot more than I've had on any other job."

"So your idea is that the same bunch stirring up the ranchers have been working on the teamsters too?"

"Doesn't it make sense?" Ferrell demanded.

"Yes, I guess it does."

"Damn it, I've got over four hundred men in these crews I'm working, Longarm!" the construction boss exclaimed. "If we get stopped, a lot of those men, maybe most of them, are going to drift away. It won't be easy to replace them when we start up again. And I guess you know we've got time limits to think about, as well. I'm two weeks behind now, and the days are getting shorter. If I don't get iron pushed over the Continental Divide before the snows start, I'm in trouble."

"How far ahead's the Divide, Jim?"

"About forty or forty-five miles. And it's a hell of a hump. We're talking about almost seventy-five hundred feet, and God knows how much cutting or filling we'll have to do to get a working grade."

Longarm was silent for a few moments. Then he asked, "Jim, did you ever hear about an outfit called the Santa Fe Ring?"

"I've heard it mentioned," Ferrell frowned. "I don't know anything much about it besides the name, though. Some kind of political bunch, wasn't it? Like Tweed's Ring in New York?"

"Pretty much the same, I'd say. If you wanted to do business in New Mexico Territory, you paid off the Ring in cash or by giving 'em a share in your business."

Ferrell nodded. "We've run into a lot of that, of course. But most of the grafting outfits we've had trouble with have been small potatoes, so we haven't had to pay off too much." He hesitated a moment before adding, "You know, there are times when it's cheaper to pay than fight. We bought mountain passes from some old Spanish *hidalgo* when we were building up north, until we finally balked."

"Governor Wallace told me about that in Santa Fe. My hunch is the rancher that pulled that deal was nothing but a front man for the Ring."

"You seem to think this Santa Fe Ring is at the root of all our troubles in New Mexico Territory, Longarm. Is it really that powerful?"

"There ain't much of the old Ring left, but I tangled with it a while back, and I got a hunch there's some of 'em still at work. And I got another hunch. This one's about that shooting a little while ago; it'd fit into the pattern you been laying out. I stopped in Albuquerque and Santa Fe on the way here, and I'm beginning to think somebody from the old Ring might've spotted me. They don't like me one little bit."

Ferrell frowned. "You just might have an answer there. But what can you do about it?"

"Backtrack and start digging. That's all I can do."

"You're heading back to Albuquerque, then?"

"Albuquerque first, then Santa Fe if I don't find answers in Albuquerque. When's your supply train going back, Jim?"

Ferrell shook his head. "It's already gone. Pulled out as soon as I checked the waybills."

"I'll take the one back tomorrow, then."

71

"Damn it, I hate to tell you this, but there isn't another supply train coming in for three days."

"Then I'll go horseback. Because if things are starting to hotten up, I don't want to give the Ring any sort of head start. I'll sleep over here tonight, and ride out at daybreak tomorrow. If what I'm thinking is right, you hit the nail on the head when you said I was in the wrong place. The answers ain't here, they're in Albuquerque and Santa Fe, and that's where I'm heading to find 'em!"

Chapter 7

A slender thread of gray was just beginning to outline the undulating eastern horizon when Longarm rode out of the Santa Fe construction camp the next morning. The camp was already astir, but Hell on Wheels was fast asleep. There were three or four pinpoints of light coming from the saloons, and the red lanterns still glowed over the doors of the whorehouses, but the rutted road in front of the camp followers' area was deserted.

Longarm had eaten breakfast in the chow car with the gandy dancers who were getting ready to go on the railhead for their day's work. After breakfast he'd drawn food enough for two days from the Santa Fe's commissary: a small slab of smoked bacon, a half-dozen potatoes, a chunk of summer sausage, and a handful of dried apples. He stood for a moment outside the chow car, putting the food in his saddlebag to join the emergency rations of parched corn, jerky, and coffee beans that he always carried, watching the camp boiling to life.

Lights shone from the farrier's shed and the timekeeper's hut and the little shanties where clerks checked lists of tools and materials. Lanterns bobbed through the darkness as men hustled to join their gangs. There was a clanging of steel on steel as tools hit the rails, and a heavier grating of metal against metal as the men lifted the handcars onto the tracks.

The popping of whips resounded sharply as teamsters moved their wagons to the supply dumps to have them loaded with rails and ties, fishplates and tieplates, spikes and bolts. The noises of the organized confusion of the camp followed Longarm for a mile or more as he headed the livery horse east into the line of dawn.

Even in the dim gray pre-sunrise gleam, the broad, rutted swath beaten beside the tracks by the construction gangs was easy enough to see as Longarm rode toward the rising sun. There was no wind, and the smoke from his after-breakfast cheroot hung in the air in a ghostly trace marking his passage. Once the noise of the construction camp had been left behind, the morning was silent except for the clopping of the livery horse's hooves.

Before turning in for the night, Longarm had looked at Jim Ferrell's maps, seeking landmarks to guide him across the high mesas west of Albuquerque, which the railroad tracks had avoided with their long, looping arc southward.

"You must've had a reason for heading south out of Albuquerque instead of going due west," he'd told Ferrell. "I ain't smart enough to be a surveyor, but it looks to me like any damned fool would've known to run those tracks in a straight line."

"Not when that damned fool's laying rails for an engine to run on," Ferrell had replied with a smile. "He'd know enough to choose a route that's as level as possible, even if it's longer. It costs the Santa Fe about twice as much to haul a train up even a three-percent grade as it does to haul that same load on level track. That's why we look for passes with as little rise as possible. We're looking at what we'll be hauling ten or twenty years from now as well as getting track down fast."

"It makes sense when you put it that way," Longarm had agreed. "But going uphill don't cost a penny more on a horse."

"Then just follow the old military road straight into Albuquerque when the tracks curve south," Ferrell had advised. "You can't get lost. It'll also cut about ten or fifteen miles off your ride."

"Now that's the smartest thing you've said tonight. I'll just do that, Jim."

It was a barren land that sunrise revealed to Longarm's eyes as he kept the livery horse on the smoother ground at the edge of the rutted trail. He rode across terrain that unfolded in a rolling, high-altitude prairie, its short grasses and infrequent shrubs as brown as the dry earth itself with the approach of winter. There were no trees, and the shrubs themselves were low-growing, gnarled, and sparse. No life that Longarm could see inhabited the vast sweep; not even a bird wheeled in the cloudless, light blue sky.

By midmorning the huge, imposing mass of Chacra Mesa rose in great jutting shoulders on his left. By noon, when he stopped for a bite of jerky and parched corn, the high, castlelike crag on which Acoma Pueblo stood had come into view on his right. Acoma remained in sight as he rode steadily through the afternoon, a thick thumb of stone thrust erect above a level plain. Not until late afternoon, when Longarm had gotten almost to the saucerlike valley in which Laguna Pueblo's terraced adobe buildings rose, did Acoma's tip slip below his horizon.

Shortly after he'd passed Laguna, the sun now at his back, the railroad tracks began their sweep south, but the military road Ferrell had pointed out on the map stretched straight ahead. Beyond Laguna Pueblo, with the sky behind him growing pink with the oncoming sunset, he reined in at the edge of a dropoff, an almost vertical cliff. The military road twisted sinuously in a series of sharp switchbacks hewn from the bluff's stone face.

Below, in the dark shadow of the high, sheer bluff, a tiny stream trickled turquoise blue in its rocky bed. Here and there, in widely spaced patches beside the stream, he saw the green of fresh grass.

Concluding that he'd given the taxpayers their due for this day, and reasoning that there wasn't likely to be any more water for some distance, he decided to camp by the stream for the night, which was rapidly approaching.

A bit of scrounging around the area he'd selected for his camp yielded enough bits and pieces of driftwood to fuel a small fire. Bacon broiled on a pointed stick, a potato cooked in the coals, and coffee boiled in his big tin cup provided a hot supper. The livery horse, tethered between two patches of grass, munched contentedly while Longarm topped off his meal with a good swallow of Maryland rye and unrolled his bedding.

Lying on the bedroll, a cheroot clamped between his teeth, his boots off and his coat folded under his head for a pillow, the bottle of rye beside him, Longarm considered the job ahead while he studied the stars that dotted the ink-black sky. A homely analogy popped into his mind as he thought, drawn from the days when, as a boy, he'd fished little streams and ponds with a green hickory limb and a short length of line in the hardscrabble hills of West Virginia.

Old son, you stepped into a puddle of muddy water, and right now you can't see the bottom for the silt. But it's a pretty safe bet that Jim Ferrell's right about there being just one big fish pulling all the strings that's giving the Santa Fe all the trouble they're having. Now, it ain't going to do one blessed bit of good for you to mess around with the minnows. You got to go right for the big fish. Thing you got to do is jump in and roil up the water so the minnows gets scared and starts heading for the big fish to save 'em. And right now, you ain't even sure where to look for the pond that big fish is swimming in. So just eat the apple a bite at a time. Find the pond and you'll find the minnows. Then, someplace in a big deep hole right in the middle of the pond, you'll come across that big fish, if you can hold your breath long enough.

Picking up the bottle at his side, Longarm half rose and tilted it. He'd gotten only one good swallow down when the bottle exploded in his hand, splashing the fragrant liquor on his face at the same instant that the sharp report of a rifle shot reached him from the cliff.

As cat-quick as Longarm's reflexes were, the shot and the spray that spattered his cheeks took him by surprise. He did not roll fast enough to avoid the second shot completely. The slug tore harmlessly through his shirt-sleeve and whistled past to burrow into the hard soil beyond the dying fire. Longarm jerked his torso in the manner of a man badly hit and let himself flop prone on the ground beside his blankets.

He lay in frozen stillness, hoping the sniper perched on the rim of the cliff above him wouldn't think of sending another shot into his unprotected back for good measure. Seconds slipped slowly by, and no third shot followed the first two. Longarm pressed his face against the hard earth, willing his muscles to stay relaxed and motionless until it was clear that the bushwhacker was satisfied.

Even when he was reasonably sure the immediate danger was past, he did not move, but continued to simulate a corpse while in his mind he reviewed his own ride down the steep, winding road that had been cut into the face of the bluff.

He could think of no spot on the way down where he'd lost sight of the little stream that ran a few paces from where he was now lying. That meant he would always be visible to the sniper, who he was certain was now coming down that trail.

Longarm stayed frozen for what seemed an endless time. At last he heard the slow, measured thudding made by the hooves of a horse being held on a tight rein. The sounds came closer until he could almost tell which hoof the animal was placing on the ground. They stopped, and for a long moment there was total silence. Then he heard the faint creak of saddle leather as the sniper dismounted, followed by the scraping of boot soles on the baked soil.

Measuring distance and direction by sound alone, Longarm waited patiently. He held himself totally still, breathing in careful, shallow inhalations that he was sure would not be noticed by the approaching man. He knew he did not dare let the sniper get close enough to detect his shamming. When he judged the time to be right, he rolled into a crouch, whipping out his Colt with a practiced sweep of his arm as he moved.

He got only a fleeting impression of the form of the sniper, outlined by the dim coals of the dying fire, as the slug from his Colt went home. The sniper buckled and went down as lead tore into his chest. The rifle he'd been carrying dropped with a clatter as the unknown man crumpled to the ground.

Still on his knees, Longarm waited. The sprawled form of his assailant did not move. Rising from his knees, Longarm walked to the fallen figure. He turned the body over and gazed at the dead man's face in the faint, ghostly light.

If he'd seen the sniper before, it had been in a crowd, for the man's face was strange to him. It was a Hispanic face, thin and swarthy, with a narrow nose in a straight line to delicate, almost penciled brows. The fellow's hat had fallen off, showing a high forehead and thick black hair. His mouth was hidden by a heavy, full mustache and his jaws bore a three- or four-day stubble of black beard.

Under a short *charro* jacket, common to working cowhands in the territory, the dead man's bloodstained shirt was an indiscriminate gray. He had on course duck trousers, faded from their original brown to a soft tan, tucked into battered, high-heeled boots. His pistol was a Rogers & Spencer .44, an old gun, but even in the dim light of the coals, Longarm could see that it had been given very good care.

After staring thoughtfully at the face of the corpse, Longarm pulled on his boots and used most of the bits and pieces of wood he'd been saving to cook breakfast to build up the dying coals of his supper fire into a small, bright flame. Moving back to where the sniper's body lay, he searched the man's pockets. They yielded a surprisingly large sum of money, almost a hundred dollars, in gold and silver coins. Except for the money and the materials for rolling cigarettes—a sack of tobacco, a sheaf of trimmed cornhusks, and matches—the pockets held nothing else.

He returned the money and cigarette makings to the dead

man's pockets, then went to the horse the sniper had been riding and rummaged through its saddlebags. He found only the utilitarian objects that a traveling cowhand might be expected to carry: trail rations, spare shells for both rifle and pistol, a few pieces of leather strapping and rawhide strings, and a pair of much-worn hobbles. The horse itself bore several brands, none of which he recognized.

Returning to the fire, Longarm hunkered down and lighted a cheroot. *There ain't any ordinary cowhands on the loose with that much money in their pockets,* he told himself thoughtfully, gazing into the dancing flames and wishing his bottle of Maryland rye hadn't been broken by the sniper's first shot. *He got that cash to do a tough job, which means killing you, old son. And you gave him two chances. No credit to you he didn't bring off either one. Question is, who paid him?*

All his thinking brought no answer, and when he'd smoked the cheroot to a stub, Longarm put the question aside. He had one final job to do. He tethered the horse, then levered up the limp corpse and draped the dead sniper across the animal's back. He secured the corpse's wrists and ankles under the horse's belly with some of the rawhide strings from the saddlebags. By morning he knew the body would have stiffened, turning it into a load that would be clumsy if not impossible for the horse to carry. Without a backward glance at the laden animal, he returned to his bedroll, took off his boots for the second time that night, and slid between the blankets.

Sunrise found Longarm on the military road again, leading the corpse-laden horse. As the sun arced up the sky, he forged onward in a steady pace. He crossed the wide, shallow valley of a long-vanished river, heading for the high mesas that loomed in the distance. The military road swept up the side of the first mesa in a series of wide curves, which the horses mounted slowly but steadily. Atop the mesa he saw the broad and relatively level expanses of the remaining mesas ahead, and beyond them the ragged peaks of the Sandia Mountains.

Accustomed to the deceptiveness of distances in the thin, clear air of high altitudes, Longarm did not let the seeming nearness of the mountains lead him to hurry his pace. At the top of each mesa he stopped to rest the horses after their climb up its side, and when both the sun and his stomach reminded him it was noon, he ate in the saddle, slivers of the sausage he'd gotten from the camp commissary.

He came at last to the edge of the last mesa. Its eastern face sloped gently down into the valley of the Rio Grande, and he reined in. Below him, shrunken to a narrow thread at this time of the year, the river wound gently between its cottonwood-shaded banks. A short distance past the stream, Albuquerque huddled around its plaza. It was a town of adobe houses, mixed now with a few of red brick, all of the houses and tin-awninged business buildings around the plaza dwarfed by the bulk of San Felipe de Neri, with its high windows now black rectangles sunk deeply into the old church's fortresslike walls.

During the day's journey, Longarm had studied out a plan. He began now to put it into operation. Kicking the horses ahead, he guided the livery horse in a northward slant that brought it to the Rio Grande above the town. The horses splashed across the shallow stream, and once they'd gained the eastern bank, Longarm dismounted.

He looped the reins of the sniper's horse around the horn of its saddle, headed the animal toward the town, and gave it a sharp slap on its rump. The horse started at a slow walk toward the line of houses a half-mile away. Longarm swung back into the saddle of the livery horse and nudged it back across the stream with his booted toe. Keeping parallel with the bank, he rode downstream to the bridge where the military road crossed, and on into the town.

A saloon caught his eye as the horse plodded slowly down Mountain Road toward the plaza. He pulled up at the hitch rail and went inside. The barkeep moved up to the mahogany, waiting.

"If you got a bottle of Tom Moore, you can pour me a shot," Longarm said, putting money on the bar. "If you're out of Moore, I'll take the best Maryland rye you got."

Wordlessly, the barkeep lifted an almost full bottle from the backbar and wiped the dust off it with a corner of his apron. He poured for Longarm, who drained the glass at one gulp and motioned for a refill. He sipped the second drink, alternating small swallows with puffs on a cheroot, picked up his change, touched the brim of his hat to the bartender, and left. Remounted, he continued along Mountain Road past the plaza, and rode on through the straggling outskirts of town to its northeastern edge, where the new Santa Fe depot stood. Circling the little frame building, he pulled up at the back door and went into the dispatcher's office.

Elmer Parsons' eyebrows went up in surprise when he looked up from the battery of chattering telegraph keys on his desk and saw Longarm. He said, "After all the stir you raised day before yesterday about getting to railhead, you sure made a hell of a quick trip out of it, Marshal."

"I took care of all the business I needed to."

"Well, what is it you want this time? I suppose you need me to get you transportation somewhere else?" Parsons asked resignedly.

"Not right away. I got business with you, now."

"What kind of business?"

"I understand the railroad's got the only telegraph wire between here and Santa Fe, is that right?"

"Yep, The brass made a dicker with the territorial government to take over the line they used to try to keep open between here and the capital."

"And you handle private messages along with railroad traffic over the wire, don't you?"

"Of course. That was part of our deal when we took over the wire. Why?"

For the first time, Longarm put into words what his careful deductions during the past twenty-four hours had led him to conclude. "Because somebody up in Santa Fe found out I was sent here on this case I'm working." Longarm didn't add that he was sure the leak had taken place in the Palace of the Governors. "Whoever it was must've got word down here to Albuquerque about me, because somebody followed me out to your railhead camp and took a couple of shots at me."

Parsons thought this over for a moment, then asked, "You think there was a message sent here from Santa Fe, telling someone in Albuquerque to trail you and try to kill you?"

"That's the only answer I can come up with, Parsons. Which means that message had to pass through your office, seeing as how it's the only telegraph line between here and there."

"If you're wondering whether I'd remember seeing your name mentioned in any of the wires we've handled during the past few days, the answer's no. It wasn't in a company message, or I'd be sure to remember it. But you've got to realize that we're open day and night. We handle a whole lot of private messages, and I don't read all of them."

Longarm smiled. "You know, Parsons, I got a little bit of a fist on a key, myself. I understand how telegraphers copy down code and never pay any mind to what it says."

"I guess I don't understand what you're after, then," Parsons replied, frowning.

"Why, I'd imagine you keep copies of all the messages you handle, your company traffic and the private wires both?"

"You seem to know such a lot about our business, Marshal, I'm sure you know we do. What're you driving at, anyhow?"

"I need to take a look through those private message files."

"Now hold on! Those files aren't Santa Fe property! We just keep copies in case somebody loses a message or claims they didn't get one, and we have to prove we handled the traffic. Nobody but the ones the messages are addressed to is supposed to be able to look at them!"

"Well, Parsons, we can do this one of two ways," Longarm told the dispatcher. "You can either let me go through those files right now, or you can make me send a message to the governor up in Santa Fe, asking him to get a court order that'll make you show 'em to me. All you'll be doing is slowing me down a little while."

Parsons frowned. "I'm not sure I've got the authority to let anybody look at the private wires in our files. Not even a federal marshal."

Longarm shrugged. "I'd as soon not get you into trouble by bringing Governor Wallace's office into this, but if you make me do it, I sure as hell will."

Parsons thought this over, obviously recalling the argument he'd lost to Longarm over transportation to the railhead. After a moment he nodded. "All right. As long as I've got your word it'll be just between the two of us, I'll let you look at them."

"Just between the two of us," Longarm agreed.

"We keep about a month of flimsies of the private traffic in that file over against the wall," Parsons said, pointing to an oak cabinet. "If you want to go back any further, I'll have to dig out the boxes we put the old stuff in when the drawer gets full."

"I'll start with what's handiest, then, and hope I don't have to dig any deeper."

Parsons nodded. "Go ahead then. Look all you want to."

Longarm pulled the file drawer open and looked at its neat rows of alphabetically indexed folders, all of them bulging with copies of the private telegrams the Albuquerque office had handled. Not knowing exactly what he was searching for, he had no alternative but to start with the "A" file and go on through the drawer in the hope of hitting pay dirt. He pulled up a chair, took out the first folder, and began flipping through the flimsies.

It took Longarm only a few minutes to discover what Parsons had failed to tell him: that the flimsies had been placed in the folders in chronological order, the lastest ones sent or received being put in the front of the folder. He also found that they had been written on two colors of paper. Messages on blue sheets were obviously those to be dispatched, and were in the handwriting of the sender, while those on pink sheets had been received by the local telegrapher and copied as they ticked out of the key in Morse code.

Patiently, Longarm worked his way through the folders. Most of the telegrams were short, routine messages; most were in English, but a few were in Spanish. They dealt with everyday affairs: an impending arrival or departure, a family birth or death or serious illness, requests for money. The bulk of the file was business messages, and these were equally routine: offers of or applications for a job, offers to buy or sell, orders from local merchants addressed to their suppliers, confirmations of orders received, notification of shipments made.

Longarm paid no attention to any wires sent or received before his arrival in Santa Fe. After scanning the copies of wires transmitted during the past several days, he returned the folder to the drawer.

Even so, some of the files held a score or more messages that had been handled within those few days. He'd worked his way down through the alphabet to the "S" file before he came across the first of the coded messages. Instead of being written in script, it was hand-printed, and the groups of letters did not form words in either English or Spanish.

"Parsons, what the hell language is this wire in?" Longarm called to the dispatcher after he'd studied the flimsy for a few seconds without being able to make sense of it.

Parsons came over and scanned the sheet Longarm was holding. "It's in some private code. We've got a few commercial customers who don't like anybody, even us, to find out anything about their private business, so they fix up a code that nobody knows except the one the wire's addressed to."

"And you send it, without knowing what it says?"

"Why, of course. What the wire says doesn't concern us

82

one bit. We're not interested in anybody's business but our own."

"How do you know a wire like this ain't from a scout for another railroad, telling something he's found out about the Santa Fe's business?"

"Well, we don't, of course. But something like that's not likely to happen. Anyhow, there aren't but a few businesses here that use codes."

"How many?" Longarm asked.

"Oh, five or six," Parsons replied. "And we know who they are, so we don't pay much attention to what they send."

"Look at this one here," Longarm said. "It's sent to the Zia Land Company in Santa Fe, and it's just signed 'QZ.' You mean you know who 'QZ' stands for?"

"Why, of course. Cynthia Evans. She's . . . well, she works for Rudy Fernandez. He's the one owns the San Ysidro Cattle Company. It's a big ranch up to the north, but Rudy stays here in Albuquerque most of the time."

"Where does this Cynthia Evans stay most of the time?"

"Here in town, of course. She sort of keeps an eye on things for Rudy while he's away."

"I'll ask you to do something for me, Parsons," Longarm told the dispatcher, his voice very serious. "You said there's not many that use these code telegrams, and you know who they are. I want you to dig out all the wires every one of them has sent in the past week. If my hunch is right, those wires might break my case for me."

Chapter 8

"You think somebody in Santa Fe sent a message in code telling them you were on the way here?" Parsons asked.

"Somebody must have. That sniper didn't just pick me out by accident, and I never had seen him before," Longarm replied.

Parsons' jaw dropped. He stared at Longarm, gaping with surprise. "Why, that means you're suspicious of Cynthia Evans! Oh no, you're wrong there, Marshal. Why, hell, she couldn't have had anything to do with that fellow who tried to kill you. She's not that kind of lady!"

"Suppose you tell me what kind of lady she is," Longarm suggested. "And who Rudy Fernandez is, too, while you're telling."

"Well . . ." Parsons hesitated, trying to find words. "Cynthia is just like any widow lady who's got to work for a living, I guess you'd say. Maybe a little bit younger and prettier than most of them. But I never would even think she'd be mixed up in something that meant breaking the law, or killing, or anything out of the way like that."

"She comes in here pretty regular, does she? Sending wires off to this Fernandez?"

"That depends on what you call regular. When Fernandez is up at his ranch north of Santa Fe, she might be in here two or three times a week. Not as often when he's in town, though."

"Does she ever send wires in just plain English?"

Parsons nodded. "Sometimes, sure. But mostly they're in that code the company uses."

"How about the telegrams she gets? Are all of them in code too?"

"Not all of them, but a lot are."

"Addressed to her by name? Or to Fernandez? Or to whatever the name of his company is?"

"I can't recall any messages coming in that were addressed to anybody special. Just to the San Ysidro Cattle Company."

"And they're in the same code that this Evans woman uses when she sends out a wire?"

"Of course. That is . . . well, I guess it's the same code. I don't know all that much about any code but Morse, Marshal. It looks the same, that's all I can tell you."

"Has she got any of these messages in code in the last three or four days?"

"I don't remember that, Marshal. Of course, I'm not the only one who handles the wire. I don't see every message."

Longarm said thoughtfully. "I guess I better have a little talk with this Cynthia Evans. Where'll I find her?"

"Why, the San Ysidro Cattle Company's got an office in the Grand Hotel. The hotel's out on Central Avenue; you won't have any trouble finding it."

"It's getting pretty late in the day for an office to be open," Longarm told Parsons. "You got any idea where she lives."

"Someplace on Roma Avenue. I'm not sure exactly where, but they can tell you at the hotels if you stop there and ask."

"All right, Parsons. Thanks. Now if you'll just take care of that other little job I asked you to do, I'll be on my way."

"You mean the other messages?" Longarm nodded, and Parsons went on, "Marshal, if you want every message that we've handled for all the people that use codes, it'll take me a while to dig them out. A couple of hours or more."

"Tell you what. Let me have the ones in code that were sent out by Hernandez or the Evans woman or that company, the San Ysidro Cattle Company. And the ones in code they got. I'll want all the other wires in code that are in your files, but you can take your time pulling them out. I'll stop by for them tomorrow."

"That'll be fine," Parsons replied. "I can get you the San Ysidro Cattle Company's flimsies in just a few minutes."

Longarm studied the coded messages as Parsons handed them to him from the file folder. They appeared to be nothing but gibberish, scrambled combinations of letters that had been grouped together without rhyme or reason. After a few futile efforts to make sense of them, he gave up trying, and simply added the new ones Parsons passed over to him to the ones he was already holding. When the dispatcher finally finished going through the file folder, Longarm had a sheaf of about twenty of the cryptic telegrams, covering a period of more than two months.

"Much obliged," he told Parsons. "These ought to do me to start with, and I'll come by in the morning for the rest."

"Glad I could help you, Marshal. I feel like I'm helping the Santa Fe at the same time. Murder's a dirty business."

In the gathering twilight, Longarm rode along the tracks toward the new section of Albuquerque that was spreading in the direction of the railroad line. When he reached Central Avenue, he turned the livery horse west. Central was a new street, beginning to take shape as a business thoroughfare. Recently finished buildings were in every block, and between them others were being erected. Most of the new buildings were of brick, in sharp contrast to the somewhat shabby-looking adobe structures that clustered around the old plaza.

Parsons had been right; Longarm had no trouble finding the Grand Hotel. It stood on a corner near the end of Central, where the avenue began to curve toward the plaza. The hotel was new, a four-story, red brick structure with an imposing colonnaded facade and a short flight of broad marble steps leading up to its entry. A hitch rail stood at one side of the steps. Longarm looped the reins around the rail and went into the hotel lobby, which rose two stories to a frescoed ceiling.

"I'm looking for the San Ysidro Cattle Company office," he told the desk clerk. "Understand they got one here."

"You'll find it on the mezzanine, sir. Rooms 104 and 105. The stairs are at the rear of the lobby. I'm not sure there's anyone there at this time of day, though."

"I'll just go up and see. Won't do any harm to look."

Longarm mounted the stairs and began looking at the numbered doors as he walked around the mezzanine's perimeter. He reached rooms 104 and 105. Neither of the doors bore a sign of any kind, and both were closed. He stood between the two doors for a moment before deciding to knock on 104. He'd just raised his hand, his knuckles folded to rap, when the door suddenly swung inward and a woman appeared in the opening. She saw Longarm's raised fist in front of her eyes and jumped back.

"Goodness!" she exclaimed. "You're not getting ready to hit me, are you?"

Longarm was almost as startled as the woman by the unexpected confrontation. He looked at her, but the light from the room behind her was much brighter than that in the corridor. All that he could tell was that she was almost as tall as he was and had a statuesque body.

"I'm sorry, ma'am. I was just getting ready to knock."

"Oh, there's no harm done. I just wasn't expecting to see a man holding his fist in my face when I opened the door."

"I came up here looking for Mrs. Evans. Cynthia Evans," he said. "Would that be you?"

"Yes."

"My name's Long. Deputy U.S. marshal out of Denver."

Riding to the hotel, Longarm had decided it would do him no good to be less than open about his identity. If Cynthia Evans and Rudolpho Fernandez were involved in the attempts to kill him, they'd know who he was without being told. If they had no part in a plot, as good citizens they would be glad to help him in his investigation.

"I see," Mrs. Evans said. She hesitated for only a fraction of a second before going on. "Would you like to come in, Marshal Long? I was just closing the office, but I'm not in any hurry, if there's something you want to talk about."

"That's right neighborly, Mrs. Evans. I appreciate it."

Longarm followed her inside. The room looked more like a drawing room in a well-appointed home than an office. It was deeply carpeted and furnished with a pair of sofas that faced one another in front of an open fireplace, and several easy chairs upholstered in red velvet to match the sofas. Small tables stood at one end of each sofa, there was a long table placed against one wall, and a tall, ornately carved cabinet against the wall facing the table.

As he moved to the couch that Cynthia Evans indicated, Longarm got a quick glimpse into the adjoining room through the connecting door, which stood open. He saw a desk, straight chairs, an oak filing cabinet, a table. Apparently the second room was the one used for the business of the San Ysidro Cattle Company.

"Sit down, Marshal," Mrs. Evans said, indicating one of the sofas.

Longarm settled back on the red velvet upholstery, and she sat down on the sofa facing him. For a moment they sat in silence, neither of them making any effort to hide the fact that each was taking the measure of the other.

Longarm's scrutiny of Cynthia Evans confirmed the impression he'd gotten in his first fleeting glimpse of her when she'd opened the door. She was a tall woman, and her body was scaled generously. Her breasts bulged under the tailored broadcloth jacket of her suit, her hips were wide, and as she'd settled onto the couch he'd seen full, rounded thighs and calves outlined by the fabric of her narrow skirt.

She was well past youth—he guessed her to be in her middle thirties—but her face was smooth and unlined and her skin had the translucent clarity displayed in the complexions of so many large women. Her face was a wide oval, her chin firm. A full, almost pouting lower lip did not quite match her upper lip, which was thin and came up to a sharply pointed Cupid's-bow arc. She had a straight, almost-too-long aquiline nose that robbed her face of the real beauty it might otherwise have shown. Under thick eyebrows, her brown eyes were large and lustrous. A fringe of blond curls showed under the line of the toque she was wearing.

"Well, Marshal Long," she began. "If you'll tell me why you're here, perhaps I can help you. But you understand that I'm just employed by the company. Mr. Fernandez is the owner, I'm sure you know that, and he's at his ranch north of Santa Fe."

Deciding he had nothing to lose, Longarm took the telegraph flimsies out of his coat pocket. "I'm curious about these wires. They're all in some kind of code."

Cynthia Evans glanced at the flimsies and her eyes opened still wider. "Why, those are copies of company messages!" she exclaimed. "Telegrams we've sent and received from people we do business with."

"That's what I understand, Mrs. Evans. What I want to know is what they say."

"What they say is private business, Marshal. And they're in code because we want them to stay private. I don't know whether you're aware of it, but gossip by telegraph-office clerks and messengers can spoil business deals. We use a code to keep our messages confidential."

"I understand about all that too. But I'm still curious about what's in 'em."

"Are you suggesting that the company or Mr. Fernandez is doing something illegal?"

"I ain't suggesting a thing. I'm just asking."

"Do you mind telling me why?"

"Because I got a right strong suspicion these wires might

be wound up in a case I'm working on."

"Then you do think somebody in the company is breaking the law!"

"Now, I didn't say that. All I want—"

"Marshal Long," she interrupted, "if you can't show that someone in this company is doing something illegal, then you have no right to those messages."

"Except that I've got 'em. And I recall an old saying about possession being nine points of the law."

"You can't have gotten them legally. You'd have had to go to court for permission to seize them, and we'd have had a chance to defend ourselves."

"I could turn that around on you, Mrs. Evans. If all these wires are only about business deals, you ought not to mind me knowing what they say. I sure don't care what you do in the course of your business, as long as it ain't against the law."

"It certainly isn't against the law for us to send coded telegrams to keep our affairs private."

"I didn't say it was."

"You're definitely suggesting it, though. As for my objecting to your having them, that's a matter of principle. Now, I'll ask you once more to return those telegrams to me, as a representative of the company."

She extended her hand. Longarm ignored it. He said, "You know I ain't about to do that, ma'am. Not until I find out what these messages say."

"Well, I certainly have no intention of decoding them for you," she told him firmly. "The only one who can do that, or who can give me permission to do that, is Mr. Fernandez, and you know he's not here."

"Looks like I'll just have to wait till he comes back, then. When do you look for him?"

She said coldly, "I haven't any idea. He might be back in a few days, he may not be back for a month."

"I guess I can find him at this ranch, though?"

"If you care to make the trip up there, I suppose you can. But I can save you a lot of time. I'm sure Mr. Fernandez will do just what I'm doing, and refuse to decode the wires for you."

"What makes you so sure he won't, Mrs. Evans?"

"Because they're private and confidential. I've told you that once."

Longarm stood up, more convinced now than ever that he'd

hit a warm trail. Tucking the flimsies back into his pocket, he picked up his hat and said, "Like you told me, Mr. Fernandez is the boss. I guess I'll have to hear what he says."

"Just a minute, Marshal," she said hastily. "Please. Sit down for a moment longer."

"Well, the way you set your foot down so hard, I don't know that it'll do much good for us to talk anymore, but I'll listen."

"I . . . I might have been too hasty," she said. She waited until Longarm had taken his seat again, then went on, "Perhaps I'm to blame for our not understanding one another."

"I don't see where there's any misunderstanding. You told me plain out from the start that you weren't about to read these wires for me. I understood that real well."

Cynthia Evans smiled. "Women do foolish things sometimes, you know, Marshal Long. First, you startled me when I opened the door, then you startled me a second time when you showed me the messages. My nerves are just now beginning to settle down."

"I'm sorry if I upset you," Longarm told her, careful to keep out of his voice any hint of the skepticism he'd begun to feel. "Now that you've got over being upset, are you about to change your mind about the telegrams?"

"I don't know. I'll have to think about that for a little while, and I'm so hungry I can't think very straight. It's quite a bit past my regular dinnertime."

Longarm refused the bait. He said, "If you'd like for me to come back in the morning . . ."

"I wasn't thinking about that. Have you had your dinner yet, Marshal?"

"No. I was in a hurry to get here before your office closed, so I didn't stop to eat."

"Would you object to having dinner with me, then? That would give me a chance to do a little more thinking about decoding them. You know, if I did that without permission from Mr. Fernandez, I might get into a lot of trouble."

"I don't see how it'd hurt for us to eat together, except that I've been on the trail for a while, so I ain't really dressed right to take a lady out to dinner."

"We wouldn't have to go anywhere," she said quickly. "The hotel has a very good restaurant, and when I'm working late, or in a hurry, I have them serve me something here in the office."

"That'll satisfy me just fine, if it suits you."

Cynthia stood up. "There's a call bell to the front desk in the office. If you'll excuse me, I'll just signal for them to send a waiter up for our orders."

She went into the next room, returning in a moment without her hat and jacket. Stopping just inside the door, she asked, "Would you like a drink while we're waiting, Marshal?" Moving to the carved cabinet, she opened it, showing bottle-laden shelves. "Mr. Fernandez likes to offer his business associates a drink when they visit the office."

"If you got a bottle of Maryland rye in there, I'd enjoy a sip. And unless you mind, I'll light up a cigar too."

"Go right ahead," Cynthia told him. She was looking at the bottles and reached to the back of a shelf, bringing out a bottle that she held up for Longarm to see. "This is rye whiskey, but I don't know whether it's from Maryland or not."

Longarm looked across the flame of the match he was holding to the tip of his cheroot. The bottle didn't bear Tom Moore's likeness, but it was a label he recognized. He nodded his approval. Cynthia took a glass from the cabinet and put bottle and glass on the small table at Longarm's elbow.

"I'll let you pour for yourself," she told him. "And I'll join you when the waiter brings up some ice. I enjoy a relaxing sip before dinner myself."

Turning to reach the bottle, Longarm poured his drink. When he settled back, he put himself unobtrusively into a position where he'd be able to reach his Colt readily. Though he wasn't able to define his feelings yet, there was something in Cynthia Evans' quick reversal of her attitude that sent him a warning signal. In fact, his instinct was whispering to him that there was something about the entire setup in the offices of the San Ysidro Cattle Company that struck a false note.

Old son, he told himself, *this place just might be on the edge of that pond you been thinking about. If it is, you can start wading, and maybe get the minnows stirred up. Only don't try to go too deep too fast.*

When a knock sounded at the door and Cynthia Evans told the waiter to come in, Longarm shifted his drink to his left hand and kept it there until the business of ordering dinner was completed and the waiter had left. Not until Cynthia resumed her seat on the couch opposite him did he relax.

"Now, then, Marshal Long," she said. "If we're going to be dining together, there's no reason for us to act so stiff and formal. I'd be a lot more comfortable if you'd call me Cynthia, instead of Mrs. Evans. Somehow, being called by my late husband's name always makes me feel old and unattractive."

"I'll be real pleased to, Cynthia. I'd a lot rather get along with folks than fight, myself."

"You must have a first name too," she suggested.

"Nobody much uses it. Folks that know me call me by a sort of nickname, which is Longarm."

"You won't mind if I call you by your nickname, then?"

"Of course not."

They were interrupted by another knock. A busboy entered in response to Cynthia's call, bringing a silver-plated bucket filled with cracked ice. He placed it on the table at Cynthia's elbow and left. With a gesture of apology, she got up and went to the liquor cabinet, poured gin and a splash of bitters in a glass, returned, and sat down before adding ice.

"Now, we can talk while we're waiting for dinner," she said. "Tell me about this case you're investigating here in the territory, Longarm. Why didn't Governor Wallace put his own men to work on it?"

"What makes you think Governor Wallace had anything to do with me being here? I disremember mentioning him."

"You didn't, but you didn't have to. Anybody who lives in New Mexico Territory knows the governor's got a finger in just about everything that happens right now. Especially when federal officials are involved."

Longarm still refused to answer Cynthia directly. He said, "I guess I wouldn't know that, seeing as how I don't live here. I get my orders from my chief in Denver. When he sends me out on a case, I just go do the best I can to close it up."

"And I'd imagine you usually succeed."

"When I don't, it ain't because I don't try."

She smiled. "I like a determined man. Especially when he's competent in his work. And I'm sure you are. You wouldn't be here if you didn't have a lot of ability."

"Now, Cynthia, I guess I might as well tell you to start out with, sweet-talking me ain't going to make me back off from the job I was sent here to do."

"That wasn't in my mind at all!" she protested. Then, when Longarm smiled, she began chuckling. "It was, of course," she confessed. "I was just trying you out. I'm terribly curious to know why you're so interested in those telegrams."

"I told you that at the beginning. Things have been happening in this case I'm here on that've got me looking into any wires being sent in code."

"Then you've got several suspects? Not just the San Ysidro Cattle Company, or Mr. Fernandez?" After a brief pause she added, "Or me?"

"There's a lot of things I got to find out before I'll call anybody a suspect," Longarm replied. "There's leads I'll be running down, folks I'll be talking to, like I'm talking to you."

"That doesn't tell me very much," she pouted.

"You're a smart lady, Cynthia. You know I ain't going to tell you a thing about my case, or how far I've got until now. Why don't we just talk friendly, instead of you trying to pry at me? Because it won't do you no good."

"That's unfair!" she protested. "I'm not trying to pry, as you put it. I'm just curious. Wouldn't you be, if you were in my situation?"

"I'd be curious," Longarm admitted. "And I'd be prying too, just like you are."

Whatever Cynthia might have said in reply remained unuttered as the waiter knocked and entered, carrying their dinners on a tray—steak and potatoes for Longarm, grilled chicken breasts and a salad for Cynthia. He also had an iced bottle of champagne on the tray, and when Longarm looked at it and started to remark that the wine hadn't been included in their order, Cynthia interrupted him.

"Our dinners will be charged to the company, Longarm. Mr. Fernandez has left instructions that whenever a meal is sent up here, a bottle of champagne is to be sent with it."

"Well, I guess it won't hurt my expenses to have a meal on your company," Longarm said. Then he added, "Your boss must treat his friends pretty good."

"He does. Most of them are customers too, of course." She indicated the dishes that the waiter had placed on the small tables at the end of each couch before moving the tables into the open space between the two sofas. "Now let's not talk about the cattle business, or this case you're investigating. Let's enjoy our dinner."

After two days of trail rations, Longarm suddenly realized he was famished. Cynthia Evans might have been on a trail too, judging from her appetite, which was as hearty as his. They made little conversation while they ate, but gradually the tension between them eased. After the food had been consumed and the champagne bottle drained, Longarm lighted a cheroot and leaned back.

"That was a real fine meal, Cynthia. I enjoyed it."

"I'm glad you did. One of the reasons Mr. Fernandez keeps this office is that it gives him a place to entertain customers—and other friends too, of course."

"How come I got to be a friend all of a sudden, Cynthia? You acted like you were ready to scratch my eyes out for a while there. Then, all of a sudden, you changed your mind."

"I suppose I realized I was doing the wrong thing."

"Then you're going to translate these messages into plain English for me?"

"Now I didn't say that, Longarm. I told you I couldn't do that until I got Mr. Fernandez's permission."

"Why don't you send him a wire and ask if it's all right?"

"I was thinking about doing that while we were eating. I haven't quite made up my mind to do it, though."

"Mind telling me why?"

"Because I still don't know what kind of case it is you're looking into. How does the San Ysidro Cattle Company come into it?"

"It ain't into it yet. It might not ever be. That'd depend on what's in those telegrams."

"What do you think is in them?" she persisted.

Now it was Longarm's turn to hedge. He said, "I ain't sure I want to tell you that much about the case."

"Why don't you tell me what you think is safe, then? Maybe it would help me make up my mind."

Longarm made a quick decision to start wading into the pond, but very carefully. He said, "Your company does a lot of business with the Santa Fe, I guess?"

"Of course we do. It's the only Eastern railroad that's come into the territory so far. The Santa Fe handles all of our cattle shipments."

"You know they have been having some troubles, I guess? Over the new surveys, and with the ranchers west of here, about water rights for their tanks? And with the teamsters who'll be put out of business on the long hauls they got now?"

"I don't suppose there's anybody in the territory who hasn't heard about the Santa Fe's troubles. In fact, Mr. Fernandez has mentioned several times that he'd like to help the railroad solve some of them. You know, he buys cattle from the ranchers west of here. He's on very good terms with almost all of them."

"How does Mr. Fernandez think he can help?"

"He hasn't told me that," she replied. "I suppose what he's thinking of is acting as a mediator of some kind between the Santa Fe and the ranchers, or the teamster companies, or whoever they might be having trouble with."

"It's an idea, I guess." Longarm was aware that Cynthia had been steering him away from the subject of the coded telegrams, and thought it was time to get back to them. He said, "You feel any different about reading me those messages, now you've had time to think about it a little bit?"

"I haven't changed my mind. I can't, Longarm. But I will do this. I'll send a wire to Mr. Fernandez the first thing in the morning, asking him if he'll give me permission."

"I guess that's a fair offer," he nodded. "I'll come in tomorrow, then, after you've had time to get your answer." He stood up and picked up his hat. "Now, I'd be pleased to see you home, Cynthia. You were about ready to leave when I butted in."

"Thank you for offering, Longarm, but I've just thought of two or three things I need to finish up. Perhaps next time."

"Next time it'll be, then," he agreed.

Walking downstairs to the lobby, Longarm made another quick decision. He went to the desk and registered, arranging for the livery horse to be put in the hotel stables, and for his gear to be brought up to his room by a porter.

There's something that don't smell right about that San Ysidro outfit, old son, he thought as he climbed the stairs to his room. *And if you're going to do any wading into that pond where the big fish is, it's a lot easier to start right at the edge, where you can get your feet wet with just a step or two And it sure is beginning to look like that's where you're standing right now!*

Chapter 9

Elmer Parsons had the coded telegrams ready when Longarm got to the chief dispatcher's office early the following morning.

"This is what you asked for, Marshal," he said, pushing the flimsies across his desk. "Here's every wire in code that we've handled in this office for the last month. You might be interested in the one on top. Cynthia Evans sent it over late last night by a bellboy from the hotel."

"To her boss in Santa Fe, I'd guess?"

"You'd guess right."

"I don't suppose there's been an answer from him yet?"

"No. But there hasn't been time."

"You'll save the answer for me when it comes in, won't you?"

"Of course I will. Damn it, I'm into this thing now almost as deep as you are. I don't know how far I've got my neck stuck out, but the way I look at it, you're on the Santa Fe's side."

"Thanks, Parsons. I'll see that you don't get into trouble for giving me a hand." Longarm added the latest San Ysidro Cattle Company flimsy to the ones already in his pocket, then looked at the pile of pink and blue tissue-thin sheets on the dispatcher's desk. "Now, you know New Mexico Territory better'n I do, so maybe you can tell me a little something about the people that sent those wires and the ones that got 'em."

"I thought you'd be interested in knowing that, so I sorted the messages out. There's only seven companies that use a code, and most of these wires are between just two of them."

"I bet I can guess who those two are," Longarm said. "But go ahead and tell me."

"When you asked me about these coded wires last night, I didn't realize how many had passed between the San Ysidro company and that outfit called the Zia Land Company, up in

Santa Fe. They seem to do quite a bit of business together."

"That's what I'd figured," Longarm nodded. "You know anything about this Zia Land Company, Parsons?"

"Not a thing. As far as I'm concerned, it's just a name on the messages we handle."

"Well, it won't be much of a job to find out. There'll be records up at the capital, if I can't find out any other way. Now how about these other outfits that use coded telegrams?"

"Well, there's the Santa Rita Mining Company—they've got an office here and one in St. Louis. There's the Hutchins Freighting Company—that's the outfit the road's contracted its construction hauling to, so I know a little bit about them."

"They've got more'n one office, I take it?"

"One here, one in Santa Fe," Parsons replied. "But they started out back in Kansas, just a little jerkwater outfit, two brothers and a few teams and wagons. They've got rich off what the railroad's paid them since we started laying tracks."

"Their rates keep going up all the time, I'd bet."

"I wouldn't know about that, Marshal. It's not in my department." Parsons riffled through the flimsies again. "The others are the New Mexico Factoring Company—they telegraph back and forth regular with a company called National Factors, in Chicago. Then there's Cabral y Hijos. I know about them, too. They wholesale grocery goods and notions, and run warehouses here and in Santa Fe. The last one is the Western Trading Company, and it doesn't get many wires, but it sends a lot."

"You've saved me a good amount of work, Parsons. Now if I can just borrow those flimsies from you for a little while, I'll see you get 'em back when I'm through with them."

"Well, you've already got the San Ysidro file. I don't guess it'll hurt for me to let you take the rest." Parsons indicated the stack of messages. "Take them and welcome."

Longarm picked up the flimsies and put them in his coat pocket. "I reckon I'll go back to the hotel and see if I can make heads or tails out of any of these," he told Parsons. "I got a room there, if you get any more of these wires and feel like sending 'em over. If I ain't in my room, I'll be down at that San Ysidro outfit, talking to Cynthia Parsons."

On his way back to the Grand Hotel, Longarm had to stop at three saloons before he found a bottle of Tom Moore. He wasn't

97

looking forward to the dry work that awaited him, and felt that his mind would need the occasional lubrication of a swallow of good Maryland rye to work its best.

In his room, he laid the flimsies on the unmade bed in seven separate piles, one for each of the senders. Then he began studying the messages from the two largest stacks, those of the San Ysidro Cattle Company and the Zia Land Company.

At first, the only similarity he could see between the messages was the two-letter signature on each one. Most of the San Ysidro telegrams sent from Albuquerque bore the two letters QZ, which Parsons had already identified as the signature of Cynthia Evans, while those that came from Santa Fe were signed BL. Longarm guessed that these letters stood for Rudolpho Fernandez, as the BL signature occasionally showed up on a wire from Albuquerque addressed to the Zia Land Company.

That's got to be the way of it, old son, he told himself as he reached for the bottle of Tom Moore and let a swallow of the rye trickle down his throat. *But about all the rest of what's in those messages is just a bunch of mixed-up letters, and they ain't going to tell you one billy-be-damned thing until you figure out how to unmix 'em and make words out of 'em.*

Pushing aside his frustration, he picked up the flimsies in the Zia Land Company stack. In these, just as in the San Ysidro messages, he could make nothing of the jumble of letters that formed the text of the wires, but the pattern of signatures that he'd recognized in the San Ysidro telegrams was repeated in those sent by the Zia firm. Messages from Santa Fe were signed with the letters "SM," those from Albuquerque with "DY."

Which still don't mean nothing, Longarm thought. The longer he'd worked over the code, the angrier he'd gotten with himself for his failure to break it. *There's just too damn many letters in them wires to unscramble. But it's a job you got to do, because all you're working on so far is a great big hunch that whoever goes to so much trouble to keep what they say a secret has got to be up to something crooked.*

More to take his mind off his immediate problem than because he felt any hope of learning anything useful, he began flipping through the other sheaves of flimsies. Halfway through the stack of wires from the Hutchins Freighting Company he stopped and stared. There, on a message from Santa Fe to the company's Albuquerque office, was the BL signature.

Now that's a nice question for you to find an answer for, old son, he thought. *Why in hell would Fernandez be sending telegrams from the Hutchins Freighting Company, unless he's some kind of a boss there, too? And if Fernandez is tied up with the freight outfit, how come nobody seems to know about it? Maybe right now'd be a good time to go downstairs and have another little palaver with Cynthia Evans. Even if she's lying, you can understand what she says, and you sure ain't making much headway understanding what all the scrambled letters on these flimsies are trying to tell you.*

Glad of a reason to escape the frustrating flimsies, Longarm reached for his coat and hat and went downstairs to the mezzanine. Without knocking he opened the door to the office of the San Ysidro Cattle Company and went in.

Cynthia Evans' large eyes grew even larger when she saw Longarm standing in the doorway. Her face looked strained, as though the night she'd just passed had not been an easy one. The strained look was quickly replaced by a smile as she gestured for Longarm to come in.

"What a nice surprise, Longarm!" she greeted him. "Do sit down. I knew you'd be coming in this morning, but I didn't look for you quite so soon."

"I like to start off a day by finishing up business that's been left over." He picked up a chair and carried it to the desk where Cynthia was working, and sat down facing her. "You were going to wire Mr. Fernandez and see if he'd say whether it was all right for you to tell me what's in all them telegrams."

"I did wire him last night, but I haven't heard from him yet. Of course, he might have gone into Santa Fe, or be out on the range inspecting stock, or even on his way back here. Where will you be, if I get an answer?"

"I got a room here in the hotel. Figure it's as good a place as any to stay while I'm in town."

"Then I'll let you know as soon as I hear from him."

"There's been one more little thing come up since last night that I thought I'd ask you about," Longarm said, keeping his voice carefully offhand. "There's an outfit in town called the Hutchins Freighting Company. I reckon you've heard of it?"

A thoughtful frown furrowed Cynthia's brow, then she asked, "Aren't they the ones who're doing all the hauling for the Santa Fe, out of their construction camp?"

"You do know about 'em, then?" Longarm countered.

"Only what I've heard. Why?"

"Besides being the boss of the San Ysidro Cattle Company, Mr. Fernandez wouldn't have any connection with this Hutchins outfit, would he?"

If the abruptness of his inquiry startled Cynthia, Longarm could not tell.

She countered his question with one of her own. Her voice level, she asked him, "Whatever gave you that idea?"

"Just something I stumbled into while I was nosying around."

"Now, Longarm, you ought to know better than to believe all the wild rumors you run into."

"I'm waiting to hear you say yes or no," he told her.

"I said it was one of those wild rumors, didn't I?"

"You're sure?"

"If you don't believe me, you'll just have to ask Mr. Fernandez," Cynthia said tartly.

Longarm saw that any more questioning might push his luck too far. He was sure he knew the answer, and equally sure that Cynthia did too. Her evasions, the way she'd been answering his questions with questions of her own, were enough to convince him of that.

"Oh, I will, when I see him. Even if I have to go out to his ranch to do it when I go to Santa Fe," he said.

"Are you going up there right away?"

"In a few days, I reckon. As soon as I get through here. There's a few loose ends I still got to pull together before I can leave Albuquerque."

"If I can help you..." she suggested.

"What you could do to help me most would be to tell me what I already asked you to."

"You know why I can't, not right now. I've—" A knock at the door interrupted her. She called, "Come in." The door opened and a youth in his early teens stood there. "Why, Jimmy," Cynthia said, "I haven't seen you for several days. Do you have a telegram for me this morning?"

"Not for you, Mrs. Evans. I'm looking for Marshal Long."

"You found him," Longarm broke in.

"Mr. Parsons told me you'd be here if you weren't in your room, Marshal." The youth took a folded paper from his pocket and handed it to Longarm. "He said you'd likely want to have this right away."

Unfolding the message, Longarm read: "FRESH GROUND OPENED YOU NEED TO DIG IN QUICK STOP ORDERING SPECIAL TRAIN LEAVE ALBUQUERQUE AT ONCE TO GET YOU HERE STOP FERRELL"

His face poker-straight, Longarm folded the telegram and put it in his pocket. Cynthia had been watching him while he read the message, a frown growing on her face as she got no indication from his expression as to the telegram's contents.

"Bad news or good?" she asked.

"Neither one. Just a little job I got to tend to." Longarm turned to Jimmy. "You mind going out the back door when you get downstairs, young fellow, and telling the hostler to saddle my horse and get it ready? I'll be down after it soon as I pick up a few things from my room."

"Sure, Marshal. Be glad to."

When the boy had gone, Cynthia asked, "You'll be back later on, won't you, Longarm? I should hear from Mr. Fernandez before the day's over."

"If I don't get back today, I'll see you tomorrow. I ain't quite sure how long this little job's going to take me."

Longarm wasted no time in collecting his rifle and saddlebags from his room and getting back to the Santa Fe depot. At the roundhouse, which stood just beyond the dispatcher's office, he could see an engine, hauling a stock car and caboose, pulling out onto the mainline. He went into Parsons' office.

"You sure don't waste much time," the dispatcher said. "And we won't hold you up. The accommodation ought to be ready to roll inside of the next few minutes."

"I saw it pulling away from the roundhouse. Any fresh word from Jim Ferrell?"

"No. I suppose he thought that wire he sent was all the word you'd need."

"It is. I don't figure Jim to be the kind of man that'll holler for help without a pretty good reason."

"Is that how you read his wire?" Parsons asked. "I don't remember it saying anything about him needing help."

"It didn't, not in so many words. And I'm just guessing, but I'd be willing to back up my hunch with a little side bet."

"Well, good luck to you. If any coded wires come in while you're gone, I'll keep the copies for you."

"You do that. Even if I ain't been able to make sense out of 'em yet, my hunch is still real strong that they mean a lot to this case."

Huffing and swaying over the newly laid rails, Longarm's special train made the run to the construction camp in a little more than half the time required by the heavily loaded equipment train he'd taken on his earlier trip. Looking ahead from the caboose, Longarm saw Jim Ferrell come out of his office and hurry to the mainline when the special began to slow at the camp. Ferrell swung aboard the caboose before the special had come to a halt.

"Glad you read my message right," Ferrell said crisply as he shook hands with Longarm. "I didn't want to spell everything out. There's no way of knowing who'll see a wire."

"I got the feeling you were telling me I'd best get here in a hurry," Longarm replied. "Suppose you tell me what all the fuss is about."

"We've got a water tower going up a few miles past the railhead," Ferrell explained. "And it's damned well got to go where the surveyors located it, because there's no water within ten miles on either side of it. When the crew went out this morning to start erecting it, there was a bunch of cowboys guarding the water hole. They told my men the rancher who owns the property has changed his mind about letting us put the tower there."

"Did they say why?"

"They didn't say a damn thing more than what I've told you, Longarm. Just stood there with their rifles ready to stoot, from what my foreman's message said."

"But there ain't been no shooting yet?"

"Not unless the cowboys have done some. Our work crews don't go out armed, but the foreman always carries a pistol. He sent two men back here on the handcar to let me know what was happening. I sent them back with instructions to the foreman that he was just to keep cool."

"When was all this? Last night, or today?"

"Today. This morning. The crew went out as usual, in time to get to where they're working by daylight. It took the handcar an hour or so to get here, and I got that wire off to you right after they started back to rail-end. I sent Mike Sullivan with them. He's the chief of my camp police force."

"Just one man?"

"One man's all I could spare, damn it! There was a big brawl at Hell on Wheels last night that took all of Mike's men to break up. Two of them got hurt, they can't get around today."

"You got any suspicion that the fight last night was a put-up job?"

Ferrell shook his head. "No. Hell, fights at the saloons and whorehouses are a dime a dozen, Longarm. There's some kind of fracas almost every night. But the cowboys keeping my men off the water-tower site is another proposition. It goes along with the ranchers trying to bar us from the passes farther west."

"It'd sure fit into the pattern of all the other troubles that've shaped up," Longarm agreed.

"That's how it struck me," Ferrell said. "I got to wondering if it might not give you some kind of fresh lead as to who's behind all of it. And I didn't think it'd do any harm if a U.S. marshal was to show up and make things more or less official."

"If I can get a fresh lead off whatever's going on at your water hole, Jim, I'll sure be glad to have it. How far ahead is the place where the trouble is?"

"Something like ten miles."

"Good enough. I'll just get your train crew to take my horse out of the stock car and I'll be on my way."

"There's no need for you to go horseback all the way to rail-end," Ferrell said. "The track's ballasted about two-thirds of the way, and the accommodation can run you out to where the ballast ends. I'll tell the engineer what to do."

A half-hour later, Longarm was in the saddle, riding beside the newly laid rails. He passed the rail-end, where the gandy dancers were filling the air with the clanging of sledges driving spikes through tieplates, and continued along the raw earthen embankment formed by the fresh grade.

He mounted a long upslope, and as he topped the rise he could see the trouble spot. In a little saucer, a dozen or so men in the nondescript garb that characterized the construction gangs were barricaded behind a stack of boards and timbers. Beyond them, in front of a small pond where the high late-morning sun danced in reflections from the water's surface, the ranch hands sat their horses. There were only a half-dozen of them, but in addition to the holstered pistols at their belts, each of the riders carried a rifle.

Longarm reined his horse over the rim of the saucer and down on the opposite side. The move placed him between the two groups. As he approached, one of the men in the railroad crew motioned for him to come to their barricade. Longarm pulled his mount aside and stopped in front of the piled-up timbers.

"You'd be Sullivan, I guess?" he asked the man who'd waved.

"That's right. You're Marshal Long?"

Longarm nodded. "You had any trouble yet?"

"Nobody's made a move yet, us or them. The boss said we was to sit tight till you got here."

"You talked to the vaqueros any?"

"Not a word, except I told 'em to clear out so we could get to work. The greasers didn't say a thing, just set there like they didn't know what I was saying."

"Let me have a word with 'em, then. Don't do anything until I see if I can find out how the land lays." He walked the horse to within a few yards of the mounted men and reined in. "Which one of you is ramrodding this outfit?" he asked. "And who sent you to start trouble?"

"I am *capataz*," the cowhand directly in front of him replied. "Pablo Gomez. We are the vaqueros of the Rancho Montemayor, and we take our orders from our *patrón*, Don Pascual Iglesias. And who are you, *señor*, to ask us questions while we protect the land of our *patrón?*"

Longarm took his time replying while he studied the vaqueros and their leader. Gomez was wide and stocky, the short stirrup-leathers showed that. Like his companions, he wore the *charro* jacket of the territorial cowhand, faded duck jeans, and high-heeled boots. His face, shaded by his broad-brimmed hat, was wide, his lips thick, his nose blunt. He wore a mustache that was luxuriantly untrimmed, and his jowls and cheeks had not felt a razor's touch for several days.

Though flashing his badge was not Longarm's habit, he could see that this was one of the times when it was necessary. Moving carefully, he took his wallet out and flipped it open to show the badge.

"My name's Long," he said levelly. "Deputy United States

marshal. And the reason I'm here is to keep any kind of trouble from starting up."

Over his shoulder, Gomez said to his man, *"Es un oficial del gobierno federal. Cuidarse que no veremos en apuros."* Facing Longarm again, he said, "It is not we vaqueros who make the trouble, *señor*. It is those men there. We are only send here by Don Pascual to guard what is belong to El Rancho Montemayor."

"You're talking about the I water hole, I guess?"

"Sí. In this country is so precious like gold, *la agua."*

"Now, what I understand is that your boss, Don Pascual, sold the railroad this water hole," Longarm said.

"About this, you must ask *el patrón* himself. He does not tell me of such things. He says, 'Go and guard *la agua.' Pues,* we do it. Like you see."

"But if your *patrón* sold the water hole to the railroad, it wouldn't belong to him or the ranch anymore," Longarm explained patiently.

"Don Pascual is tell me nothing about selling or buying. All he is say is what I have to tell you, *Señor Federalista."*

Longarm turned to the barricade and called, "Sullivan! Did Jim Ferrell give you any kind of deed or contract to show these fellows?"

"Why'd he do a thing like that? Everybody knows the Santa Fe bought these damn water rights, but whatever papers changed hands is back at the main office in Topeka. Besides, chances are them cowpokes can't read."

"Maybe not, but I don't seem to be making much headway trying to explain to these follows that the water hole don't belong to their boss anymore."

"What are we going to do, then?" Sullivan asked. "Get a gang out here with rifles and run them bastards off railroad land?"

"That's what Ferrell don't want to do. Let me take another stab at it, and see if I can work out something."

Facing Gomez again, he said, "Looks like I'm going to have to talk to your boss. Where'll I find him?"

"At the hacienda, *señor*. Where else?" Gomez shrugged.

"How far away is that?"

"Cinco mil varas, más o menos," the ranch hand replied.

This was the first time in a number of years that Longarm had enountered the old Spanish royal method of measurement, but he recalled that a *vara* was roughly the distance between the marks left by the front and rear hooves of a loping horse, a bit more than four feet. He did a bit of round-number division and decided the ranch house was between five and six miles distant.

"You come along with me, then, Gomez," he told the foreman. "We'll go see your *patrón* and maybe we can straighten all this out and not have any trouble."

Gomez shook his head stolidly. "No, *Señor Federalista*," he said. "Don Pascual is tell me to guard the *agua*, so that is what I must do. But if you fear to lose yourself, I will send Juan Alemán to guide you."

"I'll settle for that," Longarm agreed. "But while I'm gone, don't you start nothing with the railroad men over there."

"So long as they do not try to take the *agua*, all will be well," Gomez said. He called to one of the ranch hands, "Juan! *Llevarse el federalista a la hacienda, quiere diga con el patrón. Y volve tan pronto aquí. Entiende?*"

Longarm toed the horse back to the barricade and told Sullivan, "You just set tight. I'm going to ride over to the main ranch house and talk to the big boss. It ain't all that far from here. I ought to be back before too long."

"Take your time. As long as we get back to camp in time to eat supper. After last night, I'd just as soon stay out here for a while, where I can't smell Hell on Wheels."

With a nod, Longarm rode back to the ranch hands. The man chosen by Gomez to guide him to the ranch house was waiting, and Longarm followed him as he led the way across the gently rolling hills that sloped to the southeast.

Though there was no trail that Longarm could see, he knew his guide was choosing a route by landmarks of his own. The country over which they rode was not prairieland, but it had the same vast expanses of empty distance. It was marked by rolling ridges that undulated like giant outstretched snakes lying in sinuous lines across almost flat plains. Here and there small mesas rose from the flats between the ridges.

When topping one of the long, rounded ridges, the landscape ahead was hidden by the next waving rise, so that even a man on horseback had very limited vision. The ranch hand led Longarm in a nearly straight line, veering only when it became necessary to skirt the steep sides of one of the small mesas. After an hour or more of steady riding they mounted one of the low ridges, and in the wide valley, which was threaded by a small stream, Longarm saw what at first he took to be a town.

He looked more closely and realized that it must be the ranch he was looking at. Its center was an imposing, turreted structure surrounded by a high wall, with adobe huts huddling close to the wall, as though seeking its protection.

His guide reined in to allow Longarm to come abreast, and pointed to the houses. *"Es la plaza del patrón,"* he said. *"La plaza de Don Pascual Iglesias, El Rancho Montemayor."*

Chapter 10

As Longarm followed the vaquero down the sloping side of the ridge into the valley where the ranch house stood, he could see that the estate was, for all practical purposes, the small town he'd taken it to be at first glance. He counted four irregular rows of the small adobe houses that stood in a semicircle around the mansion. The stream that fell from the distant end of the wide valley had been diverted into ditches that ran down the center path separating the dwellings before it disappeared in a channel that ran under the wall circling the turreted hacienda. Children played around the houses outside the wall, and there were women moving in the wide paths between them.

Ornate iron gates closed a broad opening in the wall. A man with a rifle resting in the crook of his elbow stood just inside the gates. Longarm's guide pulled up at the opening and motioned for Longarm to rein in as well.

"Este hombre es un oficial federalista quien quiere hablar con el patrón," he called to the sentry. *"Pablo dile su aprobación."*

For a moment the sentry subjected Longarm to a slit-eyed inspection, then nodded. *"Bueno. Momentito,"* he said. Shifting his rifle, the man lifted the heavy crossbar that secured the gates and swung one of them open. Longarm followed the vaquero to the entrance of the mansion, where they dismounted. Seemingly from nowhere, a young boy came running to hold their horses. The ranch hand led Longarm to the door and tugged at a bell-pull.

After a brief wait, the carved oaken doors opened, and a man clad in funereal black appeared. He appeared to Longarm to be just short of middle age. He was narrow-faced, with a straight, thin nose that ended in a pronounced hook above a long upper lip adorned with a pencil-line mustache. His lips

108

were so thin as to be virtually invisible, and his clean-shaven jaw was exceptionally long, thrusting forward in a curve that was the reverse of the hook of his nose.

"Qué quieres, Juan Alemán?" he asked the ranch hand.

Touching his hat brim, the vaquero repeated the explanation he'd given at the gate, and again Longarm stood impassively while he received a head-to-toe inspection.

"What is your business with Don Pascual?" the newcomer asked at last.

"I'd just as soon tell him about it myself, if it's all the same to you," Longarm said levelly.

"Don Pascual does not speak to"—the man hesitated for a moment, then went on—"to everyone who knocks at the door. I am Feliciano Ramos, the *mayordomo*—I suppose your Anglo word would be 'manager'—of the Rancho Montemayor. Perhaps you can transact your business with me."

Longarm's patience had run out, but he controlled his irritation. Keeping his voice level, he replied, "I guess maybe I could, if I was a mind to. But I came here to see Don Pascual, and that's who I aim to talk to."

"Juan says you are a federal official. What kind of post do you hold with the government?"

"I'm a deputy U.S. marshal. From the Denver office, if you happen to be all that interested. My name's Long, and if you want to see my badge, I'll show it to you, or to your boss, when you finally get around to telling him I'm here."

"Indeed?" There was sarcasm in Ramos' voice. "And you have come all the way from Denver just to see Don Pascual?"

Longarm did not bother to reply. He locked his gunmetal-blue eyes with Ramos' brown ones and held them until the other man looked away.

"Very well," the *mayordomo* said at last. "I will ask Don Pascual to see you." To the ranch hand, Ramos said, *"Juan, quedarse con los caballos."* Then, with a gesture, he invited Longarm into the wide, flagstone-floored hallway and motioned to an open door a few paces from the entry. "You can wait in that room for Don Pascual." Without waiting for Longarm to reply, he closed the door and walked down the long hallway.

Longarm went into the room Ramos had indicated, and looked around. The room was of such size that although it was quite adequately furnished, it looked bare. A long table stretched most of its length. At least twenty chairs stood against the walls or were scattered in groups of two or three around the floor. Leather-upholstered divans, wide and deep, stood at each end before wide fireplaces that had mantelpieces at the level of Longarm's head.

Walking across to one of the deep-set windows that broke the room's outer wall, Longarm looked out into a courtyard. He got a glimpse of stables at one end, of a group of men squatting against the encircling wall at the other. Fishing a cheroot out of his pocket, Longarm flicked his thumbnail across a match and lighted up. He was still standing gazing out the window when he heard the clicking of footsteps in the corridor and turned around in time to see a man younger than Ramos enter, with the *mayordomo* following a respectful pace behind.

If Don Pascual was not a young man, he was at least younger than his *mayordomo*, Longarm thought. The ranch owner was both shorter and slighter of build than either Ramos or Longarm. His jet-black hair was smoothed back from a high, unwrinkled forehead. He had thick, glossy eyebrows and his eyes were a surprisingly light blue. His nose was sharply arched at its bridge, his lips were full, his chin a short, firm block. He was wearing covert-cloth trousers, a gold-embroidered *charro* jacket, and a soft, cream-colored silk shirt.

Neither Longarm nor the new arrivals spoke for a moment, but stood studying one another. The ranch owner broke the silence in that moment before it became embarrassingly strained. In a light, almost high voice, his English totally unaccented, he said, "I am Pascual Iglesias. Ramos tells me you have some kind of official business to discuss with me."

"My name's Long, Mr. Iglesias. Deputy U.S. marshal out of the Denver office. I ain't sure just how official you'll take my business to be, but what I come here for is to see if I can get you to pull your ranch hands away from that water hole you sold to the Santa Fe railroad before somebody gets killed."

For a moment, Iglesias stared at Longarm, a puzzled frown forming on his face. He said, "You speak in riddles, Marshal Long. I do not understand what it is you have said."

"Seems to me I said it plain enough. Some of the men from your ranch are about to get into a shooting fight with a bunch of Santa Fe railroad men who've come to put up a water tower at the water hole along the tracks. I'm trying to find out how come you changed your mind about the deal you made with the Santa Fe, and to stop a bad fight from starting."

Don Pascual's frown deepened. "You must be mistaken, Marshal. It is true that some time ago I sold water rights at one of my small *fuentes* to the railroad. You must know, though, that once an *hidalgo* gives his word, he does not break it. I have no knowledge of any of my people making ready to fight with anyone."

"You got a foreman named Pablo Gomez working for you?"

"Of course. Gomez is one of my most reliable men."

"Well, him and five or six more of your hands are standing off a crew from the railroad that's come to put up a tank at that water hole I'm talking about. One of your men rode back here with me, to show me the way. You can ask him if you don't believe what I'm telling you."

"I do not accuse you of falsifying, Marshal Long," Don Pascual said quickly. "I can see no reason for you to lie."

"Oh, I'm giving you the straight facts, Mr. Iglesias. Your men are holding rifles on the Santa Fe's crew, and it looked to me like they were spoiling to use 'em."

Turning to Ramos, Don Pascual asked, "Feliciano, do you know anything of this matter?"

Ramos shrugged. "Gomez is in charge of a party I sent out to look for strays on the outlying range. I gave him no special orders; it is a job he has done many times before. The Anglo marshal must be mistaken, *patrón*."

"There ain't no mistake," Longarm said firmly. "I just come from that water hole. I'll tell you this straight out, unless you pull your men back, Mr. Iglesias, there's going to be shooting."

"Perhaps I should go to the *fuente* with the marshal, Don Pascual," Ramos suggested. "There is no need for you to concern yourself with such trifles. If there is indeed trouble, I can settle the matter very quickly."

"This is no trifle," Iglesias replied. "It involves the honor of my house, Feliciano. Tell Luís to saddle a horse for me at once. I will go with you."

When they went out the front door of the *hacienda*, Longarm looked around for the man who'd guided him to the ranch house. Both he and his horse had disappeared, though the livery horse was standing where Longarm had left it, a young boy holding its reins. Before Longarm could ask the boy about the missing ranch hand, a stableman appeared at the corner of the mansion, leading two saddled horses.

"Where's the man that guided me here?" Longarm asked

Ramos. "The fellow named Juan something-or-other? He can tell your boss what's happening at that waterhole."

"I needed a man quickly to attend to an errand." Ramos spoke as much to Don Pascual to Longarm. "Juan was at hand, so I sent him."

"Where Juan has gone is not important," Don Pascual said. "We are going to the *fuente* together."

"Well, I guess you're right about that," Longarm agreed. "And the quicker we get there, the better."

Riding hard, the trio reached the water hole less than an hour after leaving the ranch headquarters. The need for speed gave them no opportunity to talk. When they topped the last of the long, undulating ridges that lay between the ranch house and the railroad tracks, and looked down the gentle slope, Longarm could tell at a glance that the situation had remained stalemated. Gomez and his men were still clustered around the water hole; Sullivan and the Santa Fe crew had not moved from their position behind the barricade. Seeing that there was no longer any need for speed, the riders walked their tired horses down the slope.

"Looks like we got here in time," Longarm called to Don Pascual as they rode down the gentle slope to the water hole.

"Thanks to you, Marshal," the rancher replied. "And I will make it my business to find out how this misunderstanding could occur."

"It's easy to see what happened," Ramos said quickly. "The foremen all have standing orders to expel trespassers from our range. Since you Anglos took our territory away from us, all the ranches everywhere have suffered from rustlers."

"Gomez should have not mistaken a crew of workmen for rustlers, Feliciano," Don Pascual told the *mayordomo*. "He is one of the best of our *capatazores*."

"All men make mistakes, *patrón*," Ramos replied. "I'm sure that Pablo was only doing his best to protect your lands."

"We shall see." Iglesias said curtly. "I would not want it to be said that I am one who breaks honest agreements."

"Far as I can tell, there ain't any harm done," Longarm put in. "We got here in time to keep a fight from starting."

They rode on down the slope in silence. As the trio drew closer to the water hole, Gomez rode out to meet them, and

112

the men of the railroad crew began moving out of the protection of their timber barricade.

Don Pascual reined in when Gomez reached the group, and Longarm and Ramos followed suit. Gomez pulled up his horse and touched his hatbrim to his employer.

Don Pascual asked the forman, *"Qué significa este asunto, Gomez?"*

"De cuál, patrón?" Gomez asked, his face showing his bewilderment.

"Este conflicto sobre los trabajadores del ferrocarril."

"No hay conflicto, patrón! Estos hombres sera encagarse su agua! Solamente dijo que la aqua tocando era suyo."

Ramos broke in before Don Pascual could question Gomez further. "You see *patrón*, it's just as I told you. Pablo was only being a little overeager to protect your property."

Gomez was looking from Iglesias to Ramos, a perplexed expression on his broad face. He said, *"Pero, Señor Mayordomo—"*

Before he could go on, Ramos waved him to stay silent, and turned back to Don Pascual. *"Pablo no es culpablemente, patrón. Si es culpa, es de mio. Debería diciendo que este fuente sera vendido a ferrocarril."*

Longarm had been following the quick exchanges between the rancher and his men as well as his smattering of Spanish allowed. He said to Don Pascual, "Looks like it's just one of them mixups that happens, Mr. Iglesias. Your foreman told me he didn't know a thing about you selling the water rights to the railroad, but I couldn't get him to believe me when I told you you had."

"Gomez is like all of Don Pascual's people, Marshal," Ramos broke in. "They are a very loyal group."

"That is true," Don Pascual frowned. "I suppose you're right, Marshal. It was just an unfortunate misunderstanding."

"It could've been worse, if you hadn't come to stop it," Longarm said. "Anyhow, there ain't no harm done. Just call your men off so the railroad crew can get to their work, and everything'll be fine."

"See to it, Feliciano," Don Pascual told the *mayordomo*. "And see that we do not have another such incident as this."

"Of course, Don Pascual," Ramos replied. "I promise you that there will be no more such misunderstandings." He turned

113

to Gomez. *"Vaminos a hablar con los vaqueros. El patrón excusete."*

Touching his hatbrim again to Don Pascual, Gomez followed Ramos to the water hole. The rancher shook his head as he watched the two men riding away.

"My people are like children sometimes," he told Longarm. "They mean well, but they need me as their *patrón*, to watch after them constantly. It is not an easy task, Marshal Long. Even Feliciano, for all his astuteness, has moments when he overlooks things of importance."

"Must be a real job, running a big spread like you got," Longarm commented. "Lucky you got a good man like Ramos to take some of the load off your shoulders. He's been working for you quite a while, I imagine?"

"Feliciano, like most of my people, was born on the Rancho Montemayor," Don Pascual replied. "Almost all my men come from families that have served us for a century or more. They look to me for everything."

"I can see where it'd be quite some job, Mr. Iglesias."

"Luckily, my father trained me well." Don Pascual shook his head. "But I still miss his wisdom, myself." He looked at the vaqueros grouped around Ramos and Gomez, listening attentively. "Well, Marshal, Ramos is explaining things to them now. I'm sure there will be no more trouble."

"No, I don't reckon there will be, now. Thanks for your help, Mr. Iglesias. You saved a nasty dustup."

"I could do no less. As I told you, my honor was at stake."

"I'll go tell the Santa Fe men everything's clear for them to start work now," Longarm said. He glanced at the sun, just beginning to drop down the sky in the west. "They'll still be able to get in a pretty good day's work. I'll probably run into you again before my job here's finished."

With a two-finger salute to Don Pascual, Longarm turned his horse and walked it down to the water hole. He avoided the group of ranch hands and rode directly to where Sullivan stood waiting.

"You sure fixed things up, from the looks of it," the railroad cop greeted him. "Them greasers backtracked in a hurry. I guess it's all right for the crew to start work?"

"Anytime they're ready." Longarm looked around at the ranch hands and asked Sullivan, "You ever see that fellow

114

before—the one in the black undertaker's suit—prowling around the construction camp?"

Sullivan squinted at Ramos and shook his head. "Not that I can recall. And I'd be pretty sure to, if he wears that kind of getup all the time."

"Well, you mark him down good, Sullivan, and let me know if he shows up there. Or any of those hombres from the ranch."

"Mind telling me why?"

"If I knew, I'd sure tell you. All I got right this minute is a hunch. He just don't smell right to me, is all."

"I'll keep my eyes peeled, and tell my men to do the same," the policeman promised. "If you're ready to head back now, how about me riding with you on that accommodation? I came up here on a handcar, and even a caboose seat beats that."

"Why, sure. I need to get back and ease Ferrell's mind, so I'm not going to hang around a minute longer'n I have to."

Back in Ferrell's caboose office at the construction camp, Longarm outlined as briefly as possible the way in which the dispute over the water hole had been settled.

"But there's something that sticks in my craw about that ranch strawboss—the *mayordomo*, Mr. Iglesias calls him. It ain't anything I can tie down quite yet, though."

"You're thinking that Ramos and Iglesias are tied in somehow with this Santa Fe Ring you told me about?" Ferrell asked.

"Ramos, maybe. I ain't sure about Iglesias. He acted right upset when he finally heard what was going on."

"How could one of them be working for the Ring without the other being in on it too?"

"I ain't certain-sure about much of anything yet, Jim," Longarm replied. "But I commenced wondering about that Ramos right off, when I had to put my head down and push like a bull just to get him to let me talk to his boss. I told your man Sullivan to let me know if he sees Ramos nosying around here, and you might keep a lookout, too."

Ferrell frowned. "If Ramos is in with the Ring and Iglesias isn't, that'd mean Ramos is going behind his boss's back to stir up trouble between the Santa Fe and the ranchers."

"I got a sneaking hunch it might be something like that. For what it's worth, Jim, I don't think Mr. Iglesias knew a damn thing about what those hands of his were up to. He said a few things that gave me an idea he pretty much leaves it up to Ramos to run things for him."

"You said Iglesias told you Ramos was born on the ranch, and never has worked for anybody but Iglesias. That doesn't sound like he'd be selling Iglesias out," Ferrell objected.

"Hell, Jim, you been bossing men long enough to know there's a lot of reasons a man can give himself for turning his coat inside out."

"But you didn't have any real trouble with Ramos, did you?"

"Not anything big. We butted heads right off, when he tried to sidestep bringing out his boss, and I set tight till he did. Of course I was careful not to let on to Ramos, or Mr. Iglesias either that I'd seen anything I thought was fishy, but that Ramos fellow . . ." Longarm shook his head. "I've seen too many like him to get took in, I guess."

"Longarm, just what in hell are we going to have to do to stop all this trouble?" Ferrell asked. "When I add what you've told me to what I saw happening before you got here, I'm beginning to think the Santa Fe might have a tiger by the tail."

"I'd say you're right enough about that, Jim. I bucked the Ring before, you know. Thought I'd busted it up pretty good, but there must've been enough of the bastards left to start up in business again after I left and things cooled down."

"You've never told me any of the details of the old Ring, Longarm. I know it was some kind of crooked operation, but just how bad was it?"

"Pretty bad, toward the last. I heard the Ring started up years ago, only it wasn't called a ring, then. It was just a few of the old Spanish merchant traders that felt like they were getting a raw deal from the new traders and merchants coming in from the East. Hell, that was even before we had that little war with Mexico back in the forties."

"How did the merchants turn into the Ring, then?"

"Why, after New Mexico was made into a territory, it didn't take long for the old Spanish families that had run things before to see that they'd have to play our kind of politics if they wanted to hold on to what they'd got."

"And they turned it into a political party?"

"It never got that far. Some crooked Anglo politicians joined up with the old bunch, and after a while there got to be more crooks than decent people in it."

"I suppose it's happened before, almost any place you want to look," Ferrell nodded.

"Sure. But the Ring got to be so big that if you wanted to do anything at all in New Mexico Territory, you had to work in cahoots with it. Pay off politicians, give 'em special deals, if you wanted to do business in the territory."

"Well, that's pretty common back East, Longarm. It wasn't but a few years ago when it came out that Credit Mobilier had paid off congressmen and senators, even the Vice-President, and some say the President, to close their eyes to grafting on the Union Pacific's construction."

"Oh, there's nothing new about political bribery and graft, I'll grant you that. It wouldn't surprise me if the Santa Fe didn't have to do a little bit of it to get that line over Raton Pass away from the Denver & Rio Grande."

"Now, you're wrong about Raton Pass, Longarm. I was there, and I know. Sure, we used a carload of gunfighters, but I'll tell you what wasn't talked about. They had orders not to shoot, even if the Rio Grande gang shot first."

"If you say so, I'll believe you. I always figured having that bunch of gunmen on hand was more bluff than stuff. But I imagine there's been a few payoffs here in the territory."

"If there have, I don't know anything about them," Ferrell replied. "Not that it'd surprise me, either. But that's out of my department."

"I'll tell you one thing straight out, Jim. If the old Ring is back in business, or even part of it, they'll be coming around with their hands stuck out sooner or later."

"When that happens, I'll just refer them to the main office. I can't make any payoffs out of my construction allotments."

"If somebody does try to collect, watch yourself, Jim."

Ferrell looked up, frowning. "You sound serious, Longarm. Maybe you'd better tell me exactly what you're hinting at."

"When the old Santa Fe Ring didn't get what it wanted, the men that didn't give it to 'em had a way of dropping out of sight or dying from lead poison."

"Shot?"

Longarm nodded soberly. "That's what got me into the case. They'd begun hiring killers to get rid of the men they couldn't bribe. That didn't just scare the ones that were still trying to stay honest, it gave the Ring a job to fill with their own man."

"And that's when it got broken up?"

"Put it this way, Jim—it got bent, but not busted all the way. And my bet is that whoever's at the bottom of all the trouble your railroad's having right now is what's left of the old Santa Fe Ring."

"So now you've got to—" Ferrell began. But before he could finish what he'd started to say, the door of the caboose was opened with a bang and a big hulk of a man stamped in.

Remembering the attempt made to ambush him on his earlier visit, Longarm was on his feet, Colt in hand, before the bulky man was fully through the door. When he saw that the newcomer's hands were empty, he lowered the revolver's muzzle. Then, when Ferrell showed no signs of alarm, he holstered the weapon.

"You're quick with that gun, me boy," the man said in a thick Irish accent. "You won't be after needing it, though. I'm just here to talk business with Ferrell. But I haven't seen you around here before. Would you be a new man on Mike Sullivan's force, now?"

"I'm a deputy U.S. marshal. Name's Long."

The bulky, red-faced man grinned. "Sure now, I remember hearing your name. You was here a day or so ago, and somebody had a shot at you, wasn't that the way of it?"

"Maybe you remember my name," Longarm replied, "but I can't say I've had the pleasure of hearing yours."

"O'Reilley," the fellow answered. "The one and only original O'Reilley."

Longarm studied the Irishman closely, putting together a physical description to go with his name, which had rung a vague bell with him. The man was big all over; his face was as round as a pie plate, with small eyes set deep between beetling brows and high, ruddy cheekbones. His arms were long and gangling, his hands hamlike. He wore a soiled and wrinkled suit, a shirt without a collar, and a derby hat pushed far back on his head, revealing a fringe of reddish hair.

"It's good manners to knock before you come barging into a man's office, O'Reilley," Ferrell said.

"To hell with manners," the big man snapped. "I'm in a hurry. And I'll ask you to get rid of your friend here before we start talking business."

"What's happened now that's got you in such a tearing big hurry?" Ferrell asked.

"It's not what's happened, Ferrell," O'Reilley said. "It's what's *going* to happen."

"Well, suppose you tell me what that is, then," the construction boss said.

"I told you, it's private business," O'Reilley replied, jerking his head toward Longarm.

"I'll wait outside, Jim," Longarm volunteered. He went out, leaving the door cracked just enough for him to hear what was being said inside.

"All right, O'Reilley," Ferrell said. "Suppose you tell me what's going to happen that's so private and important."

"What's going to happen is that you're going to pay three cents a pound more for every wagonload that my men haul, beginning tomorrow morning."

"Now hold on, O'Reilley!" Ferrell protested. "We've got a contract with Hutchins, and I can't pay a penny more than it calls for until I get permission from the head office."

Longarm remembered now where he'd encountered O'Reilley's name before. A few of the coded telegrams sent to the Hutchins Freighting Company had been addressed to O'Reilley personally.

"Your head office be damned!" O'Reilley snorted. "You're the man in charge here, and it's you I'm telling to deliver or my boys won't turn a wheel."

"Do you know how much three cents a pound more on freight is going to cost the Santa Fe?" Ferrell asked.

"What do you care? It's not coming out of your pocket," the teamster said. He dropped his voice to a whisper that Longarm could barely hear. "But one cent of the three goes into that pocket of yours, Ferrell."

"No!" Ferrell snapped angrily. "I won't cheat the people who pay my wages, O'Reilley. Take your dirty three-cents-a-pound proposition and get the hell out of here!"

"Don't be in a big hurry to say no," O'Reilley warned. "I'm going to give you a few days to think about it, Ferrell. Maybe you'll see things differently after you've slept on it."

"I told you to get out," Ferrell repeated. "I've never taken dirty money before, and I won't start now."

"Be after thinking it over," O'Reilley said. "You've got a few days. And just remember, I'm letting you off light at three cents. If you don't watch your step, I might go up five."

Longarm moved away from the door and busied himself

119

lighting a cheroot while O'Reilley came down the steps of the office-caboose and started toward Hell on Wheels. Going back into the office, Longarm found Ferrell taking the bottle of Irish whiskey out of the cabinet.

"Do you know what that son of a bitch O'Reilley wants?" he began.

Longarm nodded. "I was listening outside the door. I didn't think you'd mind. And I'll tell you again, Jim, watch your step in any dealings you have with O'Reilley. I've got a hunch that the Ring's coming out in the open. If I'm right, that's the thing I've been waiting for 'em to do. I been trying to stir up the minnows, and they're scurrying around now. With any luck, they'll lead me to the big fish I'm after."

Chapter 11

Ferrell stared at Longarm, his jaw dropping in a surprised gape. He recovered quickly, though, and poured drinks from the bottle he'd taken out of the cabinet.

"Sit down, Longarm," he said. "I think we'd better start talking where O'Reilley and I left off. What makes you think he belongs to the Ring?"

"I ain't saying he belongs in the way you mean, Jim. What I am pretty damned sure of is that whoever owns that freighting outfit he's working for is taking orders from the Ring, and might even be part of it."

"Well, from a practical standpoint, that'd amount to the same thing as O'Reilley being part of the Ring, wouldn't it?" Ferrell asked.

"Just about. It's like we were talking about with Iglesias and Ramos. They might not belong to the Ring, but one of 'em is certain to be doing any dirty work the Ring tells 'em to."

"What're you going to do about O'Reilley, then?"

"I'll figure out something. Right now I got a question or two I want to ask him about the Hutchins Freighting Company and some coded telegrams. What happens after that's going to depend on the answers I get."

"What if you don't get any answers at all?" Ferrell asked. "Paddy O'Reilley's a rough customer, Longarm, but he's smart as a fox. You saw that."

"If he don't come up with answers, all I can do is keep on pushing as hard as I know how to. And keep asking questions until I dig up some answers that make sense. Where does O'Reilley hang out?"·

"He's got a shanty down by the corrals that he uses for an office. If he's not there, you'll just have to look in the saloons until you find him."

121

"Don't worry, I'll find him. But as long as I'm here, I might as well push from this end of the line and see where it takes me."

"How long will you be staying? Overnight?"

"Not if I can help it. If I get lucky, maybe I can make it back to Albuquerque tonight."

"I'll have your accommodation moved off the mainline, then, and tell the crew to stand by. It'll be waiting on one of the spurs whenever you're ready to go." Ferrell raised his glass in salute. "Well, here's to your good luck."

Longarm touched his glass to Ferrell's, drained it, and took a final puff from his cheroot. He tossed the stub of the cigar into the spittoon beside Ferrell's work table, stood up, and said, "I'll be back after while, then."

O'Reilley's office was a small, square, shedlike building of unpainted and weatherbeaten boards, perched on a foundation of railroad ties. The shanty was deserted, but its door wasn't locked. It held a bed, a chair, a sheet-iron stove, and a small table. Longarm looked around, found no papers of any kind, and concluded that like many men who had reason to be careful, O'Reilley must keep his business records in his pockets. With a shrug, Longarm left the shanty and started across the tracks to Hell on Wheels.

It was the shank of the afternoon, and activity was beginning to shift here from the construction camp across the tracks. Teamsters who'd returned from their last haul of the day were taking the harnesses off their teams, turning the animals into the corrals, and heading for the dining tent. The train crews, having banked the fires in their locomotives and loaded the tenders with tomorrow's fuel, were straggling across the tracks toward Hell on Wheels. Most of the gandy dancers were still at rail-end, and it would be fully dark before their handcars began rolling into the camp.

Hell on Wheels was starting to come to life. A few women, their faces pale and the collars of their coats pulled high, were scurrying along the unpaved street. One by one they disappeared into the shacks where red lanterns had already been lighted above the doors.

From one or two of the bigger saloons, the tentative tinkle of pianos filtered out as the "professors" limbered up their hands. Few of the saloons had windows, and the soft glow of kerosene lamps or the harsh white glare of carbide lanterns showed in the spaces above and below their batwings. In front of most of them, pale, well-dressed gamblers lounged—dealers and house men waiting for customers, engaged in low-voiced, professional chats. The store doors gaped open, and there were even a few customers moving from one to another.

Longarm walked on to the far edge of Hell on Wheels, where the last of the saloons stood, and began methodically working his way back down the street, pushing open the batwings of each saloon and scanning the drinkers at the tables and bar before moving to the next. He'd covered a bit more than half the length of the street without success when he spotted O'Reilley crossing from the construction camp. With him was another man who carried in a coil over his shoulder the heavy wooden-handled whip that identified him as a teamster. They reached the street and angled away from the spot where Longarm stood, heading across the rutted thoroughfare toward a saloon.

Covering the distance between them in long, purposeful strides, Longarm caught up with O'Reilly and his companion before they reached the saloon. The two men were walking slowly, absorbed in a quiet conversation. He came up behind the pair in the middle of the street and fell into step with them.

"We got a little bit of talking to do, O'Reilley," Longarm said in a quiet voice.

O'Reilley turned with a start. He recognized Longarm, and stopped and grunted. "Umph. The U.S. marshal. And what would you be wanting to talk about now?"

"There's a few questions I'd like to ask you."

"Ask away, me boy. But don't look for me to answer them unless it suits me."

Longarm indicated the teamster boss's companion and said, "I'd just as soon we talked by ourselves, O'Reilley. You might like it better that way too."

O'Reilley scowled, his piglike eyes almost closing, and for a moment Longarm thought he was about to refuse to talk. Then the teamster boss told the man with him, "Step on ahead of us, One-Eye. I'll catch up with you as soon as I've satisfied the marshal's curiosity."

Longarm got his first good look at the man with O'Reilley. He was heavy-jowled and unshaven, his face shaded by a battered felt hat with a wide, floppy brim. His right eye gleamed, a bloodshot orb of blue in a grimy face; his left eye was missing, the socket a twisted mass of wrinkled scar tissue. He glared at Longarm as though he bore the world a grudge, then snorted and moved away, readjusting the whip that was coiled around his shoulder.

"All right, me boy," O'Reilley said. "What is it you'd be after asking me?"

"Who told you to raise the rates you've been charging the Santa Fe, O'Reilley?"

"My boss in Albuquerque. You ought to know that."

"How'd they get the word to you?"

"Just like they always do. Sent me a letter from the office. It came out yesterday on the regular supply haul."

"And you waited until today to pass the word to Ferrell?"

"I was busy."

Longarm stabbed in the dark. Keeping his voice casual, he said, "Suppose you tell me the name of the man in Santa Fe who gives orders to your office in Albuquerque."

Longarm's request was designed to take O'Reilley off guard, and it succeeded. The teamster boss's little pig eyes blinked as he stared at Longarm for a moment. Then he blustered, "Your brain's addled, Marshal. I said my orders was sent from Albuquerque, not Santa Fe. The Hutchins brothers haven't got a place in Santa Fe."

"How about the Zia Land Company?"

O'Reilley opened his mouth to reply, hesitated long enough to swallow, and then asked, "And what might that be, Marshal? The name's a strange one to me."

"Stop lying, O'Reilley," Longarm said sternly. "You know—"

He did not get to finish what he'd started to say. O'Reilley leaped backward, shouting, "Take him, One-Eye!"

Disturbed air whistled in Longarm's ears, a thin rush of wind brushed his face, and he was suddenly caught in coils of braided leather that encircled his torso in a series of tightening loops that pinned his arms to his side. The leather coils drew tighter, and their binding grip was followed by a backward jerk that sent him staggering off balance, almost bringing him to his knees.

O'Reilley stepped forward quickly, yanked Longarm's Colt out of its holster, and jammed the muzzle in his ribs. "Haul him off the street fast, One-Eye," the teamster boss commanded. "Take him between Tim's saloon and Masie's place! We'll get him there in back of the saloon, where nobody can see us!"

Instantly the coils encircling Longarm's body began to unwind, whirling him around. Longarm got a glimpse of the one-eyed teamster hauling on the butt of the whip that had swept around his chest, but deprived of the balance his arms would have given him, if they had not been pressed tightly against him, Longarm was staggering, trying to keep from falling as his body twirled. O'Reilley grabbed him by the shoulder and steadied him.

With O'Reilley holding him erect and the one-eyed teamster hauling on the butt of the whip, Longarm was helpless to do anything except run with them as the two men dragged him to a narrow gap between the saloon and the whorehouse next to it. Longarm glanced back as he was hauled toward the passage between the two buildings, but the few men walking along the street who were watching made no move to interfere.

Longarm realized belatedly that street violence must be fairly common in Hell on Wheels. Even if any of the spectators had been inclined to help, they could not have moved fast enough. Less than half a minute had passed between the moment when the teamster's whip had imprisoned him and the time when the three of them disappeared into the gap between the buildings.

Longarm's captors led him around the corner of the saloon, where a high board fence enclosed an area bigger than the building itself. A gate leading into the enclosure was open wide enough for them to squeeze through, and O'Reilley pulled the gate closed behind them. Longarm looked around and saw that he must be in an arena where fights were staged, for the fenced square was empty except for four posts with ropes stretched around them that stood in the center of the enclosure.

"We'll be private enough here," O'Reilley announced. He stepped away from Longarm and leveled the Colt. "Tim only uses the place for his payday boxing matches. You can let him go now, One-Eye."

With quick upward flips of the whip handle, the teamster unwound the braided leather coils. "You want me to leave him with you, Paddy?" he asked. "Or shall I stick around?"

"You'd better stay," O'Reilley said. "I want to get the son of a bitch to talking, and that whip of yours might come in handy to persuade him if he balks."

"You're the boss," One-Eye replied. He laid the whip out full length with one quick, practiced stroke of its four-foot wooden handle. Longarm's eyes involuntarily followed the ripple of the braided leather as it stretched sinuously to its full twenty-foot length. At its butt, the leather braid was almost as big around as a man's wrist, and it tapered down to a thin popper made of leather strips at its finger-thick tip.

O'Reilley noticed the flick of Longarm's eyes when he looked at the whip. "It's a fearsome weapon, Marshal," he said softly. "And nobody knows how to handle it like One-Eye Mercer there. He can give you an eye like his left one is, or he can take off a chunk of your hide that you can't cover with both hands." He held up Longarm's Colt. "And since you've got nothing to argue against One-Eye's whip with, I'll expect you to answer whatever questions I'll be asking without giving me any lip."

"That'll depend on the questions," Longarm said quietly.

"Flick him easy, One-Eye, on the leg, maybe, just enough to show him how it feels," O'Reilley said.

Mercer's whip hand seemed barely to move, but the long leather braid rose like a striking snake. It rippled from stock to popper, the lash snapped at Longarm's thigh, and he felt a biting sting as the thin thongs hit. It took all of Longarm's self-control to keep his muscles from responding to the bite.

"Saints preserve us, but he's a tough one, ain't he, One-Eye?" O'Reilley said mockingly. "Maybe you'd better do it again, but this time show him how easy it is to take off a man's fingers one at a time."

Involuntarily, Longarm clenched his fists and thrust his hands behind him. Mercer must have expected him to make just such a move. Slowly the lash coiled back upon itself, then, faster than Longarm's sharp eyes could follow, midway of its braided length the tip reversed itself and darted forward, the popper shooting sidewise as it reached him. Longarm's left hand jerked as it struck, popping like a firecracker, with the burning bite of a hot coal.

"Doesn't he make it look easy, now?" O'Reilley asked, an evil smile wreathing his thick lips. "You've no protection, you see, me boy. Save yourself hurt, now, and answer me nicely."

"You still ain't asked me anything," Longarm reminded him.

"Ah, but I'm about to. Now let me see." The teamster boss frowned, then nodded and went on, "You were wanting me to talk about the Zia Land Company a wee bit ago, and it's a good place to start. Suppose you tell me what you know about them."

Longarm's mind had been racing while O'Reilley talked. He said, "If I knew anything about them, I wouldn't need to ask you, O'Reilley. Even a damned fool like you ought to know that much."

O'Reilley dropped his pose of mocking solicitude. "Hit him where it hurts, One-Eye!" he snapped angrily. "Pop his balls a time or two!"

As fast as One-Eye Mercer moved his whip hand, Longarm moved a fraction of a second faster. O'Reilley's harsh voice had not died away when Longarm launched in a half-dive, half-leap that carried him sideways through the air, to drop on the already moving braids near the center of the whip. While he was still moving through the air, his right hand was reaching for his watch chain, and when he landed he had his derringer in his hand.

Twisting as he fell, he swung the derringer at O'Reilley and triggered it just as the teamster boss was bringing up the Colt. O'Reilley got off a shot, but the heavy lead slug from the little derringer was tearing into his shoulder as his finger closed on the Colt's trigger. The bullet from the Colt slammed into the ground a foot or more from Longarm's side, bringing up a puff of brown dust.

Mercer was tugging at the handle of the whip, trying to pull it from under Longarm's body. Longarm did not interrupt the fluid flow of his movements to watch O'Reilley as he lurched and then toppled backward under the impact of the derringer's slug. He swiveled the stubby little weapon, took snapshot aim, and Mercer's head flew back, blood gushing from the socket of what had been his remaining eye. The derringer's flat report was still hanging in the air as Mercer dropped to the ground in the limp, boneless fall that only death brings.

O'Reilley was twitching, trying to regain control of the muscles that the bullet's impact had shocked into immobility. Longarm rolled to his feet and covered the distance between them in two long strides.

He reached the teamster boss just as O'Reilley was reaching with his left hand for the Colt that had fallen from his right. Longarm took an extra half-step, planted his boot heel with crushing force on the teamster boss's outstretched wrist, and ground down hard.

O'Reilley groaned as the bones in his wrist creaked under Longarm's weight. Longarm stooped and retrieved his Colt before removing his foot. Then he stepped back and looked down at the wounded man.

Hatred and fear struggling in his piglike eyes, O'Reilley glared at Longarm. He saw no pity in Longarm's set, stern face. With a groan, the teamster boss slowly pulled himself into a sitting position and clamped his left hand over the wound in his right shoulder.

"You've wounded me, you son of a bitch!" he gritted. Then he caught sight of Mercer's body. "And One-Eye, too!"

"No. Your whip-man ain't wounded, O'Reilley," Longarm said harshly. "He's dead." The teamster boss opened his mouth as though to protest further, but Longarm cut him off before he started to speak. "And you'd be dead too, if I'd had time to aim. This derringer shoots a mite high, twenty feet off."

O'Reilley was tough, Longarm gave him credit for that. The Irishman sat silently on the ground for a moment while he digested the fact that his one-eyed whip-wielder was dead. Then, with an effort at a shrug, he said, "You can't win all the time, can you, me boy?"

He tried to bring his feet under him, to stand up, but with his left arm slung across his chest, its hand grasping his wounded shoulder, he could not get the necessary leverage. Longarm was putting a round into his Colt to replace the one that had been discharged. He holstered the revolver and re-loaded both barrels of the derringer.

Still holding the stubby little pistol in his hand, he looked at O'Reilley and asked, "What's your choice, Reilley? Are you ready to talk?" He fixed his eyes on O'Reilley while he hefted the ugly little derringer suggestively.

"Ah, wait now!" O'Reilley gasped. "You're a federal marshal! A peace officer! You wouldn't shoot a man in cold blood, would you?" When Longarm did not answer, but kept his gunmetal-blue eyes unwaveringly fixed, the teamster boss said thoughtfully, "I suppose you would, at that," Then, trying to salvage what he could of a bad situation, he said, "I'll tell you whatever I know, Marshal. But only if you'll spare my life and get me to a doctor. Do we have a deal, now?"

"That'll depend on you," Longarm told him, his voice as cold as his eyes. He made time for himself to think by pulling out a cheroot and lighting it. Through a cloud of blue smoke he told the worried O'Reilley, "Let's start off with the question you never did get around to answering while we were talking out in the street. Tell me about the Zia Land Company."

"I was afraid that's where you'd be after starting." O'Reilley shook his head sadly, winced as the movement hurt his wounded shoulder, and said, "You can believe me or not, Marhshal. I don't know a blessed damned thing about the Zia Land Company. I was hoping I'd find out about it from you."

"You're right, O'Reilley. I don't believe you." Longarm kept his voice hard. "But I know there's a connection between them and the Hutchins Freighting Company."

"Sure and I didn't say there's not! I've had orders from Clem Hutchins that I'm to do whatever somebody at the Zia Land Company tells me to do, and ask no questions. Only don't be asking me why, because that's what I don't know."

"Clem's one of the Hutchins brothers." Longarm frowned, talking more to himself than to O'Reilley. "Who's the other one?"

"Len. He stays back in Kansas at the main office, mostly."

"But you got your instructions direct from Clem?"

"I did that. From Clem himself, about six months ago. And he didn't give me any reasons."

"And you've had orders from the Zia Land Company since then?"

"Only three times. Once it was to hire on a man they were sending to the job here to work as a wagoner's helper. He showed up, and I put him on. He hung around a few days, did nary a lick of work, and one morning he didn't show up."

"What about the next time?" Longarm asked.

"That was just a few days back. It was another man they were sending me. This one wasn't to do any work. All I had to do was take him around and acquaint him with the camp—when the men were busiest, where things was, Ferrell's office and the paymaster's records, and when the supply trains ran and suchlike."

"Wait a minute. How many days ago was that fellow here?"

O'Reilley thought briefly and said, "It was the day before

you showed up. I recall now that I wondered if the man could've been the one who shot at you, when I heard about it. He wasn't dressed like a railroader or a teamster, more like a ranch hand. And he looked ugly enough to take on that kind of job."

"What did he look like?" Longarm asked.

"He was one of the natives. Greasers, I call 'em, but not to their faces. I learned better than to do that when I was on the line building down from Raton. Hispanic, they want you to call 'em. But you'd know that. Had a mustache, needed a shave. A dirty kind of man, I thought to myself."

"And he just disappeared?" When O'Reilley nodded, Longarm said, "All right. Tell me about the third time the Zia outfit sent you orders."

"That was yesterday, to tell Ferrell the rate was going up."

"How'd you get these orders, O'Reilley?"

"They always come in a special envelope in the office message pouch. The Santa Fe sends the pouch from Albuquerque, like they do such of their own office messages that don't go by the telegraph. The supply train conductor brings the pouch to me."

"Whose name is signed to the orders?"

"Nobody's. They're just orders."

Longarm shook his head in disgust. "That's the most unlikely bunch of lies I've ever heard, O'Reilley! Suppose you start all over and tell me the truth for a change."

"Dammit, Marshal, it's the truth! On me sainted mother's grave, I swear it's the truth!"

"You're going to have to prove it, then."

"How? How can I? With a bullet hole in my shoulder that's hurting me like original sin, and no doctor here to look after it, I'll be lucky if I'm alive by morning."

"That little scratch ain't gonna kill you," Longarm told O'Reilley unfeelingly. "But I'll figure out a way to make you prove what you've told me." He tucked the derringer in his vest pocket and leaned down. Putting a hand under O'Reilley's left armpit, he helped the teamster boss to his feet. "Come on."

"Where? Where you taking me?"

"To Albuquerque. I'll find a doctor to fix up that wound, and then me and you are going to that office the Hutchins brothers have got there. I figure with you along, I might have a chance to get to the bottom of this."

"Wait a minute!" O'Reilley protested. "I've got a job to do

here, Marshal! How're my men going to know what to do if I'm not around to tell 'em? And One-Eye's got to be buried."

"Your friend Tim, the saloonkeeper, can take care of the funeral. And don't worry about your men. They'll figure out what to do, or somebody else can boss 'em until you get back. Now let's go."

"How do you expect to get me to Albuquerque? The supply train won't be making another trip until day after tomorrow."

"I've got an accommodation waiting on a spur to take me back tonight. The one that brought me here. Now come on."

After putting O'Reilley under the care of the head brakeman on the accommodation, with instructions not to let the Irishman get off, Longarm made a quick trip to Ferrell's office while his horse was loaded and the accommodation was pulled off the spur and onto the mainline.

"What do you mean you're taking O'Reilley to Albuquerque to get a gunshot wound treated? Who in hell shot him?" Ferrell demanded when Longarm told him his plans.

"I shot him. Now don't go plaguing me for a lot of hows and whys, Jim, because I'm in a hurry. I'll tell you the whole story when I get back."

"When's that going to be?"

"Damned if I know. Maybe tomorrow, maybe not for two or three days. But O'Reilley's the best lead I got to cracking this case, and I don't aim to slow down."

"Wait a minute!" Ferrell said. "What about the teamsters? Who's going to boss them if O'Reilley's gone?"

"Put one of your men on it. They won't need much bossing, anyhow. You'll get along all right."

Ten minutes later, Longarm and the head brakeman were putting a temporary bandage on O'Reilley's shoulder while the wounded man lay on one of the berths in the caboose. Outside, the lowering sun cast a long shadow of the speeding train as it rocked over the newly laid track on its way to Albuquerque.

Chapter 12

Although the engineer of the accommodation had run on a full head of steam during the trip back to Albuquerque, it was almost sunset when they pulled to a halt in the Santa Fe yards. The sun had gone down completely and the short high-altitude twilight was darkening into night by the time Longarm had finished seeing that O'Reilley was safely taken care of for the night. After going to the trouble of nursing the teamster boss back to Albuquerque, Longarm had no intention of letting him slip away while he was busy elsewhere.

Knowing that brakemen got more than their share of injuries, Longarm had asked the accommodation's head brakie for advice, and the brakeman had told him of a doctor who ran a small private clinic. Bundling O'Reilley into a hired hack, Longarm had taken him there. After Longarm had shown the medic his badge, the doctor had agreed to keep O'Reilley in a locked room and heavily sedated with laudanum until Longarm returned to take custody of the wounded man.

When he saw the bruise on the back of Longarm's hand where One-Eye Mercer's whiplash had landed earlier in the day, the doctor had offered to apply a salve to it. Though Longarm had been aware that his hand had been stiff and slightly swollen and was by now beginning to throb painfully, he had no time to think of anything except work unfinished. Refusing the offer, he had the hackman take him back to the Santa Fe yards.

Dismissing the hack, Longarm found the livery horse waiting at the freight station hitching rack. As he prepared to swing into the saddle, his stomach began sending him urgent messages, and suddenly he remembered that, aside from a few bites of jerky and parched corn on the accommodation riding back from the construction camp, he'd had no food since breakfast.

He debated stopping for supper, but quickly decided that finding out about getting the coded messages turned into readable English was more urgent than responding to the signals he was getting from his stomach. Cheating his hunger with a swallow of Maryland rye from the bottle in his saddlebag and a cheroot, he swung into the saddle.

Trailing a plume of fragrant tobacco smoke, Longarm rode down Central Avenue. Darkness had taken over by now, and lights inside the new stores along the street lighted his way to the Grand Hotel. Hurrying up to the mezzanine, Longarm knocked on the door of the San Ysidro Cattle Company offices, but when his repeated rapping brought no response, he returned to the lobby.

"I got back later'n I figured on, and the San Ysidro Cattle Company office is already closed," he told the desk clerk. "Now, I'd imagine you got Mrs. Evan's home address around somewhere. Could you tell me what it is?"

"Why, of course, Marshal Long," the clerk replied. He took a small ledger from the desk drawer and consulted it. "Mrs. Evans lives at 806 Roma Avenue. I don't recall seeing her leave, but I'm sure you'll find her there."

"I will if I can find Roma Avenue in the dark. I don't know Albuquerque streets all that well."

"It's not very far from here, Marshal. Just turn left when you leave the hotel, go right on the first corner, and Roma Avenue will be the fourth street you come to. Turn left on Roma, and Mrs. Evans's house will be between the third and fourth cross-streets."

Even without the benefit of street signs, a cultural refinement that had not yet reached the fast-growing town, Longarm had no trouble following the clerk's directions. Cynthia Evans's house was a new yellow brick cottage, with a narrow veranda supported by white wooden pillars. Light shone through two of the front windows on one side of the door and through a pane of etched glass set into the door itself.

Longarm reined in and looked around. Like most of the similar dwellings around it, the house had a brick walkway leading from the door to the curb. At the end of the walk there was a carriage-step with a hitching ring set in its stone side. Longarm dismounted, looped the livery horse's reins in the ring, and went up the walk to the house.

Through the translucent pane in the door, Longarm saw

Cynthia Evans's form in silhouette as she came to answer his knock. She began speaking the instant she had the door ajar.

"I really didn't look for you until tomorrow—" she said; then, as the door opened wider and she saw Longarm, she stopped short, gasped, recovered her composure, and went on with a barely noticeable hesitation, "Why, Longarm! What a pleasant surprise. Come in."

"I hate to come butting in on you at home this way," Longarm said, "but your office was closed up tight by the time I got back to town, so I asked the desk clerk where you live."

"I'm glad you did. I was just beginning to feel lonely."

"You sure you ain't expecting company?"

"No. Of course not. Now come in, Longarm. I'm very glad to see you."

Longarm stepped into a small entryway. In the light that spilled into the little hall from a door at Cynthia's right, he could see her in half-profile. She was wearing a cream-colored silk wrapper trimmed with lace, and her golden hair was caught up in a loose bun at the nape of her neck. Her translucent skin picked up tiny highlights from the lamplight reflected off the fabric of the wrapper, which somehow managed both to reveal and conceal the opulent body that Longarm remembered from the evening before, when her figure had been emphasized by a fitted suit.

"Hang your hat on the rack," she said. "We'll go into the parlor. I've just lighted a fire in there." She brushed past him to enter the door leading to the lighted room, and Longarm got a whiff of her perfume—a rich, musky scent that somehow seemed to fit her statuesque proportions.

He followed her into the parlor and scanned the room in one quick glance. It was much more richly furnished than the outside of the cottage suggested. A curve-backed sofa with petit-point upholstery occupied most of one wall. The opposite wall was taken up by a low, wide whatnot cabinet filled with pieces of china and glassware. Two straight chairs flanked the cabinet; like the sofa, they had petit-point upholstery.

An oval library table stood near the center of the room, and an Aladdin lamp with a china shade decorated in a floral design was on the table. A pair of easy chairs had been drawn up at facing angles in front of the fireplace, where a fire of fragrant piñon branches glowed with flickering flame. Small tables stood beside the chairs. A purple and red Turkey carpet covered the floor.

"You got a real homey place, Cynthia," Longarm said.

"It's comfortable, at least. Sit down, Longarm." She indicated one of the easy chairs, and when Longarm moved toward it, she settled into the facing chair in front of the fireplace. "I really am glad to see you, you know. Evenings seem to drag when you're by yourself."

"I figured on getting back in time to stop at your office, but my business out at the construction camp took a little bit longer than I'd allowed for."

"I thought something like that must have been the case when you didn't get back before closing time."

"For a while, I just about decided not to bother you this evening, but those coded messages commenced fretting at me, so I just came ahead."

Cynthia hesitated for a moment before saying, "Even if you'd gotten to the office before I left, I still couldn't have decoded those messages."

"You didn't get a wire from Mr. Fernandez, then?"

"Oh, I got a telegram from him today. It'd be silly of me to lie about that, because I know you only have to ask the Santa Fe for copies of any wires you want."

"But Mr. Fernandez said you weren't to tell me what's in those coded messages I want to know about?"

"He didn't mention them at all. His wire just said that he's coming back from Santa Fe. He'll get in tonight or in the morning, I suppose, and then you can talk to him yourself."

"I bet you figured it was him at the door when I knocked a while ago."

"As a matter of fact, I did. He often stops by when he gets in late, to ask me about things that've happened at the office."

"And you were surprised when it was me instead of him."

"Surprised, but not at all disappointed, Longarm. I wasn't just being polite when I said I was glad to see you."

Longarm took out a cheroot, and belatedly remembered that some women discouraged smoking in their parlors. He started to put the cigar back in his pocket.

"I don't mind you smoking at all," Cynthia said. She stood up and went to the whatnot, took a china ashtray from one of the shelves, and placed it on the table beside his chair. Then she shook her head and went on, "I'm being a thoughtless hostess, I'm afraid. I haven't even offered you a drink, and I'm sure you'd enjoy one after such a busy day."

Longarm had already lighted the cheroot. Through the smoke that wreathed his head, and without really thinking of what he was saying, he replied, "I'll settle for a smoke right now, and wait for a drink until after supper."

"You mean you haven't eaten yet?"

"I guess I just disremembered to stop and eat. Like you said, I been right busy today."

"Let me fix you something, then. You must be starving."

"Now, Cynthia, I wasn't hinting for you to feed me. I'm not all that hungry. I'll pick up a bite after I leave."

"Please, Longarm. I'd like to fix you something. I've got roast beef that's still warm from my dinner, and a loaf of fresh bread in the kitchen. At least let me make you a sandwich."

Longarm hesitated. The mention of food had started his empty stomach to demand that it be filled. "Well," he said, "if you don't think it's too much trouble..."

"It's no trouble at all. I'd enjoy doing it. I'll make you a roast beef sandwich, and wait to have my drink until you've eaten. Then we can have an after-dinner brandy together."

"I don't like to act picky, Cynthia, but I ain't such a much for brandy. But I got a bottle of rye out in my saddlebag. If you don't mind, I'll step out and get it while you fix the sandwich."

"Go right ahead. Don't bother to close the front door, just come on back inside and be comfortable. I'll be in the kitchen."

Cynthia was not in the parlor when Longarm returned carrying the bottle of whiskey. He put it on the table beside his chair and was turning to sit down when Cynthia's voice reached him through the door that stood open opposite the fireplace.

"Longarm?" she called, "Come in the dining room. I'm just finishing your sandwich. Sit down, I'll be right there."

Instead of stopping in the dining room, Longarm went through it to the brightly lighted kitchen. Cynthia was just cutting the thick sandwich into halves.

"Why don't I sit right down here and eat at the kitchen table?" he asked her. "It'd make me feel right at home, and then you won't have to fret about crumbs on your dining room carpet."

"If that's what you'd rather do." She pulled a chair out from the table. "Make yourself at home. I like the idea of having a man in my kitchen, anyhow. It's been a long time."

Longarm sat down and rested his hands on the pine tabletop. Cynthia put the sandwich on a plate, picked up a dish containing pickles and a dab of mustard, and set it in front of him.

"Now, if that's not enough, I'll make you another one," she said, smiling. "I'll sit down with you while you eat."

Longarm reached for one of the halves of the sandwich, and in the bright light of the kitchen, Cynthia saw for the first time the bruise that had gone unnoticed in the softer light of the parlor.

"Why, you've hurt yourself!" she exclaimed. "Longarm, have you been fighting? That's what it looks like."

"Oh, that ain't anything to worry about. A man that knocks around the country a lot has almost always got a bruise or two someplace on him."

"Well, it needs to be attended to. Some arnica or salve or something. I know you're hungry, so eat first, then I'll fix it up for you."

Longarm made short work of the sandwich, and the thick slice of beef and yeasty bread did a bit more than cut the edge off his hunger. He leaned back in the chair and reached for a cheroot.

"Why don't you wait until I've doctored your hand before you light your cigar," Cynthia suggested. "Then we'll go into the parlor and you can smoke it while we have an after-dinner drink."

"Well, my hand don't really bother me all that much, but if you're dead set on tending to it, I won't object."

"Come in the bathroom, and I'll see what I can find. I know there's some liniment and some salve in there."

Picking up the lamp from the kitchen cabinet, she lighted their way across a narrow hall and through her bedroom. Longarm got only a glimpse of her bedroom as he followed her, a quick impression of a wide, high bed with a satin coverlet and a frilly dressing table. Putting the lamp on a marble-topped washstand beside the tub, she bent to open the doors of the stand, and began rummaging on the shelves of the bottom compartment.

In the intimacy of the small bathroom, Cynthia's movements sent waves of the musky aroma of her perfume into the air. She stood up with a brown medicine bottle in her hand, saw Longarm's eyes on her, and smiled.

"I suppose you're thinking I'm being very forward on such

short acquaintanceship, Longarm. But I'm sure this isn't the first time you've been in a bathroom with a woman."

"It's been a while since I been in any room with such a pretty woman," he told her.

"That's a nice compliment, but it's not going to take my mind off fixing your hand," she said. "I know most men don't like to be doctored, and I don't suppose you're any exception. Now take off your coat and let me hang it up while you roll up your sleeve so I can attend to that hand."

Longarm slid his arms out of his coatsleeves and Cynthia hung the coat on a hook beside the bathtub. Longarm sat down on the edge of the tub. He'd rolled the sleeve of his shirt to his elbow by the time she turned back to face him, the bottle still in one hand. She drew the cork and a sharp, tangy scent of alcohol and arnica filled the air, driving out the more subtle aroma of Cynthia's perfume.

"This isn't going to hurt, you know, it's only liniment," she told Longarm, taking his hand and spreading it flat, pressing her palm to his to hold the back of his hand upright. She looked at the purple welt and said, "You never did tell me how you hurt yourself."

"Oh, I got careless and let my hand get in the way of a fellow that was showing how good he was with a bullwhip."

"And he did this to you accidentally?" Cynthia let a bit of the liniment trickle on his hand and began rubbing it in, gently at first, then with a bit more pressure. "I hope he apologized for his carelessness."

"Well, he wasn't what you'd call being careless, but I'm real sure he won't do it again." Longarm felt the warmth of the liniment beginning to ease the throbbing that he'd been ignoring since the whip had struck him. Cynthia's gentle massaging hurt, but at the same time felt good.

She reached for the liniment bottle and misjudged its distance, knocked over the bottle, and it rolled across the marble top of the washstand toward the edge. Trying to reach the bottle before it fell to the floor, Cynthia turned while leaning forward to reach the bottle. Somehow the full skirt of her robe got entangled with her feet. She lunged and would have toppled to the floor, but Longarm caught her before she fell.

For an instant they both stood motionless, unsure of their balance. Longarm suddenly became aware that he was holding Cynthia in a close embrace, her back pressed to his chest, her

138

full, soft breasts grasped in his big hands, her head thrown back to rest on his shoulder. The scent of her musky perfume was much stronger than that of the liniment, now.

Cynthia seemed in no hurry to break the unplanned embrace in which they'd suddenly found themselves. She turned her head without lifting it from Longarm's shoulder and rubbed her smooth chin across his cheek; her hands found his and pressed them even tighter into her breasts.

"I like the way your hands feel on me," she whispered. "Big, strong hands, like every man should have."

Longarm was very much aware of her sensual perfume and of the pressure of her soft body against his. He was also aware that Cynthia was wearing nothing under her robe, for he could feel her nipples budding beneath the pressure of his fingers. He tried to release her breasts, but Cynthia held his hands firmly where they were. Their lips were only an inch or so apart, and suddenly, as though by common consent, they closed even that small gap.

Cynthia's lips began to writhe in a slow, pulsing motion. Longarm felt the tip of her tongue running along his lips and opened them to meet her tongue with his. She let go his hands, and when Longarm reacted instinctively by slackening the tension of his embrace, she whirled in his arms so that they stood face to face and body against body, the generous mounds of her breasts pressing on his chest. She shifted her feet and he felt her hips push against his. After a moment of motionlessness, she began rubbing her soft hips across his groin.

Her tongue was stabbing into his mouth now with deep, flickering darts. Longarm felt an erection beginning, and Cynthia must have felt him starting to swell, for she pressed herself still harder against him and her rubbing became a rotation of her hips. Breathlessly they broke the kiss that they had been holding for so many moments.

"You sure about what you're doing?" Longarm asked her in a low voice.

"Of course I am, or I'd never have started it. I'm a grown woman, Longarm."

"You don't have to remind me of that."

Longarm nuzzled his chin along Cynthia's soft neck and buried his face in the soft, pulsing hollow between her neck and shoulder. She shuddered as the tip of his tongue traced a path over her warm, scented skin, and returned to explore again

139

the soft spot where the caress had started. Her hand found his crotch, and he felt her soft fingertips stroking the length of his growing erection.

Her voice soft and throaty, she said, "Let's go into the bedroom where we can be comfortable."

Taking Longarm's hand, she led him into the bedroom. The lamp in the bathroom shed a soft light into the larger room. Cynthia nodded toward the bed.

"Sit down and take your boots off. Then I'll help you undress. I want to see if what I've been feeling is real."

Longarm perched on the side of the bed and levered off his boots. Cynthia's hands were on his belt before he could stand up. He pushed them away gently to unbuckle his gunbelt and hang it on the head of the bedstead, where the Colt's butt would be within easy reach. Leaving Cynthia's fingers to work busily at the buttons of his fly, he slipped his watch into the right-hand pocket of his vest, where the derringer nested, and slid the vest off. He laid it across the chair that stood beside the bed.

While Longarm was unbuttoning and removing his shirt, Cynthia succeeded at last in freeing the buttons of his trousers. She pulled them down to his thighs and began on the buttons of his balbriggans, her hands meeting Longarm's as he freed the buttons from the top. Avidly now, she grasped the sides of the ballbriggans and pulled the undergarment down with one swift jerk.

"My God, I don't believe it!" she gasped when she saw the jutting cylinder she'd liberated. "I knew you were a lot of man from the first minute I saw you, but I didn't expect this much!"

Reluctantly releasing her grip on him, Cynthia stood erect and pulled at the sash that held her robe together. With a quick shrug she let the robe drop from her shoulders to fall in a crumpled heap around her feet. As large as her breasts were, they stood erect without drooping, great hemispheres of translucent white skin tipped with bright pink rosettes, their nipples protruding in a darker rose. Her waist flowed in gently, only to flare out in wide hips that blended into ample thighs, and between them, a mass of dark blond pubic curls.

"You're a real lot of woman yourself," Longarm told her.

He rose from the bed to embrace her. Cynthia stepped out of her soft bedroom slippers and came to meet him. She grasped his erection and tucked it between her thighs, and Longarm at last became completely hard when he felt himself engulfed by the soft flesh of her inner thighs and the moist heat of her crotch.

Cynthia's breath was gusting now, as she felt him still growing in the soft recess between her thighs. Her arms went around him and he let her turn their bodies so that her back was to the bed. She relaxed her arms enough to allow herself to slide down his body until she was sitting on the side of the high bed. She fell backward, opening her thighs, and her hand sought Longarm to place him inside the pink lips that now gaped beneath her triangle of blond curls.

Longarm lunged and went into her swiftly, with a single sustained thrust that brought a cry of pleasure from deep inside her throat. Longarm bent over her to seek her nipples with his lips, but Cynthia put a hand on his chest to stop him.

"Later, Longarm. Right now I want you this way."

She raised her legs and rested their rounded calves on his chest. Longarm felt her inner muscles tightening around him as her thighs came together again. He wrapped his arms around her legs and lifted her a bit higher, until her soft buttocks were pressed against his thighs. Then he began stroking lustily, going into her deeply and holding himself against her body firmly for a moment before withdrawing full length to begin another swift, hard lunge.

He looked down at Cynthia as he stroked. Her arms were outstretched across the bed, her hands grasping the coverlet. Her chin was raised high, the white column of her neck tautly stretched, her eyes squeezed tightly shut. Her full lower lip was drawn into her mouth, and in the soft light he could see the white line of her teeth clenched against it. The nostrils of her aquiline nose were dilated as she breathed in sighing gusts, the only sound other than the soft collisions of their bodies that broke the silence of the dimly lighted room.

Cynthia's high-standing breasts were no longer outthrust. Their mounds had taken on softer contours that emphasized the pebbled center rosettes and the rosy tips that jutted from them. They were rising and falling as she breathed in soft, sighing gasps, and at the same time shaking and quivering in rhythm with his thrusting as he drove into her.

Now Cynthia's ankles had locked behind Longarm's neck. He released his embrace around her legs and sunk his hands into the soft flesh of her buttocks, lifting her and supporting her as he increased the tempo of his deep lunges. He felt the muscles in her buttocks growing tauter in his hands.

Cynthia's body began writhing and tossing on the bed. She rolled her shoulders from side to side and the gusting of her breath became deep, groaning sighs. Longarm felt the muscles that had grown so taut begin to quiver. Cynthia's mouth flew open and her full, moist lower lip glistened in the obscurity. Then she opened her eyes and looked up at Longarm.

"Are you ready now?" she asked. "Because I certainly am."

"You let go when you want to, Cynthia. I feel like I can keep on going for a spell."

"I want to wait too, but I can't."

"Then don't hold back."

"If you're not ready—"

"I won't be for quite a while."

"Don't stop, then. Because I . . . I . . ."

Her hips rose in a sudden, convulsive spasm. A small scream burst from her throat. Her tossing grew swiftly into a series of rippling tremors that came closer and closer together until she keened with a final high cry, her hips twisted and heaved, her outthrust hands beat soundlessly on the bedcover, and then her body was limp, her muslces slack. With a deep sigh she closed her eyes again, and as she sank back into the pillow, the ridges in the white column of her throat disappeared.

Longarm eased the tempo of his stroking. Cynthia lay supine and motionless, though he could still feel small, involuntary twitches in the muscles of her buttocks. He stopped his slowed thrusts and pressed hard against her thighs, holding himself in her at full depth.

Cynthia's eyes opened and she looked up at him. "I feel wonderful now, Longarm, but you must be getting tired."

Longarm withdrew halfway and gently eased his full length into her wet hotness. "Not yet, Cynthia. I can still go on when you've rested a little bit."

"Wouldn't you like to stay inside me and just lie on me while we rest a few minutes? I need to rest, even if you don't."

"Why, sure. We don't have to be in any hurry."

"I hate to have you leave me, though, even for a minute."

"There's no need for me to. Here."

Longarm leaned forward and braced his knees on the side of the bed. He slid his hand under Cynthia's ribs and started to lift her. She put her arms around his shoulders and lowered her legs to clasp them around his waist. Longarm carried her with him as he moved on his knees to the center of the bed. Then lowered her gently and stretched out on her soft body.

Cynthia lay quietly for a moment, then stirred, and Longarm felt her inner muscles tightening around his shaft, still buried in her. She started kissing his shoulders and neck, rubbing her moist lips hard on his skin, until she reached his mouth. Then her lips opened and she thrust her tongue deeply into Longarm's mouth.

They held the kiss only briefly, though. Cynthia moved her head and whispered, "I thought I was tired, but I'm not. Feeling you inside of me still hard does something to me, Longarm. Go on and start again as soon as you're ready."

Longarm responded with a short, hard thrust, and Cynthia opened her thighs in a wide sprawl, her feet planted on the bed beside them, her knees in the air. Longarm raised his hips high and pounded into her. The short rest had both refreshed him and brought him closer to a climax. He began stabbing into her ready body. He lunged faster and faster, with Cynthia raising her hips to meet his driving strokes, until he felt himself close to the point where his brain could no longer control his body.

Cynthia sensed Longarm's growing readiness. She spread her thighs wider, inviting him to pound as deeply as he could penetrate, and as Longarm speeded up, her thighs began trembling, her hips started rolling from side to side. She caught Longarm's face in her hands and pulled their lips together. Their tongues met and rubbed together wetly and hotly as Longarm continued to pound until she threw back her head, breaking the kiss.

"Hurry now!" she urged. "You must be ready too! I want to come with you this time, and I'm getting to the place fast!"

Longarm did not answer. His breath was whistling in his throat as his hips rose and fell faster and faster until the building tension in his groin suddenly dissolved. He shook and fell forward on Cynthia's writhing body, holding himself firmly in her while her hips rose and fell until he was drained and spent, his quick, sharp breathing lost in the sound of her gratified sighs.

Outstretched on Cynthia's flesh, Longarm almost fell asleep. Her stirring roused him and he raised himself on his hands to look down at her.

"You're going to stay with me the rest of the night, aren't you?" she asked.

"If you'd like for me to."

"You know the answer, Longarm."

"Then I'll stay."

"You won't be sorry." Cynthia sighed happily. "Right now all I can think of is sleeping for a while. But if you're going to stay, there'll be lots of time. Time for everything, including time for us to talk. No, you won't be sorry, I'll promise you that."

Chapter 13

In the parlor, the clock chimed four times. Puffing on a cheroot, Longarm counted the number of chimes, just as he'd counted them each hour since he and Cynthia entered the bedroom. He wondered, aₒ he had through the night when the clock had reminded him of time's passing, how he was going to get her started on the talking she'd promised they would do.

He glanced at Cynthia out of the corner of his eye. She was lying beside him, her head on his shoulder, her blond hair spread in tousled disarray, mixing with the darker curls of his chest. Her naked body was pressed close to him, both hands clasping his wrist, holding his hand cupped over a bare breast. Her eyes stared at the ceiling through the half-light that spilled into the bedroom from the lamp in the bathroom.

Cynthia sighed and stirred. She said, "I hate to think the night's almost over. It's been too short."

"Time goes by fast when you're enjoying something," Longarm replied.

"And I've certainly been enjoying it. But I don't need to tell you that, do I?"

Longarm did not answer her; he was making a long reach with his free hand to pick up the bottle of Tom Moore that stood on the chair beside the bed. Pulling the cork with his teeth, he let it fall to the pillow while he tilted the bottle and let a swallow of the liquor trickle down his throat. He put the bottle back on the chair without bothering to recork it, and turned his head to look at Cynthia.

"We still ain't found a chance to have that talk you promised we would," he reminded her.

"I haven't forgotten," she said. "I've been waiting for you to get tired and want to rest, but you've just stayed inside me until you're hard again and kept on going. You're the first man I've known who's been able to do that."

Longarm had shared enough pillow-talks to recognize that the time he'd been waiting for had come. The incandescence that had sustained Cynthia had burned out, leaving her in a conversational mood. He knew also that he'd have to steer their talk into a gradual transition, away from sex to subjects that now interested him more.

"You mean to say a pretty woman like you ain't got a steady man friend or two that can keep her satisfied?" he asked.

"Most of the men I know are too old and settled to be interested in me or for me to be interested in them. The younger ones want younger women." There was no bitterness in Cynthia's voice; she spoke flatly, merely stating a fact.

"I guess I was wrong in what I figured, then."

"What was that?"

"Why, the way you were standing up for your boss, fighting me all the way to keep me from finding out about those telegrams, I sort of got the idea there was something more than business between the two of you."

"Rudy?" Cynthia chuckled. "Oh no. Anybody but him."

"You said that like you really meant it."

"I do." She hesitated for a moment before continuing, but the mood to talk had taken hold of her now. "Rudolpho Fernandez isn't interested in me or any other woman. He likes young boys, the younger the better. Oh, sometimes when we've been working late he'll take me to dinner, and once in a while he used me as a smokescreen, if you understand what I'm saying."

"Sure. I've seen it before. So it's strictly business between the two of you, then."

"Strictly. Rudy pays me a lot more than I could make doing anything else. I don't think I'd enjoy standing behind a counter in a store, waiting on women all day. So I do the very best job I can for him."

"I guess that means you ain't going to tell me much about those messages, then."

Cynthia sat up and looked at him angrily. "Is that why you took me to bed, Longarm? Just to get me started talking?"

"Ain't it funny, now? I been wondering the same thing about you, Cynthia. I changed my mind when you said what you did a minute ago about your boss. But the truth of it is,

I didn't have any plan but for us to talk when I came to see you tonight. Anything else just happened."

"I'm sorry, Longarm. I know that our being in this bed right now was as much my idea as yours, maybe more my idea than yours. But it's an idea that's been in my mind almost since the first time you came into the office."

"Well, I ain't been exactly blind about you, either. Except that you were on one side and I was on the other, and it didn't seem like such a good idea."

"You're a very interesting man, Longarm," Cynthia said, her eyes fixed on his face. "How did you ever get into such an unrewarding job as the one you have?"

"Now, I wouldn't call it that. Of course, it ain't a job that'll ever make me rich, but it suits me."

"If what I suspect is true, Rudy and his friends are going to offer to make you rich." She had no sooner finished speaking than her eyes widened and she bit down hard on her lower lip. She saw Longarm's eyes fixed on her and added hastily, "Damn! I shouldn't have said that!"

"Now that you did say it, maybe you'll tell me what you were getting at."

"No. I can't do that, Longarm. I've already said more than I should have."

"Seeing as how you've said so much already, it looks to me like a little bit more wouldn't hurt."

Cynthia hesitated, undecided, then told him, "Longarm, even if I'd wanted to decode those messages for you, I couldn't have."

"I don't exactly follow you," he frowned. "You told me you know what they say."

"Yes. I do. That is, I know what they say, but I don't know exactly what they mean."

"That don't make much sense, Cynthia."

"There are names in those messages that don't match the names of anybody the San Ysidro Cattle Company does business with."

"Sort of one code inside of another one, you mean?"

"It has to be something like that. And there's a great deal of money going through the office that doesn't have any connection with buying and selling cattle or land."

"You figure there's some kind of funny business going on,

but you can't find out what kind, is that it?"

"When Rudy hired me, he made it very plain that he'd tell me what he wanted me to know about his business, and that I wasn't to pry or to ask too many questions. I haven't, and that's why I still have a job there."

"You done some pretty good hinting a minute ago, Cynthia. If you'd just tell me what you were getting at . . ."

She shook her head, her lips set firmly. "Longarm, I've already said a lot more than I should have, more than I intended to. I can't tell you anything else. You'll have to come to the office later this morning and talk to Rudy."

"Oh, I aim to do that. There's a man I've got to look after, and likely another little call I'll make first, but I'll be looking for your Mr. Fernandez as soon as I can. And don't worry, Cynthia. I won't give away anything you said to me, not a thing at all."

Longarm got to the clinic shortly after eight o'clock. He'd left Cynthia Evans before daybreak, slept for an hour or two in his room at the Grand Hotel, and then taken the time to sit down and enjoy a leisurely breakfast in the hotel restaurant before hailing a hack and going to the clinic to check up on the teamster boss. The doctor greeted him sourly, shook his head with a resigned expression on his face, and escorted him to a locked room. The doctor unlocked the door, and Longarm found O'Reilley groggy but unrepentant, his arm in a sling.

"Let's go talk to your boss," Longarm said without wasting any time in greetings. "I've got other things to do today, and I want to settle this business with him first."

"You're forcing me to do a thing I wouldn't do to oblige even me own sainted mother, Marshal!" O'Reilley protested. "And me with a bullet hole in me and a head that won't give off aching from whatever kind of devil's dose it was you paid the doctor to give me!"

"Well, you got a choice, O'Reilley," Longarm said unfeelingly. "You can go with me to talk to your boss, or you can go to jail for attempted murder."

"So it's Paddy-be-damned if I do, and Paddy-be-damned if I don't!" O'Reilley complained.

"It's more like Paddy-you-do-what-I-tell-you-to," Longarm retorted. "Now make up your mind. Which is it going to be? Go with me to talk to Clem Hutchins, or go to jail?"

"We'll go see Clem," O'Reilley agreed after thinking it over for a moment. "And if it costs me my job, it's better than going to jail."

The Hutchins Freighting Company occupied a small two-room building at the edge of the Santa Fe yards. Longarm prodded O'Reilley through the door. A wooden counter ran across the room they entered; doors behind and in front of the counter led to the second room. Behind the counter, a young Hispanic sat at a paper-littered desk. He was coatless, but wore black India rubber sleeve protectors and a felt eyeshade. He looked up when Longarm and O'Reilley came in.

"If you men are looking for work, we have none," he said.

O'Reilley was staring at the youth. He demanded belligerently, "Who might you be? And where's Clem?"

"If you're looking for Mr. Hutchins, he is not here. Perhaps I can help you. My name is Flores."

Longarm decided quickly that his best course would be to keep silent. Though there was no resemblance between the two men, he'd noted instantly that the youth behind the desk had the same distant manner he'd noticed in Ramos, the *mayordomo* of the Rancho Montemayor, and he wondered if the young man, like Ramos, might be a new breed of Hispanic.

"What happened to Gorman?" O'Reilley growled.

"I am replacing Mr. Gorman," Flores replied. "He has gone back to Kansas. If you'll tell me who you are and what you want, I'm sure I can—"

"I'm Paddy O'Reilley, the boss of the Santa Fe railhead job, and I come to see Clem Hutchins! Now tell me where the hell he is and what's going on here!"

"Ah, O'Reilley," the youth repeated with an understanding nod. "Of course I know your name, Mr. O'Reilley, even if this is the first time you've been in the office since things changed."

"Damned if they haven't!" O'Reilley snorted. "But I'll let Clem tell me what it's all about. Where'll I find him?"

"Mr. Hutchins has gone back to Kansas, too."

"You mean you're in charge now?"

"No indeed, Mr. O'Reilley. I'm in the same position as yourself. I just have a job here. Mr. Tafolla is the manager now."

"Then where's he at? Dammit, I feel like a fool, not knowing about what's happening! Where's this Tafolla at?"

"Perhaps you had better talk to Mr. Tafolla, at that. He's in his office. I will find out if he has time to see you."

Longarm saw a flush of anger creeping redly up O'Reilley's neck. He waited until Flores had gone through the door to the inner office before cautioning the teamster boss in a low voice, "Better put a snaffle on that temper of yours, O'Reilley, or you might find yourself out of a job."

"Be damned if I will! It ain't like Clem to go off without saying a word to me! I've been with him and Len a long? time!"

"I got a hunch that ain't going to matter a hell of a lot. Something's going on here that I don't savvy."

"No more do I!" O'Reilley retorted. "But I'll damned soon find out what's what!"

"Watch your step, just the same," Longarm said. "You—" He stopped short as the door in front of the counter opened and a man whom he assumed was Tafolla appeared.

He looked from Longarm to O'Reilley and asked, "Which of you is Señor O'Reilley?"

"That's me. And maybe you can tell me what happened to Clem Hutchins?"

"Señor Hutchins has returned to Kansas. He has left me in charge of this office."

"You're my boss now, is that it, then?" O'Reilley asked.

"If you put it this way, yes, Mr. O'Reilley. Now that we understand the situation, suppose you explain to me why you are here instead of at the railhead, doing the work for which you are being paid?"

O'Reilley was quick-thinking enough to indicate the sling. "I had to come in to the doctor's. Thought I'd pay my respects to Clem before I went back. There's a thing or two I got to ask him about, anyhow."

"Then you can ask me," Tafolla said.

"Maybe I better not take up your time, Mr. Tafolla," O'Reilley said. "Most of it was personal, between Clem and me."

Longarm had no intention of letting O'Reilley get off so lightly. He'd been studying Tafolla, and again saw a resemblance between him and the ranch factotum.

"Mr. O'Reilley was wondering about one thing, Mr. Tafolla—that rate raise he was ordered to put in on the Santa Fe job."

"Ah." Tafolla nodded. "I was wondering why you had come here with O'Reilley. Your interest is with the Santa Fe, then. I am sorry, but I did not hear your name, and I am not yet well acquainted with all of the men of the railroad."

Longarm gambled that O'Reilley would be reluctant to admit to his new boss that he'd been brought to the office by a U.S. marshal. Since it was against his principles to lie, he replied obliquely, "My name's Long. Jim Ferrell, the construction superintendent out at railhead, told me he don't like the idea of that new rate one bit."

"No one wishes to pay more for a commodity or a service, Mr. Long," Tafolla replied smoothly. "The increased rate is regrettable, but necessary, I'm afraid. If Mr. Ferrell intends to protest, I suggest he go through the proper channels. It was put into effect by an authority higher than mine. Unfortunately, I cannot change it."

"I sort of had a hunch that's what you'd say." Longarm nodded and turned to the teamster boss. "Well, O'Reilley, if you're finished, so am I. No use in taking up Mr. Taffolla's time."

"What the hell was the idea of shutting me up in there?" O'Reilley demanded angrily when they were back in the hack. "You didn't give me a chance to ask about the messages, and I thought that was what we come for. And I was all primed to give that greaser a piece of my mind!"

"You ain't got enough mind to afford to give any of it away," Longarm told him. "You couldn't even see that I wanted to get out of there before you set off a bunch of fresh trouble. I didn't like the smell of things."

"Nor did I," O'Reilley agreed. He looked at Longarm, his bushy eyebrows raised. "Well? What's next?"

Longarm had been asking himself the same question, and had come up with only part of an answer. "You get on the next supply train and go back to see Ferrell. Tell him you got the Hutchins Freighting Company to call off the rate raise."

"Now hold on, Marshal! You can't expect me to do that. If my new boss says he can't put the old rate back, how in hell do you expect me to? If I did that, it might get me into a lot of hot water!"

"Then you'll just have to be smart enough to swim out of it, O'Reilley. Don't worry about it. They won't find out here in Albuquerque until the Santa Fe makes its next payment, and my guess is that they won't do anything right away, until after they find out why. So you got some elbow room, and so have I."

"Elbow room for what?" O'Reilley demanded.

"To find out what's going on, and stop it."

O'Reilley shook his head. "I don't like it."

"I'm not asking you to like it," Longarm said coldly. "I'm telling you to *do* it. Because if you don't, I'll be looking you up to find out why, and if you make me do that, I promise you I'll take good aim before I pull trigger."

O'Reilley looked at Longarm for several moments. Longarm kept the teamster boss's eyes fixed with his own gunmetal-blue gaze. Finally, O'Reilley said, "You'd be about mean enough to do in anybody that crossed you, wouldn't you, Marshal?"

"You be the judge of that, O'Reilley."

"I already have been. And I don't think I want to risk it." He shook his head. "All right. I'll do what you said, and hope to all the blessed saints you'll be handy to get me out of whatever trouble I get into."

O'Reilley's expression and the feeling that he put into his words left little doubt in Longarm's mind that the teamster boss would do what he was told. He had no hesitation about dropping O'Reilley off at the central supply depot near the Santa Fe yards to fend for himself until the next supply train left for the construction camp. He rode back to the hotel alone and dismissed the hack, then climbed the stairs to the mezzanine and knocked at the door of the San Ysidro Cattle Company's office."

Cynthia's voice called, "Come in." Longarm opened the door and saw her seated at her desk. As though they hadn't parted only a few hours ago, she looked coolly at Longarm and said, "Good morning, Marshal Long. Mr. Fernandez is expecting you. I told him you'd be here sometime fairly early. Come in."

Longarm entered; forewarned by the formality of Cynthia's greeting, he glanced at the room's second desk. It was occupied by a burly man with a complexion swarthier than was common to the natives of New Mexico Territory. The midnight-black of his full, waxed mustache above thick cherry-red lips made him look even darker than he was in reality.

Gray flecked his black hair at the temples, and the bushy, outcurving sideburns that covered most of his cheeks also

152

showed a touch of gray. His eyes were black under puffy lids that gave them a vaguely Oriental appearance. He was wearing a well-cut business suit; his double chin was pushed up by the high collar of a stiffly starched shirt and a puffy gray cravat ornamented by a large diamond stickpin puffed up from his vest.

"Mr. Fernandez," Cynthia said, "this is U.S. Marshal Long. I told you what his reason is for calling."

Fernandez did not rise or offer his hand. He looked at Longarm with obsidian eyes and said, "Long, Mrs. Evans said you've been asking her questions about some of our private telegraph messages."

"So I have, Mr. Fernandez. Some that are in code, that is."

"This is a private code, Long, like those used by many companies to keep their business from becoming the gossip of telegraph clerks and messengers."

"I don't have any argument about your right to use a code."

"Then what interest does the federal government have in my business affairs?"

"It's in connection with a case I'm working on, Mr. Fernandez. That's all I can tell you right this minute."

"Are you saying that the San Ysidro Cattle Company is suspected of some kind of crime in connection with this case, Marshal?"

"I ain't saying a thing except that I'm here working on a case and I'm pretty sure those coded messages will help me close the case out."

Fernandez frowned. "How do you happen to have copies of these messages? Where did you get them?"

"That ain't any concern of yours, Mr. Fernandez."

"I don't agree. I think I must be very much concerned about the way you obtained copies of private messages." Fernandez raised his voice slightly. "Cynthia! Do you know how our telegrams came to be in the marshal's hands?"

"When Marshal Long asked me to decode the messages for him, he told me he'd gotten them from the Santa Fe Railroad."

"But you did not decode them for him, you said."

"No," Cynthia replied. "I told him I couldn't do that without your permission."

"Quite properly too. I also forbid you to do so in the future." Fernandez turned back to Longarm. "And I will not decode the messages for you, Marshal. I think that settles the matter."

153

Fernandez extended his hand. "The messages, Marshal."

Longarm shook his head. "It don't settle a thing."

"But they are useless to you unless you can read them!"

"Oh, I might have to send those telegrams clear to Washington to find somebody who knows how to turn 'em into English, but I sure ain't going to give 'em back."

Fernandez was showing his anger now. "You are an unreasonable and stubborn man, Marshal Long!"

"Maybe so," Longarm replied calmly. "But I'll just keep on trying till I find somebody who can tell me what's in those wires. You and Mrs. Evans ain't the only ones that know the code. Some of those telegrams were sent you by the Zia Land Company, up in Santa Fe, if I recall rightly."

"Do you know the people in charge of the Zia Land Company, then?" Fernandez asked.

"Not yet. But I aim to talk to them as soon as I get around to it."

"They are my friends and business associates, Marshal. I can assure you, they will refuse to decode the messages, just as I am refusing. You can save yourself a great deal of time and inconvenience by handing me the telegrams now, and forgetting about this entire affair."

"You know I ain't going to do that, Mr. Fernandez," Longarm said quietly.

Fernandez sat silent for a moment, then said, "You seem to feel the messages are important to this mysterious case you've mentioned, Marshal Long. Why, if you do not know what they say?"

Longarm decided the time had come to stir the water a bit harder, and get the minnows more agitated. He said, "Because I know enough about the case from what I've already dug up to know those telegrams might be all I need to wind it up."

If Fernandez was bothered, he did not show it. He asked, "But if you do not know what is in the messages, how could you tell me, as you did a moment ago, that my company is not connected with your case?"

Longarm had played enough poker to recognize a bluff when he met one. He replied levelly, "You must've disremembered what I told you, Mr. Fernandez. That ain't exactly what I said."

Fernandez changed tactics. He said thoughtfully, "I suppose you had authorization from your superiors to seize my property without a warrant, Marshal?"

"Why, I didn't seize a thing, so I didn't need any warrant. I just borrowed copies of some messages I was curious about."

"I have a number of friends in the federal government," Fernandez went on. "You might be in danger of losing your job if I call their attention to your illegal action."

"You go ahead and call anybody's attention to it you want, Mr. Fernandez. I'll look after my job."

His inability to make progress was obviously irritating Fernandez. He pounded the desk with his fist as he said angrily, "Be careful, Marshal! There are laws that protect private property from illegal government seizure! Do you want to force me to take this affair to court?"

Fully aware that his bluff might be called, Longarm replied, "Why, if that's what you feel like doing, I sure can't stop you. You might think about something, though. Court trials are a mite different from you and me talking in private."

Fernandez's eyes closed to even narrower slits than normal. He said, "I do not see your point, Marshal."

"Why, if you go to court, the judge might just make you tell him what those messages say, to prove I did something wrong when I borrowed them."

Fernandez fell silent and began drumming his fingers absently on the top of his desk. Finally he looked at Cynthia and said, "I want to speak in private with Marshal Long. Go into the other room, and close the door." When Cynthia had left, he turned back to Longarm. "It has occurred to me that I may have been taking the wrong approach to solving this problem, Marshal."

Longarm knew what was coming next, but gave no indication of his awareness. His voice blandly innocent, he asked, "How's that, Mr. Fernandez?"

"It's possible that I have not taken you into my confidence enough. Now, I will tell you this much. The messages you are so interested in concern an important business transaction, and if my competitors learn what they say, it could cost me a great deal of money. It would be worth my while to . . . well, shall we say, buy them from you."

"They ain't for sale, Mr. Fernandez. And I'll save you the trouble of trying to buy me along with the wires. I ain't for sale, either."

"My offer would be very high," Fernandez persisted.

"Save your breath," Longarm snapped. He started for the

door, but turned back to say, "I found out a long time ago that any man who sells himself ain't worth buying. Now if that's all you got to say, I'll bid you good day. I got more important business to take care of."

Chapter 14

Longarm reviewed the immediate past and planned his future moves for an hour and a half, while the northbound Santa Fe train climbed from Albuquerque to the transfer station at Lamy, where passengers headed for the territorial capital boarded a stagecoach for the last fifteen miles of their journey. He sat by a window in the smoking car, lighting one cheroot after another, paying no attention to the rolling fields of the wide valley through which the train first passed, or to the sparsely wooded foothills of the Sangre de Cristo mountains, around which the train looped before it began chugging up the steep incline that led to Glorieta Pass, beyond Lamy.

He was the first to swing off the train when it ground to a halt at Lamy's small wooden depot. The piñon and juniper grew thicker at this altitude, and a few tall pine trees towered over the underbrush. When Longarm dropped the stub of the cheroot he'd been puffing and ground its coal out on the narrow platform of the high, angular little station, the pines' resinous aroma filled his nostrils with an unaccustomed fragrance.

Old son, he thought as he drew in big breaths of the tangy air, *you got to quit smoking them damn cigars. This fresh air sure beats breathing in tobacco smoke.*

For a moment, Longarm stood on the platform in front of the depot, inhaling the tangy air. Then, tucking the stock of his rifle into his armpit, he walked up to the baggage car to make sure that his saddle gear was transferred to the stage that was waiting to carry the passengers the rest of the way to Santa Fe.

After his long and fruitless exchange with Rudolpho Fernandez, Longarm had gone down to the barroom of the Grand Hotel. He lighted a stogie and, with a bottle of Tom Moore on the table in front of him, puffed and sipped while he pondered the tangled web into which he'd stumbled.

157

Very little deliberation had been needed to convince him that during his earlier encounter with the Santa Fe Ring, he had failed to make a clean sweep of its conspirators. He'd sensed this at the time, but had been called back to Denver to handle another case. Now it was apparent to him that the remnants of the old Ring had re-formed and enlisted new members, and that the Ring was presently not only resuming its predatory activities, but expanding them.

Which ought to be a lesson to you, old son, Longarm told himself, studying the amber depths of the glass he'd just refilled with Maryland rye. *If you set out to do a job, do it right the first time around, or you'll just have to go back and start from the beginning and do it all over again. When Billy Vail called you off to send you on that other case, you ought to have told him you hadn't finished the one you were on, and stayed till you wiped the Ring out, from asshole to appetite. But the milk's already been spilled, so it's up to you to do the best you can. Which means starting all over to dig the rats out of the cellar.*

Because the old Ring had been based in Santa Fe, Longarm quickly concluded that the capital was the place to begin his work. He'd ruled out both Tafolla and Fernandez as the top leaders of the new Ring. Neither of them had the characteristics he'd learned to look for in men heading a large criminal organization. Longarm was convinced that he'd stirred up only some of the minnows while in Albuquerque. Never one to waste time, he'd checked out of the Grand Hotel and, after leaving word with Elmer Parsons as to where he could be located, boarded the train for the territorial capital.

Standing now beside the railroad tracks in Lamy, he watched the baggagemaster take his saddle gear from the coach and load it on top of the stage. Satisfied that his equipment hadn't been overlooked, Longarm walked back to the station, where the other four Santa Fe–bound passengers were waiting to get on the stage. Two of the passengers were nuns carrying large net bags loaded with parcels, their white coifs gleaming with starched freshness against their sober black habits. They stood a few paces apart from the other two passengers, men whom Longarm judged by their appearance to be sheepherders or ranch hands.

With a creaking of harness leathers as the driver hoarsely geed up his team, the stage rolled away from the baggage coach. The train whistled and started up the grade at a crawl.

The stagecoach reached the corner of the small wooden depot and Longarm stepped up to meet it, but the stagecoach went past him and the driver pulled up where the other passengers stood. He waited at the back of the high-wheeled Concord coach, standing beside its boot. The two men stepped away from the stage to allow the nuns to board first.

One of the sisters handed her net bag to the other, got into the stage, and held out her hand to take the bag. The second nun handed the bag up, but the one already in the stage dropped it, spewing parcels out on the ground around the Concord wagon's wheels. Longarm, closer to the stage than the other men, leaned forward at once to pick up the spilled parcels, and the act of courtesy saved his life.

Just as he bent down, reaching for the first parcel, a rifle spat from the concealment of the thick stands of trees and brush on the hillside. The slug punched into the wood of the Concord's boot, where Longarm's head had been an instant earlier.

When he heard the shot, Longarm did not stop with bending. In a cat-quick continuation of his forward movement, he dropped flat and rolled beneath the stagecoach, then scrambled to cover behind its rear wheel. A second rifle slug raised dust from the dry, powdery mountain soil behind him as he reached shelter under the coach.

A puff of smoke from the second shot had fixed the location of the sniper for him. Longarm had not really stopped moving before he was triggering an answering shot into the brush where his attacker was concealed. He bracketed the spot where he'd seen the muzzle blast with shots on either side and on the slope above it, but no more firing came from the brush. Then the muted thudding of hoofbeats told Longarm that his would-be assassin was making a quick getaway.

From the stage above his head, Longarm now heard the startled screams of the two nuns, the excited voices of the two men, and the indignant, angry shouts of the stagecoach driver.

"It's all over," he called, scrambling from beneath the stage. "Whoever was doing the shooting's gone now." He rose to his feet and turned to the Concord. "You folks ain't in any danger, it was me that bushwhacker was aiming at."

"Why should someone be trying to kill you, *señor?*" one of the nuns asked. "Are you such a dreadful sinner?"

"Yeah," the driver seconded. "Just who are you, mister?"

Longarm chose to answer the nun first. "I don't reckon I'd

qualify as a saint, sister, so I guess you could call me a sinner, all right." Then, looking up at the driver but speaking to all of them, he went on, "My name's Long. I'm a deputy U.S. marshal, working on a case. I got a notion it was some of the men I'm after that took those shots at me."

"You make it sound so unimportant," the nun said quietly, frowning. "As though taking life is a small thing."

"I sure didn't mean it to sound that way, sister," Longarm replied. "Being shot at is something that men in my line get used to, though. This ain't the first time they've tried it since I've been after 'em, and I don't reckon it'll be the last."

"Maybe you better get to Santa Fe on shank's mare, then," the driver said. "The hombre that let off them shots might be waiting up the road to have another try, and I don't want none of them folks in the coach to get hurt."

Longarm shook his head. "He ain't likely to hang around." Before the man could protest, he vaulted up into the high seat beside the driver. "But just in case, I'll ride with you, where I can keep an eye peeled for him."

After a glance at Longarm's set face, the driver said nothing more. He slapped the reins over the team's backs, and the stage rolled ahead.

There were no more shots from ambush as the coach bounced over the ruts of the dusty, winding road that led to the territorial capital. Just the same, the driver inched as far from Longarm as he could, and Longarm kept his Winchester across his knees until the low brown adobe houses of Santa Fe came in sight. The trip from Lamy had taken almost as long as the train had required to cover the distance to the transfer station from Albuquerque, and the shadows were stretching across the plaza when the stage stopped in front of the hotel at the end of the trail.

Longarm looked across the plaza at the Palace of the Governors, and saw that lamps had already been lighted inside. The carved double doors of the entry were open, and vertical slits of yellow showed between the drawn curtains of the deep embrasured windows of Governor Lew Wallace's office. He told the driver to have his saddle carried into the hotel, and walked at an angle across the plaza toward the entrance of the Palace. Sergeant Higgins was sitting at his post just inside the entry.

"Marshal Long," Higgins said, a salute in his voice. "You'd be wanting to see the governor, I suppose? He's going to have to leave soon; he's the guest of honor at a dinner at the fort this evening."

"I won't keep him but a minute," Longarm promised. "All I want to do is tell him what I found out in Albuquerque, and get him to open up a door or two so I won't waste time starting work in the morning."

"I'll take you in, then, Marshal," Higgins said.

"Longarm!" Governor Wallace exclaimed when Higgins opened the door to his office and ushered Longarm inside. "I didn't expect you'd be reporting back so soon."

"I ain't exactly got a report, Governor. I'm still trying to fit a bunch of bits and pieces together."

"Well, report or not, I'm glad to see you. Cristina was asking about you just the other day, before she left."

"She's gone back home, then?"

"Oh no. She just went up to the northern Pueblo country to paint Indians."

"She had somebody with her, I guess? From what I heard, that part of the territory's pretty wild yet."

"Why, I wouldn't have allowed her to go alone. I sent two of my household servants with her, to handle the camp jobs and look after her." The governor indicated a chair. "I hope you do have at least a little progress to report."

"A little bit, Governor." Longarm sat down in the chair the governor indicated and waited until Higgins closed the door before going on. "I'd say you were right when you guessed that the old Ring was setting up for business again. Oh, it ain't exactly the same bunch, but it's just as bad. Maybe worse."

"You've had trouble, then?"

"Some." Forgetting his latest resolution to quit smoking, Longarm took up a cheroot and touched a match to its tip. "I was shot at a few times, and I've dug up a few names that need to be looked into. That's why I come up here, to see if you can give me a little bit of a hand."

"How can I help?" Wallace asked.

"I want to poke around in whatever records the territory keeps. Lists of ranches and businesses and who owns 'em. I been digging up some names that I need to find out more about."

Wallace frowned thoughtfully. "Well, let's see. There's the brand register, that gives the names of the ranchers and the location of their home range. The territorial treasurer has a record of company names and the men who own them, and his office is also supposed to keep records of corporations and their stock issues. Of course, the land office keeps track of title transfers and deeds, when land changes hands."

Longarm remembered the frustrations he'd run into before when he'd been compelled to search through records. It was not one of the aspects of his job that he enjoyed. He asked the governor, "How far behind do all those offices run in keeping their books up to date?"

"That's a hard question to answer, Longarm." The governor shook his head. "You know the situation where political appointments are concerned. What counts is who a job seeker knows, not how efficient he might be, when there's a job to be filled."

"When we talked about this right after I got here, Governor, you told me you suspicioned there was still a bunch of men in territorial jobs that used to work with the old Ring. You'd have some of your own people in all those offices too, I suppose?"

"Not very many. I've appointed a few men who served with me in the War, but—" Wallace stopped abruptly and asked, "Do you know what the territory's unofficial policy is in making appointments?"

"Can't say I do."

"It's a long-standing agreement, going back to the days of the occupation during the Mexican War. Half the jobs in the territorial offices are supposed to go to the native Hispanics."

"That sounds fair enough to me, seeing it was their country to start out with."

"True enough, and it was certainly politically expedient. But I've found the territorial offices I've looked at closely to be anywhere from six months to two or three years behind in their record-keeping."

"Governor, I've got to have the latest information I can get, or I'm just wasting my time. There's got to be records of some kind that I can get it out of."

A rapping sound at the door before the governor could reply. Higgins opened the door and stuck his head in.

"Excuse the interruption, Governor," he said. "There's that dinner at the fort—"

"I hadn't forgotten, Higgins." Wallace turned to Longarm and asked, "Look here, Longarm, didn't you serve in the War?"

"Well, I signed up soon as I thought I was old enough, and got shot at a time or two."

"Come along to the dinner with me, then, if you don't think the speech I'm going to make will be too boring."

"I was just a buck-ass private in the War, Governor. I don't belong at any officer's shindy like this one."

"Nonsense! This isn't a big formal affair. It's just a regimental dinner. And there won't be a big crowd, because so many of the officers are in the field."

"It's right kind of you to ask me, Governor, but I—"

"I'm not going to take no for an answer," Wallace insisted. "There's nothing you can do this evening, the territorial offices are closed by now. You've got to eat somewhere, and I can promise you this won't be the usual mess hall meal. After dinner we can come back here and you can bring me up to date on what you've found out so far."

"If you put it that way, Governor Wallace, I'll be proud to join you."

Fort Marcy sprawled southwest of the plaza, a short distance from the Palace of the Governors. The regimental officers' mess hall had been draped in red, white, and blue bunting, and most of the men wore dress blues and their ladies had donned evening gowns, but the atmosphere was surprisingly informal. Longarm found a bottle of adequate Maryland rye on the refreshments table, and a quiet corner in which to stand when Governor Wallace became the center of the crowd.

At dinner he found himself sitting between two very junior second lieutenants, newly arrived from the East, and spent most of his time between bites answering their questions about New Mexico Territory, which they were seeing for the first time. The dinner was winding on toward dessert, coffee, and speeches when Longarm saw Higgins come in and lean over the governor's chair. Wallace's lips compressed, and he glanced quickly around the table until he saw Longarm, then turned to Higgins and said something to the aide. Higgins made his way to where Longarm sat.

"Marshal Long, the governor would like to have a word with you in private," he whispered. "He's going to excuse himself from the table and wants to meet you in the dayroom, next door."

As soon as the governor had left the mess hall, Longarm followed him into the dayroom. Wallace stood with his hands clasped behind him, facing the fireplace in the low-ceilinged chamber. When Longarm came in, he turned, his face drawn into a worried frown.

"I've had some very serious news, Longarm," he said abruptly. "Cristina's been taken prisoner by a band of Jicarilla Apaches."

"You said she'd gone up to the northern Pueblo country," Longarm remembered. "That's quite a ways south of the Jicarilla range, as I recall. Don't they hole up in the Rio Arriba?"

"Yes. Teena didn't mention going that far north, though. She told me the pueblos were what she wanted to paint, so I didn't worry too much when she insisted on going."

"How about the people you sent to look after her?"

"Esquivel Baca and his wife, Adelita," the governor said. "I sent them because they're reliable and know the country. Esquivel has just gotten back. Higgins told me he's wounded and that Adelita was killed."

"How'd this Baca get away from the Jics?"

"I don't know all the details yet. All I'm concerned with is getting Cristina free as soon as possible."

"Well, there's plenty of soldiers here. You can send a troop or two up there at a quick march, and they ought to be able to get her back pretty fast."

"No!" Wallace said quickly. "That's the very thing I don't want to do. I have all the respect in the world for the army, Longarm, but it's trained to fight Indians, not liberate prisoners from them."

Longarm nodded slowly. He was beginning to get an idea of what Wallace had in mind. He said, "Guess I got to agree with you about that, Governor. The army's a lot better at fighting than it is at parleying."

"I know that better than most, I suppose," Wallace went on. "If I sent a troop up into the Jicarillas' stronghold, they'd gallop in with their guns blazing and try to rescue Teena by force. And I'm afraid all they'd rescue would be her dead body."

Longarm said nothing. He waited, sure of what was coming next.

"This is a job for one or two men," Wallace went on. "Men who know what they're doing and can keep cool while they do it." He hesitated, then said, "I don't have any authority to take you off your case, or to order you to do anything, Longarm, but will you take on the job?"

"I reckon you know the answer to that, Governor," he replied without hesitation. "Give me one good man who'll stand rear guard, and I'll do my level best to bring her back safe and sound."

"Thank you, Longarm. I suppose I knew what your answer would be," Wallace said, trying to smile and not quite succeeding. "I don't know who you'll want to go with you, though."

"Higgins," Longarm said promptly. "He'll do fine if you can spare him, and if he'll go."

"Don't worry about Higgins going. You're a good judge of men, I couldn't have picked better myself. And for a job like this, I'll certainly spare him."

"If that Baca fellow ain't all chopped up, I'll want him to go too. We'll need a guide, and you say he knows the country."

"I don't know how badly Esquivel was hurt. You'll find out soon enough. He's with Higgins, in my office."

"Then I'll go on over there and see what I can find out. I reckon if you're aiming to keep the army out of this, the best thing for you to do is go ahead and make your speech. We can talk later on, after I find out the lay of the land."

Wallace nodded. "Yes, that's the best plan. It's too late for you to set out tonight. There'll be things you'll need—a horse, supplies—and I'm sure there are plans you'll want to make. I'll go ahead with the speech, even if I don't know how it's going to sound. I'll see you in my office as soon as I can get there."

In the governor's office, Longarm found Higgins sitting with the wounded man. Esquivel Baca could have been any age from thirty to sixty, but Longarm suspected that he was closer to the latter. Baca was a small man, wiry, with a badly pockmarked face and a thin mustache. He did not seem to be injured too seriously, though his clothing was ripped in places and bore a few bloodstains. His face was scratched and his head had been bandaged in an amateurish fashion; Longarm suspected that Baca had put the bandage on himself.

Longarm decided to let Governor Wallace inform Higgins that he'd been drafted, and devoted his attention to Baca. When the sergeant offered to leave, Longarm shook his head. "There's no need for you to go, Higgins. You might think of something that I'd miss when I'm asking Baca questions." He turned to the wounded man. "Esquivel, tell me how it happened up there in the Rio Arriba country."

"We were not in the Rio Arriba, *señor,*" Baca replied in reasonably understandable English. "It ees to the far pueblos that *la señorita* say she want to go, so we are stay the first night at Nambe, on our way to Picuris and then Taos."

"You mean the Jicarillas jumped you right inside of one of the pueblos?" Longarm frowned.

"No, no," Baca replied, shaking his head. He winced and his face wrinkled with pain, but he went on, "It is after we are go from Nambe, maybe we get halfway to Picuris. We stop to make *la comida.* Adelita is go gather wood for fire, *la señorita* is make the painting from *la vista,* I am tend horses and take off them the food for cook. Then, so quick—*ay, caramba!* is much yell, is all around *los Apaches!*"

Didn't you have a gun along, Esquivel?" Longarm asked.

"*Seguro, señor!* I am take rifle, I am take *pistola.* But I am not think we are in danger, so far from *Apacheria* like we are. I do not have guns unpack."

"So they took you by surprise. What happened then?"

"There is some shooting. I am get hit. I fall down, then is nothing I know until I am wake up. Is gone *la señorita,* is gone *caballos, mulo, todas.* Is noplace Adelita, too."

"You got that bandage on your head," Longarm frowned. "Did the Apaches scalp you?"

"No, *señor.* You weel onderstan', I am fall down into *la cañada,* ees so narrow they do not find me."

"All right. When you come to, you were down in a ravine, and you crawled out. Miss Teena and your wife are gone, and all your animals and gear. What did you do next?"

"I am look for them," Baca replied. His voice grew unsteady as he continued. "Soon, Adelita I am see. She is on ground, all over with blood. *Los Apaches diablos se arranca su cuero sobre matala.*"

Esquivel stopped and buried his face in his hands, thinking of the moment when he found his wife dead, scalped. Longarm let him grieve for a few moments before continuing to question him.

"Esquivel," he said after Baca raised his head, "I'm sorry I got to ask you all this, but I need to know what happened."

166

"*Seguro, señor*. This I onderstan'. *Preguntame*."

"You looked for Teena and the horses and mule after you saw you couldn't help your wife?"

"*Sí, señor*."

"You didn't find any signs they'd hurt Teena, did you?"

Baca shook his head. "No, *señor*. Tracks I am find, *sí*, I am follow them a little way, but I am *cansado*, I do not go so far. How am I to fight so many Apaches, with nothing but only my hands?"

"There wasn't much else you could do, Esquivel. All of us know that. You started back to Santa Fe, then?"

With great dignity, Baca drew himself up and said, "No, *señor*. I am carry Adelita to Nambe. Is take most of the night, but is there the church. I am not to put *mi Adelita como un animal, en tierra disconsegrada*. Is make her funeral mass, there in Nambe, *el padre*. Then he is fix for *un indio* to help me back *en mulo* to Santa Fe."

"You won't have any trouble finding the place where those Apaches jumped you, will you?"

"*No, señor. Este puesto recuerdo hasta que morir!*"

"I guess you will, at that," Longarm nodded. "I'd remember it too, if I was you." He looked at Baca's bandaged head, then asked, "You think you'll be fit to start back tomorrow, and show us where the Apaches hit you?"

Esquivel looked up at Longarm, his dark eyes blazing. "You are to go take *la señorita* Cristina from them, *señor?*"

"We're sure going to make a try of it."

"Then I will go back. I will go back if you give me gun. I have *venganza* to take on them, *señor!* If you are wish to go tonight even, I am ready!"

"Tomorrow'll be time enough," Longarm told Baca. "All right, you set still and rest. You hungry?"

"No, *señor*. Is bring food, *el indio*, we are eat on way back."

"Just rest, then," Longarm told him. "Governor Wallace is on his way back here, he ought to get here in a few minutes. He'll see about getting a doctor to fix up your head and whatever else you need."

After his explosive vow of revenge, Esquivel seemed to have reached the end of his strength. He nodded, sagging in his chair. Longarm looked at him for a moment, then signaled to Higgins to join him in the hall.

"What do you think, Marshal?" the sergeant asked, as they stood outside the closed door of the governor's office. "Is there a chance of getting Miss Teena back alive?"

Longarm frowned. "I don't know. Maybe if I can get up there fast enough to pick up their trail, and push like hell chasing after those Jicarillas, I might get her away from 'em."

"You're going after her yourself?"

"Unless the governor's changed his mind since I left him a few minutes ago."

"But what about the case you're working on?"

"I'll pick it up when I get back. It ain't going to take more'n two or three days to find out what's happened to Teena and get her back here, if she's still alive."

Higgins hesitated for a moment, then said, "You wouldn't be wanting some help, would you, Marshal? Governor Wallace has treated me real fine, and the few times I saw Miss Teena, she was always such a nice lady. I'd give a lot if I could go with you!"

"I was going to let the governor ask you, Sergent, but when he told me to pick out somebody to go along with me, you were the man I asked for."

"Saints be praised! You've got yourself a man, Marshal! When do we start?"

"Early tomorrow. Before daybreak. But don't get any wrong ideas about what we'll be up against. It ain't going to be easy, and before we get back, the chances are we'll know we been in a scrape. If you want the bare bones, Higgins, there's a right good chance we might not get back at all."

Chapter 15

Since midafternoon the three men—Longarm, Higgins, and Esquivel Baca—had been following a trail that led them steadily northwest from the spot above Nambe Pueblo where the Jicarilla Apaches had captured Cristina Albee.

It was a trail that was at best faint, at worst invisible. Time after time the tracks were so clearly defined that they were able to move ahead confidently for several miles, only to have the prints of the Apaches' unshod horses vanish in a wide area of soil baked to the hardness of stone. At such times there was nothing to be done but to range in widening circles where the baked earth ended until the hoofprints appeared again in softer dirt.

One good thing—good in comparison with the alternative—that their tracking revealed: since leaving the place that Esquivel identified as the one where the Apaches had attacked, they had not found Teena's body. To Longarm and his companions that meant one thing, that she was still a prisoner of the Jicarilla band. The thought had given them a constant beacon of hope as they'd followed the Apaches' tracks.

Until an hour ago the tracks had led them upward, then they had crossed the spine of the Sangre de Cristo Mountains and started down the western slope of the range. Shortly after they began to descend they could catch an occasional glimpse of the Rio Chama flowing far below in its ragged, winding gorge.

As the three had moved west, so had the sun. At their altitude, almost nine thousand feet, it was in their faces now, appearing to be suspended in the sky squarely in front of them, and Higgins squinted anxiously into the glare, measuring its angle.

"We're going to have to make better time," he said. "It'll be too dark to track pretty soon."

"Luck's been riding with us so far," Longarm observed. He spoke with the patience of an experienced tracker. "We've been able to keep on the trail ever since we picked it up. But the Jics ain't been trying to hide their prints. Likely they figured they'd finished off Esquivel too, and didn't look for somebody to be after 'em this quick."

They moved along in silence for a while. As they descended, the pine trees gave way to low, wide-bodied cedars, and these became smaller, the growth of underbrush around their bases thinner and scantier. The soil took on the light tan hue that gave the area its name, Tierra Amarilla, and the tracks began to grow fainter. The three were still high above the lip of the river gorge when Longarm reined in and held up a hand to halt his companions. He pointed ahead and to the south, where the tiniest wisp of thin smoke rose against the sunset sky.

"That might not be the bunch we're after," he said as they studied the thread of white that wavered in the red glow of the late evening sun. "But we can't take a chance it ain't. We better go have us a look-see."

Turning their horses, they started at a long slant that would take them to the place where the smoke rose, but would place them on the slopes well above it. They did not hurry. After a long day of trailing, most of it uphill and in the oxygen-poor air of high altitude, their mounts were no longer fresh. The cavalry horses they'd gotten from the Fort Marcy remount station were baldy out of condition, requiring frequent rest stops, and even resting did not improve the performance of the packhorse that Esquivel was leading. It was showing signs of serious fatigue.

By the time they'd reached a point on the sloping mountainside where they could look down on the source of the smoke, only half of the sun's bright orange disc was visible behind the ragged crests of the ancient volcanic cones that made a jagged line along the western horizon. They pulled up and gazed into the twilight that had now engulfed the bottom of the steep gorge through which the river ran.

Below them the Rio Chama had widened, but it was in deep shadow now. The small fire that had guided them was not alone on the riverbank. Others had been kindled around it, and there were now a half-dozen tiny blazes winking up at them from a lopsided break in the gorge where the river had gouged a huge chunk of one wall to form a flat running back from the

170

riverbank to a precipitous cliff that enclosed in a rough semi-circle the level area between cliff and river.

Huddled on the flat were more than a dozen wickiups—crude, dome-shaped shelters made by thrusting pine branches into the earth in a circle and pulling their tops together. Figures moved in the area around the wickiups and the fires that glowed between them. At the far end of the flat there was still enough light to see a small herd of horses.

"Looks like we found 'em, all right," Longarm told his companions. He took a cheroot from his pocket, shielded a match with his hands, and lighted the slim cigar.

"I'd say we have," Higgins aqreed. "It's not likely there'd be two bunches of Jicarillas at the same time traveling across the country we've just covered."

"Creo lo mismo," Esquivel put in. He was lifting himself in his stirrups, peering down at the wickiups. "These are *los diablos* who kill Adelita and take *la señorita.*"

"That ain't just a camp down there, though," Longarm said after he'd studied the huddle of huts. "Apaches don't bother to make a camp like that when they're just stopping for the night. If I recall rightly, the women build their wickiups, not the fighting men. I'd say we've found 'em where they live."

"All we've got to do now is figure a way to get to them," Higgins said. "They wouldn't build a village at a place where they couldn't get their horses down to it. There's bound to be a trail of some kind."

"We better scout around and find it before it's full dark, too," Longarm said. "For all we know, we passed it on the way here, while we were watching their smoke-sign instead of paying attention to their tracks."

"It'll be in a cut, a little ravine leading down," Higgins said thoughtfully.

"Likely," Longarm agreed. "If there was a switchback trail on the face of the cliff, we'd see signs of it from here."

"I'll slip down to the edge of the cliff," Higgins volunteered. "It'll be easy enough to work along the rim on foot, and there's less chance of them seeing me that way."

"We'll both go," Longarm told him. "If we start about the middle of the cliff, you can scout toward the river going one way, while I'm looking in the other direction. Esquivel, you stay here with the horses."

Scrambling down the steep slope, Longarm and Higgins

separated a few yards before they reached the rim of the cliff that enclosed the flat. Keeping well back from the edge, Longarm walked slowly along the slope until he got to the point where the cliff angled into the wall of the river gorge. Darkness was almost full by the time he reached his objective; only a narrow rim of the sunset's dying glow remained in the sky.

He stood for a moment looking down at the Apache settlement. With the coming of darkness the fires around the wickiups seemed to give more light. He tried to count the people he saw moving around between the huts, but after losing track of some of those he'd tallied, or getting them mixed up with others, he gave it up as a bad job. There were between thirty and forty Apaches on the flat, he guessed, with not quite half of them fighting men.

That still gives 'em a pretty good edge, old son, he told himself. *And most of 'em—maybe all of 'em—have got guns. Even if some of those guns are oldtimers, they'll kill a man just as dead as a new one. Looks like you're going to have to figure a way to do some sneaking and planning to get Teena out of that place down there. And there ain't a bit of doubt, that's where she's bound to be.*

Longarm turned back and skirted the cliff's rim back to his starting point. He watched the settlement as he went, hoping to see Teena, but saw only the Apaches moving around the wickiups. Higgins had already returned when Longarm got back to the level spot on the slope where they'd left Esquivel with the horses. The sergeant could not hold back his news.

"I found the trail," he burst out as Longarm came up. "It's a ravine, just like we'd thought it'd have to be. It's nothing but a narrow slit, just about wide enough for a horse to pass through, and it's pretty steep in places, as far down as I went."

"You didn't go plumb to the bottom, then?"

"I was afraid to follow it down too far. I got to thinking they might have a sentry posted at the bottom. I just went far enough to be sure."

"And I'll bet silver cartwheels to plugged pennies that there ain't only the one way down to that flat," Longarm said reflectively. "If there is, I sure didn't find it along the part I scouted."

"I went on to the end of the cliff and back before I went down the cut," Higgins told him. "It was the only one there is." He paused and breathed deeply, almost a sigh. "I watched all the time I was working along the cliff, too, but I didn't see a sign of Miss Cristina."

"No more did I," Longarm said. Then, forcing a cheerful note into his voice, he added, "Well, you found out what we needed to know, Higgins. Which means we done about a third of the job we set out on, and still got two-thirds left."

Esquivel had been looking from Longarm to Higgins as they talked. Now he asked Longarm, "How is it you say, *señor?*"

"It's thisaway, Esquivel," Longarm replied. "We tracked the Apaches all the way and found 'em here, that's the first third of our job. Now we got to make sure Teena's down there and get her away, that's the middle third. Then we got to get away without leaving our scalps, and that's the last third."

"Ah, *sí.*" Esquivel nodded. *"Es verdad."*

"And the last two-thirds are going to be the hardest," Longarm concluded. "But I reckon we can handle it if we take it like eating an apple, one bite at a time till we hit the core."

"Our next bite's going to be to make sure she's down there, then," Higgins said.

"That's how I see it," Longarm told him. "We got to do that before we can start trying to figure out the rest of it."

"If we're going to watch, we'd better move up to the rim," Higgins suggested. "From what I saw on my way back, they were getting ready to cook their supper. I'd say that's a likely time for us to be spying. Chances are, they'll bring her out of wherever they've been keeping her, to feed her."

"Best time of all," Longarm agreed. "Let's do it."

Within moments they'd tethered the horses and were lying flat on the rim of the cliff, their eyes fixed on the Apaches that were moving around between the wickiups.

Pottery cooking pots were resting on almost all the fires by now, and women wearing long, shapeless deerskin dresses were watching them. Occasionally one of the women would stir her pot with a long stick. There were few children. Longarm saw only a handful, though from that distance and height it was impossible to distinguish between adults and almost-mature adolescents.

A discussion of some sort was going on around a large fire in the center of the village, where the men were gathered. No cooking was being done at the central fire. The men were standing three or four deep in a rough circle around the blaze, and now and then one of them raised a hand in a quick gesture to emphasize a point or to express disagreement. A few of the men wore long deerskin leggings or trousers, and none were wearing any kind of upper garment. There were no rifles visible, though two or three of them had holstered pistols dangling from their waistbands, and all of them wore sheath knives.

"What d'you suppose they're powwowing about?" Higgins asked Longarm.

"Whatever it is, they're sure taking it serious. It's easy to see they ain't got their minds on anything else."

They watched while the discussion continued. After a few moments the women began calling, their distance-attenuated calls reaching the watchers through the thin air.

"I'd give a pretty to know what they're yelling about," Longarm said.

Surprisingly, Esquivel spoke up. "They want the men to come and eat *la comida*."

Longarm looked at Baca in surprise. "You didn't tell me you savvied Apache lingo."

"*Pues,* Señor Long, you do not ask me."

"Guess I didn't, at that. Well, if you hear anything that's likely to interest us, be sure to let us know about it."

Family dining was obviously not an Apache custom. A few men left the central fire in response to the women's calls. They went to their own cooking fires and fished pieces of meat out of the utensils with their knife points. Without waiting for the strips of meat to cool, they cut off gobbets with the knives and ate while standing, or hunkered down on their heels beside the blaze. The women and the few children stood away from the fires until the men had eaten their fill. As soon as one of the men finished his meal, he returned to the discussion around the fire in the center of the wickiups, and the women and children moved up to the cooking fire to eat.

Though there was little about the scene to stimulate their appetites, the mere sight of others eating reminded the watchers that they'd had nothing since nibbling bits of cold jerky and thin slices of hard *chorizo* sausage in the saddle at noon.

"If I wasn't afraid I'd miss something, I'd go back to the horses and get a bite to eat," Higgins said, his eyes fixed on the scene below.

"I don't look for much to happen till all the men have had their grub," Longarm told him. "We can take turns going, if everybody's getting hungry."

174

"You go first, then," the sergeant replied. "Right now I'd rather watch than eat."

"Me too," Longarm said, his eyes fixed on the Apaches.

Esquivel did not express a preference. He'd edged a bit apart from Longarm and Higgins and was straining his ears trying to pick up scraps of conversation from the flat.

For the better part of an hour the discussion around the main fire continued while the men straggled to and from the cooking pots. A short while after all of them had eaten, and only women and children remained at the individual blazes, what had apparently been a preliminary talk became serious. None of the men left the group now, and occasionally a voice, raised in argument, trickled up through the thin night air to the watchers on the cliff.

"You make anything at all out of what they're saying?" Longarm asked Esquivel.

"Nada de nada, señor." Baca shrugged. "Is one word I am hear many times—'woman.' Is *la señorita* they talk of now, I am sure."

"And you can't tell what they're saying about her?"

"Not enough I hear to know this," Esquivel replied.

"Well, keep listening. Sooner or later you'll get an idea of what they're talking about."

They returned their attention to the village, where the discussion around the fire had grown even more heated. At last one of the men spread his arms and stepped out of the circle of his fellows and shouted commandingly. Slowly the individual arguments that had been raging subsided and all the Apache men gave their attention to the one who'd taken command.

He began speaking, his voice raised, and in the silence that had settled over the disputants, the clifftop watchers could hear him plainly. Esquivel began translating in a loud whisper.

"Is *la señorita* they are to argue about. This one, he is *jefe*, I think. He say not to make more *alboroto*, more fuss. Four of men say they capture *la señorita*, all of them they want her. He tell them they must make fight *mano a mano* to see who will get her."

Longarm's mind began racing even before Esquivel finished his translation. "That means she's likely all right. I'd guess they got her tied up in one of those shanties. Question is, which one is it?"

"You've got in mind trying to sneak Miss Cristina from

them while they're watching the fight?" Higgins asked.

"I can't see as we'll have a better time. They ain't got their rifles handy, and they ain't expecting anybody to move in on 'em. We sure as hell can't wait till that chief hands her over to whichever one of them wins the fight."

"You're right about that," Higgins said. "But we've got to find out which of the wickiups she's in before we can move."

Longarm looked back down at the flat. The men around the central fire were beginning to scatter, going to the different wickiups or gathering in groups of two or three—probably, he thought, to talk about the fights that were to take place. He told Higgins, "That's what I'm trying to figure a way to do right now. If you got any ideas, trot 'em out."

"I'm afraid I haven't, Marshal. Not unless we go look in each one of them, and we wouldn't last long if we tried that."

"I am think I know this thing, Señor Long," Esquivel said diffidently.

"What in hell gives you that idea?" Longarm asked brusquely.

"I am see *mujer* take pot with food into wickiup," Esquivel explained. "Only one *mujer* do this. I am think she is take to give *la señorita.*"

"And you're probably right, Esquivel!" Longarm exclaimed. "Which one is it?"

Esquivel pointed to the one cooking fire from which the clay pot had been removed. *"Esto, ahí."*

"You saw the woman who was cooking take the pot into the wickiup?" Higgins asked.

Esquivel nodded. *"Sí.* I am think why, then I am wonder if is maybe to feed *la señorita*, because we do not see her."

Longarm nodded. "That'd make sense, all right. Far as I can tell, that's the only one of the wickiups that anybody took grub into. I'll bet you're right, Esquivel."

"It's good enough for us to take a chance on, isn't it?" Higgins asked. He started to push himself back from the rim.

"Wait a minute," Longarm said, seeing what the sergeant was doing. "We better not go off half-cocked. Let's just stay right where we're at until we do some figuring."

"It doesn't look to me like there's much figuring needed, Marshal," Higgins said. "We wait until the four Apaches start their fight, then we go down and grab Miss Cristina and get the hell out of there."

Longarm nodded. "Sure. But we better know just who's going to be doing what before we start down that cut. The way I'm figuring to handle it is for you and Esquivel to stay up on the rim here and cover me while I sneak down and get hold of Teena. If I'm lucky, I can make it to the wickiup where she is while they're watching the fight, maybe even make it up before any of 'em spots us moving."

"You're taking all the risk," Higgins objected.

"One man ain't as likely to be spotted as two," Longarm said. "And if you and Baca move sideways every time you shoot, the Apaches'll think we got a lot more men up here."

"Momentito, señor," Esquivel said excitedly. *"Hay más de sobra Apaches ahí para uno hombre puede combate."* Realizing that he was speaking Spanish, he added, "Is more Apaches as you can fight alone. I am go with you, no?"

"He's right, Marshal," Higgins said. "Take him along."

"Sí!" Esquivel exclaimed.

"Considering the number of men they got down there, I guess you're right," Longarm agreed. "You stay up here and cover us, then, Higgins. It's all settled, I reckon. We might as well start."

After moving the horses and tethering them at the head of the cut that led down to the flat, they walked to the rim again to see what had happened below while they'd been unable to watch. The Apaches had been busy. The central fire had been replenished and was blazing brightly. The Apache men had formed a perimeter with twigs stuck into the ground, which enclosed a square area around the blaze. The women were slowly moving to join the men, taking their places at the back of the crude arena.

As far as Longarm could tell, none of the men around the fire carried rifles, though here and there he saw one with a pistol at his belt. He was inspecting the Apaches for arms when the first fight began. If a signal or command was given, Longarm missed it. Two of the men simply stepped out of the lines of spectators that framed the combat area. They were stripped to their breechclouts, and were armed only with sheath knives. They were about of a size, stocky and chunky, with the short, bowed legs inherited from generations of their horseman ancestors. Each man's black hair was drawn up into a figure-eight knot at the back of his neck, and both had on narrow, greasy headbands.

For a moment the two men stayed close to the spectators, then one leaped forward, the other moved to face him, and the fight was on. Both combatants drew their knives as they came together, and for a moment they faced one another warily, a yard or so apart. Each of them stood in a half-crouch, left arm brought up as a guard against a sudden slash or thrust, knife hand extended at waist level, ready to attack. They circled, sparring and feinting, not yet ready to close.

"Time we moved," Longarm said tersely. He turned to Higgins. "I figure they're bound to spot us sooner or later. Hold off shooting until they do."

"You're leaving yourself a mighty thin margin," the sergeant warned. "But I can see why. All right, Marshal. Good luck."

With Esquivel close behind him, Longarm walked back to the head of the ravine that led to the flat and started down. The cut was narrow and steep, but it had been widened at the narrowest spots, and the ground underfoot had been beaten fairly smooth by the hooves of horses passing through it. The ravine did not run straight. There were curves and bulges in its sides, and in places there was room for the two of them to go abreast for a few yards before the walls narrowed again, coming together so closely that a horse would barely be able to squeeze between them.

For the final few yards, the ravine's floor leveled out as it met the flat. Longarm stopped while they were still shielded by the walls of the cut, which now towered high above their heads. He peered from the slit in the wall, and saw no sign of anyone moving between the cliff and the wickiups.

"You stay here," he told Esquivel. "Keep a close watch, and don't start shooting till you're sure they've spotted me."

"*Entiendo, señor.*" Esquivel patted the breech of his rifle, a Spencer repeater that Higgins had given him from the small stand of firearms stored at the Palace.

During the time they'd watched the village from the rim of the cliff, Longarm had taken careful note of the wickiup in which he was sure Cristina was being held. It stood in the center of the sprawl of circular huts, and after he'd left the cover of the ravine and gone a few yards, he stopped to orient himself. When he was sure he'd located the wickiup he wanted, he started toward it.

Only small red coals remained from the cooking fires that had burned earlier beside the brush shelters. The close-packed bodies of the Apaches surrounding the big central fire shielded its glow and kept the ground between the wickiups in deep shadow. Longarm could hear the voices of those watching the fight, calling encouragement to the duelists. The voices and the clash of steel as the fighters parried covered the scraping of his boots on the hard ground as he made his way to the hut in which they'd decided Teena must be imprisoned.

He reached the hut and circled it until he found the door, a low, unshielded gap between the branches that formed the walls of the wickiup. Bending low, Longarm ducked inside. Slight as the fireglow had been on the flat, the inside of the hut was much darker. For a moment he stood motionless, straining his eyes as he tried to penetrate the murky darkness.

"Teena?" he whispered.

"Longarm?" Her voice reached him in an unbelieving whisper.

"Where are you?" he asked. "Say something, so I can find you!"

"Here. Across from the door."

Longarm groped his way around the brush wall. His hands encountered cloth, then he could trace the outlines of Teena's arms. Laying his rifle on the earthen floor, he felt until he found the leather thongs that bound her.

"I didn't look for you to—" Teena began, as she felt his hands touch her.

He was aware of a rising noise outside, a cacophony of shouts and shrieks. The thought flashed through his mind that the first fight had ended, and he realized he must move faster.

"Hush!" he commanded, taking his penknife from his pants pocket and sawing at the tough rawhide around her wrists. "Your feet. Are they tied up too?"

"Yes. Oh, Longarm, if you only knew—"

"Don't talk!" he repeated.

Teena fell quiet. Outside, the noises began to subside. Longarm felt along Teena's legs to locate the thongs that held her ankles together, and sliced at them until they parted.

"All right," he commanded. "Stand up now. We got to get away from here fast!"

"I haven't got any feeling in my feet!" she said.

Longarm grasped her arm and lifted her. Teena tried to stay on her feet, but even with his help she kept collapsing.

"It's no use!" Teena gasped. "I can't walk! My feet have

179

been tied almost all the time since they caught me."

"Never mind that. Here, get across my shoulders."

Bending forward, Longarm helped Teena to arrange herself over his broad shoulders. He picked up the rifle and turned. His eyes were dark-adjusted now, and the opening that led out of the wickiup showed as a lighter slit against its brush walls. His body bent forward, he carried Teena out of the hut.

Chapter 16

As Longarm passed through the door of the wickiup and turned toward the cliff, he realized that the friendly shadows that had shielded him before were gone. There was no longer an almost solid mass of spectators around the big central fire; evidently, when the first fight ended, the Apaches had scattered into small groups. Through the gaps between them, the light from the blaze now flooded the ground around the wickiups.

Turning toward the cliff, Longarm began running as fast as he could, burdened by Teena's limp form lying across his shoulders and the added weight of his rifle in his left hand. He was beyond the last of the huts before a harsh shout and the flat bark of a pistol shot told him he'd been spotted. Glancing ahead, he saw that there was still a distance of almost a hundred yards between him and the mouth of the cut.

More shouts were sounding behind him now. A second pistol shot split the air, then a third, but the range was long for handguns and he did not hear any lead whistling close. He saw the muzzle blast of Esquivel's rifle at the mouth of the cut, and its sharp bark overrode for a fraction of a second the duller booming of the outranged pistols that were barking behind him.

Almost before the crack of Esquivel's rifle died away, the report of an Apache rifle sounded behind Longarm. He risked slowing his pace for a moment while he turned to check on the pursuit. The Apache wickiups looked like a small stand of disturbed beehives, except that the bees were angry warriors of one of the fiercest of all Indian tribes, and their stings were the bullets that were now whizzing past Longarm. He resumed his run for the cut, and got safely inside its protecting mouth an instant before a hail of lead from the Apaches' rifles peppered the high walls of the cliff around the slit.

Letting Teena slide from his shoulders, Longarm joined Esquivel Baca at the mouth of the cut. Outlined against their own fire, the Apaches were clear targets, even in the darkness. Longarm brought down three with as many swiftly aimed shots, and Esquivel's lead accounted for another.

For the first time, Longarm could hear Higgins' shots ringing out from the top of the cliff. The Apaches reacted in a way that showed they were veterans of many fights. They did not retreat, but began dropping to the ground where they would not be outlined against the fire, and began resorting to their familiar tactic of squeezing off a shot and at once rolling a bit to one side. Most of the Indians were now within pistol range, and the thudding of bullets into the earthen sides of the ravine was constant.

"We got to get out of here fast!" Longarm called to Esquivel over the noise of the constant fusillade that was raking them from the flat. "Teena can't walk, her feet are all numbed up. You take her and start for the horses!"

"No, señor!" Esquivel called back. "You go with her!"

"I ain't leaving you," Longarm retorted. "Those Apaches'll be swarming in here like ants inside of a few minutes!"

"All the better for me to take my revenge on them!" Esquivel said quietly. "I will make the savages pay with many lives for killing *mi querida Adelita!*"

"Don't be a damn fool!" Longarm urged. "Come on!"

"No! I am stay and kill Apaches! You take *la señorita* to where she is safe! I am come *poco a poco.*"

Longarm whirled, with Teena still clinging to his shoulders. Shooting from the hip, he emptied his Winchester at the charging mob, joining his fire to Esquivel's, raking the flat with bullet after bullet until the rifle's hammer clicked on an empty chamber. The rapid fire from the two rifles brought the Appaches to a momentary halt. They scattered to each side of the slit, where the slugs from the rapid rifle fire laid down by Longarm and Esquivel could no longer reach them. From the brow of the cliff above them, Higgins' shots still sounded, spaced out now as the sergeant picked his targets.

Longarm tried once more. "Come on, Esquivel! We got time to get partway up before they rush us again!"

Esquivel's tone told Longarm that further pleading would be useless, and there was no time to waste in arguing.

"Give 'em another magazine full and come catch up with us, then," he said.

"I will follow when I am ready," Esquivel replied, busy with reloading. "It is best you go now. *Adelante!*"

Without stopping to reload his own gun, Longarm began scrabbling up the cut, carrying Teena. He'd almost reached the top when he heard the sharp barking of Esquivel's rifle resume amid the flatter reports of the Apache pistols.

There was nothing he could do to help Esquivel. He concentrated on getting to the end of the cut, and emerged from the mouth of the narrow, steep-walled gulley to find the horses waiting.

Higgins was kneeling at the edge of the cliff, firing down at the Apaches.

"Let's go!" Longarm called. "We ain't got much time!"

"What about Baca?" the sergeant asked.

"He's holding 'em off till we get away. Come on, Higgins! We got to move if we're going to make it!"

"You can't leave Esquivel to die!" Teena objected. "The least we can do is to stay here and help him!"

"He don't want any help, Teena." Longarm's voice was somber. "All he wants to do is kill as many Apaches as he can before they send him to join his wife."

"If that's the way of it—" Higgins began.

Longarm cut him short. "It is. I seen it happen before."

From the gorge behind them a few scattered shots sounded. The firing grew in intensity as Longarm and Teena reached the spot where the horses were tethered.

"We sure had better move," Higgins said. He joined them at the horses. "I don't suppose there's much reason to leave him a mount."

"No. Teena can ride his horse."

"What a terrible thing!" Teena said, her voice angry.

"Be quiet, Teena!" Longarm said sternly. "Esquivel don't want to live any longer. He meant to stay down there as soon as he figured out how this fracas might wind up. Now quit feeling bad about him and let's us get a move on!"

"Just the same, it's a brave thing for him to do," Teena said as Longarm bent to let her slide off his shoulders.

"Grant you that," Longarm replied. He stopped to listen as the firing below rose to a crescendo, then faded to a scattered

183

shot or two. Then there was silence. He went on, "Esquivel bought us some time, but it's run out now. Let's be riding!"

He lifted Teena to Baca's horse. Higgins swung into the saddle of his mount and Longarm hurried to follow suit. They rode off into the blackness, letting their horses pick their way between the trees and through the scanty underbrush.

"Do you think the Apaches will follow us?" Teena asked after they'd ridden for a while in silence.

"Not tonight," Longarm replied through the smoke of the cheroot he'd felt it was safe to light when no sounds of pursuit sounded from behind them. "Not even Apaches can read much sign on a night as dark as this one. We'll push on as fast as we can. By daybreak we ought to have enough lead on 'em so's they can't catch up with us all that easy."

They fell silent then, as they rode on through the blackness.

If the Jicarillas did indeed try to follow the trio, the Apaches did not succeed in catching up with them. The three reached Nambe Pueblo in the early morning, where they stopped only long enough to rest and feed the horses before pushing on toward Santa Fe. Darkness had fallen when their tired horses plodded up the rise where the Taos road cross the Arroyo del Rosario, and they saw the lights of the territorial capitol shining through the thin, clear air.

"I don't think I've ever been so glad to see a town before!" Teena exclaimed as they reined in before descending the slope to the arroyo. "This time yesterday evening, I didn't think I'd see anything much, ever again."

"We cut our luck pretty thin, all right," Higgins agreed.

"If it hadn't been for Esquivel—" Teena began.

"He did what he wanted to do," Longarm reminded her, his voice flat. "It wouldn't have made any difference even if he'd been there by himself."

"I suppose you're right," Teena agreed slowly. "But I never will forget him. Or you and Higgins, either."

Later, after they'd reached the Palace of the Governors to find her uncle still at work by lamplight, and had gone to supper at the sprawling, somewhat dilapidated adobe house between the Palace and Fort Marcy, which served as the official mansion, Governor Wallace had listened without comment while Teena, Longarm, and Higgins told them of her rescue and the short, fierce fight that had followed. Teena faltered while telling of the last few minutes, when Esquivel had insisted on fighting a foredoomed rearguard action against the Apaches, and the governor broke into her story to repeat almost exactly what Longarm had told her earlier, but Longarm could see that the thought of Esquivel's sacrificial action would haunt her for a long time.

After Higgins had returned to his quarters, Governor Wallace insisted that Longarm occupy one of the guest bedrooms. Teena crept quietly in to join Longarm after the house had grown quiet.

"I know you're tired," she said. "So am I, but I just couldn't stand being by myself. Especially knowing you're in here by yourself. Just hold me awhile, Longarm, if that's all you feel like doing."

Their caresses went beyond holding, of course, and Teena fell finally into a deep, restful sleep. Longarm slept too, and it was Teena who woke up first. Seeing the warning hint of dawn graying the curtains at the ceiling-high embrasured windows, she roused him with a kiss. Longarm snapped awake, fully alert the instant her lips touched his. He put his arms around her, but Teena pulled back.

"I've got to hurry back to my own room," she whispered. "Uncle Lew gets up early. But you're going to stay here in Santa Fe for a few days, aren't you?"

"Depends on how long it takes me to dig into some reports at the land office and the treasurer's office. If I'm lucky, I'll find what I need today, and take the evening train back to Albuquerque."

"If you're lucky, then I'll be unlucky." Teena's lips puckered into an impish grimace. "I suppose it'll be dinnertime before I find out what you're going to do?"

"Wait a minute, Teena. The governor ain't asked me to dinner, and I don't see why he would, anyhow."

"If he doesn't, I will," she promised.

After another quick kiss, she was gone. Longarm reached for a cheroot, missed his morning swallow of Maryland rye, and regretted that he hadn't thought to provide himself with a bottle the night before. Then he shrugged and leaned back against the pillows to think of the things he'd be looking for during the day ahead.

At breakfast, Governor Wallace asked Longarm the same

question Teena had posed to him in bed. "You're going to stay in Santa Fe a few days, aren't you, looking up the information you want from the land office and treasurer?"

Longarm glanced across the table at Teena while he chewed and swallowed the mouthful of eggs and bacon he'd just put in his mouth. She looked back guilelessly. Longarm took a sip of coffee to help the mouthful down and said, "I aim to stay until I dig up some answers, Governor. If they're there for me to dig up, that is."

Wallace frowned. "I'd offer to give you notes of introduction to Lucero at the land office and to Ramirez, the treasurer, but I'm not sure whether they'd help you get cooperation or hinder you."

"Sounds like you don't get along too good with 'em," Longarm commented.

"I try, but I can't shake off the feeling that the Hispanics in the different government offices have agreed to ignore me as much as they can." Wallace shook his head sadly. "Resentment seems to die hard here. I suppose they can't forget it was the United States Army that took over from Mexico back in '46."

"Don't feel bad about it, Governor," Longarm replied. "A lot of folks I know still act like the War Between the States didn't end about fifteen years ago."

"Yes, I've run into them," Wallace agreed. "Well, if you think it'd help, I'll give you notes to Lucero and Ramirez."

"Suppose I see how I get along on my own," Longarm suggested. "If I run into a blank wall, there'll be time enough for me to ask you for some help."

"You'll be here for dinner this evening, then?" Teena asked him, her voice carefully casual.

Longarm began, "I don't aim to impose, Teena—"

"Nonsense!" the governor said firmly. "Even if you do go back to Albuquerque tonight, the train leaves late enough for you to get the Lamy stage after we've dined. And I want to know how your investigation's going. We've had very little chance to talk about it, as yet."

"Whatever you say, Governor," Longarm agreed. "Even if I ain't got a lot to report right now, I might run into something today that'd give me an idea or two."

If Longarm ran into no actual obstruction in unearthing the material he'd come to the territorial capitol to find, he got very little help, either. He began by going through the land office registers, tracing the Zia Land Company back to its beginning days. Because real estate was involved, the massive, dusty ledgers at the land office yielded the names of all the individuals who shared in the Zia Land Comapny's ownership at present, or who had owned a part of it in the past.

He spent most of the two hours it took him to get all the names he wanted waiting for a totally uninterested clerk to bring him files from a storeroom. Then he spent another hour laboriously checking all the transfers of ownership interests in the Zia firm. He recognized a few of the names he'd copied from the files, which went back to the firm's original formation. Most of the names he'd recognized from his old battle with the Santa Fe Ring were those of men long dead.

"I got another bunch of files I want to look at now," he told the land office clerk who'd spent so much time bringing him the files from the storeroom. "I hear you got cross-files on all the people that've ever owned part of any company dealing in land, like this Zia outfit does. From what I heard, those cross-files show what other land they hold here in the territory."

"You have heard correctly, *señor*."

"Good. Those are the files I want next."

"Very well, *señor*. If you will give me the list, I will find them for you."

"Why can't I just go in that storeroom and find the files myself?" he asked the man.

"It is not allowed for anyone but land office workers to go into the file rooms, *señor*."

"Now look here," Longarm suggested. "There ain't any use in both of us wasting time. I know the way the letters of the alphabet go, and I got enough sense not to mess with anything that ain't what I'm looking for."

With a shrug, the clerk shook his head. "I do not make the rules, *señor*, I only obey them. Now, if there is something more you wish for me to do . . ."

Longarm didn't follow his first impulse, which was to tell the man what he'd really like for him to do. He'd learned from experience in his own bureaucracy the difficulty of breaking rules that were primarily designed to protect the jobs and powers of the head bureaucrats. He handed the clerk the sheet of paper on which he'd written the names of the men whose cross-files he wanted.

"I'd appreciate it if you'll find those files for me sort of quick-like," he said. "I got a lot of other things to do today."

"Alas, *señor*," the clerk sighed as he saw the number of names on the list, "there are many names here, and I am only one person. But I will do the best I can. And if you do not finish all your tasks today, there is always tomorrow."

Within another two hours, Longarm got the stack of tape-tied files, thick with the dust of the storage room. He spent another hour going through them, copying dates of land purchases and land transfers, and by late afternoon he had compiled most of the information he was seeking.

Late as the hour was, he went into the office of the territorial treasurer, where he encountered a roadblock that he hadn't anticipated. The clerk in the treasurer's office, who could have passed as a twin to the one in the land office, took the list Longarm handed him, glanced at its length, and shook his head.

"What you ask me to do is impossible, *señor*."

"I don't see why," Longarm said, holding his impatience in check. "You got all the files in here, ain't you?"

"*De seguro, señor*. But the hour is growing late, and I cannot provide you with all these files in the time left before the office closes. By the time I have found the folders, it will be time to leave for the day. You would not be able to read all the files before I would have to return them to the storeroom."

"Then bring me out as many as you can find real easy. I'll do what work there's time for, and whichever of the files I don't get around to, you can just leave out on the table here, then you won't have to look for 'em in the storeroom tomorrow."

"You do not understand. I must return each file to the storeroom before the office closes. It is against rules to leave them here in the office when we are closed."

"I don't reckon you can overlook those rules of yours just this one time?" Longarm asked, knowing as he did so what the answer was going to be.

"I am indeed sorry, *señor*, but rules cannot be broken. And even to find two or three of these would require more time than is left in the day. You must come back tomorrow, early, and I will get them for you then."

Tucking his lists into the inside breast pocket of his coat, and stifling his frustration, Longarm left the treasurer's office and walked thorough the cooling air of the late afternoon, along the Alameda to Galisteo Street and the Plaza. Higgins was sitting at his accustomed station outside the door of Governor Wallace's office.

"From the way you look, you've had some trouble today," the sergeant greeted Longarm. "Anything I can help out with?"

"I don't know that anybody can help me with what I'm trying to do right now," Longarm admitted. "Not even the governor. But I'll go in and talk to him, if he ain't too busy."

"He's just winding up the day's business," Higgins replied. "He told me you were supposed to stop by and catch him up on whatever it is you're trying to find out for him, so go on in. Oh yes. He's got a telegram for you from Albuquerque. It was sent in care of the office here, just delivered a while ago."

Governor Wallace looked up from his document-strewn desk when Longarm opened the office door and stuck his head in. "Come in," he invited. "I thought you'd be showing up as soon as the land office or the treasurer's office started closing. As nearly as I can tell, they begin to close an hour or so before their regular business hours end."

"They sure do. And nobody in 'em is about to stay two minutes after business hours, either. Not even to oblige a federal marshal."

"You did find at least part of what you're looking for, though?" the governor asked, indicating a chair at the corner of his desk, the only chair not piled high with books.

"Part of it. Enough to get me started. But I've still got a long ways to go, and a right big puzzle to work out." Longarm settled into the chair and lighted a cheroot. "I run across a lot of names in those files I was going through, but most of 'em belong to men that are dead. Thing is, I got enough to connect some of those dead men with a bunch that's still alive, and if my suspicion is right, they're the ones that are trying to bring the old Ring back to life."

"I haven't just been whistling up ghosts, then," Wallace said with a satisfied nod. "Well, maybe I can help you make the connections you're looking for. But before we get started on that, here's a telegram that was sent you in care of my office. It was delivered less than an hour ago."

Longarm took the folded sheet of yellow paper and unfolded it. "BIG RUCKUS ABOUT TO BLOW UP STOP NEED YOU HERE IN TIME TO STOP IT STOP ACCOMMODATION

WAITING ALBUQUERQUE ROUNDHOUSE FOR YOU TO GET TO RAILHEAD FAST AS POSSIBLE STOP FERRELL"

"Bad news?" the governor asked as Longarm refolded the wire and tucked it away in his pocket.

"I can't say yet, Governor. But I'm going to have to catch the evening train to Albuquerque. There's some kind of fracas brewing up at the Santa Fe's railhead, and the construction boss wants me to try to stop it."

Wallace glanced at the tall mahogany-cased grandfather's clock that occupied a corner of his crowded office. "Well, you have plenty of time before the stage leaves for Lamy. Time enough to bring me up to date on what you've discovered. There might be something I can do to help you here in Santa Fe while you're attending to the business that's taking you south."

"Maybe there is. Like I said a minute ago, I didn't get as much digging done today as I'd figured to. By the time I was finished at the land office, the treasurer's office was getting ready to close up."

"Just exactly what are you trying to establish, Longarm?" Wallace asked with a thoughtful frown.

"Well, when I come close to busting up the old Ring a few years ago, I didn't corral all them that was part of it. Now, I figure there was enough left to start the Ring up again, and what I got to dig out is evidence that'll stand up in court."

"What kind of evidence?"

"That the ones left from the old Ring took over land and jobs and tucked-away cash that the dead ones couldn't take with 'em. And I figured some of what was left had to be shifted to men that the old Ring members enlisted when they started up again."

"Yes. I'd say that's a sound deduction," Wallace agreed. "The new Ring would need cash for bribes, and they certainly wouldn't let go of anything the dead members left."

"I've found out that crooks are pretty quick to use the law to protect what they steal," Longarm went on. "Hard cash, now that don't leave no tracks. But when you come to land and shares of stock in a business that's built on political graft, that's a horse of a different color. That kind of critter leaves tracks a man can pick up from records like the ones in the land office and the treasurer's office. So what I been doing is looking for names in the old records, names that'll show where the surviving members of the old Ring shifted land titles and stock shares to new members they brought in."

Wallace nodded. "I can see that as a chain of legal evidence, but how do you plan to tie the old and the new Rings together?"

"Except for one thing, it ought not be too hard to do," Longarm replied, pulling out the sheaf of coded telegrams that had been exchanged between the office of the San Ysidro Cattle Company, the Zia Land Company, and the other firms he suspected of being fronts for the operations of the re-forming Ring. "I got all these telegrams, but they're in code, so nobody can read 'em. If what I suspect is right, they'll give me a key to where I can dig out real evidence tying everything together."

"Codes aren't too difficult to break," the governor said thoughtfully. "You know, the conspirators in the plot against President Lincoln used codes a great deal. I happened to be one of the panel of judges that sat at their trial, so I learned a bit about codes and how they can be broken from the evidence that was brought out then."

"Now that's something I didn't know," Longarm said, sitting up straighter in his chair.

"Most people have forgotten. But my interest in codes and ciphers didn't stop there. I think I mentioned the book I'm now writing, about the young Roman charioteer named Ben Hur, who was converted to become a follower of Christ?"

"You said something about your book the day I got here," Longarm nodded. "But if you'll excuse me saying so, Governor, I don't see how it applies."

"Why, the early Christians used codes and ciphers a great deal, to hide their activities from the Roman officials," the governor explained. "They had symbols—a fish, for instance, to identify their meeting places—and there were other messages that were coded before being passed among the converts. So I've had to brush up on coded messages. I'm not yet sure how I'll need to use them in my book, but I want to be prepared if I do."

Keeping his voice level to avoid betraying his interest, Longarm asked, "You mean you might be able to read these telegrams I got?"

"I don't see why not, if they're the kind of simple letter-substitution codes that are the most common. I'll certainly be glad to try to decipher them for you, if you want to leave them with me."

191

Longarm shook his head. "You lost me there, Governor."

"A letter-substitution code just replaces one letter of the alphabet with another. And there are key words to look for that make them fairly easy to break. 'There' and 'where' and 'that' and 'what,' for instance. Words such as those form patterns that will eventually help in identifying other words."

"I guess I see what you mean," Longarm said. "It's about like recognizing a track made by a boot or a horseshoe. Once you see it, you don't forget it."

"Something like that," Wallace agreed. "If you want me to look at those telegrams and try—"

"I sure do, Governor!" Longarm exclaimed. He handed Wallace the sheaf of messages. "Now, there's a thing or two you ought to know that might make it easier for you to unravel these. They're all signed with letters that have got to stand for names of people in the businesses that sent 'em."

"Of course it'll help, if I have a starting point."

"I got a hunch that the San Ysidro Cattle Company telegrams from Albuquerque are mostly signed by a lady named Cynthia Evans, and the ones from Santa Fe are signed by Rudolpho Fernandez."

Wallace nodded. "Yes, that should help." Then he frowned and said, "If I do break the codes, I imagine you'll want the messages back as soon as I can get them to you. Suppose I send Higgins down to Albuquerque with them, if I do make any progress with them?"

"That'd be first-rate. I'll be at the Grand Hotel if I'm in Albuquerque, or at the Santa Fe railhead camp if I'm not." Longarm glanced at the clock and stood up. "Now, I better be getting on, if I'm going to catch the Lamy stage. I still got to gather up my gear and tell Teena not to look for me at supper. But I'll tell you one thing right now, Governor. If you can give me what those telegrams say in plain English, I might just be able to crack this new Ring wide open before it gets any bigger!"

Chapter 17

After making sure that the accommodation train that Ferrell's wire had promised was waiting for him at the roundhouse in Albuquerque, Longarm delayed his departure only long enough to take care of a few necessary details.

Taking a hack to the hotel, he got his horse from the stable and a bottle of Maryland rye to put in his saddlebag. He rode the horse back to the roundhouse and loaded it in the cattle car, which, with the caboose, engine, and tender, made up the short train called a bobtail. Then he tossed his gear into the caboose and caught a few winks of sleep in one of the bunks while the special train rattled and screeched over the newly laid roadbed. He stepped off the accommodation at the construction camp a little before midnight and, while waiting for his horse to be unloaded, looked out over his surroundings.

In spite of the late hour, Hell on Wheels was booming. The wide stretch of rutted ground between the rails and the jerry-built buildings and tents of the camp followers was crowded with gandy dancers, teamsters, roustabouts, and other railhead workers. The red lights over the whorehouse doors glowed their invitations. The batwings of the saloons flip-flopped constantly, the acetylene lights inside shuttering across the area between tracks and buildings, alternately revealing and hiding the roiling mass of men that roamed the road in front of the joints.

On the other side of the tracks, the construction camp was dark and relatively quiet. Near the big shanty that served as a temporary roundhouse, the locomotives stood silent, their headlights dark, looking strangely short now that their tenders were uncoupled to be left standing on another siding, beside the coalstacks. A few squares of light showed in the board-inghouse cars on the farthest sidings, and a sound of hammers hitting hot metal on an anvil rang out from the shed that sheltered the forge, indicating that some of the foundrymen were working late on an emergency repair job to a piece or two of the camp's rolling stock.

Here and there along the sidings, lanterns bobbed where grease monkeys were still busy repacking the wheel bearings of the flatcars and boxcars and gondola cars that hauled the ties, rail, fishplates, spikes, tools, and roadbed gravel to the end of the track.

When he'd seen his horse safely in the corral, Longarm tossed his saddlebags over his shoulder, picked up his saddle in one hand and his Winchester in the other, and started for Ferrell's caboose-office. As he drew close to it he saw lamplight shining between the cracks of the boards that had been nailed over the windows broken when the first bushwhacker had tried to kill him and the construction boss. After a perfunctory rap on the door, Longarm pushed it open and stuck his head into the car.

"You made quick time getting here, I'll give you that," Ferrell said, looking up from the maps and drawings that were spread over his table. His voice was casual; he might have been greeting Longarm on his return from an absence of only a few minutes.

Longarm stepped up into the car and dropped his gear on the floor beside the door. "From what you said in that wire you sent me in Santa Fe, I got the idea you were in a hurry for me to get back."

"I was hoping you wouldn't waste any time," Ferrell admitted.

Longarm bent over his saddlebags and pulled out the bottle of Tom Moore. "If you're going to bend my ear with a long, sad story, we might as well enjoy ourselves as much as we can while you're unraveling it."

"I don't know how sad the story is, but unless you can figure out a way to stop it, we're going to have a little war on our hands starting late tomorrow," the construction superintendent said, watching Longarm's fingers working the cork out of the bottle of whiskey.

"That so?" Longarm passed the bottle across the desk. "Who's going to be doing all the fighting?"

Ferrell produced glasses from the drawer and shoved one to Longarm while he poured for himself into the other. He said,

"The teamsters and a bunch of gunslingers the company's sending here on a special train."

"Hold on, Jim. I figured I straightened out those teamsters when I took Paddy O'Reilley's measure and hauled him in to Albuquerque to talk to his new boss."

"You can't blame Paddy this time, Longarm. I don't know all the ins and outs of what happened, but the wagoneers got wind of that rate increase the Hutchins brothers were trying to get."

"Seems to me they'd have liked that, Jim."

"Oh, they would have, except for one thing. They found out at the same time that the Hutchins boys weren't going to give them any of that extra money."

"I can see where that'd really put the fat in the fire," Longarm said, lighting a cheroot to follow the smooth bite of his first sip of rye. "Wonder who spilled the beans to 'em?"

"I never did find out, but it sure set off the wagoneers. They got their heads together and quit. It didn't take the smarter ones very long to figure out that if they could make their own deal with the railroad, they'd get the cut the Hutchins brothers have been keeping."

"It wouldn't surprise me a bit if it was Paddy himself who let the word leak out. Clem Hutchins has gone back East, and there's a new boss at the Hutchins office in Albuquerque, man named Tafolla. He gave Paddy the rough edge of things when we stopped in there for a few minutes."

"I'd thought about it being Paddy, but I couldn't understand why he'd turn on the Hutchins brothers. If he found a new boss in Albuquerque that he didn't think he could get along with, that'd sure explain it," Ferrell said.

"Go ahead and tell me the rest," Longarm suggested, pouring himself another drink.

"I don't know whether you realize it or not, but most of the teamsters working this job own their own teams and wagons. The Hutchins outfit's been hiring men and their wagons along with them. Hutchins only has a few pieces of rolling stock of their own. So the upshot is that it's every man for himself now, and Paddy O'Reilley's out in the cold along with his boss."

"That still don't explain what the war you mentioned is all about."

"I'm getting to that part of it. What the teamsters didn't stop to think about is that the Hutchins brothers have a contract with the railroad, and they haven't. Hell, Longarm, I'd like nothing more than to be rid of the Hutchins outfit for the rest of this job. I've got a lot more miles of rail to put down, and if I could hire independent teamsters all the way from here to California, I could cut a big chunk of money off the cost."

"Seems to me that'd make your bosses happy."

"It doesn't, though. The Hutchins brothers say they'll have all the teams we need rolling in a few days, and that they'll pay whatever the railroad's lost because of this teamster ruckus. But they also say they'll sue if the Santa Fe doesn't honor the contract."

"I never did figure a railroad would back off from going to court. Seems to me that railroads like lawsuits."

"That's what most people think, but it's not true. Court cases cost money and slow down construction. I think that's why the brass in the head office decided to fight this time."

"Which leaves you caught between a rock and a hard place. But you still ain't explained what the ruckus you're expecting is all about."

"It's taken me this long to get to it. Right now, the teamsters who've quit have got the right-of-way barricaded at that water hole where we had trouble the other day. They say we'll have to fight 'em to build on past the roadblock they've put up."

Longarm nodded. "So your bosses back East have told you to fight."

"Told me, hell!" Ferrell exploded. "They've taken that decision right out of my hands. They've already got that bunch of gunslicks I mentioned on the way here. Their special's running on a red-flag highball. It'll get here sometime tomorrow."

"What'd you have in mind for me to do?" Longarm asked, his voice casually innocent, knowing pretty well what Ferrell's reply was going to be.

"Dammit, I want you to keep the gunslingers and teamsters from starting to fight! Look here, Longarm. I'm the superintendent of a construction job, not a general commanding an army. All I want to do is lay rail. I don't want to be responsible for men getting killed."

"I don't reckon anybody does, Jim. But when the chips are on the table and the cards are turning up, somebody's got to hold high hand."

"That's fine. As long as it's not me."

"So you're passing the buck to me, is that the way of it?'

"You know damned well it's more in your line than mine."

"Oh, I ain't arguing that. And I sure don't figure on turning my back on it." Longarm fell silent while he refilled his glass. Finally he asked, "How many gunslingers are you expecting to show up, Jim?"

"Ten or a dozen, I'd imagine. The only other time I know of when the Santa Fe got into a shooting fight was when they were facing down the Rio Grande Northern at Raton Pass, and I think they sent about twenty men there."

"They didn't put up such a much of a fight, either. As I recall, there wasn't any shooting to speak of at that Raton Pass dustup, and nobody got hurt or killed."

"You can't go by what happened there, Longarm. Things here might be completely different."

"I know that, Jim. There never was two fights just alike. I'm just trying to fit this blowup into the case I'm working on."

"You told me your case was mainly to help the railroad keep on our construction schedule. Stopping what might turn into a nasty gunfight seems to me to be right in line with what you were sent here to do."

"I never said it wasn't." Longarm looked at his empty glass and shook his head. He put the glass back on the desk, stood up, and stretched. "Well, I'll see what I can do with the teamsters tomorrow morning. There sure ain't a lot I can do tonight, and I been chasing around New Mexico Territory so fast the past few days, I'm running a little bit behind on shut-eye."

"You look like you could use some sleep, all right. Why don't you just crawl into the spare bunk I've got here in the office? It won't have any bedbugs in it, which is more than you can say for the boardinghouse cars. And we can talk some more while we have breakfast, maybe come up with an idea or two. There might be some wires come in from the head office overnight that'd help us plan what to do."

"That makes more sense than anything you've said so far. Just show me the bunk. I'm more'n ready to turn in."

While Longarm and Ferrell ate an early breakfast the next morning, the construction superintendent quickly scanned the sheaf of flimsies that had been received at the railhead's telegraph office during the night.

"Looks like our gunfighters' special will get here about six this evening," Ferrell said, flicking his thumb at a flimsy near the bottom of the stack of messages. "That means we're going to have to do what we can to get the teamsters in a peaceful frame of mine before the day's out."

"I guess I better get on out to where they're forted up, then," Longarm replied. "I'll get saddled up and start as soon as I finish eating."

"You want me to go with you?" Ferrell asked. Then, before Longarm could answer, he added, "I don't know that I could help you much. The teamsters sure haven't been inclined to pay any attention to what I've said before."

Longarm frowned thoughtfully. "It might be better if you don't go along, you being their boss, so to speak. As long as you'll back me up if I got to make some promises that they'll get what they want out of the railroad."

"You know how I feel about that. I told you last night."

"Then you're ready to go against your bosses back East?"

"If I have to. It wouldn't be the first time. They're not all that unreasonable, and they know a shooting fight won't do the Santa Fe's reputation any good. Yes, I think I can talk the brass into calling the Hutchins brothers' bluff after I tell them how much money we'll save on the rest of this job if we hire the teamsters as independents."

"I'll do my best, then, Jim. Only don't expect any miracles, then you won't be too disappointed if things don't work out the way you want them to."

With the morning sun warm on his back, Longarm rode along the rutted road beside the newly laid tracks; the terrain was familiar to him from his earlier visit. He reached the upslope leading to the rim of the little saucer containing the water hole that had been the scene of his earlier confrontation with the vaqueros from the Rancho Montemayor.

Rails had been laid up the slope now, through a narrow cut that began just below the rim of the saucer, and as he came to the cut he saw just beyond it a chest-high barricade that had been erected across the tracks. The barrier was made from crisscrossed ties buttressed by a dirt embankment. He rode on up the slope and saw the pugnacious teamsters—thirty or more of them, he judged at a glance—scattered in small groups behind the roadblock they'd erected.

A few small cooking fires behind the barricade sent threads of smoke into the clear morning sky. Close to the water hole, wagons had been formed into a rough square to make a temporary corral for the teams. It looked to him as though the teamsters were not only ready to fight, but had prepared for a long siege. Longarm's experienced eyes flicked across the position they had prepared and saw that the Santa Fe's gunfighters were going to have a rough fight if they tried to storm the barricade.

When the men saw him approaching, they dropped whatever they had been doing and clustered behind their improvised breastworks. Longarm reined in fifty yards from the barricade and spread his arms out as a sign that his intentions were peaceful.

"I guess most of you know who I am," he called. "Name's Long, deputy U.S. marshal out of Denver, in case some of you don't recognize me."

"We know who you are, Marshal," one of the teamsters said. "What we don't know is why you're butting into something that's between us and the Santa Fe. You sure as hell can't arrest us just because we decided we didn't want to work for the railroad no longer."

"I didn't come out here to arrest anybody. All I got in mind is doing a little talking," Longarm answered. "You can see I'm by myself, and I sure ain't fool enough to try to take you men on singlehanded."

For a few moments there was silence as the teamsters drew into a close group and discussed the situation. Longarm fished a cheroot out of his pocket, flicked his thumbnail over the head of a match, and lighted the long, slim cigar. He watched the men impassively while they carried on their conference.

At last one of them came up to the blockade and called, "All right, Marshal. You can ride on up. We'll talk to you, if that's what you've come for."

Longarm toed his horse up to the barricade and swung out of the saddle. "Mind if I come over to your side?" he asked. "It's sort of hard to talk friendly if we got to yell back and forth."

"Come ahead," the man who seemed to be the leader replied. "Like I said, we got nothing against you, Marshal."

"I guess that makes us even," Longarm answered, scrambling over the embankment and dropping to his feet behind the barricade. "I got nothing against you men, either."

"You didn't ride all the way out here just to tell us that," one of the teamsters said as the others clustered around to hear what was being discussed.

"No I didn't. What I did come to tell you is that there's a bunch of hired gunmen on the way here in a special train to get you men rooted out of this roadblock you built here so the Santa Fe can get back to laying track."

"Let 'em come, by God!" one of the men at the rear of the group said angrily. "We'll be ready to give 'em a lesson when they get here!"

"Damn right!" another agreed. "We got guns, and we can shoot just as good as any hired shootist, too!"

Raising his voice to override the men around him, Longarm said, "Now hold on! There ain't no use in you fellows fighting the Santa Fe! Jim Ferrell wants to hire you back, without any kind of deal with the Hutchins brothers, if you're ready to go back to work."

A babble of excited voices broke out following Longarm's words. The men were quieted by a shout from their leader.

"All right! Let's talk about this without getting all hottened up!" he shouted, overriding the others. He waited until the men were quiet, then turned to face Longarm again. "You're talking for Ferrell, I guess?"

"I ain't talking for him. I'm just telling you how he'd like to handle things."

"Ferrell's all right, as construction bosses go," the teamster leader said, frowning. "But he's still got to do what the big bosses back East tell him to. That's why we been working through the Hutchins outfit. They do our talking for us to the railroad."

"Or did, till they got the idea they could cheat us and get away with it," one of the men called.

"As far as Jim Ferrell's concerned, you're rid of the Hutchins brothers," Longarm assured them. "But you're going to have to—"

He broke off as a thudding of hooves sounded at the bottom of the slope that led up to the teamsters' barricade. The teamsters gave their attention to the hoofbeats too, turning to watch as a half-dozen vaqueros swept through the cut at the top of the slope and down toward the barrier. Longarm recognized the lead rider at once; it was Feliciano Ramos, the *mayordomo* of the Rancho Montemayor. At the edge of the dirt embankment, Ramos raised his arm, and the riders behind him reined in. The *mayordomo* recognized Longarm, and his eyes widened.

"Señor Long!" Ramos exclaimed. "I did not expect to see you here today."

"Why not, Ramos? My business takes me to a lot of places. Looks like yours does too. I didn't look to see you here."

Ramos shrugged. "What I am doing here is easily explained. Don Pascual has heard rumors of trouble between the railroad and its workers. He sent me to make sure that his lands do not suffer by becoming the scene of a disturbance these troubles might cause."

"Sort of hoping there might be enough trouble for him to use it as an excuse to go back on his deal with the Santa Fe for this water hole, I'd guess?"

A flush of anger swept over Ramos's thin face, but he ignored Longarm's question. He asked, "It is true that there is trouble, then?"

"You don't see none, do you?" Longarm countered.

"Not at the moment. But I see that preparations have been made for a fight here."

"Well, even if there was to be a fight, it wouldn't be any of Mr. Montemayor's business. As far as he's concerned, this land belongs to the Santa Fe railroad now."

"But not the land around the tracks. That is still part of the Rancho Montemayor."

"Sure." Longarm nodded. "You don't need to worry, though. There ain't going to be no fighting, not if I got anything to say about it. You can ride on back home and tell your boss not to lose any sleep over what he's heard."

"Are you ordering us to leave as an official of the federal government, Marshal?" Ramos asked.

"I ain't *ordering* you to do anything. You can set there all day, as long as you don't get in nobody's way. Including mine."

"I did not come here to interfere in any lawful activity, Marshal Long," Ramos said stiffly. "I will make my report to Don Pascual and tell him you have guaranteed that the property of the Rancho Montemayor will not be harmed."

"You do that, Ramos. Tell him I'll let him know if anything happens along the tracks that's some concern of his."

"Now, what in hell did all that have to do with anything?" the teamsters' spokesman asked Longarm as the vaqueros followed Ramos down the slope and out of sight.

"You got me," Longarm replied. He kept his voice casual and unconcerned, but wondered how word of the railhead troubles had reached the Rancho Montemayor, and searched his mind for a reason why Don Pascual would be interested in the Santa Fe's problems. Turning back to the teamsters, he went on, "Well, I've said what I come here to say. You men want to talk about Jim Ferrell's proposition, or you want to make up your minds now?"

"How do we know Ferrell can get his bosses back East to go along with what he's saying he'll do?" the spokesman demanded.

"You men know Jim," Longarm answered quickly. "You know he ain't going to promise you anything he ain't sure he can deliver."

"How about that extra money the Hutchins brothers was going to get?" one of the teamsters at the back of the group called. "If we take up Ferrell's proposition, do we get it?"

"If there's any extra money going, it'll be yours," Longarm said, hoping he wasnt sticking Ferrell's neck too far out.

"What about them gunfighters the railroad's got coming?" a man in the rear asked. "Can you call them off, Marshal?"

"I sure as hell can," Longarm promised. "And will, the first thing, as soon as I get back and talk to Ferrell."

"Let's don't jump at anything too fast," another of the men suggested. "We better be thinking about what's going to happen to us after this damn tracklaying's finished. Once the railroad starts hauling to California, we're out of business!"

"Yes," another chimed in. "What's left for us?"

"It'll be a long time before the Santa Fe can push spurs out from this mainline," Longarm said. "You men stand to make more on short hauls from the tracks to the towns and ranches that ain't on the right-of-way, and with a lot less trouble than you have on long hauls, like to California."

"How do we know we'll get that short-haul business?" the first objector asked. "What if the railroad blacklists us?"

"You'll only get the short-haul business if you go out after it," Longarm shot back. "But I'll make sure that there won't be any blacklist put up."

For a moment there was silence, then the leader asked, "Well, what're we going to tell Ferrell? We got to make up our minds sooner or later."

"Hell, if the marshal says he'll speak up for us, I'd say we

202

go along," a teamster close to Longarm said. "If he set his mind to it, he could talk the balls off of a stud horse."

"But we don't move from where we're at until we get Ferrell to put what he says he'll do in writing," another said. "If we give up too easy, all we're likely to get outa this is what the little boy shot at."

"That's for sure!" the leader agreed. He looked at the men, and one by one they nodded or spoke their agreement. "All right, Marshal," he told Longarm. "You go back and tell Ferrell what you said and what we said. And when he comes out here and gives it to us all wrote down nice and neat, we'll go back to work."

"That's good enough for me," Longarm told them, trying to hide his relief that he'd been able to settle at least one side of the dispute without having to draw a weapon. "I'll get on back, and you can look for Ferrell to come out tomorrow and make the deal official."

Riding back to the construction camp, Longarm began once more to wonder how news of the trouble between the teamsters and the railroad had gotten to the Rancho Montemayor so swiftly, and why Don Pascual had been interested enough to send his second-in-command to the teamsters' barricade to look into the matter.

It just don't signify, old son, he told himself as the livery horse picked its way over the rutted ground beside the railroad tracks. *That Don Pascual, he's a big man in this part of the territory. He's got more land than a lot of them little squinched-up states back East, I bet. The little bit of land he's signed over to the Santa Fe for right-of-way don't mean diddledy-squat to him. So why'd he send that Ramos fellow out to nosey around? Or was it Ramos's idea to come take a look? It just don't make sense for him to be so concerned. Unless there's more to it than I can see right now, something about those men riding all the way to that teamster camp just don't smell right. And when things begin to stink, old son, it's time you got busy and found out why.*

Longarm mulled over the question, but he was still searching his mind for a reason when he pulled up in front of Jim Ferrell's caboose-office.

"Well, how'd you do?" Ferrell asked.

"Middling good, I'd say." Using as few words as possible, Longarm sketched the agreement he'd made with the teamsters.

He concluded, "It's up to you to say whether I done the right thing, Jim. But I'll guarantee that if you go along with the deal those fellows want, and get your bosses to say it's all right, you won't have any more trouble with 'em on this job."

Ferrell nodded. "I'm inclined to agree with you. I think I can get the Santa Fe brass to agree on the deal you worked out, because it not only makes sense, it saves money. A lot more money than the Hutchins brothers could win in a court settlement, I'd guess, especially since it was them who broke the contract. So I'd say you've solved the problem pretty well."

"Maybe. Except for one thing."

"Oh? What'd I overlook?"

"That bunch of gunslicks that's on the way."

"Surely they won't object to not having a fight on their hands when they get here," Ferrell frowned. "They'll get paid for their time just the same."

"I ain't so sure they'll like it, Jim." Longarm lighted a cheroot while he tried to find the words to explain so that Ferrell would understand. "Hired gunmen's crazy to start out with, Jim. It ain't the money they fight for. It's what it does to 'em inside. I know, I run up against too many of that breed."

"You think we'll have trouble with them, then?"

"I'm hoping we don't, but I ain't really sure. And I won't be until I see 'em and talk to 'em."

"Well, we won't have long to wait to find out," Ferrell said a bit grimly. "I got a wire from the Albuquerque station just a few minutes ago. The red-flag special just passed through there. In about an hour or so, it looks like your question's going to be answered."

Chapter 18

In spite of the especially good steaks that he and Ferrell ate for supper while waiting for the red-flag special, Longarm counted the hour or more that passed as one of the slowest he could remember. The train finally rolled in, and was switched off the mainline to a siding where Ferrell had instructed the yardmaster to spot it.

There were only three cars to the special: a baggage car, a passenger coach, and a parlor car. Darkness had fallen by the time the short string pulled off the mainline and was braked to a stop by the engineer. The baggage car was dark, but lights glowed from the passenger coach and the parlor car. The passenger coach halted at the point where Longarm and Ferrell were standing, waiting. They looked into the windows of the coach and exchanged questioning glances when they saw that none of the seats were occupied.

"All of them must be in the parlor car," Ferrell muttered.

He led the way to the open vestibule between the two coaches, and he and Longarm swung aboard. When they pushed open the vestibule door, they discovered why the passenger coach was empty.

At the rear corner of the parlor car, the compact bar was piled high. The scrag-end of a carelessly carved ham stood beside what remained of a wheel of cheese, an opened jar of mustard crowded between them. Bags of soda crackers spilled their contents across a corner of the bar and onto the floor. Opened cans of peaches and tomatoes shared the bar top with liquor bottles, empty or almost empty. An assortment of rifles and shotguns leaned haphazardly together in the corner where the bar met the side of the parlor coach.

Cigar smoke hung thickly in the air, layered in the bright glare of the twin acetylene lamps that hung from the center of the ceiling, and the sweet, flat aroma of chewing tobacco rose from the spittoons that dotted the carpeted floor. Deep indentations in the spattered carpet marked the spots where two half-round tables usually stood, on opposite sides of the coach between its wide windows. The tables had been pulled into the center of the car and pushed together to form a single table big enough to accommodate the eleven men who sat around it.

Though they were sitting in the wicker lounge chairs that normally were scattered along the sides of the coach, the men were not lounging. They were leaning intently over the table, their eyes fixed on the cards fanned out in their hands. In the center of the joined tables a scattering of gold and silver coins surrounded a single card that lay facedown.

None of them looked up when Ferrell and Longarm entered; they were too engrossed in studying the cards they held or trying to read the faces of the other players.

Once he'd taken a quick look at the layout and counted the number of players and the number of cards each one held, Longarm readily identified the game as whiskey poker. It was a common enough variation of poker, one played when there were too many players to allow each man to be dealt a full five-card hand.

In whiskey poker, each gambler was dealt four cards. One of the remaining cards was then placed facedown in the center of the table. When the betting was over and the time came for the showdown, this single card was turned up, and became a common fifth card for each player. The hand that the single card made the highest took the entire pot.

"I hate to break up your game," Ferrell began, "but I have to talk to whoever's in charge here."

Without taking his eyes off his fellow players, a man sitting with his back toward Longarm and Ferrell said, "I guess you'd be Ferrell. That's who they said would meet us and show us the ropes when we got here. Just hold your horses a minute, till we get this hand played out. I grant you, whiskey poker's a half-assed game, but it's the only one this many of us can play, and we're going to finish this hand before we quit."

Across the table from the man who'd spoken, another one said, "All right, if everybody's in the pot, let's lay 'em down and see who got lucky this time."

One by one, the players laid face up the four cards each of them had been holding. Moving his hand slowly, almost delicately, the one who'd called for the cards to be shown reached to the center of the table and turned up the single card.

For a moment there was silence as the players studied the hands that had been exposed. Then the man who'd greeted Ferrell and Longarm said angrily, "Ain't that my goddamn luck! Another fucking busted flush!"

"Looks like it's my pot," chuckled the player sitting next to him. "That hole card fills out my aces and four to an ace-high full house, and I don't see anything that'll top it."

"Take the money and stop crowing," snorted the man who'd spoken first. As the man sitting beside him began raking the coins across the table, he kicked his chair back and stood up.

"Name's Nobs Pelter," he said as he turned to face Longarm and Ferrell. "My friends here tagged me to talk for the bunch of us. Now which one of you two is the boss, and when do we start to work?"

"I'm Jim Ferrell," the construction superintendent replied. He extended a hand, but Pelter ignored it, nor did he show any inclination to introduce his companions. Slowly lowering his outstretched hand, Ferrell went on, "This is Deputy U.S. Marshal Long."

"Long?" Pelter repeated. Under the brim of the dark brown fedora he wore pushed far back on his head, a frown began to crease his brow. His eyes slitted as he stared at Longarm. "You wouldn't be the one that works out of Denver, would you? The one they call Longarm?"

A low gabble of chatter and laughter had begun around the table, but when Pelter mentioned Longarm's name it died away. The men who'd been laughing or griping about their poker hands fixed their attention on Longarm. Two or three of them pushed their chairs back and stood up.

"Some of my friends call me that," Longarm said quietly.

"Huh," Pelter snorted. His eyes were in constant motion. He was examining Longarm as a scientist might study a new species of animal that was strange to him. He said, "I've heard that name Longarm mentioned, here and there."

"Oh, I've heard your name too, Pelter," Longarm told the gunfighter. He was examining Pelter in the same fashion that the gunman was studying him. He went on, "But as I recall, your main stomping ground's around Fort Smith and over in the Indian Nation, along the Arkansas brakes. Maybe that's why we ain't met up before."

One by one, the men who had not risen before stood up and slowly began to move into a solid group behind Pelter. Their eyes were shifting from Pelter to Longarm to Ferrell. The faces of the hired gunmen were as varied as their clothing. Four or five of them wore full beards, and only two were totally clean-shaven. Some had the tanned cheeks of men who spent most of their time outdoors; one or two showed the veined complexions that marked them as heavy drinkers; the others had the pasty white skins of men who shunned the sunlight. All of them had a common characteristic, though: the cold and always-moving eyes of men whose lives depended on keeping constantly aware of their surroundings.

About half of the gunfighters wore rough clothing; calf-high boots into which were tucked tan or brown duck jeans; gingham or denim shirts with neckerchiefs at the collar; broad-brimmed Stetsons of the sort favored by men who spent most of their time outdoors. Those wearing outdoor garb had on gunbelts, with holstered revolvers dangling low on the right hip or worn butt-forward, high on their left sides, in the cross-draw position.

Among the remainder, dark business suits predominated, in shades of brown or of the deepest blue or black wool serge. A few wore their collars open, without neckties, and one of them had no collar at all; his corded throat rose from the neck-band of his shirt, which was held closed by a gleaming gold collar button. Two had derbies on; the rest, like Pelter, wore felt hats with narrow rolled brims.

Only the man who'd been calling the play at the table stood out as being dandified. The coat of his dark blue suit had wide cuffs of dove-gray, adorned with peal buttons; his cravat puffed out in soft gray silken perfection from a high choker collar, and was dotted by a huge pearl stickpin in an ornate gold setting, and his well-brushed homburg was a deep blue that matched to perfection the shade of his suit. He moved very little, but when he did, it was with the grace and precision of a dancer.

Longarm and Pelter concluded their session of mutual examination almost simultaneously. Pelter turned to Ferrell and asked, "What business has Long got here, Ferrell? As far as I know, there's no federal warrants out on any of us."

Before Ferrell could speak, Longarm said, "I'll answer you on that one, Pelter. I'm here on a case that started a long time before the Santa Fe hired you and your friends."

'Meaning you're going to stay out of this?" Pelter asked.

"Meaning I've got no cause to get interested in any of you, not right this minute. You're right about one thing, Pelter. Even if I don't know all of your friends by name, I been looking 'em over right close, and none of 'em match any of the wanted flyers I've looked at lately." Longarm ignored the smug smile that had crept over Pelter's face while he'd been talking, and put down the temptation to wipe it off the gunman's countenance.

"What about this job we've come here for?" Pelter asked.

Trying to keep his words from showing the reluctance he felt, Longarm told the gunman, "Far as I know, you wouldn't be breaking any federal law if you were hired by the Santa Fe to protect its rights and property. And unless a local lawman asks us to help, federal marshals try to steer clear of butting into local cases."

Pelter's smile was no longer a smug smirk when Longarm finished talking; it was a full-blown grin. He bobbed his head curtly and turned his attention from Longarm back to Ferrell.

"All right, Ferrell," he began. "You heard what your friend just said. If that's the way its going to be, you better tell the marshal to make himself scarce while we take care of the job we were sent here for. You expect us to start tonight, or do we wait until tomorrow morning to begin?"

"It looks like you don't have a job any longer, Pelter," Ferrell replied. "The trouble's all been settled."

Ignoring the murmur that rose from the men crowding up behind him, Pelter asked Ferrell, "What d'you mean, settled?"

"I mean there's no fighting to be done. The job you men were sent out here to do doesn't exist any longer."

"Wait a minute, now!" It was the dandified gunfighter who protested. "If we don't fight, we don't get the extra pay the railroad promised us to settle up whatever trouble there was."

"That's right," one of his companions chimed in. "If I'd known this was going to be a dry run, I'd've stayed home."

"Now just take it easy!" Ferrell told them. "I don't know what you men were supposed to be paid, but we'll work something out. I'll have to find out from the main office—"

"To hell with your main office!" Pelter snapped. "We're all going to get what's due us, and you better write that down in your little book, if you got one."

"That's putting it to 'em straight, Nobs!" said one of the

209

bearded gunmen. "Hell, none of us needed that long by-God train ride that we taken to git here, and we want what we was promised!"

A murmur of agreement swept through the group ranged in back of Pelter. A few hands crept to gunbelts and hitched them up, and then the tension of silence made itself felt in the rear

Longarm stood stock-still, trying not to draw their attention, while he gauged the changing mood of the gunslingers. He'd recognized at the outset of the quickly developing dispute that the problem was one he'd better stay out of and let Ferrell resolve. Little as he'd liked to admit the fact to Nobs Pelter, Longarm realized that he had no authority to make a move of any sort. Whatever his feelings might be, officially his hands were tied until a federal law had been broken or until some local lawman asked him for assistance.

Ferrell raised his voice to override the protests of the hired gunmen. "You men be quiet and listen to me! We had some trouble with the teamsters on this job, and it looked for a while like there was going to be a showdown fight. Now, that trouble was settled just a little while ago. You were already past Albuquerque by then, and it was too late for me to wire the head office that I didn't need you. Now, I'm sorry you made the trip out here, and—"

"Hold up, Ferrell!" Pelter broke in. "Sorry just don't signify All we give a damn about is cash money, so you better put up or shut up."

"If you'll give me time to finish, I'm getting to that," Ferrell snapped. "I know that each of you got a hundred dollars in advance, and you didn't pay a penny for transportation or food and liquor on the trip. I'm ready to pay you something more, and send you back to where you started, and feed you on the way. But that's as far as I feel like I'm obliged to go."

"How much more you figure to pay us?" called one of the gunmen at the back of the group.

"Since you haven't earned anything, I think about twenty-five dollars apiece ought to cover it," Ferrell answered.

"Like hell it will!" Pelter retorted. "You say a hundred more apiece, and we might start to listen."

"I can't go that high!" Ferrell protested. "The Santa Fe doesn't give me all that much cash to hand out for something like this!"

"Out here where there ain't no banks, you having to pay

off a lot of men every week, the railroad's bound to let you keep a pretty good-sized chunk of cash in hand," Pelter countered.

"You're wrong about that. Every payday a train comes out from Albuquerque with the payroll money," Ferrell replied. "All I keep in my office safe is a few hundred dollars."

"Hell, Nobs, let's just make him hand over whatever cash he's got in the safe and split it and go back home." The suggestion came from one of the bearded, roughly dressed gunmen.

Longarm had kept out of the discussion, but now he decided it was time to start bringing the gunslingers back down to earth. He said in a quietly level voice, "You're forgetting something."

"What the hell are you getting at?" asked the man who'd made the suggestion.

"Ferrell's the only man out here who can give the order to turn your train around and start it back to wherever you come from. He sure ain't likely to do that with a gun stuck in his belly."

"Shit!" snorted another of the group. "There ain't no trick to running a steam engine. I can do it, so can a lot of us."

"And if the Santa Fe don't pony up with what we got coming to us, we'll wreck this whole damn place so bad it'll take you a month to start working again!" another of the bearded shootists threatened.

"They'll do it, too, Ferrell," Pelter said with the quiet confidence of one who knew what he was talking about.

Longarm had been watching Nobs Pelter unobtrusively. The leader of the hired guns was again grinning hugely, obviously enjoying the situation he'd done so much to create. It was equally obvious to Longarm that the time had come for him to take a hand in settling the dispute the gunslingers had started. Pelter was engrossed in his argument with Ferrell, and the eyes of the other hired guns kept moving from their leader to Ferrell to Longarm. Watching the gunmen closely and timing his moves carefully, Longarm began moving imperceptibly closer to Pelter.

"You'd never get away with wrecking the camp," Ferrell was saying. "I've got too many men for a bunch your size to handle. You begin tearing their places up, they'll smother you."

"Don't count on it," Pelter said coldly. "We've got the guns and we're not bashful about using them. Your men won't stand up to us, even if they got odds of fifty to one in their favor."

Ferrell's face showed that he recognized the truth of the gunfighter's statement. He said, "Look here, Pelter, why don't you settle for what I've offered you and save us all a lot of trouble? There'll be times when you'll want to work for the Santa Fe again, you know."

"Not after this, there won't!" Pelter said hotly. "Your damn railroad got us all the way out here to this godforsaken place, and promised us that if we put up a good fight we'd get paid. Now it's up to you to deliver."

"It's not my fault there's no fighting to be done," Ferrell remonstrated. "It's not the Santa Fe's fault or your fault. It just happened that way."

"How it happened has got nothing to do with anything," Pelter shot back. "We're ready to fight. We lived up to our end of the deal, now you better toe up to yours."

Longarm was within reach of Pelter by now. He was aware of the occasional flickers in the eyes of the other gunmen as they noted his slow moves, and he realized that a motion to draw his Colt would bring a hail of bullets. Even with his speed, the odds against his being able to trigger the gun, even if he succeeded in drawing it, were too high to make a try.

He took a cheroot from his inside pocket and, while putting it in his mouth, clumsily let the cigar fall to the floor. He saw the eyes of at least three of the gunfighters following him as he bent to pick up the cheroot, but he'd gotten the distraction he needed in the single act of bending to pick up his cigar.

Longarm brought himself erect in a single swift motion, the derringer concealed in the palm of his hand. Before the watching gunslicks could move, he had the muzzle of the ugly little snub-nosed weapon pressed to Nobs Pelter's temple, and he'd swung Pelter's body in front of him so that in order to hit him, any of the watching gunmen would be forced to kill their leader. During the half-second while the watching gunhands were still frozen with surprise, he made a left-hand draw that brought the entire group of them under the menacing muzzle of his Colt.

All the men facing Longarm were professionals. He'd counted on this as well as his own reputation for good shooting when he'd planned his move. He was gambling on a coppered bet that no professional gunfighter would be foolish enough to try to draw while another, equally proficient, was covering him with a hair-triggered Colt. When a few seconds had ticked away and the men in front of him remained motionless, Longarm knew his gamble had been a safe one.

Pressing the derringer's muzzle even harder against Pelter's head, he announced in a steel-hard voice, "Now, I've had about all I can stand of this fool jawing. Let's get down to cases." Without turning his head, he went on, "Jim, there's a couple of sawed-off shotguns in that corner by the bar. Why don't you ease past those fellows real careful and pick out one that's loaded, then stand over here by me. I aim to settle this argument once and for all."

Ferrell wasted no time. Without hurrying, keeping his eyes on the group of gunfighters, he selected one of the shotguns from the corner and edged back to where Longarm was holding Pelter.

"You keep that scattergun on the others while I take a load off Nobs's hip," Longarm said.

Holstering his Colt, he lifted Pelter's revolver from its holster, ran his hands quickly over the other man's body to make sure he had no knife, sleeve-gun, or derringer on him, and gave him a shove toward the group.

He told Ferrell, "If this was any other kind of bunch, I'd just tell 'em to hand over their guns. But I can't trust these yahoos not to hold out on me. I got to search every one of 'em myself. You keep that shotgun steady while I'm doing it." To the gunmen he said, "Now I want you men to step up one at a time, and I'll give you the same treatment I gave Nobs."

Having no other choice, the gunfighters obeyed meekly. Longarm searched each man carefully, tossing to the floor behind him an assortment of weapons: heavy revolvers from holsters, a boot-gun from the dandified gunfighter, a backup gun of some kind from several others, knives from most of them. When he'd finished with the last man, Longarm was ready to swear that none of them was carrying a weapon more dangerous than a toothpick.

"Now, then," he said when he'd finished searching the last man, "Maybe we can set down and get this business wound up without everybody running off at the mouth." He waited until the gunfighters had settled down at the table, and looked around its perimeter at the sobered group. "Well? Nobs, you was running off at the mouth pretty free a minute ago. What've you got to say now?"

"I underestimated you, Long," Pelter said bitterly. "That's my own fault. I didn't think there was a man living who could move as smooth as I'd heard you can. But don't worry. I won't make the same mistake again."

"I don't aim to give you a chance to," Longarm told Pelter. "Except that ain't what I asked you. Now, Jim's offered to give you men twenty-five dollars apiece over and above the hundred you got before you set out. In my book, getting paid that much for not fighting is just about as good as getting paid a hundred for fighting. You said a while ago it wasn't, but I was wondering if maybe you've changed your mind."

"It looks like we don't have much choice but to change our minds, Nobs," one of the roughly dressed bearded men said before Pelter could reply. "I say we better settle for what we can git and go back home."

"You're right, Ed," another of the subdued gunslingers said. "Twenty-five's not a lot, but it's better'n a boot in the ass."

Around the table, heads began to nod in agreement. Pelter finally acknowledged defeat. He said, "All right, Ferrell. It looks like the boys are ready to take your offer. But I'll tell you this. It'll be a cold day in hell before any of us will take on a job from the goddamn Santa Fe railroad again!"

"If I've got anything to say about it, it'll be an even colder day in hell before the Santa Fe ever offers any of you a job again," Ferrell retorted. He looked at Longarm. "You want to hold the shotgun while I go get the money?"

"That's what I figured to do," Longarm replied. "And while you're getting things, you better get a couple of gunnysacks."

"Sacks? What for?"

"Before these yahoos pull out of here, I aim to unload all these guns and stow 'em in those sacks. The engineer and fireman can look after 'em in the cab until the end of their run," Longarm told him. "I'd hate for this bunch to get a few miles along and change their minds about the deal they made. Some of 'em might be tempted to come back here and make trouble."

"You're too damn smart for your own good, Long," Pelter growled after Ferrell had gone on his errand. "If your business ever brings you into my home territory, I guess I don't need to warn you to step mighty soft and careful."

"Oh, I'd do that without you ever saying anything, Nobs. A man needs to watch where he's going, this day and age."

Pelter glowered at Longarm, but said nothing more. Ferrell returned with the money, a bag of double eagles and half-eagles, and handed each of the gunfighters the twenty-five dollars they'd been promised. Then he relieved Longarm of the shotgun and stood guard while the confiscated weapons were emptied and placed in the gunnysacks. Even with half the weapons in each sack, they made a heavy load.

Hefting the sack he was carrying, Longarm faced the table and said, "Jim and me are going to stand watch outside until the engineer gets up steam and you men are on your way. I don't guess I need to say anything else."

None of the gunslingers answered. They did not need to say anything, the angry glares they were directing at Longarm and Ferrell spoke volumes.

As they left the parlor car, half-dragging, half-carrying the heavy sacks containing the guns, Longarm said to Ferrell, "I missed a bet, Jim, not taking time to look in the passenger coach and baggage car. I'll bet these fellows got spare guns tucked away in both of 'em."

"You want me to hold the train while you search them?"

After a moment's thought, Longarm shook his head. "No. It might just turn out to be time wasted. Anyhow, I don't imagine they'll be coming back. They got more'n they deserved as it is."

"I sure owe you—hell, Longarm, the Santa Fe owes you—for getting that mess straightened out."

"Well, I sure wasn't going to stand by and watch 'em put the spurs to you, Jim. Not that I'm too fond of professional gunmen anyways. I didn't want to push this bunch too hard, though. The Santa Fe covers a lot of territory, and I'd guess any business as big as it is has got enough enemies so it don't need new ones."

"No." Ferrell peered through the door pane at the gunmen and added, "You know, there's no need for both of us to stay here and stand watch. You can see the whole car from right here. Let me have that sack of guns. I'll drag both of them up to the engine while you stay here and keep an eye on those jaspers."

Longarm watched the gunfighters through the vestibule door until the special began to lurch slowly forward, then swung out of the vestibule and dropped to the ground. After a moment, Ferrell joined him.

"I don't know about you," the construction boss said, "But I think we've earned a couple of drinks. Let's go over to the office and enjoy them."

"I sure don't need to be begged to do that." Longarm took out a cheroot and lighted it. "And I sure won't need any sweet lullabyes to put me to sleep tonight."

"You'll be going back to Albuquerque tomorrow, I guess?"

"As early as I can get away. This whole damned case is coming to a boil, Jim. I need to be where I can keep track of a lot of things, which I can't do out here at the rail-end."

"You've really gone that far with it?" Ferrell asked. "Of course, there hasn't been too much time on this trip for you to bring me up to date, but I'm certainly interested."

"Oh, I'm a ways yet from pulling all the strings together, but if a little luck comes my way, I ought to be seeing daylight pretty soon."

They'd barely sipped their drinks after settling down in the caboose-office when a rapping sounded at the door. "Mr. Ferrell? Are you in there?" a man called.

"Come on in," Ferrell replied.

Saunders, the construction camp's telegrapher, stuck his head in the door. He saw Longarm and sighed with relief. "I was hoping you'd be here," he said. "I was just about to close the wire down for the night when this message for you cleared from Albuquerque."

He stepped inside and handed Longarm the folded flimsy. Longarm smoothed out the creases and read, in the telegrapher's hasty scribble, "Army Sergeant Higgins here with urgent papers for Deputy U.S. Marshal Long. Says will come to rail head on morning work train if Long unable return here tonight. Parsons."

Longarm passed the wire to Ferrell. While the construction boss read the message, Longarm told the telegrapher, "You better wire back for Higgins to meet me at the Grand Hotel. I'll be there as soon as I can make it." Turning to Ferrell, he went on, "This just might be the break I was talking about, Jim. Can you get the accommodation I rode out here on steamed up and ready to go back right away?"

"Sure. That's easy enough to do." He told Saunders, "Pass the word along to get the bobtail ready to roll. They ought to have it in shape to pull out in less than an hour." Then, turning

216

back to Longarm, Ferrell said, "What about that good night's sleep you were going to have?"

"I'll catch what I can on the train. If my case is ready to break, I better get my butt to Albuquerque in a hurry. I can sleep anytime."

Chapter 19

Longarm found a sleepy-eyed Sergeant Higgins waiting in the lobby of the Grand Hotel. As anxious as he was to learn what fresh information the governor's aide had brought from Santa Fe, Longarm took a single look at the sergeant's drooping eyelids and led him across the lobby to the bar.

"I don't know if you're a drinking man, Higgins, but you need something to wake you up before we start talking," he said.

"A sergeant's pay in this man's army don't run to buying many drinks at saloons," Higgins said through a wide yawn. "I guess I am pretty sleepy, though. The governor's kept me going day and night since you left Santa Fe."

"A man that's half asleep can't think very good. I need a little eye-opener myself, even if I did get a few winks of sleep on the way back here. We'll have a quick one in the bar."

Crossing the lobby, Longarm glanced at the clock over the registration desk and was surprised to see that it was just a few minutes before midnight. He felt that it should be a lot later, after the long day he'd had.

There were only two other customers in the bar. Longarm led Higgins down to the end of the long stretch of polished mahogany and ordered drinks.

After the barkeep had left, he said to Higgins, "I hope you got good news from Governor Wallace for me."

"He seemed to think you'd be glad to get the papers I've brought you, a lot of copies of telegrams, and some lists of names that I copied from the files at the treasurer's office. And the governor wrote you a long letter, too."

Higgins reached into his inner jacket pocket, but Longarm shook his head. "Let's go up to my room," he said. "There ain't any way of telling who might wander in here. It might be somebody who'd recognize us and those telegrams."

A few minutes later, in the privacy of his room, Longarm had his first chance to examine the material Higgins gave him. He read the governor's letter first, which was written in a fine Spencerian hand:

"As I'd thought, the telegrams were in a very simple substitution code. They were really no trouble to decipher, though after my first efforts I became almost convinced that the messages by themselves had very little significance. Then I discovered that there was a code within a code, the second code hiding names of individuals mentioned in the telegrams. I quickly changed my mind about the value of these wires after I had solved the inner code.

"When the names which occur in the telegrams are matched with those on the lists you left, and the other lists Higgins got after your departure, the wires show very clearly that the Zia Land Co. is acting as a central command office for a new Ring, and that Zia and the San Ysidro Cattle Co. are very closely intertwined.

"I was surprised and shocked at the details of bribes paid to members of the Territorial Legislature and to some of the Territorial officials whom I have heretofore trusted and considered to be honest. I can see dimly the outline of the plotting which is aimed at extracting tribute from the Santa Fe Railroad, and I strongly suspect that when you look at the material I am sending by Higgins, you will find a number of details which I've overlooked.

"You are closer to the case than I am, and I am confident that your further investigation will uncover the evidence that will enable me to bring this matter to a close."

Longarm put the governor's letter aside and glanced at Higgins. He could see that the sergeant was very close to going to sleep in his chair.

He said, "Look here, Higgins, I'm going to need a little time to take a close look at this stuff you brought. There ain't a thing more that you can do tonight. You go downstairs and have the clerk fix you up with a room, and I'll put the rent on my expenses. I want you to stay close by until I finish reading all these papers, in case there's anything I need to ask you about."

"I'll be glad to stay right here, if you think I can help."

Longarm shook his head. "No. Do what I told you to. I'll wake you up if I find anything that can't wait, but there ain't a bit of use in both of us staying up."

When Higgins had gone, Longarm went back to studying the material the sergeant had brought. There were sums of money and transfers of property listed as bribes and payoffs that surprised him by their size. Many of the names in the messages were new to him; for instance, he did not recognize the name of the man who'd signed the Zia Land Company telegrams. There were other names with which he was familiar, Rudolpho Fernandez among them. The initials of Cynthia Evans were signed to many of the telegrams, and her name or initials also appeared frequently in the wires exchanged between the San Ysidro Cattle Company and the Zia Land Company.

One sequence of messages dealt with the Zia firm's manuevers in connection with the Hutchins Freighting Company. Though many of the telegrams were worded cryptically to hide their real meaning, Longarm could read between the lines and deduce the sequence of bribery and threats of murder that the Zia operators had used to take control of the Hutchins operations in New Mexico Territory, and to replace Clem Hutchins with their man Tafolla.

In another series of telegrams Longarm found his own name, the date of his arrival in Santa Fe, and details of his first trip to the railhead construction camp, and for the first time he learned that it had been the Zia Land Company that had ordered the attempts to murder him during his first visit to the railhead construction, and later, on the trail to Albuquerque.

You might've set out to stir up a pond full of minnows, old son, Longarm told himself when at last he put the sheaf of papers aside, *but what it looks like right now is that the pond you jumped in is bigger than you figured, and there's more sharks than minnows in it. You're apt to get bit real bad if you can't swim faster'n they can. And just getting away from a few of the little sharks ain't going to do much good. What you need is to get to shore before they get close enough to snap. And that being the case, you might as well start right now.*

Longarm reached for his pistol belt, which he'd hung in its usual place, on the headboard of his bed. He stood up to buckle on the belt, followed his usual routine of checking his Colt, and slid the weapon into its holster. He had not yet taken off his vest. He took out his derringer and gave the stubby little gun and its two .44-caliber cartridges a close look, donned his coat and hat, and walked downstairs.

For a moment he debated getting his horse out again, but quickly decided the distance he'd be covering wasn't great enough to justify waiting while a sleepy stableman saddled the animal. Making his way through the deserted hotel lobby, he went out into the fresh air of the cool night.

No lights showed through the etched-glass door panel of Cynthia Evans's bungalow when he reached it after a short, brisk walk. Longarm tapped at the door and waited. A dim light appeared in the doorpane, growing steadily brighter, and in a moment he saw Cynthia's form in the small hallway, her silhouette hazy through the diffracting glass inset.

"Who is it?" she called.

"Longarm."

"Oh. Just a minute."

He watched her hazy silhouette through the glass, saw her hand go up to smooth her hair and adjust her robe at the throat, then the lock clicked and the door opened. Cynthia was wearing the lace-trimmed robe of creamy silk that he remembered from his last visit. She swung the door wider and smiled invitingly.

"What a nice surprise, Longarm!"

"I thought twice before I knocked. It's pretty late at night, and I don't want to—"

"I hadn't really gone to sleep," she said. "I was lying in bed, half-awake, thinking. And don't ask me what I was thinking about, because I won't tell you. Come in, Longarm. I'm really glad to see you."

Cynthia closed and locked the door as Longarm stepped inside, and led him through the hall into the living room. Putting the lamp on a table, she indicated the sofa and settled down beside him. Sitting close to her, Longarm was at once aware of the faint aroma of her familiar perfume, enhanced by the subtle fragrance that clings to the body of a woman just out of a warm bed. He looked at her face, its soft translucent skin still flushed with sleep, framed by loose tendrils of her unbound golden hair.

Cynthia's full breasts strained at her silk wrapper; he could see their nipples pushing at the fabric as she turned to look at him squarely. In spite of what he'd learned about her in the past hour, in spite of the unceasing activity that had kept him

221

busy for the past several days, Longarm felt himself being aroused by her.

She said, "I was wondering this afternoon when I'd see you again. I thought perhaps I'd made you angry the last time we were together."

"Now, why would I get mad at you, Cynthia?"

"Well, I wasn't very helpful when you asked me about Rudy and his business affairs."

"You'd more'n made up for that before I asked."

"Then you've forgiven me?"

"I wouldn't've knocked on your door at this hour of the night if I hadn't wanted to see you."

"That makes me feel very good."

Cynthia's perfumed warmth engulfed him and he felt the pressure of her breasts against his chest as she put her arms around him and pulled herself close, offering him her lips. Longarm bent to kiss her, and when the kiss grew prolonged, her tongue parting his lips to twine with his, her hand trailing down to his groin to knead and stroke him, the stirring that he'd begun to feel a few moments earlier from her proximity began to be transformed into the beginning of an erection.

She broke their kiss to whisper, "We couldn't be together long enough, the last time. You've missed me, just like I've missed you, Longarm." Squeezing him gently, she added, "I can feel how much you've missed me."

"I got to admit, I've thought about you more'n once."

"If you're thinking what I've been thinking, there's no use wasting our time in here, is there?"

"Not when you put it that way."

Cynthia rose from the sofa, extended her hand to Longarm, and led him to the bedroom. The aroma of her perfume was stronger here; it rose from the thrown-back sheets of the wide bed, which still bore the imprint of her body. Longarm folded his coat and laid it over a chair, turned his back while he put his watch into the pocket that held his derringer, unbuckled his gunbelt, and carefully laid the holstered Colt on the chair that stood at the head of the bed.

She'd been watching him, her hand holding her robe together at the base of her alabaster throat. She said, "You're a careful man, aren't you, Longarm?"

"In my line of work, a man's got to keep thinking ahead if he means to go on living."

"Yes," she said thoughtfully. "I suppose that's right. But you're not out on a case, now." She stopped with a frown, then asked him, "Or are you? Am I just another case to you? Did you come here to see me because you wanted to, or because you've got more questions to ask me?"

"I ain't going to lie to you, Cynthia. I wanted to come see you, sure. And maybe later on we can talk. Not questions, not unless you feel like me asking you about some things after we've talked it over."

"That sounds terribly mysterious, but I'm not going to worry about later on. All that I can think of right now is that you're here and I'm here, and we're wasting time again."

Stepping to Longarm's side, Cynthia released her hand from the neck of her silken robe. It fell open, revealing the deep cleft between her upstanding breasts, the gentle bulge of her abdomen, and the tawny curls of her pubic hair. She started to unfasten the buttons of his soft gray flannel shirt.

Longarm could see that undressing him gave her pleasure, so he made no move to help her; instead he slipped his hands through the opening of her robe and began to caress her with his palms, cupping them around her sides and bringing his palms gently down the soft flesh that covered her ribs.

As Cynthia removed his shirt and her fingers got busy on the buttons of his fly, Longarm turned his hips to one side to give her busy fingers more freedom. He bent his head to kiss her breasts, rubbing his cheeks over their smooth softness. The tempo of her breathing increased. Longarm found the rosettes of her breasts with his lips, taking them in turn into his mouth and running his tongue over them until their tips pushed out round and firm under his caresses.

He felt her warm hands pass over his bare shoulders as she pulled away his balbriggans, and interrupted his caressing long enough to pry off his boots and kick off his trousers. Cynthia freed herself of her robe with a swift shrug. Her hands were on his erection now, her fingers encircling him, pulling him toward her. Her legs parted and she guided him into her, bringing her hips forward with a sudden lunge to take him as deeply as she could in their standing position.

"I've been wanting you inside me again ever since we were together that first night," she gasped, her breath hot on his ear. "But I want you in me all the way now. The bed, Longarm, the bed!"

Longarm brought his arms around Cynthia's waist and placed his hands under her buttocks. She let him lift her until her feet left the floor before she brought up her legs and clamped her ankles around his waist to keep him from slipping out of her while they moved. The bed was only a step or two away. Longarm carried Cynthia to its side and fell on top of her, driving full length into the wet softness that was now enclosing him.

Cynthia gasped and caught her lower lip with her teeth as she felt him sinking into her. Longarm lifted himself to begin stroking, but she tightened her legs around his hips and shook her head, tossing her loosely gathered golden hair into even greater disarray.

"Wait, please wait, Longarm!" she said. "Don't move for a minute! Just let me feel you in me this way a little while!"

Longarm lay quietly on Cynthia's yielding body, feeling himself swelling to a full erection as her inner muscles grasped him in slow, pulsating ripples. When he felt her muscles growing quiet he began to stroke, slowly and almost gently, withdrawing until their fleshy connection was almost lost before he lowered himself to go into her once more with a smooth, firm push that brought a gasp from deep in her throat.

"Hurry now!" she urged in a breathy whisper that ululated between the rasping of her deep breaths. "Because I'm almost ready to come, and I don't want to let go until you do."

"You let go whenever you feel like it, Cynthia. It'll take a while longer yet for me."

"Are you sure?"

"I'm sure."

"Then I'll let go now," she told him, her voice trembling and unsteady. "But go faster just the same! Because the faster you go...oh, go, go, go, Longarm! Now, oh, now, now!"

Longarm drove harder as he felt Cynthia convulsing beneath him. He pounded with swift, deep lunges until her gasps no longer shook her body, then slowed to a more deliberate pace while the tremors that had shaken her subsided and stopped. He held himself buried in her for a few moments, lying motionless, while Cynthia lay supine, her eyes closed, her full, firm lips parted to show even rows of pearl-white teeth.

Several minutes passed before Cynthia opened her eyes and looked up at Longarm with a smile. "You can't imagine how good it is just to lie here and feel you all big and hard, filling me up and making me want to turn inside-out."

"It makes me feel right good to be in you, making you feel good."

Longarm bent to meet Cynthia's upturned lips, which she opened to let her tongue slip into his mouth, thrusting it in and around in time with his more sturdy thrusting into her other, more intimate and secret lips. They held the kiss until the need to breathe more freely forced them to pull their lips apart, and Longarm could feel her body beginning to grow taut once more.

"Longarm?" she said, when they were breathing easily once again. She paused and then repeated with the same tentative inflection, "Longarm? You don't mind stopping just a minute, do you?"

"Of course not, if you're getting tired."

"I'm not tired. I could enjoy this forever, but I know you must be getting about ready to come, and I want you to go in even deeper. So stop just long enough for me to turn over."

Longarm withdrew from Cynthia's hot wetness and stood beside the bed while she rolled over and brought her knees up under her, lifting her buttocks high and resting her body on her elbows. He poised himself and went in slowly, deliberately, until he heard Cynthia's sudden, sighing inhalation. Then he lunged in still deeper, and felt her buttocks quivering under his hands.

"Now ride me, Longarm!" she commanded, her voice a mixture of pain and pleasure. "No matter if I yell or cry, ride me and don't stop until you have to!"

Longarm rode her. He pulled away for a short moment, then jabbed into her with a bull-like thrust that she answered with a sobbing laugh of ecstasy. Again and again he drove full length, with all the power he could muster. Cynthia writhed in his firm grasp, her buttocks twisting wildly, her blond hair flying as she tossed her head back and forth while sobs of pleasure broke from her lips.

She came to her climax swiftly, within a few moments after Longarm's first deep drive. Longarm gripped her hips with his strong hands and kept up his powerful, swift, pounding strokes while she shook and cried out wildly, until her spasm had ended and she was a limp burden in his grasp.

Longarm's swift pace was too fierce for any man to keep up very long. He let himself build almost to his orgasm and held back only until he felt Cynthia's hips begin to roll and jerk in her second quick climax. Then he let go, while still stabbing hard and fast into her quivering depths, until he was drained and suddenly tired. He held her hips firmly when his shaking ended, for her buttocks were still jerking and her body shivering in the fading moment of her spasms. Then he heard her final sigh and left her, and dropped to the tousled bed beside her.

They lay quietly for a long while, the only sound in the room the broken rasping of their deep breaths. Cynthia still lay facedown, her face covered by the tangled tendrils of her bright blond hair. Longarm sprawled beside her, his body limp. After several minutes she stirred and brushed her hair away from her face. She looked at Longarm for a moment and shook her head.

"I feel disgracefully good," she said. "And I think I've got enough strength in my legs to move around, at least a little bit. Wait where you are. I'll be right back."

Rolling off the bed, Cynthia disappeared into the bathroom She returned in a moment, carrying a warm, damp towel. Kneeling beside Longarm on the bed, she washed him gently, her fingers lingering lovingly on his groin as she slowly cleansed him, lingering over the task as though she hated to bring it to an end.

She went back to the bathroom, and Longarm rolled off the bed and took a cheroot out of his pocket. He lighted it and sat down on the bed to wait; Cynthia came back in a few moments and sat down beside him.

For a moment neither of them spoke, then Cynthia sighed happily and said, "There's never been a man who can do what you've done for me. I feel so good I'm not even going to be jealous of the other women who must've told you that."

"You're a lot more woman than most," he told her.

"I like to hear you say things like that, Longarm," she said throatily. Then her voice grew serious. "You're not fooling me a bit, of course, and I'm not one to fool myself. You didn't come here tonight just to see me, or even because you knew I'd be only too damned ready to fall into bed with you."

"I didn't have your bed on my mind when I started over to see you, I'll grant you that," Longarm replied, his seriousness matching hers. "I come because I needed to talk to you, and what just happened between us . . . well, it happened, that's all."

"Let's leave it at that," she told him flatly. "Why did you come to see me, Longarm?"

"To keep you from getting into more trouble than you or me or anybody else can handle. Even more than your boss can handle, because he's going to be in a lot more trouble than you are."

"That sounds serious," Cynthia frowned.

"It is. I'm guessing it's a lot more serious than you got any idea of right now."

Standing up, Cynthia reached for her robe. "Sitting naked on the side of a bed is no way to have a serious talk, is it? Let's go into the parlor, Longarm. I think I might need a drink. You sound a lot different than you usually do."

"You go on. I'll slip back into my clothes and be there in just a minute."

When Longarm joined Cynthia in the parlor, she'd already poured a drink for herself and was struggling to get the cork out of an unopened bottle of Tom Moore.

"I remembered your favorite liquor, and got a bottle so I'd have some for you, even before I knew whether you'd ever visit me again. Now I can't get the damn cork out," she said.

"Here." Longarm held out his hand for the bottle. "There's a trick to opening Tom Moore's Maryland rye. I learned it a long time ago. Let me do it for you."

Longarm grasped the bottle firmly in his right hand and hit its base a sharp blow with the heel of his left hand. A quarter-inch of the cork popped up from the neck. Closing his strong teeth on the protruding rim of the cork, he gave the bottle a twist and a pull. The cork came out easily. He handed the bottle back to Cynthia.

"You make it look easy," she said. "I hope I can take what you're going to say as easily."

She poured his drink and passed him the glass. Longarm took out a cheroot and lighted it.

"You better sit down," he said, settling down in one of the easy chairs that stood before the dark fireplace.

Cynthia had taken a step toward the sofa, but she shrugged and sat down in the other easy chair. "Well?" she asked. "What is this bad news you've got to tell me?"

"To start with, I read all them coded telegrams."

Cynthia shrugged. "I don't understand why you think those

227

messages are so important, Longarm. All they're about is simple business deals."

"They're a lot more than that. You know I went up to Santa Fe the other day, after I'd had that talk with Mr. Fernandez?"

"I knew you'd gone somewhere. How could I know where?"

Longarm ignored her question and pressed on. "While I was there, I did some digging in the land office and the territorial treasurer's office. Cynthia, don't you know your boss is one of the bigwigs in what's setting out to be a new Santa Fe Ring?"

A worried frown spread over Cynthia's face. "You mean like the old Ring? The bunch of important people who were behind all the crooked deals and bribery and even murders, a long time ago?"

"It wasn't all that long ago. Or maybe it does look that way to you. But this new Ring's starting out to do all the dirty kind of work the old one did."

"And Rudy Fernandez is part of it?"

"He's one of the main spokes in the new Ring's wheels. And that means you're in it too, maybe not that you know what's going on, but just because you work for him. You can connect him up with killings and bribes and payoffs and crooked deals of just about every kind there is."

For a long moment, Cynthia sat silent. At last she said, "You can believe this or not, Longarm, but I didn't know about any of these things you're telling me have been going on."

"You were pretty much in charge of things while he was away from the office," Longarm reminded her.

"Here in Albuquerque, yes. I never knew much about what Rudy did when he was in Santa Fe, of course."

"You mean he just never mentioned what he did up there?"

"Rudy can be very secretive, Longarm. I wondered at times why he'd be that way, but I thought—well, you remember, I told you he loves young men instead of women. I just thought he was dodging around, trying to keep people from finding that out."

"Now, I believe you when you say that, Cynthia," he said thoughtfully. "I ain't so sure a judge and jury would."

"You mean I might get arrested? Be brought up in court?"

"There's only one way I can see for you to get out of it."

"How? Turn myself in and testify for you?"

"Not just for me. First of all, it's Governor Wallace's case, not mine. You'd be doing the territory a favor if you helped

228

him, and I can just about guarantee that I can get the governor to let you off free and clear if you do."

Cynthia sat thoughtfully silent for a moment, then said, "I don't see that I've got much choice, have I?"

"Not a lot. Unless you feel like you owe it to your boss not to turn on him."

"Which I don't, Longarm. Oh, I've been well paid, but not enough to pay me for several years in jail." She shrugged. "All right. I'll do it. But you'll have to tell me what to do from tonight on. I can't keep on working for Rudy, can I?"

"No. I think the best thing you can do is lay low until tomorrow, and I'll take you up to Santa Fe on the evening train, and you can talk to Governor Wallace. After that, it'll be up to you and him."

Cynthia nodded slowly. "If that's what you think is best."

"Just stay in your house, and don't open the door for anybody but me. I've got some things to tend to yet tonight, but I'll bring somebody I know I can trust to stay with you until I can take you to the train tomorrow." He looked at the ormolu clock on the mantel. "I've got to go back to the hotel now and do some more work. Remember, stay in the house until I get back, and don't let anybody in. Especially Rudy Fernandez."

"He's the last person I'd want to let in. Don't worry about me, Longarm. I'll be all right."

Chapter 20

A quarter moon low in the sky turned the smoke trailing from Longarm's cheroot into a luminous ribbon as he walked down Roma Avenue to the corner where he would turn to get to the hotel. The houses on Roma were all dark at that hour of the morning, and the street itself was deserted. He turned at Eighth Street; the houses facing it were equally dark, the street equally deserted. As he started toward Central Avenue, he almost stumbled on a patch of broken bricks in the narrow sidewalk and decided to cross to the east side of Eighth, where the dim moonlight shone brighter and he'd be able to see any other broken areas of the sidewalk he might encounter.

Longarm was in no special hurry to get back to the hotel. Cynthia had occupied his mind only for the first few minutes after he'd left her, for thinking of how she could help him in bringing his case to a quick finish had led him to thoughts about other aspects of the investigation.

Now his mind was occupied with the mass of documents that Higgins had brought from Santa Fe, and the job he still faced of going over the papers he hadn't taken time to examine. After he had gone through the rest of the file, he could foresee that there would be names of a lot of people who must be proved to have been connected with one another. That was the job he still had to do in order to give Governor Wallace the evidence that would be required to smash the new version of the Santa Fe Ring before it became as powerful as the old one had been.

Longarm strolled at a leisurely pace, recalling some of the names he'd want to ask Cynthia about later in the day. He saw the three men approaching on the opposite side of Eighth Street, and even though he'd seen no one else abroad at that early hour of the morning, he paid little attention to them as they passed in the shadows on the west side of the street.

Not until he'd gone by two more intersecting streets and was crossing Grand Avenue did the thought occur to him that there had been something vaguely familiar about two of the three men he'd passed. The familiarity was more a recollection of the manner in which they moved than anything else. It had been far too dark, and the distance across the street too great, for him to see their faces or any other details of their appearance.

Longarm stopped in the middle of the street he was crossing, searching his memory for signs that he knew he must have noticed without being aware of them. Recollections flashed through his mind, and with the flashes came recognition of two of the three. One of them was Rudolpho Fernandez, Cynthia's employer. One of the others was Feliciano Ramos, the *mayordomo* of Rancho Montemayor. He whirled instantly and started retracing his steps at a fast walk, almost a run.

His heels clicking sharply on the brick sidewalk, Longarm rounded the corner of Roma Avenue and started toward Cynthia's bungalow. A light still showed through the etched-glass panel of the front door. He broke into a run now, but was still some distance from the house when the sudden, flat bark of a heavy-caliber pistol broke the night's stillness.

Longarm drew his Colt as he ran, and was holding it ready when he turned up the short walkway that led to the pillared porch. He could see where the inset glass pane had been shattered. A ragged-edged hole gaped in one corner of the etched panel, a hole big enough to allow a hand to reach inside and turn the latch.

At the steps leading up to the porch, Longarm stopped to listen. No sound came from inside the house. He mounted the steps silently, walking on tiptoe. Reaching for the doorknob, he turned it, careful to make no noise. The knob yielded easily to his pressure. He went inside, closing the door soundlessly, still walking on his toes.

He stopped short when he heard men's voices, pitched low, almost in whispers, coming from the parlor. The door leading from the hall to the parlor was ajar. Longarm stopped again to listen. The men in the parlor were conversing in Spanish, and Longarm's smattering of the language did not allow him

231

to follow it as rapidly as he could identify the voices of the speakers.

"*Su maldito pistolero!*" Rudolpho Fernandez was saying. "*No sera necesario matar la mujer! Cynthia no conocis nada de importancia que trate de mis asuntos!*"

Anger rushed over Longarm in a hot sweeping flood. He had understood enough to realize that the shot he'd heard had killed Cynthia. He fought down the temptation to rush into the parlor and start shooting when another voice sounded, replying to Fernandez.

Sí, Rudolpho, convieno," the second man said. Longarm knew he had heard the voice before, but could not place it at once. The second speaker went on, "*Lo siento, pero suceden algunas engaños.*"

Now Longarm recognized the second voice as that of Feliciano Ramos. He wondered who the third man could be, and what Ramos was doing there, but his attention was drawn back to the parlor when Fernandez spoke again.

"*Qué tontería!*" he said angrily. "*Mira, Feliciano! Inmediatamente tenemos la policía, preguntas, retrasos! No tenemos tiempo para algunas cosas!*"

"*Sí, sí! Conozco, Rudolpho!*" Ramos replied soothingly. "*Serenese, amigo! Todas justamos ahorita!*"

Longarm had heard all he needed. It was obvious to him that two such differently situated men as Fernandez and Ramos could have only one thing in common: the new Santa Fe Ring.

One step took Longarm to the open door of the parlor. He entered the room with his Colt leveled.

''Just stand right where you are and don't so much as move a finger!" he rasped.

Ramos and Fernandez froze, their eyes fixed on Longarm and the threatening revolver in his rock-steady hand. Longarm looked around for the third man, but he was not in the room. He saw Cynthia's body, then, sprawled on the floor in front of the sofa, the breast of her cream-colored silk robe stained with blood, her golden hair swept across her face.

"There was three of you walking together when I seen you on the street back there. Where's the other man that was with you?" Longarm demanded.

Almost before he finished speaking, he got an unpleasant answer to his question. The hard muzzle of a revolver was jabbed into his back and a harsh voice grated, "Let the pistol fall from your hand! And do not try to trick me, or you die!"

Longarm recognized the voice; it was that of Gomez, the foreman from Rancho Montemayor.

Longarm had long since learned the stupidity of arguing with a man who was sticking a gun into his ribs. He let his Colt fall to the floor, where it thudded on the carpet. The pressure of the muzzle of Gomez's gun eased when the Colt hit the floor.

Ramos stepped forward and picked it up. He did not bother to raise the weapon, but looked past Longarm and said, *"Buen cocido, Gomez! Y tiene cuidado, es hombre astuto!"*

"Sí, jefe!" Gomez replied. *"Sera alerta!"*

Fernandez said to Longarm, "We wondered if you might not have recognized us when we passed, Marshal. It is well that we put Gomez on watch!"

"Well, you got me right this minute, Fernandez," Longarm replied. "But what are you going to do with me? Shoot me in cold blood, like you did Cynthia Evans?"

"Of a certainty," Ramos nodded, his voice casual. "A dead man cannot arrest anyone, Marshal Long. It will save us a great deal of trouble if the police find your bodies lying here side by side, you holding your gun with two shells fired, a bullet through your head. A lover's quarrel, they will be sure to say. Rudolpho will tell them, of course, how angry you were with the Evans woman because she rejected your advances."

"You made your move a little bit too late, Ramos," Longarm said. "There's a lot of people, from the governor on down, who know what I've dug up about you and your friends. Whether I'm alive or dead, you and the new Ring you've been trying to put together are done for!"

Ramos shook his head, smiling coldly. "No, Marshal. We can move more swiftly than you think. Before the governor can act, there will be no evidence against us. You do not give us enough credit, you see. Our people are already taking care of those small details."

"Maybe we'd better find out what he knows before Gomez kills him, Feliciano," Fernandez suggested nervously.

Ramos retorted swiftly, *"Callate, Rudolfo! No se tonto! Es nada, que se dice!"* He motioned to attract Gomez's attention and held out Longarm's Colt. *"Vente 'ca, Gomez. Tome esta pistola y matarle!"*

Longarm felt Gomez's pistol muzzle bite into his back once

again as the pistolero prodded him to move forward. He welcomed the pressure; it signaled that the time he'd been hoping might come had arrived. As long as Gomez kept the muzzle of his revolver out of contact with Longarm's body, Longarm had no way of knowing the exact location of the weapon. Any effort he might have made then to grab the revolver would have been risky, based on pure chance. Now, knowing exactly where the gun's muzzle was, Longarm stepped forward in response to the pistolero's prodding, tensing himself to move quickly.

Gomez leaned forward to take the gun Ramos was holding out for him. When he saw Gomez's hand go past his side, reaching to take the pistol, Longarm struck.

He swiveled his hips, sliding his derringer from his vest pocket as he moved. The muzzle of Gomez's gun, pressed to Longarm's back, was dislodged when Longarm's body turned. The pistolero's revolver was swept harmlessly aside, and the shot Gomez instinctively triggered thudded harmlessly into the far wall of the parlor.

Before Gomez could swing his revolver back for a second shot, Longarm had the derringer up to Gomez's head. Its heavy conical slug plowed into the gunman's brain. Gomez's pistol fell from his lifeless hand as he sagged to the floor.

Longarm completed his turn before Ramos could reverse the Colt in his hand to grasp its grip. The stubby barrel of the derringer in Longarm's hand was only inches from Ramos's face when Longarm triggered the second barrel. The derringer's slug tore through Ramos's left eye and into his brain. His face went blank and he began to crumple to the floor.

Longarm scooped his Colt out of Ramos's hand before the dying man's muscles went limp. He swung the Colt to bring Fernandez into its sights, but Fernandez was already falling to his knees, his arms held up in surrender.

"Do not shoot!" he called. "I have no gun, Marshal! Spare me and I will pay you well for my life!"

"You ain't got enough money to buy your life or anything else from me!" Longarm snapped. "But I might let you off if you swear you'll tell me everything you know about this Ring that you and your friends were trying to put together."

"Yes, yes, Marshal! I can tell you all of it! And I will do so gladly, if only you will not shoot me!"

Longarm slackened the pressure of his trigger finger. He

234

holstered his Colt, picked up the derringer that he'd let fall to the floor, and restored it to his vest pocket. Fernandez kept his fear-widened eyes on Longarm, but did not rise from his knees.

"All right, Fernandez," Longarm said reluctantly. "I'd a hell of a lot rather see you dead, but I ain't cold-blooded enough to kill a man that ain't holding a gun on me."

"You will not regret it, I promise you," Fernandez babbled. "Ask what you wish to know, and I will tell you! I will tell you of the deceitful plotting of Don Pascual Iglesias de Montemayor, who became the head of the old Santa Fe Ring when his uncle, Don Emiliano, died! It was Don Pascual's scheme to build a new Ring with those who were left of the old one. I will give you names and—"

"Shut up!" Longarm almost shouted, his eyes fixed on the lifeless body of Cynthia Evans. "You can talk later on, Fernandez, and I'll be glad to listen to you. So will Governor Wallace and some judges, when we get your bunch into court. Now get up on your feet and come along with me. There's a man at the hotel that'll look after you until I can get around to closing my case. But right now I got to see about cleaning up the mess you and your friends made here."

Longarm stood at the station in Lamy, waiting for the northbound Santa Fe express.

Cristina Albee, standing beside him, looked up and said, "Maybe you'll have time to give me some attention, now that the trial's over. I've barely seen you or Uncle Lew either, since you got back to Santa Fe."

"You seen both of us every day in court, Teena."

"That's not the same thing, and you know it." She paused, a small frown flitted across her face, and she went on, "Tell me something, Longarm. That Cynthia Evans who was murdered, the one whose name I heard mentioned so many times in court—did you know her very well?"

"I knew her, sure."

"That's not what I asked you!" Teena said. "The way you acted when you talked about her, I got the idea . . ." she stopped short and shrugged. "Well, I suppose it's none of my business, is it?"

Longarm's voice was carefully neutral when he replied, "No. No, Teena, I reckon it ain't."

"Forget I asked you, then. Let's talk about something else. If I do decide to stop over in Denver, are you sure you can get some time away from your work?"

"I'm sure. I got it coming and I aim to take it."

"I'll stop over, then, if you're sure. Having you show me around Denver, Longarm, is a treat I wouldn't miss for anything in this world!"

Teena pulled Longarm's head down and kissed him as the first faint whistle of the approaching train reached them from down the track.

SPECIAL PREVIEW

Here are the opening scenes
from

LONGARM AND THE STALKING CORPSE

thirty-seventh in the bold
LONGARM series from Jove

Chapter 1

Longarm crossed Larimer Street feeling mighty peeved with himself that Saturday morning, for he saw he was going to be late getting to the office again. While this would come as no great surprise to his boss, U.S. Marshal Billy Vail, Longarm knew he faced a longer-than-usual chewing out. The office was only open half a day on Saturday, and with the federal courts closed, business would be slow. So the marshal would have time at his disposal to discuss his tall deputy's shortcomings in tedious detail.

The cool dry morning breeze sweeping into Denver from the nearby Front Range was clearing Longarm's head of the cobwebs he'd picked up the night before in the Black Cat Saloon, along with a right athletic gal who'd answered to the name of Sue. As he squinted in the painfully bright morning sunlight, Longarm was still walking sort of stiffly, but he figured he was sober enough to ponder out an excuse for oversleeping, which was a right polite way of putting what he and old Sue had been doing when he'd heard the bell on City Hall ring nine times.

He didn't think Marshal Vail would accept a morning quicky as a valid excuse for his being this late. Old married gents like Billy Vail tended to forget that it was important for a man to leave a lady purring contentedly while he shaved. So, as Longarm got to the corner of Arapahoe and 17th, and spied the blue uniforms of the Denver P.D. amid a milling crowd down the block, he grinned and headed that way. As a professional peace officer, it was his simple duty to assist others in the same line of work, and he could see that the Denver coppers were up to something he might be able to say he'd found more important than checking in with the durned old clerks at the Federal Building.

239

When he reached the scene, he saw that coppers and civilian passersby had gathered about a man in bib overalls, who was spread like a bearskin rug on the sandstone walk. The man was groaning too much to be hurt badly, and as Longarm nodded to a copper he knew, the gent on the ground asked someone to help him to his feet. But the copper told him, "Lay still till the ambulance gets here, dang it. I already told you, both your durned ankles are busted or sprained."

Longarm asked the copper what had happened. The man in blue pointed up with his chin and said, "Suicide attempt. The way we put her together, that farm boy throwed hisself out that open window up there, landed on the awning yonder, and somersaulted to the pavement to land on his fool feet, which must have stung some. He ain't hurt bad."

Longarm stared up at the open window of what he now saw was a cheap hotel and mused aloud, "Suicide leap, from a second-story window?"

"I never said he was smart. I just said he leaped. Two stories likely seem high, to a furriner off a farm."

The injured man sat up, groaning some more as he clutched one of his ankles with his knee drawn up to his chest. Longarm didn't think Billy Vail was going to like this excuse all that much unless he did something important. So he dropped to one knee beside the farmer and said, "Don't try to stand. Let me have a feel of that ankle before you go busting it up worse."

"Are you a doctor?"

"I'm better than some doctors when it comes to horrible injuries. I'm a deputy U.S. marshal and I see more of them than the average sawbones does."

He put a hand gently on the man's ankle and added, "You ain't hurt all that horrible, despite the swelling. Can you wiggle your toes and does it hurt when you try?"

The man shook his head and said, "My foot feels all right, but I can't bend my ankle."

"Don't try, then. It's sprained or maybe busted a mite. They'll take you to the dressing station directly and wrap you right. Sprained or busted, you ain't going to run after any trains for a while. Why in hell have you taken to diving out windows of late, pilgrim? Don't you know a gent could get hurt that way?"

"I noticed," the farmer groaned. "It was a sudden feeling that come over me as I faced a dismal future, broke and sober.

I don't reckon I'll do her again. As I've been laying here, it's passed through my mind that I was trying to kill the wrong fool. As soon as I'm able, I aim to get me a gun and do it right."

"Shooting yourself is against the law, friend."

"Ain't fixing to shoot *me*. Gonna shoot *him*, the man who robbed me! Mary Lou ain't never going to speak to me either way, after the way I lost the wherewithal to marry up with her. But at least I'll have the satisfaction of putting the man who ruined my life in his grave."

Longarm grimaced and informed the farmer, "There's a local regulation against that, too. Man could wind up in jail, putting folks in graves. I've heard the part about you being broke, and from the red in your eyes I'd say you've been drunk as a skunk in recent memory, too. Things may look brighter after you simmer down with some plaster around your ankles."

One of the coppers craned his neck to demand, "Where's that infernal meat wagon? I can't stand here all day guarding this lost sheep. I got me a beat to walk."

Longarm smiled to himself as he added that to the excuse for Billy Vail. He said, "You boys can go on about your business and leave this poor victim of circumstance to me, seeing as how I'm a peace officer too, right?"

They nodded but stayed put, the bastards. Longarm decided he'd better investigate further. The idiot who'd tried suicide from a second-story window had said he'd been robbed, and no peace officer worth his salt would walk away from a tale of robbery before he'd heard all the facts. Even old Billy Vail knew that.

He asked the farmer to tell his tale, and then, as the latter did so, the tall deputy's eyes glazed over, for the man's story, while sad, was all too dumb and familiar.

"There was this street hawker, selling soap off a barrel down on Larimer when I come outten the bank after cashing the check for my produce yesterday noon. He said it was good soap and I meant to buy a bar for my Mary Lou. But business must have been slow, for the hawker unwrapped a bar and said he aimed to put a ten-dollar note around one bar, to make the sale more exciting."

Longarm glanced up at one of the coppers, who winked at him and said, "Let me guess what happened next. The soap salesman rewrapped the bar and mixed it with the others on his barrel, saying the bars were all a dollar apiece and that the lucky gent who bought the one with the ten-dollar bill around it would be taking home a fine bar of soap and a nine-dollar profit."

The farmer on the pavement winced and said, "Gosh, that's just what happened. Are you gents saying he's done her afore in Denver?"

"Many, many times," Longarm said. "I'll tell you what happened next. You bought a bar of soap, right?"

"I did. I said it was for Mary Lou and the hawker told me it was from France. I never expected to get the bar with the ten-dollar bill wrapped around it, but I did."

Longarm nodded. "That's what I just said. Naturally, since you were nine dollars ahead of the game, it only seemed right to buy a second bar for your sweet Mary Lou, and you were surprised as hell when you won a second ten spot, weren't you?"

"Surprised, deputy? I was plum thundergasted! I've never been very lucky at gaming, but guess what happened when I plunked down a dollar for the *third* bar of soap!"

"You won again. I told you we knew how it works. He must have spied you coming from the bank. After beating him three times in a row, you must have felt right friendly toward this gent, right?"

"As a matter of fact I felt sorry for him. He looked so flummoxed, and when I whupped him another time he confessed I'd cleaned him out and that the game was over. He said he'd never seen anybody so lucky. He said he only did that trick with the ten-dollar note to drum up business, and he'd never expected anybody to beat the odds like that. He said he was not of a mind to buck a man who was on such a lucky streak."

Longarm looked up at the copper he knew and asked "Reckon it's old Soapy Smith?"

"Has to be," the copper replied. "Most of 'em ain't that generous with their flash money. Modest street cons palm the bill and just use the temptation to sell nickel bars for a dollar to the great unwashed. Smith's the one who plays it for high stakes."

Longarm nodded, turned back to the injured man, and said "You likely know how you were suckered, pilgrim."

The farmer groaned and said, "It come to me, just afore I

jumped out the window. The soap hawker asked me if I'd buy him a drink, since I'd about cleaned him out. I figured it was only Christian, since he was being such a sport about losing thirty dollars so sudden. He said he knowed a place across the way where we could drink in private and maybe get some gals to sit on our knees. But I said I was fixing to marry up next week, so a drink or two would have to hold him."

"Right, and after you got to the Silver Dollar and settled down comfortable, old Soapy Smith just happened to notice some other gents playing monte across the way, correct?"

"Well, it was blackjack and not monte they were playing, but I see you are ahead of me on brains. It only come to me recent that them other gents must have been in on it with, uh, what'd you call him? Soapy?"

"Soapy Smith, one of Denver's better-known educational institutions. I'll tell you what you did with your produce money, pilgrim. You let Soapy sucker you into the game, full of good cheer and feeling smug as hell about the winning streak he said you were on. The details get tedious after that. Suffice it to say you won the first few hands and then, as you were fed congratulatory drinks, things went sort of fuzzy until you came to your senses this morning, short of cash."

"I was swindled outten my whole spring crop, and now I'll never be able to face Mary Lou again. But as soon as I can walk, I'll get me a scattergun and we'll see who's laughing last around here!"

The horsedrawn ambulance came around the corner and Longarm said, "No you won't. I told you it's unlawful. I know where they'll take you in yon meat wagon, so no matter what the sawbones says, stay put there until I come by with your purloined cash. Are you listening to me, old son?"

"You mean it? You reckon you can get them rascals to give me back the money I was meaning to marry up with?"

Longarm rose, dusting off the knees of his brown tweed pants as he readjusted the cross-draw rig under his frock coat and asked one of the coppers, "Where's old Soapy staying these days? I doubt like hell he'd be at the Silver Dollar."

The copper shrugged and said, "He drinks in Henry's, down by the stockyards, when he ain't working the street for marks. But I don't see what we can do about this gent's misfortune, Longarm. Arresting Soapy Smith seems to be a waste of time as well as a mite dangerous. He's sort of nasty for a con man, and when you *do* get the drop on him, he's got more damned witnesses on tap than you can shake a stick at. This farm boy's tale rings true to me, but you know it'll never hold up in court."

"I ain't figuring on arresting anybody," Longarm said amiably. "Ain't sure that what he did comes under federal law, in any case. I just mean to have a friendly word with Soapy Smith."

"Want us to come along?"

"Wish you wouldn't. It might not be *that* friendly ."

"Oh." The copper grinned.

Longarm was grinning too, as he retraced his steps to the west and consulted his pocket watch. He was now so late that Billy Vail would be losing interest in chewing him out, and starting to worry. The boss would know that when Longarm was really late, he was onto something. It really wasn't any business of the Justice Department, but Longarm was sure there was something, somewhere in the Constitution, that covered keeping Miss Mary Lou from dying an old maid.

Henry's was a serious drinking place for cowhands, railroad workers and such, down near the Burlington yards. There were no fancy gals and no piano to distract gents as they wet their whistles at the long bar running the length of the single narrow room. It was early, so the stuffed buffalo head over the bar stared down on only one customer as the elderly barkeep read the *Police Gazette* spread on the mahogany. The customer was a tall, dapperly dressed gent with a mustache rivaling Longarm's. The pearl grips of a serious-looking sidearm peeked out from the shoulder holster under his left armpit. He ignored Longarm as he stood facing the bar and the bottle of redeye he'd ordered, with one booted foot hooked over the brass rail.

Longarm nodded to the bartender and drew his pistol as he stepped up to the solitary drinker with no preliminary remarks. The man stiffened at the unexpected move and went for his own weapon, but didn't make it. Lonarm pistolwhipped him across his face, knocking him to the sawdust-covered floor, and then kicked him in the head to stretch him full-length on the floor, dazed and moaning.

The bartender knew who both of them were, so he went on reading as Longarm sat on the chest of Soapy Smith to relieve him of his pearl-handled Walker Colt and toss it in a corner. Soapy Smith shook his head to clear it as he muttered, "I'll

244

kill you for this, as soon as I can figure out who you are and where I might happen to be. What the hell did you hit me for? I ain't done nothing to *you* in recent memory, stranger!"

"Let's put this down as a friendly negotiation, Soapy," Longarm said. "I came here to discuss a pilgrim you took advantage of last evening, and I said I was sure you'd be a gent about giving his crop money back. I sure hope I told him true."

Soapy Smith said, "Damm it, get off my infernal chest and let me have some air. You weigh a ton."

"Old son, you haven't felt my full weight yet. You see, this farm boy needs the money to marry up, and I'm sure you wouldn't want to stand betwixt a bride and groom now, would you?"

"Look, I suckered that yokel fair and square. I never pistolwhupped him and sat on his chest. I takes pride in being a gentle drifter, and it seems to me your methods border on sheer highway robbery, stranger."

Longarm shoved the muzzle of his .44 in one of Soapy Smith's nostrils and agreed. "I'll admit to a certain high-handedness this morning, since I am in a hurry and you have a rep for being testy to folks who approach you gentle. But, friendly or firm, I mean to recover that poor fool's roll, so where's it at? Do I have to run my hands over your shrinking flesh, or do you aim to hand it over polite?"

Soapy Smith rolled his eyes toward the bartender and growled, "Damn it, Henry, are you going to just stand there and watch a man get robbed at gunpoint?"

The bartender answered, "He ain't robbing me, Soapy, and if I was you, I'd give him the money. Modesty may forbid him to say it, but the man sitting on your chest with a double-action .44 in your nose answers to the name of Longarm. So, if it's all the same to the two of you, I mean to stay out of this discussion entire."

"Longarm?" Soapy gasped. "Hell's bells, why didn't you say so? Get off my chest and let's drink to it!"

"About the pilgrim's money, Soapy—"

"Shit, I'll give it back if it means all that much to you. I thought you were just some fool *mortal*, Longarm! Let me up and we'll do this friendly."

So Longarm rose and holstered his .44 as he extended a helping hand to the bruised and battered Soapy Smith. The latter moved to the bar, poured himself a stiff one, and downed it before he wheezed, "I got the money here, in this roll."

He took out a roll of bills wrapped in a rubber band and added, "I figure I took that chump for a rough eight hundred. I'll just out it out and we'll say no more about it."

But Longarm reached out, took the whole roll, and stuffed it in his coat pocket, saying, "He never gave exact figures, but I'm sure you'll agree a wedding present is in order, Soapy. After all, it ain't like you don't have a trade."

Soapy Smith's eyes widened as he saw his whole roll vanish as Longarm added sweetly, "I'll pay for the bottle there. It's only fair."

"Goddammit!" protested the con man. "There's over a thousand in that roll and I only took the chump for eight hundred!"

"I'll take you at your word. The extra two hundred's for damages and maybe a ribbon bow for Mary Lou."

"Damm it, I don't like being robbed of my own gold, Longarm."

Longarm said soberly, "Few people do, Soapy. But if I know you, you'll go on robbing them anyway. It's been nice jawing with you, but I have to get to the office before it closes for the day. So adios, you son of a bitch."

Longarm turned away, dropping a coin on the bar as he headed for the swinging doors. Behind him, Soapy Smith stared in confused rage for perhaps a full second. Then he growled deep in his throat and darted across the room toward the gun in the corner. Longarm turned with a weary smile, and as the con man dropped to one knee and snatched up the pearl-landled Walker, the more businesslike .44 in Longarm's big fist coughed a round into Smith and bounced him off the wall. Soapy Smith lay facedown, moaning in pain, and the bartender observed, "You only winged him, Longarm."

Longarm nodded, walked over to pick up the con man's gun again, and placed it on the bar, saying, "Better put this away and make sure no more kids play with it." He kicked Soapy gently and added, "I can see you'll likely live. Henry, here, will see about getting you a doc. Are you listening to me, Soapy?"

"I ain't going to forget this, Longarm. You've robbed me and I'm shot in the breast, but if I live, I'll come looking for you, hear?"

"That's what I wanted to talk to you about. You ain't shot

in the breast. I aimed for your shoulder and that's what I hit. I didn't kill you just now, because killing folks in Denver is tedious as hell, with all the paperwork and such involved. But by now you ought to have learned I *could've* killed you if I wanted to. Are you paying attention, old son?"

"Go ahead and crow, you bastard. This day is your'n, but mine will come as soon as I'm up and about again."

"They were right," Longarm said. "You are one testy cuss, considering your chosen profession. What I was about to say, Soapy, is that I don't want to see you in Denver anymore. I was polite this time, because I figured eight hundred wasn't worth a killing. But it's come to me, as I've gotten to know you better, that you're a mighty worthless specimen. So I don't want to see you around here anymore. I have to get back on the job, and you'll likely want to bed down somewhere and nurse that gunshot shoulder. But as soon as you're up and about, I want you on a train to other parts. You've made your brag and I'm taking you up on it. So the next time I see you in Denver, even in church, I mean to gun you down like the dog you are."

"What if I gun you first?"

"Old son, you just had a chance to try that, so you know how dumb you're talking. You're leaving town, Soapy Smith. I ain't asking you, I'm telling you. Why don't you go to Canada, or better yet, Alaska? I doubt I'll ever be sent to Alaska, and I'll kill you sure the next time we meet. So, seeing this is the last time we'll ever be talking man to man, let me leave you with a piece of advice. You're going to have to cool that ornery temper of yours, Soapy. It ain't natural in a con man. Most marks tend to forgive a *jolly* con man, if he gives 'em back their gold with a sheepish smile. But your surly manners are going to get you killed. If not by me, by somebody else."

"You can just up and fuck yourself, you grinning bastard!"

Longarm chuckled and said, "That's what I mean, Soapy. I already said adios, so I'll be leaving. Don't ever let me see your ugly face again, for, like the Lakota say, I have spoken."

Billy Vail accepted Longarm's excuse, not because he liked it all that much, but because it was getting late and Billy had a lot on his mind. As Longarm sat in the red leather chair across the desk from his boss, the bald and pudgy chief marshal said, "I know you expected the afternoon off, but tell the ladies it'll have to be another time. You remember that gent called Timberline that you said you killed over in Salt Lake City a while back?"

"*Said* I killed him, hell! I killed him deader than a turd in a milk bucket. We shot it out on the marble steps of the Salt Lake Federal Building and he rolled to the bottom with a busted neck as well as my lead in him."

Longarm fished out a cheroot and reflected, "It was an interesting case, as I think back on it. Timberline got his nickname from being taller than any gent has a right to grow. His real name was Cotton Younger, and they say he was kin to the Younger brothers, so when I figured out who he was—"

"Damn it," Vail cut in, "I know who Timberline was, or is. I sent you on the case in the first damn place."

Longarm struck a match and was about to light his smoke as Vail's last words sank in. Holding the flaming match, he frowned and repeated, "*Is*, Billy? Don't you mean *was*? I had it in my report about our shootout, and like I said, he lost."

"That's what I thought, too," said Vail. "But it seems we were fooled. Timberline's alive and kicking and making more mischief than you can shake a stick at!"

The match burned down to Longarm's fingers as he stared, slack-jawed, at the serious florid face of Marshal Vail. He cursed and shook the flame out. He knew Vail didn't josh much, so he was likely serious. Longarm shook his head and said, "Somebody's telling fibs, Billy. I didn't just shoot that tall drink of water. I shot him in front of federal employees, and the way I know he busted his neck on the way down those marble steps is because I was at the autopsy."

"Did you see him buried, Longarm?"

Longarm took out another match, did it right this time, and blew some annoyed smoke out his nostrils as he replied, "You know I caught me a train back to Denver right after the gunplay, so I can't say I acted as one of Timberline's pallbearers. But, buried or stuffed, I left him cold and dead on a zinc table in the Salt Lake City morgue. I don't know who's been raising Ned in the name of the late Cotton Younger, but it can't be him. Like I said, I killed him fair and square."

Vail picked up a flyer from his green blotter and read off, "Suspect around seven feet tall, has pale, rabbitlike eyes and snow-white hair, although he appears to be no older than thirty."

Longarm nodded. "Yeah, he had his hair dyed black when we last tangled. That's why I didn't know who he was right off. They used to call him Cotton because of that cotton top. He's likely a part albino—or I mean he *was*."

"A man of this description just shot up the Aurora post office, Longarm."

"Do tell? Aurora's just outside the Denver city limits, Billy."

Vail looked disgusted and growled, "Tell me something I don't know. Tell me how many gents answering a freak description like that there might be west of the Big Muddy, old son."

Longarm took a drag of smoke and observed, "Well, giants ain't all that unusual . . ."

"*Albino* giants, robbing post offices and such when they could make a good living in a tent show?"

"Hell, Billy, maybe this new freak is sensitive about his appearance. Whoever he may be, he can't be Timberline! You want me to ride out to Aurora and see if I can get a line on what this new owlhoot may be using as his handle?"

Vail shook his head and said, "Deputy Grenoble and some postal dicks are working on it in the first place, and we know what to call him in the second. He was with two other riders. The holdup went sour and they had to crawfish out. Witnesses say one of them called out to somebody named Timberline about getting out sudden and alive. So, as I study on this, Longarm, we have us a gent who looks like Timberline, who's called Timberline, following the family trade of the James-Younger clan that Timberline was raised to follow. How do you like her so far?"

"Not much. I'll allow that finding a double for Cotton Younger would be a chore, but bringing the original back to life would be too. I don't want to upset your stomach just before you go home to eat, Billy, but I was there when they cut him up on that autopsy table, and even if I was bragging about my bullet in him, *that* should have finished him!"

"Maybe he was tougher than he looked. He was a big tough jasper, right?"

"Billy, nobody comes that tough! I'll bet my life and throw in my retirement that the man I gunned in Salt Lake City was Cotton Younger in the first place and killed permanent in the second. Some old boy who read about it in the paper is having some fun with us. Remember me telling you how I've always suspected there must be two or more runty jaspers bragging they are the one and only Billy the Kid? The Kid can't be all the places people have seen him, so—"

"You're not after that rascal, Longarm. You're after Timberline. He's working in my backyard and I feel foolish as hell about the way I marked that case 'closed' after you told me you'd nailed him."

Longarm's face went wooden-Indian and his voice took on a coldly polite tone as he asked quietly, "Are you accusing me of lying, Marshal Vail?"

Vail knew his tall deputy well enough to reply hastily, "Don't get your bowels in an uproar, old son. I don't doubt for an instant that you thought the man you gunned over in Salt Lake was Timberline. But you admit his hair was black when you shot him, right?"

"*Dyed* black, like I said. It was white at the roots when we looked him over careful, on the table. Aside from looking like Cotton Younger, let us not forget he was *acting* like Cotton Younger when I caught up with him. If you'll dig out that old report, you'll see he was shooting folks a lot as I hove into view."

Vail sighed and said, "I was reading your report just before you got here. The man you gunned surely had a gunning coming. But if we can assume he's dead for certain, what we have is his twin. Do you remember anything like that, Longarm?"

Longarm blew a thoughtful smoke ring. "No. I spent enough time on the trail of Cotton Younger to know him pretty good. He was an only child. I reckon his poor ma didn't have it in her to birth more than one such critter. He hailed from Clay County, and was distant kin to both the James and Younger lads. He rode on a couple of early jobs with the gang and then joined the army to avoid discussing his recent activities with the law. He deserted the Seventh Cav just in time to miss the Little Big Horn. He was up in the Bitter Creek country pretending to be an honest cowhand when you sent me after him on a false lead that turned out lucky. The man in those parts that everyone thought might have been him was somebody else, but seven-foot gents are sort of rare, and between one thing and another, I figured this other tall galoot fit better, so in Salt Lake, when I tried to arrest him peaceful—"

"Dammit, Longarm, I told you I've just been going over the report on that case. Back up and reconsider that first lead.

What if the one we had down as Cotton Younger was Cotton Younger after all?"

Longarm looked disgusted and said, "He wasn't, and even if he was, he's dead too. Timberline shot lots of folks to throw me off. So everybody connected with that old case has been cleared or buried." He blew another smoke ring and added, "I just came from a discussion of razzle-dazzle with a professional called Soapy Smith. I'd say someone was trying to con us, Billy. You'd hardly expect a man holding up a post office to use his right name, would you? Besides, lots of tall cowhands are called Timberline. It's a natural nickname for a man walking about with his head in the sky."

"What about the albino hair?"

"Snow on the peaks? How the hell should I know why a man has funny hair? Maybe he bleached it. The real Timberline dyed his white hair black so's we'd overlook his past. Maybe some old boy who thinks he's cute heard about the recent rider from the James-Younger gang and reversed the trick with a bottle. One thing's for sure, we won't find out by sitting here and jawing about it!"

LONGARM

Men love his rip-roaring, shoot-'em-up adventures...

Women delight in his romantic exploits!

This sexy lawman is as adventurous with the ladies as he is with his gun! Explore the exciting Old West with one of the men who made it wild!